Paula was born in Hammersmith, West London. She received her education and spent most of her childhood in Middlesex. After working in banking in the City of London, she moved to the Isle of Wight and worked for the Civil Service. She is now living in a Hampshire town with her husband, immediate family and her cat, Bebo.

To my high school English teacher, Mr Haynes, for inspiring me to write and enjoy English literature. To my husband, Paul, and my dad for their continued support and love.

Paula Evans

THE WHITFIELD CLAN

To Jackie
Hope you enjoy this novel.
Paula Evans
Dec. 2020

AUSTIN MACAULEY PUBLISHERS™

LONDON • CAMBRIDGE • NEW YORK • SHARJAH

A CIP catalogue record for this title is available from the British Library.

ISBN 9781528937672 (Paperback)
ISBN 9781528969215 (ePub e-book)

www.austinmacauley.com

First Published (2020)
Austin Macauley Publishers Ltd
25 Canada Square
Canary Wharf
London
E14 5LQ

Thank you to the team at Austin Macauley for all their help and assistance with both of my novels. Your assistance and experience are greatly appreciated. To my friends, Kelly and Kirsty, for helping me market my novels. To my husband, Paul, for traipsing around locations for my research.

Chapter 1

Saturday, 21 December 1912, London, England

Everything at home had been hectic for the past week. The Christmas party preparations had taken precedence. Home is a Georgian town house in Royal Crescent Notting Hill, painted white with steps up to the front and a pillared entrance to the big green door. It has three storeys and a basement. The garden also had a small building that had been the home of Sally, the cook and her husband, George, who was the butler.

Grace had been making sure that all the table linens, napkins, candlesticks and place settings were all in order and ready to use. Her mother, Elizabeth, had consulted with Sally on the menu required. Her father, Frederick, was trying to keep out of it all by staying at work later than normal. Ruth, Grace's sister-in-law, had helped her dress the Christmas tree that was placed in the sitting room. They had done that about a week ago. Ruth had also gone shopping for gifts with her. Grace liked Ruth. Ruth was only eighteen months older than her. She had been one of Ruth's bridesmaids earlier this year at her wedding to Grace's beloved brother, Michael.

Grace and Michael had always been close. They shared common interests, had the same sense of humour and had been tutored together in their early childhood. Upon the death of their older brother, Charles, ten years ago, they had become closer still; worried over losing another sibling.

Charles had been away at school. He belonged to the Rugby team and had continued playing although he had felt ill with a cold. The cold developed and eventually, the school sent him home. The doctor had been called and pneumonia was diagnosed. He seemed to improve being at home with his family, but another cold snap in March 1902 took its toll on the weakened Charles and he deteriorated. His death was a shock to all the family and friends. He had been a strong and vibrant fourteen-year-old. Frederick and Elizabeth pulled their family even closer. Grace remembered that every winter would mean mountains of clothes piled on whenever she and Michael went out; most summers were not much different either.

Again, the fear of losing another child was foremost in their parent's minds.

Ruth hadn't quite seemed herself while they were shopping. She was a little peaky and had got hot quite a few times. They had stopped for refreshments and Ruth had said she felt better. This was Ruth and Michael's first Christmas together and Ruth wanted to make it extra special.

Frederick owned another property not far from the family home in Notting Hill. It was a flat in a mansion block, and Ruth and Michael had moved in upon their marriage.

Michael was a teacher at a private school in Barons Court. Ruth had been a Governess who had to meet her charges from school. It hadn't taken them long to get to know one another and fall in love.

They married in May 1912.

Michael and Ruth had already arrived to spend the day helping with the preparations. Around 4 o'clock in the afternoon, Grace went to her room. If something was not ready now, it would never be. She had chosen a dark green dress of chiffon and lace; not too low cut but pulled in to show off her tiny waist, then the skirt fell to the floor. She wore her long hair up in a chignon. For her eighteenth birthday, that year, her parents had bought her a diamond necklace and earrings, which she decided would suit very well for this occasion. Looking at her reflection in the mirror, she approved. She applied very little makeup and a little of her favourite scent. She was looking forward to the party. Her family always threw a good do.

As she left her room close to 5 o'clock, Michael and Ruth were also ready to go down. Michael, as handsome as ever with his blond hair, blue eyes and at six feet tall, looked dashing in his dinner suit.

Ruth's dress was much like her own but in a pale pink. Ruth had brown hair and dark eyes, so the colour suited her perfectly. They chatted as they descended the stairs and went into the dining room.

"Did Uncle Roderick say he was coming this evening, Grace? Or is he still unwell?" Michael asked.

"No, neither he nor Aunt Edwina are coming. He fears his cold will develop," replied Grace. Then carried on, "Apart from them, all the normal crowd will be here."

Elizabeth and Frederick then joined them.

"Let's have a drink to toast the family," said Frederick. At the age of 54, he still looked young and fit and dashing in his dinner suit. He poured whisky for the men and sherry for the ladies.

"To the family and a happy Christmas," he boomed.

"To the family and Christmas," everyone chorused.

Ruth looked at Michael and nodded.

"As we are all together, I would like to make an announcement. Ruth is going to have a baby." As he spoke, he had put his arm around his wife's waist.

"That's wonderful news," said Elizabeth. "You're both happy about it, aren't you?"

"Yes," replied Ruth. "We've known about the baby for two months but we just wanted to ensure everything was going well."

"When is the baby due?" Grace asked.

"July," Michael replied, beaming with pride.

Grace remembered Ruth not feeling well while they were Christmas shopping and it now made sense. She went over and gave both Michael and Ruth a hug and so did Elizabeth. Frederick shook hands with his son.

"It will be lovely to have a new baby around. The first of many, I hope," and he kissed Ruth on the cheek.

"Oh, it's wonderful news," Elizabeth said. "It's the best present I could have had." The doorbell rang.

"Here we go then, come on Elizabeth, let's start greeting our guests." Frederick took her arm and led her out into the hall. George, the butler, had already answered the door and was taking coats from Elizabeth's sister, Mary and her husband, Stephen.

Soon, the house was full. Everyone had drinks, exchanged presents, chatted and laughter could be heard. Grace had cornered Ruth and spoke again about the pregnancy. Marriage and children were not high on Grace's list of life choices, but she was excited for her brother and his wife and she would be an auntie. Just before dinner was announced, the doorbell rang again. Michael put his glass down on the drinks cabinet and went to answer the door. Grace hadn't noticed the new arrival immediately, because she was talking to her cousin, Eloise. Eloise was about to be engaged, so was animated talking about her arrangements for her engagement party. Grace only noticed this new guest when he went to greet her mother.

"Good evening, Alex. It's good to see you again." Her mother hugged this man affectionately. *She obviously knows him*, she thought.

"Thank you for the invite. I'm so sorry I had lost track of the time; I hope I haven't missed dinner," as he finished, he smiled at her mother.

"No, my dear, you made it in good time. Michael, would you like to get Alex a drink?"

"You're looking well, my boy." Frederick shook hands with Alex. "How's the job going?"

"I feel like a small fish in a big ocean, sir," Alex replied. "But it's interesting and I'm looking forward to learning and progressing." As Michael returned with a whiskey for Alex, Ruth joined him.

"Hello, Ruth. You are looking exquisite," Alex took her hand and kissed it gently.

"Thank you, Alex. You are as charming as ever."

Michael told him about the pregnancy and he hugged Ruth and shook hands with Alex.

Grace had lost track of her conversation and excused herself. Who was this man? The rest of her family seemed to know him well. She was mesmerised. He was slightly taller than her brother. Apart from their height, he was a striking contrast to her brother. He was dark-haired, almost black. He had a thin face and overall expression that appeared rather sombre, but he would smile and his eyes would light up and sparkle. He had a small mouth, but again, upon smiling, he gave a dazzling mischievous grin that took away that sombre look. Making her way through her relatives, she stopped briefly chatting to them, but she really wanted to get this new guest. As she reached the group, Alex turned to look at her. He had green eyes that penetrated and she caught her breath.

"Michael, is this your sister, Grace?" The circle opened to include her.

"Yes, it's been a while since you've seen her," Michael said.

"I don't want to embarrass you, Grace, but you have grown up a lot since I last saw you, but it was about five years ago." He took her hand as he had done to Ruth, raised it to his lips and kissed it. All the time, his eyes never left hers.

Think girl, say something.

"I'm sorry, I don't remember you."

"I'm Alex, we met at a sports day at the university. I went to the same college as Michael."

Grace thought. "I remember the sports day but I don't recall meeting you," she blushed. "Sorry, Alex." His face broke into a delicious smile. "I obviously made a good impression then." The group laughed. At that point, George the butler announced that dinner was served.

"Can I escort you to dinner, Grace?" He lifted his arm for her to take hold.

She took hold of his arm; it felt strong. "I'll be glad to," she replied.

They didn't speak again. Everyone found their seats. Alex pulled out the chair for Grace and pushed her seat into place.

"Thank you, "she said quietly.

He was sitting almost opposite to her and as he took his place, he looked over and smiled. He introduced himself to Grace's Uncle, Stephen and her cousin, Eloise. Grace was sitting with her father's colleague of many years, John and his wife, Constance. She had known them for most of her life and were like family.

The first course of soup was served and everyone tucked in. Sally's cooking was always superb and received compliments every time. The next course was duck. The conversation carried on throughout the meal; her father telling jokes with raucous laughter. Sometimes, the levels raised and then died down as each course arrived.

Periodically, Grace would glance in Alex's direction. He was enjoying himself. He laughed and conversed and seemed relaxed. She kept thinking of those green eyes and the way they made her heart skip and she'd caught her breath. They had melted her instantly. How had she not remembered him? He was handsome. She had been introduced to a few eligible bachelors, but although some had been interesting to talk to or may have been a suitable escort for an odd dance, no one had captured her imagination the way Alex had done and in such a short time. She kept stealing a look at him. What was he like? What was his profession? What would it be like to have him kiss her? As if reading her mind, he glanced in her direction and winked at her. Colour rushed to her face. She smiled as demurely as she could and looked down at her plate. For the rest of the meal, she tried to concentrate on her food and the guests next to her. Unknown to Grace, Alex was also resisting the urge to keep looking at her. He remembered meeting her when she'd been about fourteen. She was pretty then, but she had grown into a beautiful young woman.

Her hair was not as blond as her brothers'; hers was flecked with auburn streaks that shone like bronze in the candlelight. She has amber eyes and a pale complexion and was a lot like her mother. She wasn't small in height for a woman, but she had a slight build and a very tiny waist. He definitely liked what he saw. When he'd winked at her, she had blushed. What had she been thinking about? Did she like him? She was bewitching. They had hardly talked but he was shaken by her effect on him.

He had recently moved from Yorkshire to start at a law firm in the City of London. He had kept in touch with Michael after they had left university and Michael had helped him to find local accommodation.

Michael had found Alex a small apartment in Barons Court. Little pricier than he hoped, but this was London and he had more potential to earn more here than back home. He had lost little of his accent at college, but working in London, he still seemed to have much more of a northern twang than others. He would have to work on that for this job.

Now here, he was at the Christmas party of his friend, enjoying the food and company far different from home and there was Grace, with whom he was completely smitten. After blushing, she hadn't looked in his direction again, but as the dinner ended and the ladies were to retire to the lounge, they looked at each other again. He half-smiled and nodded in her direction as he stood, as the ladies left. She looked directly at him, smiled and nodded. *So polite*, he thought, when really, his thoughts were of wanting to hold her, dance with her, kiss her. Grace was struggling with her thoughts and expected conduct. His smiles and nods had meant so much to her. Did they mean the same to him? She wasn't sure. She recalled his kiss on her hand and she tingled. What was happening to her? She thought, *I have never been affected by any man like this*. As she left the room behind her aunt and cousin, she glanced over her shoulder. Yes, he was watching her; those eyes burning into her.

She felt as if her body was on fire and involuntarily shuddered. She had read of passion and love. Her mother and father had always seemed to be in love, as did her brother and sister-in-law. Grace had wondered if she was immune. No other man, however good-looking, talented, well set up in business had brought on this sensation.

"Ruth, dear, do you feel up to playing for us?" Elizabeth asked.

"Of course, I'd love to, Mother. Do you want to accompany me Grace? Eloise?"

Relieved in a way but also reluctant to come out of her thoughts of Alex, she agreed, as did Eloise. While the girls sang and played, Elizabeth and her sister, Mary, ensured everyone had drinks; asking Sally for tea for those who hadn't wanted alcohol. Elizabeth had told Mary of her impending grandmother role. Pleased, she hugged Ruth at the end of one of the tunes and eventually, the whole room was congratulating Ruth. She wasn't used to so much attention and quickly got back to playing the piano.

Everyone was relaxed and happy. The up-to-date tunes had changed to carols—O Come All Ye Faithful, Once in Royal David's City and others. There was a knock on the door of the lounge and in walked Stephen.

"Ladies, would you like to re-join us? I believe the dancing is about to begin."

Music from the gramophone started to trickle into the lounge and the ladies returned to the dining room. The tables were removed and the chairs were now around the edge of the room. Most parties at her home had to include dancing, as her father liked to dance.

"I will start the proceedings, "Frederick declared. "Where is my lovely wife?"
Elizabeth stepped forward.

"My dear, would you give me the pleasure of dancing this waltz with me?"

She curtsied, took his hold and began to dance, whirling around the room. Stephen and Mary joined in. Ruth had sat down, feeling a little tired. She'd told Michael she'd wait for an even slower tempo.

Grace was suddenly aware that she couldn't see Alex and disappointment filled her. He couldn't possibly have left without saying goodbye. Surely, he would have wanted to dance with her. More people partnered up and now, there was little room to move. She then sensed someone was behind her; she knew it was Alex. It was his cologne she recognised earlier—it was fresh, but also spicy scent. His body was close to hers. He leaned in closer, his breath close to her cheek and in a low voice; almost a whisper said, "Dance with me, Grace."

He had moved to her side and she looked at him again, melting from his intense look. She smiled, could she speak, she didn't think so. They joined the other couples and started to dance. He led her with expertise, glancing at where to take in their dance, but rarely wanting to look anywhere than at her face.

He held her closer than required. Grace could feel from his hold that he was strong; he was slim but muscular. She didn't want the music to end but it did.

"Don't anyone move," bellowed Michael. "Here comes another." The tempo was slower. Grace and Alex hadn't moved. They were still in hold, close to each other, neither wanting to break the spell. The music started; Alex looked down into Grace's face, they smiled and again, they were dancing. Neither of them really knew what the other was thinking; but actually, they were thinking and feeling the same thing.

They were in a world of their own. Some of the couples had sat down, while Ruth and Michael had got up but they hadn't noticed. *Can he feel my heart beating so fast?* Grace thought. It felt like it was about to jump out of her chest. By the end of the second dance, a strange understanding had fallen over the pair.

When he said, "I ought to dance with your mother or some of your other family and not monopolise you, but I will be back." He brought her hand to his lips and kissed her again. Their eyes met and held. He escorted her to a seat and went to ask Elizabeth for a dance. Just a short while ago, she would have been disappointed by his absence, but now she was sure he would be back. She would soon be back in his arms; moulding into his hold, looking into his eyes and back in their own world.

He hadn't wanted to stop dancing with her, but Alex had only just come into this house. How would it look if he didn't mingle? Grace had left the room to get a glass of water. Her heart had slowed a little but still jumped around in anticipation of her next dance with Alex. She entered the room to the rhythm of the Foxtrot and was quickly pulled into the dance by her father and then was swapped for her sister-in-law, and then, she was then dancing with her brother. A group dance was next and there, by her side, was Alex. They changed partners throughout the dance but ended together ready for the next dance. It was a much slower Waltz and they were now close again.

Their partnership had not gone unnoticed by Elizabeth and Mary.

"Do I sense a romance on the cards?" Mary leaned towards Elizabeth.

"I think you could be right. I've never seen Grace so taken with anyone before. I hope he doesn't get his hopes up going on her normal form, but they do look good together. Perhaps, not only a grandmother but a wedding to look forward to," she chuckled. Really, Elizabeth was hoping her daughter had fallen for the dashing young man. Having lost one child, Michael and Grace became her world. Seeing Michael married and becoming a father made her ecstatically proud and happy, but she had worried about Grace.

She was a strong, intelligent girl. Both her and Fred had debated when Grace asked to go to Bedford College for women in Regent Street, but thought it was the best if she put her intelligence to good use.

Grace had wanted to work once she had finished college, but her mother had insisted that ladies of her class didn't. The compromise had been that Grace did the accounts for the local church and the women's charity group. Seeing her daughter so taken by a man was wonderful. Perhaps, things would change now; she could only hope.

As the evening progressed, Alex and Grace made no attempt to talk, dance or speak to anyone else.

When they weren't dancing, they would sit and talk. He would get refreshments and then would dance again. She learned that he had a law degree and was working in the city. He liked to dance and wanted to go to the theatre here in London. He wanted to see a lot of the sights and hoped she was willing to show him around

He learnt that she had a good education and wanted to work but wasn't allowed. She loved music, dancing, going to the theatre and wanted a bicycle as she thought it would be excellent exercise. Their eyes rarely left each other's; only occasionally, to check that everyone was still around. His hand held hers most of the time too.

I don't want to let go, he thought.

The evening was coming to an end. People were happy, full and tired. Merry Christmas wishes were bountiful. Alex was offered a ride by one of the family, which he gratefully accepted. Grace had been saying goodbye to family and friends and Alex had been thanking her mother and father for a great party. He shook hands with Michael and hugged Ruth and then he was back with her.

"I've had a wonderful evening, Grace. Thank you," he lightly touched her shoulder and bent to kiss her cheek. A soft kiss and one she would always remember.

"I've had a great time, too. Are you going home for Christmas?" she hoped he wasn't.

"Yes, I'm leaving on the 24th but only for a couple of days. Can I see you when I get back?"

"I would like that very much. Have a lovely Christmas. I'll look forward to seeing you after the holiday."

Again, he leant forward and kissed her cheek, lingering a little longer this time.

"I'll see you soon, Grace."

"Goodbye, Alex." And he was gone.

Suddenly, she felt exhausted but also lost, like she'd lost her best friend or something equally as important. Her mother was by her side as she closed the front door. Elizabeth gave her a hug.

"I'm surprised you hadn't remembered Alex. He's a nice young man, don't you agree?"

Grace smiled at her mother, kissed her cheek and said, "Merry Christmas, Mother. It has been another successful Richardson party. Had we better tidy up?"

They headed back into the house, did little tidying but decided they were too tired. Back in her bedroom, Grace was hanging up her dress, removing her make-up, unpinning her hair and remembering the dances and conversations with Alex.

I can't wait till after Christmas to see him again, she thought. She put on her nightdress and got into bed. She held a pillow close to her, wishing she was still in Alex's strong arms. While recalling the scent of his cologne and his breath on her ear as he whispered into her ear during the dances, Grace thought: *I'm never going to be able to sleep; I can't stop thinking about Alex. Is this love?* Eventually, so exhausted; she fell asleep to dream of Alex.

Chapter 2

Grace woke when Cassie brought in her breakfast. She still felt tired and there was a knot of anticipation in her chest. She was grateful there was only tea and toast, because she really couldn't eat anything. Each dance and each conversation played over in her head as she washed and dressed. Her mother and father were finishing breakfast in the dining room.

"Are you ready for church?" her father asked.

"Yes, Father. Sorry, I feel a little tired still. Good party, wasn't it?"

"Yes, it went very well. I think we're a little tired and behind in the day's routine, but it is Christmas. We can make some allowances."

The day seemed to drag. After church, they returned home and Grace helped finishing the tidying that the staff had almost completed to get the house back to normal. She ensured all the silver ware had been cleaned and put away, although it would be back out for Christmas dinner. Ruth and Michael were staying till Christmas; they helped too. Soon, she would be able to escape to think. After dinner, that was when she slipped away to her room. Still excited and nervous, she couldn't bring herself to do anything except lay on her bed. After about an hour, there was a light tap on the door. It was Ruth.

"Are you feeling alright?" she asked.

"Yes, I'm little tired, that's all."

"Your dress last night was so you, you were dazzling. You seemed to have caught Michael's friend, Alex's eye. He didn't let you out of his sight all night."

Grace said nothing for a moment. *Should she ask her sister-in-law for advice? Was it too soon anyway?* She hardly knew Alex. Then she blurted out, "Ruth, how did you know Michael was the one for you? Did you know instantly?"

Ruth smiled. She had guessed what was on Grace's mind.

"I'd met Michael twice briefly at the school. Each time I'd picked up the children, he had said 'Good Afternoon', smiled and enquired after my health. I immediately thought he was handsome and charming. On our third meeting again, I was picking up the children; he asked me if I'd like to go to the theatre. I couldn't wait to say yes. He had been on my mind for a week. I could hardly concentrate on my work. He looked at me Grace, in a way that no one else ever had, as if he could see right into my soul. He came for me for our date at the theatre. He had bought me flowers—yellow roses, which I left my mother holding as we left. We talked all the way to the theatre and during the performance, he held my hand. When we arrived back at my home, he asked to see me again and I replied, 'Yes, I'd love to,' and a little eagerly I said, 'and soon.' She smiled again, recalling her memories of falling in love. That evening at my door, he asked if he could kiss me. I nodded; a little nervous, but I really did want him to kiss me. It was a light kiss over in a moment, but if I hadn't been sure before, I was then convinced I loved this man. How did I know? I'm not sure. As I said, it was the way he looked at me; that he seemed to instinctively know what I was thinking. What interested me, what I liked, yellow roses are my favourites and of course, he was handsome. All I can say is I just knew," she stopped for a moment then said, "Does that help?"

"I think so, it sounds a lot like my predicament."

"Alex?" Ruth asked.

"I just can't think straight, Ruth. I've never felt like this. I didn't want last night to end. I just wanted to carry on dancing in his arms. It made me shiver with pleasure when he whispered in my ear so I could hear him above the noise and merriment."

"He is handsome and he has good prospects with a career in the law. He's been Michaels's friend for some time and he thinks a great deal of him."

"Don't say anything to anyone yet, Ruth. Promise me."

"Promise," Ruth said solemnly.

"I cannot wait to see him again. I want him to hold me and kiss me and…" Grace trailed off.

"It sounds serious to me, dear sister-in-law. It sounds like the cupid's arrow has got you," Ruth hugged her. "You can always talk to me and I promise I won't say anything, but I do think Alex feels the same about you, too. Michael remarked last evening that he had never seen Alex pay so much attention to one girl and one girl only at a party before. He would normally dance with everyone, but last night, he couldn't take his eyes off you, let alone dance with anyone else. He held you very close, didn't he?"

Grace blushed, recalling his strong muscular body.

"Enjoy the feeling," Ruth said. "There's nothing better." She kissed the top of Grace's head and made for the door.

"Thank you, Ruth. I needed to confide in someone. I feel like I'm going to explode."

"Maybe you and I should go for a walk and use up some of that energy. I'll get Michael and we can walk to Holland Park."

Wrapped up warm against the cold, the three took a walk to the park. While walking, the conversation turned to the subject of Alex. His home was Yorkshire, his parents owned and run a cotton mill, how he and Alex had met at college, played rugby, socialised together; but obviously had been in different classes, as Michael had majored in English, while Alex, in law. The whole time they were out, Michael was in the middle of the ladies, linking arms with them. Grace was enthralled that she was hungry for information on Alex. She asked more about his family, why had he wanted to go into the law. Question after question, Michael gave her more information which gave her a fuller picture of this man. Ruth had been right. The walk had done her good and inadvertently, she had been able to talk about Alex most of the time.

The rest of the day passed; she felt calmer. She couldn't wait to see him again. She hoped he would call again. Monday was taken up with final preparations for the family Christmas, delivering presents to neighbours, buying fresh fruits and vegetables and wrapping presents. Elizabeth had gone to the kitchen to speak to Sally about Christmas dinner for about the tenth time in the last few days. Ruth was in her bedroom wrapping presents when there was a knock at the front door. Grace glanced at the clock in the lounge—1:45 pm. Who could that be? George was out at the moment so Grace answered the door. As she opened the door, Alex turned around and was looking straight at her. A potted poinsettia wrapped with ribbons in one hand and a small package in the other. Her heart started to beat faster.

"Alex, what a wonderful surprise! Please come in."

Stepping into the hall, he put his two presents down on the hall table and his briefcase on the floor.

"Shall I take your coat? Are you stopping for a while?" Grace asked imploringly.

Taking off his coat and putting it on the coat stand, he said, "I'm sorry, I can't stay too long. I'm heading home soon and I need to collect my case from the flat to get the station on time." He picked up the plant and parcel and followed Grace into the lounge.

"Have you time for tea?"

"I would love to, but really, I only have a few moments."

He took a seat by the roaring fire. "That's good. It's getting cold out there now. I expect there's snow back home, I'll have to get used to the colder climate again."

Grace sat in the armchair opposite to him.

"I really wanted to see you again and I couldn't wait till after the holidays," he said. "So here I am, the flower is for your mother." He put the plant on the side table and stood up and went over to Grace, "And this is for you."

The box wasn't very big and had been wrapped in gold paper. "Should I save it for Christmas Day?" Grace asked.

"You can, if you wish."

"No, I want to open it now."

Her hands were shaking, but she unwrapped and opened the box to find gold drop earrings with small amber stones in them.

"They are beautiful, Alex. Thank you."

"They reminded me of the colour of your eyes."

She stood up to look in the mirror above the fireplace to put in her new earrings. Once she'd put them in, she turned to face Alex.

"How do they look?"

"Lovely." Their eyes locked again.

"I've bought you a little something. I didn't think I would see you till after Christmas, but I wanted to get you something anyway." She moved past him to get to the tree. She knew exactly where she'd placed his gift. As she handed the box to him, their hands touched and their eyes met; each realising the feelings they felt for each other as they had done the night of the party.

"As you've opened yours, I'll open mine." Onyx cufflinks were in the box. "Thank you, Grace. I will look very professional with those on for work. I'll treasure them."

"Would you like to go to the theatre when you return?" Grace asked.

"Yes, I was about to ask you to come out with me. The theatre would be good and there's a tea dance at my local church on Saturday, 4th January. We'd get to dance together again."

"So the theatre…when?"

"I'll be back Saturday, so Sunday."

"Sunday and then the tea dance on the 4th."

Elizabeth had entered the room. "Afternoon Alex, to what do we owe the pleasure of your company?"

"Good afternoon, Mrs Richardson."

He picked up the plant from the table and handed it to her.

"I wanted to wish you a merry Christmas."

"Thank you my dear. That will look delightful as the centre piece of the table for Christmas. It's a shame you are heading home as you would be welcome to spend the festive time with us."

"I would have liked that Mrs Richardson, but I had promised mother and father that I would be home."

"Alex bought me these earrings," Grace stepped forward so her mother could see them.

"They're lovely, should you have opened them yet?"

"Alex has opened his gift too, we agreed to open them as we won't be seeing each other on the day."

"Well, Alex, it's nice to see you again. You are always welcome and please call me Elizabeth. Mrs Richardson reminds me of my mother-in-law and she's rather old and grumpy."

"I'll do that," he smiled. "I have just asked Grace if she would like to go to dance and the theatre upon my return, I hope that's all right with you?"

She looked at both Alex and Grace, both appeared nervous at this request. She and Mary had been right. There was a spark and romance was in the air for these two. Elizabeth was pleased. She liked and admired Alex and thought him a good catch for her daughter. Not quite of their class, but he was bright and had a good future ahead of him and he had made Grace behave like a lovestruck girl which was no mean feat.

"If Grace has agreed, then so do I. "She gave him a peck on the cheek and lightly touched his arm. "Merry Christmas, Alex. I'd better get on, still a lot to do."

"Merry Christmas, Elizabeth," and then she was gone. "So, your mother approves of us seeing each other."

"Yes. I'm glad you came to visit today. I wasn't sure what you thought of me," she stopped suddenly. Should a lady really speak out about her feelings before she knows how the man feels? He came towards her. His fingers lightly touched her cheek.

"I thought I was too obvious the other night. I monopolised you, I can hardly remember anyone else. I'm sorry I have to rush off, but I'm pleased that I got to see you and I got an unexpected present too."

They were so close. *Kiss me Alex*, she thought, *kiss me*. He must have read her mind as he came closer still. She closed her eyes and then his lips were on hers. The kiss was firm and meaningful and as they parted, she sighed with pleasure.

"I've wanted to do that for the last two days."

"Do it again then," Grace surprised herself with her request. This time, he took her into his arms and kissed her for longer. They parted.

"I really wish I could stay but I'd better go."

Reluctantly, they went to the hall, still holding hands and Grace helped him on with his overcoat.

"Thank you for the earrings. I'll look forward to our two outings."

"Can I kiss you again? As I won't be seeing you for a while."

"You don't need to ask."

Once again, their lips met.

"Till Monday then," he said as he opened the door.

"Monday. Merry Christmas, Alex. See you soon." He took her hand, raised it to his lips and kissed it.

"It will seem an eternity, Grace. Merry Christmas."

As he got to the gate, he turned and blew her a kiss and then he was gone. Grace closed the door and rushed up the stairs to her room. At the dressing table, she sat and looked at her reflection. Did she look different? She felt different. Alex had kissed her three times, four, if you counted the one on the hand, five, counting the one blown to her at the gate. *He has stolen my heart*, she thought. Her heart was still hammering in her chest and not in an anxious way this time. He did like her and he did want to see her again. Without realising, she looked again at her reflection and said, "I love you, Alex Whitfield."

Chapter 3

Christmas Day was the same family fun as usual. Breakfast first, then around the tree to open presents. George and Sally were the only staff that lived in, so they would join the family after present opening for a drink. If the family didn't go to the Christmas Eve church service, which they hadn't done this year they would have lunch, they will have a rest and then go to the evening service at All Saints Church.

Grace felt happier than usual. Her heart was light and she felt extremely excited. She was in love with Alex. Michael and Ruth were expecting a baby and her mother and father were in good spirits. She couldn't wish for more. Boxing Day saw her Uncle Stephen, Aunt Mary and cousin Eloise visiting for the day. The whole family played games, played music, sang and ate for most of the day. *Only two more days,* thought Grace, *and then Alex would be back.* Finally, it was Sunday. Now, a lot more nervous, Grace was trying to pick an outfit for her trip to the theatre. Ruth and Michael had left yesterday, so she couldn't ask Ruth for advice. She finally decided on a brown silk dress. She would have to wear a coat against the December chill but the brown would show off her new amber earrings. She was just finishing her hair when her mother called to say Alex had arrived. She was so excited. She wanted to run down the staircase, but that wouldn't be the act of a lady. So as slowly as she could, she descended the stairs and entered the lounge. Her mother and father were both there talking to Alex. As she entered the room, Alex turned around then stood.

"Good evening, Grace. You look lovely."

Grace moved towards him, "Thank you."

He looked as handsome as she remembered him. He was wearing a dark suit, was freshly shaven and was wearing that cologne again. Grace was feeling giddy with excitement.

"Your mother and father have invited me to the New Year celebration at your Aunt's and I have accepted. I hope that's fine with you."

"Of course. It will be fun having you there," she blushed.

"What time does the show begin?" Frederick asked.

"At 7:30," Alex replied. "I think we better go."

He finished his drink and got up. In the hall, he helped Grace on with her coat and then put on his top coat. Elizabeth wished them a good time and they left. Alex hailed a taxi and all the way to the theatre, they chatted. He told her about Christmas in Yorkshire with his family.

"I've told them all about you, Grace."

"Have you?" she said a little nervous.

"I've only told them good things."

Grace laughed.

"I missed you," he said quietly, so the driver couldn't hear.

"I missed you too."

He took her hand then and didn't let go till the taxi stopped and they got out. It was a Midsummer Night's Dream. They were seeing but it could have been anything, thought Grace. She wouldn't have cared she was with Alex. During the performance, he held her hand, occasionally stroking the back of it. Tingling sensations rippled through Grace's body. She could hardly concentrate on the performance. Alex got her a drink in the intermission and again, held her hand throughout the second act. After the play, they took a taxi home and Alex asked the driver to wait while he saw Grace to her door.

"So, Tuesday then," he said. "I'll be around at seven to go to your aunt's party."

"Are you working tomorrow?"

"Yes," he replied, "why?"

"I just wondered. I thought you might like to take a walk."

"I would be honoured, but this a new job for me and I'd better show willingness."

"Of course, I understand."

"Tuesday's not too far away. Will there be music and dancing like at your party?"

"Sometimes there is, perhaps we can suggest it," Grace wanted him to hold her in his arms again. He moved a little closer and Grace closed her eyes, his lips were on hers. This time, he was more demanding. It lasted longer and she didn't want it to end. Both were a little startled at their passion. Alex said goodnight and left in the waiting taxi. Frederick was still up and walked into the hall as Grace was taking off her coat.

"Did you have a good evening, good performance of, what was it you saw?"

Grace told him and said, "I had a wonderful night, Father. I'll see you in the morning." She kissed her father's cheek and made her way up to bed. *Was that what life was going to be like from now on?* She thought the next morning, getting through the days as quickly as possible when she wasn't seeing Alex, to the hoping time stood still when they were together.

New Year's Eve was a wonderful night. Alex arrived at the time he said he would and the family went to the party together. They had dinner, danced as Alex had suggested it, played more games and stopped momentarily to count in the New Year. Having wished all her family 'a Happy New Year', Grace was finally in front of Alex.

"Happy New Year, my darling Grace. I think this will be a good year for us," and then he kissed her.

Then Grace said, "Happy New Year to you, too and I'm looking forward to all our times together."

When they returned to Grace's home, Frederick said it was too late for Alex to leave and offered him the guest room. Michael and Ruth had gone to their room straight away. Grace, Alex, her father and mother had another drink in the lounge.

After about half an hour, Elizabeth said, "I think us ladies should retire now." Everyone said goodnight and the ladies left.

The two men talked for a while about Alex's job then Frederick said, "You seemed to have formed an attachment to Grace."

"Yes, I have. I like her very much."

"I obviously don't need to tell you to act as a gentleman at all times with her."

"Of course, that goes without saying. I would appreciate your blessing, sir. I would like to court your daughter." Alex was nervous.

"Does that mean you want to marry her?"

"Yes, it does. I know we haven't known each other very long but I am sure of what I feel."

"Does she know you are thinking of marriage?"

"No, not yet. I wanted to ask your permission first."

Frederick was silent for a few moments. "I give you my blessing on your courtship. Let's see how things are going by Easter. If you are both still happy with each other, I'll give you the go-ahead to marry. Does that sound fair?"

"Yes, it does, thank you. I'll await your say so."

Alex was pleased that was over with. He had wanted to ask but had been worried at how he would be received. He was after all from a different class and didn't know if they thought him good enough for their daughter. He said goodnight and Frederick gave instructions as to which room he should use. In the guest room, he laid on the bed thinking of Grace and wondering how soon he would be able to ask her to marry him.

Alex stayed throughout New Year's Day. He was already like a part of the family. Grace didn't see him again till Saturday, when he took her to the tea dance as promised. The next day, she went to church with her family. And so, the month of January passed into February. On Valentine's Day, red roses were delivered to her door. The following Saturday, Alex took Grace out for lunch. When they arrived back at her home, they were alone in the library. As he was ready to leave, he sat with her on the couch and put his hands up to cup her face. They were more relaxed with each other now. She seemed to understand that he really did like her and that he did want to see her again and again.

"Those roses were beautiful and a lovely surprise," said Grace.

"Only the best for you, my love," and he kissed her.

Her lips parted as the kiss prolonged and suddenly, his tongue touched hers. She had heard of this type of kissing from some of the girls who had been at the college. It was strange, but it did excite her. He moved away from her gently. He looked deep into her eyes. He wanted to be sure he hadn't scared her, but he could see she was a little startled perhaps and excited. She smiled, leant forward as if reading his thoughts and kissed him. Her lips parted for him to kiss her the same way again. Every feeling of pleasure she could ever imagine soared through her body. *Don't let it end*. His arms were around her and she put her arms lightly on his shoulders. They were so physically close; she could feel the heat of his body. They should stop, she thought. Her parents could be home at any time, but she didn't stop. When they did release one another, he didn't let her go completely.

"I love you, Grace."

"I love you, Alex."

His kiss was light this time, barely like a whisper on her lips.

"I had better go; Grace or I might not be able to stop myself from kissing you again and for longer."

"I would like that."

As she saw him out, they kissed again, tongues touching. It would never be any other way from now. On she thought, it was just so delicious.

Chapter 4

Life for Grace felt like it was in two parts—life before Alex and life now that he was in it. She couldn't believe that she had fallen so helplessly and completely in love when that had been the last thing on her mind. Wasn't she going to be a new woman, have a career and leave love and marriage till later?

Alex spent a lot of time at her home. He had lively debates with her father, brought flowers for her mother and would offer to help Elizabeth with any charity events she organised. They also spent evenings with Michael and Ruth, either for dinner or outings to the theatre. This was normal life now and Grace felt that she had known Alex for far longer than she actually had. With the weather permitting them, they took walks in Holland Park. They would shop in Oxford Street on Saturdays and have tea. They would talk for hours about his childhood, his home and how his family had made a living. His parents worked in the textile trade and owned a mill. He spoke of his hopes for his career, wanted a home of his home and eventually a family. Alex knew Grace was intelligent and never treated her as if she wasn't interested in politics and world affairs. He was pleased he could talk about so much with her on so many subjects. They had even argued over political issues to such a lively degree they had had to call the debate a draw. Unknown to Grace, her father had called on Alex one lunch time before the Easter holidays.

Frederick had arrived at the law firm and asked to see Alex.

"Good afternoon, Frederick," said Alex as he entered the reception of the office, extending his hand to shake Frederick's.

"Afternoon, Alex. Do you have a spare hour for lunch?"

"Yes, right now, actually."

Once sitting in a local restaurant and having ordered their meal, Frederick asked, "Do you want to marry Grace?"

"Yes, I do."

"Do you think it's a bit soon? You haven't known each other that long."

"I know, but it feels like I've known her longer. She's beautiful and intelligent..." Alex paused for a moment. This was a little embarrassing; he was talking about love with potentially his father-in-law.

"Do you love her?" Frederick asked.

Alex looked directly at Frederick, "Yes sir, I do. I want to make her happy, provide her with a good life and hope to have a family and spend the rest of our lives together. I understand this is a big step, but I am ready and believe Grace and I could have a good life together."

Frederick didn't say anything straight away. He was amusing himself making Alex sweat. His little Grace was a woman now and it was inevitable that she would meet a man and marry, but she was still his little girl. Now, here was Alex. Was he good enough for Grace? He was smart and had good career prospects. Having observed the pair together, they were so obviously in love. Wasn't it like he and Elizabeth had been? Yes, Alex was a good prospect for a son-in-law and as a husband for his Grace. He took a sip of wine.

"Alex, I give you my permission to ask for Grace's hand."

Alex had been nervously waiting for Frederick's response, smiled and said, "Thank you, I promise to be a good husband to your daughter."

They shook hands and carried on chatting as they ate their meal. As they were leaving, Alex asked, "Do you mind when I ask Grace? It's just that I'd like to ask her over Easter, if you have no objections."

"No, of course not. Will you be able to get a ring by then?"

"I have been planning and saving. I was just waiting for you say so."

"Then Easter it is."

Alex had problems concentrating for the rest of the day at work. He was excited but also nervous. He knew Grace loved him but was he wanting too much too soon? He wanted more. Grace excited him like no other woman had. He had little sexual experience but he knew how he felt about Grace was different and he wanted to spend his life with her. He had picked out a ring several weeks ago, ordered it and paid half of the cost. He was relieved Frederick had given his permission now because he really wanted to propose. After church on Easter Sunday, the whole family were together for lunch. Alex was getting jumpy; he wanted to get Grace alone. After eating and as if Frederick sensed his tension, he made the suggestion that Alex take Grace out. It was a bright day and Grace jumped at the chance to be alone with Alex. They spent a lot of time together but not a lot alone and she desperately wanted to be alone with him. They got to the park chatting comfortably as they always did, but as they approached the first bench they came to, he stopped talking.

As they sat Grace asked, "Are you all right? Alex, you look nervous!"

"I am. I've something very important to ask and it's making me nervous." He slid off the seat and on one knee in front of Grace, he said, "I love you, Grace and would you do me the honour of becoming my wife?" He had taken a ring box from his pocket and opened it while he spoke.

Grace couldn't take her eyes away from him. Had he really asked her to marry him? She glanced at the ring—it was a row of three diamonds sparkling in the early spring sunshine. It was beautiful. Seconds passed but it seemed like hours. She looked back at him and his expression had taken on a more concerned look. People passed and whispered, but she couldn't have cared less. She loved this man and he loved her.

She lifted her hand to touch his cheek; he sighed. "I would love to be your wife," Grace surprised herself at how composed and grown-up she sounded. "I want to spend the rest of my life with you and I am sure we will be happy," she said. He rose and sat beside her. He took her left hand and placed the ring on her ring finger. "It's beautiful," she said.

"Not as beautiful as you," and then he kissed her. "Are you sure this is what you want?"

"I've never been so sure about anything, Alex. You make me so happy and marrying you makes me feel complete. Have you asked my father for permission?"

"I didn't have to. He gave it before I asked."

"When would you like to marry?" she asked enquiringly.

"I don't mind, sooner rather than later," he looked longingly at her. "I don't like saying goodbye and leaving you each night."

Grace blushed; she had been feeling different of late and had been dreaming of intimacy with Alex and had woken up hot and breathless.

"There's a lot to organise but I don't want to wait too long," and he kissed her again.

"Ruth's baby is due in July, so perhaps we shouldn't marry that month. Maybe June or August."

"You wouldn't want to be away on honeymoon when the baby is born so early in June, but I think August would probably be better," Alex concluded.

"I don't think I can wait that long," Grace said as she snuggled into his body, "but we have to be sensible, as there is a lot to prepare and we wouldn't want to steal the limelight from Michael and Ruth's special time. August is the most ideal time."

"August it is then and then you will be Mrs Grace Whitfield."

Grace kissed him with passion, "I can't wait."

Arm in arm, they hurriedly walked back to the family to tell them their news. She was filled with happiness. She felt the ring on her finger and realised she was a grown-up woman and this man loved her. She really couldn't wait to be his wife.

Chapter 5

Grace had a sneaky suspicion that their news, when they returned to the house, wasn't a total surprise. She suspected that her father had engineered their outing. Nevertheless, everyone was happy for them and congratulations were given all round. Ruth and Elizabeth admired her engagement ring while Frederick shook hands with his future son-in-law and Michael bearhugged Alex.

"Welcome to the family, brother," Michael said.

Then Elizabeth enquired, "I know its early days, but any ideas when?"

"August," Alex replied.

Grace went on to explain why, "It will give Ruth time to recover to be my head bridesmaid."

"Really?" Ruth was excited. Grace nodded and the women cuddled.

Frederick checked his diary. "Might I suggest 2nd August."

Grace looked at Alex and he smiled, "Sounds perfect, Frederick. The 2nd it is. Grace and I can check with the vicar next Sunday if the date is free and we can start planning from there."

Frederick laughed, "I think the girls will be taking over from now on."

"Why would it be any other way," laughed Elizabeth, gathering her daughter and daughter-in-law in each arm and cuddling them.

The 2nd was free at All Saint's Church and the date was booked. Elizabeth started by telling all the family. Cards and gifts were soon turning up at the house, congratulating the couple on their engagement.

Alex had some exams coming up so he did spend some time studying, but Grace didn't mind as there seemed a mountain of things to arrange. Invitations to choose have made and sent. The reception was to be at home and what were they all going to eat? Ruth was an obvious choice, but who else to have for bridesmaids? Dress, what would be the best style? Honeymoon, Alex would organise that and who to invite? There was a lot to do.

Ruth and Michael with the baby on the way were going to buy a house in Chiswick. So she and Alex were going to start married life in the family apartment that Ruth and Michael were leaving. She was excited but this was coupled with worry and anxiousness. Alex was a great organiser which did relieve some of her worries. Whenever possible, they tried to forget the wedding arrangements and would go out to just enjoy themselves at Chiswick House and Gunnersbury park, just to walk and enjoy the spring weather. They went to the Chelsea Flower Show and to Wimbledon to watch the tennis. Sometimes, with family or friends; other times, just the two of them. Elizabeth had remarked to her husband that their daughter had blossomed into a woman in the last few months and that the impending nuptials were certainly agreeing with Grace and had matured her.

Alex did well in his exams and was rewarded with an increase of his salary. By the end of June, the wedding plans were all in place, so when Ruth went into labour on 2nd July, everyone's attention could focus on the new mum and baby. On 3rd July at 7:06 am, Rachael came into the world, weighing in at 6lbs 9ozs. The new mum and baby were doing well and Ruth had had a reasonable labour and delivery. Grace couldn't wait to see her niece. When the family arrived at the hospital, they couldn't all visit at the same time, so when it was Grace's turn, she practically ran into the ward. Michael was holding his daughter and Grace could see a look of pure love radiating on her brother's face. She leant over the bed and kissed Ruth.

"How are you feeling?"

"A little tired now. Once everyone has met Rachael, she will be back in the nursery and I can get some sleep."

"You look wonderful, not a bit tired," Grace said then went to the other side of the bed to her brother to look at Rachael. "She's beautiful."

"She certainly is."

Alex had joined them having rushed from work to see the baby. Grace kissed him and they both admired the new arrival.

"We'll leave you now," said Grace. "Let you have a little time alone before visiting ends."

"Thank you," said Ruth.

"Well done you two, you have a beautiful daughter," said Alex.

"Take care and get some rest."

Grace blew a kiss to the new family. As they left the hospital, Alex asked Grace, "How do you feel about having children?"

"I'd like a large family, Alex. Maybe three or four children but not for a year or two, as I want you all to myself for a while."

"Sounds good to me."

The baby's arrival gave Grace something other than the wedding to think about, which was a relief. It was Grace's family and Ruth's help, in turn, to organise the move to Michael and Ruth's new home and help with Rachael.

Elizabeth, in a quieter moment in all the upheaval, took Grace to one side and gave her the mother to daughter talk about the wedding night and what to expect. Grace wasn't that naive, but she had to admit to herself that as the wedding day drew closer, she was becoming nervous about the expectation of the wedding night.

After the last fitting of her wedding dress two weeks before the day at Ruth's house so that Ruth's dress could be fitted too, Grace cornered her sister-in-law and asked about sex. Ruth wasn't at all embarrassed as she spoke lovingly about her relationship with Michael without going into intimate details.

"Alex loves you, Grace. He would never do anything to hurt you. Talk to each other, you'll learn from each other. Your love life can be fulfilling and enjoyable and you can be blessed with children." Ruth always said the right thing and Grace felt a little easier, but she was overwhelmed with excitement and worry as to whether Alex would find her attractive and good in bed. Their times along in the last couple of weeks had been more passionate. He kissed her harder and had stroked her breast. She had felt the muscles in his chest and her breathing quickened and her heart did somersaults. She needed to talk to Alex. He was to be her husband soon and shouldn't she be able to talk to him about anything?

On Friday, Alex arrived at Grace's home earlier than expected. He sensed she had something on her mind, so he asked her and she explained her worries about their wedding night.

"I want it to be good, memorable but... I don't know... I am just nervous, really."

"You trust me, don't you, Grace?"

"Of course, I do."

"Then everything will be all right," he smiled. "Let nature take its course."

She didn't seem convinced. They were in the lounge and he led her to a seat by the fireside, set her down and set a foot stool in front of her and sat on it. He took her hands in his and looked straight at her.

"You know what happens between men and women, I know you do." She nodded. "It can be a bit uncomfortable the first time, but I promise you, you will be relaxed. We will be enjoying ourselves and everything will be wonderful."

God did she love him. Was he always going to make her feel special, safe and secure? He kissed her then. She felt the passion between them rise and her whole body cried out for his touch. He kissed her with such intensity that her body was on fire. Her heart beat faster and she clung to him, as if her life depended on him. When they parted, she was breathless with desire.

"We will be good together, my darling Grace and we will both enjoy our sex life, I promise you that. I have never felt like this and I know we will be fulfilled, so do not worry, my love."

"Thank you, my darling. You have made me feel a lot happier and I too, believe we will be great together." Despite her worries she wanted this man and couldn't wait to become Mrs Whitfield in every way.

Chapter 6

It was 2nd August 1913 and it was her wedding day. Although she was a little nervous when she woke that morning, she was getting more excited as the morning wore on. Her dress of silk and tulle draped over her breast and was secured there by a brooch of tiny flowers. Her waist was pulled in and the flowing skirts fell to the floor with a train at the back. Her hair was piled up, the veil secured with flowers was put around her head. She wore the diamond necklace and earrings her parents had bought her. Her bouquet of yellow and white lilies and roses was laying on her bed.

"You look beautiful, my darling," Elizabeth said with a tear in her eye.

"Thank you, Mother."

Her bridesmaids, Ruth and cousins Eloise and Iris were all ready. Their dresses were similar in design but in a creamy colour with pale yellow details. A few photographs were taken in the garden before they left for the church. Grace and her father arrived by carriage at the church a little after 11 o'clock. Holding her father's arm, she made her way up the aisle to meet her love. Alex was waiting for her along with his best man, Grace's brother. She felt womanly and very grown up and when she reached Alex, he whispered in her ear that she looked beautiful and he smiled with joy. All nerves disappeared; she was where she wanted to be more than anywhere else in the world. She was marrying Alex. She faulted on her vows due to her emotions. He put a ring on her finger and the Vicar said, "Alex could now kiss his bride." She was married. She was Mrs Alexander Whitfield.

They signed the register and proceeded back down the aisle to the sounds of 'The Wedding March.' There were more photographs taken and well wishes from friends and family and then everyone went back to the house for the wedding breakfast. The meal went well. All the speeches were made then Grace excused them both to go to her room. He had brought his going away case around a couple of days ago; she had prepared hers yesterday.

He helped her out of her dress. "Well then, Mrs Whitfield, are you happy?"

"Absolutely," and she kissed him.

She started to put on her going-away outfit—a suit with a skirt and jacket in pale yellow and a white blouse and to complete, a hat. Alex changed from his dress suit into a day suit. Strangely, she thought, they were undressing in front of each other and it hadn't been awkward at all. She felt liberated by this and really couldn't wait for tonight.

"Where are we going?"

"Wait and see." He opened the bedroom door, "Ready?"

She nodded and he picked up their cases. In the lounge, they said their goodbyes and Michael took them to Waterloo Station. They were going to Torquay in South Devon.

"I'm sorry. It's not abroad, but we will go to France, Italy or anywhere else you want to in the years to come."

They could have just gone back to their home, she thought, as long as they were together. It was a plush hotel and they had the honeymoon suite. They had a light dinner in their room and then Alex suggested they go for a walk along the seafront. A band was playing at the band stand and the music wafted in the air as they walked along the promenade in the late sunshine. They chatted about their special day and after about half an hour, Alex turned to her and said, "Shall we go back now?"

"Yes."

Anticipation and any worry of their first night seemed to melt away when they were alone in their room. She wondered if she should undress in the bathroom, but the decision was taken from her. He kissed her immediately when they entered the room and started to undress her. Within moments, they were naked in front of each other. He was already excited and she wanted him too. He took her hand and guided her into bed. They kissed and caressed each other. He told her he loved her and started to kiss her all over. As he had said, nature took its course. They were soon two bodies entwined, lost in the rapture of each other, kissing and caressing.

She had only a split second of pain before the explosion of pleasure of their climax took over her body. As she realised him from her hold, he moved to her side, leaning onto her, a hand caressing her breast, "That was amazing," he said breathlessly. He had been right; they were perfect together, sex was wonderful. After a few moments, he pulled himself up and leaning on his elbow. He looked down on her and admired her slender body.

"It was good for you, Gracey, wasn't it?"

She looked into those wonderful green eyes and felt empowered she was a woman and she wanted him again. She put her hand on his chest and played with his chest hair feeling his muscles flex at her touch. He was a handsome man and his body definitely excited her.

"It was wonderful Alex and I never want to stop loving you." They kissed again; slowly, they caressed and touched each other learning every inch of their bodies. When they were aroused again, he took her. He held back this time till Grace could bear it no longer and cried out for him to take her. They fell asleep exhausted.

When she woke, Alex wasn't in bed. Where was he? She could hear running water; he was in the bathroom. She rose from the bed and put on her robe. A tray of breakfast had been brought in; she hadn't heard anyone knock. She sat at the table by the window and poured some tea. The bathroom door opened and out walked Alex with only a towel wrapped around his waist; he was dripping wet.

"Morning, Mrs Whitfield. How are you feeling?" he made his way to her, leant over and kissed her full on the lips. Droplets of water fell on her face. He smelt fresh of soap and she was immediately aroused.

"Top of the world, husband. I thought you had already bored of me when I woke up alone."

"Never," he sat on the chair opposite. "I thought a breakfast in our room would be better this morning instead of the dining room."

"Good thinking, was the shower good?"

"Refreshing."

After eating some toast and having some tea, Grace said, "I think I'll try the shower now." As she passed, he caught the belt of her robe and it opened. She turned to him.

"Or would you rather do something else?"

He opened the robe fully and let it drop to the floor. His hands were either side of her waist. She moved closer, moving the towel from him and he looked up and kissed her lips. Holding her tightly, he got up, her legs wrapped around him. They made their way to the bed and surrendered to the pleasure of lovemaking. Once recovered, they bathed together.

"We'd better think about contraception," Alex said. "You didn't want children yet."

"I know, but at least for a couple of days, I think we'll just take the chance. I don't really want to think about anything other than us and now."

They did finally leave the room that day at about 3 pm. Both of them were not wanting to get out of bed, not wanting to put on any clothes and not wanting to stop touching and caressing each other. They went for a walk, had dinner at a local restaurant and went back to bed. Each day took on the same sort of pattern. Their lovemaking was either slow and sensual, learning about their bodies or urgent and passionate, depending on how long between each coupling. They did spend some time on the beach, they learnt to tango in the ballroom which made them feel sexy. They had a trip to Paignton and Brixham resorts all on the bay, but they didn't take in much of the scenery because they only had eyes for each other.

They made love the afternoon of the last day of their honeymoon. They had gone to the town earlier to buy presents to take back to her family. Sex this time was more frenzied and passionate than any time before. They were exhausted after.

"It's a shame real life isn't like this," Grace said.

"Why can't it be?"

"Well, I don't think you'll be able to leave work at 2:30 just to come home to make love to your wife."

"No, maybe not but you can be ready for me at 6:30 each night and there's always the weekends for afternoon loving." But he knew what she meant. This week had been wonderful, magical. Only a week ago, they had barely touched each other and now, he knew every inch of her. She was incredibly passionate and he couldn't get enough of her; he was truly lucky.

Their journey back was a little sombre. Neither had wanted to leave the idyllic life they had experienced this past week. Michael met them at Waterloo and took them to their apartment. Grace gave him the gifts she had bought for the family and he left.

Alone again, she led Alex to the bedroom and said, "Let's christen our home, I'm not about to settle into real life just yet." She led the way as they both started to undress.

Chapter 7

So, married life began. Grace wanted to run her new home but found that she wasn't as adept as she thought. Still helping with all the church work she'd done before; she now wanted to cook and have dinner parties. She also wanted to have any spare moment with Alex. They still couldn't keep their hands off each other. Their appetite for sexual pleasure was well-matched. Apart from their lovemaking, Grace seemed to be floundering with the domestic duties of being a housewife. Elizabeth suggested she gets a cleaner to come in for a couple of days a week to help with the washing and ironing, Grace thought this was a good idea. She wanted to learn to cook better though and she had always enjoyed watching Sally at her parent's home, so she asked Sally to teach her. She had a great time and discovered she was a good pupil and had a talent for making excellent food. Her first dinner party was for her brother and sister-in-law. She'd been a little nervous, but they all enjoyed the meal and no one was ill afterwards, Alex had joked. She was pleased it had turned out well. She knew there would be some of Alex's colleagues to entertain in the near future and she wanted to impress them for the sake of Alex's career.

By Christmas, she felt more confident in her new role. On her first birthday with Alex he bought her a necklace to match the amber earrings he'd bought last Christmas. She wore them both all day and matched her outfit with them, to go out to dinner that evening as a special birthday celebration. The couple was invited to several parties leading up to Christmas, but Christmas Day and Boxing Day were to be at her parent's home with all the family including Alex's parents. Fun and celebration were had by all and it was good for Grace to get to know Alex's mother and father better. Valentine's Day brought roses.

They had arguments and more minor disagreements as the months wore on. Real life was infiltrating in their idealistic romantic haven. They had to get used to each other's ways and live together and fortunately, they always got though the hard times with either of them saying sorry and then making up passionately.

Rachael's first birthday in July was celebrated with a party at Michael and Ruth's. Grace had been out and bought a teddy bear and a pretty dress in the palest pink as a gift for her niece. She adored Rachael and started to feel like she too wanted to be a mother.

"The first anniversary is coming up, Gracey. How do you think you will be celebrating?" asked Michael while they tidied after the party.

"I'm not sure. I think Alex would like to go back to Torquay."

"Same hotel," Michael grinned, teasing his sister.

"Probably," Grace replied blushing.

Torquay was their destination on Saturday, 1st August 1914. They took the train and stayed in the same hotel as they had for their honeymoon. The weather was hot and they were enjoying their anniversary and holiday all in one. They were reminiscing about a year ago and spent a great deal of time in bed. But their joy was short-lived. On 4th August, Britain declared war on Germany. A string of events starting with Archduke Ferdinand's assassination caused the Austrian/Hungarians to declare war on Serbia. Russia backed Serbia; Germany declared war on Russia. Germany needed a passage through Belgium to get to France and a treaty with Belgium brought Britain into the war.

"What will it mean for us, Alex?"

"Not sure, Grace," he held her close. He really didn't know what impact this would have on the country and all their lives. Nothing changed for the rest of their week, all be it that most people had only one topic of conversation. Upon their return, they had dinner with Elizabeth and Frederick.

Frederick explained, "When the war was declared, there were crowds outside Westminster, Union Jacks flying high and people singing. It's thought it will all be over by Christmas."

"I do hope so," said Elizabeth. "I only hope that you and Michael are not called to fight." She was looking at Alex.

"It's to be single men between the ages of 18 and 30 that will be called on," Frederick continued.

Grace couldn't help being relieved. Alex went back to work the following Monday. Some things were changing; many young men were joining up. A couple of Alex's colleagues had volunteered. By 28th August, 100,000 men were called up and the age limit was raised to 35. Grace's fear was growing.

The church was asking for help. Groups of women from the congregation were forming to knit gloves and balaclavas for the troops. They were getting blankets and other useful items together to send abroad. Grace and Elizabeth got involved immediately and they wanted to help and do their bit. In general, little changed for the family. The reports from the front weren't good though.

Christmas 1914, the family were all together but the atmosphere was a little sombre. Earlier in the month, German cruises in the North Sea had bombarded Scarborough, Whitby and Hartlepool and about fifty civilians had been killed. An air raid over Dover had done little damage, but the war was creeping ever closer. The short war the country had hoped for was not in sight.

Throughout the early part of 1915, Alex would read the newspaper. He and Grace would see news reels at the cinema about the men at the front and he would say he should join up. It was his duty, so many men were fighting for their country. Grace would try to ignore the turmoil he was in. He knew she was worried, didn't want him to be enlisted but he was feeling guilty. If he wasn't married, he would have already gone. Grace knew all this but she was selfish, she didn't want him in danger, she may lose him. The horror of what was reported terrified her, she couldn't bear it. Many wives had lost husbands, mothers had lost sons and siblings and friends had been killed. She knew she was wrong, but selfish she would remain.

Alex's position in work was improving all the time, more responsibility and involvement in cases Grace became more and more involved in the church's war effort. Charing Cross Hospital had started to take in injured soldiers. It was suggested that Grace and Elizabeth visit the hospital. This was to talk to the soldiers and help them by writing letters to loved ones, but they were finding they were there to comfort and, on some occasions, be the last person these poor soldiers spoke to before they died of their injuries.

Private Edward Wilson, aged 19, had thought Grace was his sister. "Tell mother I'm sorry, June. I tried to get better and get home. I love you all," that had been his last words as he had died of the wounds to his head. Grace had cried as he passed away and had cried again at home that evening. Alex had taken her in his arms, let her explain, and then he suggested she take a bath and go to bed early. The visits were taking their toll on her and he knew it was making her more anti-war and it would be harder on her when he would eventually have to go and he knew he would have to go sooner or later.

On 7th May 1915, the Lusitania was sunk off the west coast of Ireland by a German U-boat. 1,198 men, women and children were perished. This had been a direct attack on civilians. A few days later, there were anti-German riots across Britain, the war was creeping closer. With so many men fighting, there were many vacant jobs. Women now wanted more than ever to do their bit for the war and country. The Voluntary Aid Detachments or VADs had been set up in 1914. Many women had joined and some had been sent to France to work as assistant nurses, ambulance drivers and cooks. In the rain of July 1915, Mrs Pankhurst marched through the streets of London along with 30,000 women, demanding the right to work. Women started to work in various jobs once done by men, including work in munitions factories. Grace had pondered over her choices but had decided to stick at helping at the hospital. It was becoming an addiction. She really thought she could give some hope and comfort to the soldiers, even those who were rude and abusive. She felt she was doing her bit.

Grace knew that it was not going to be too long now before Alex and her brother would have to go to France. She tried to keep their home life and time together as light and cheery as possible, at times, pretending that the war was far away. Their lovemaking was still passionate and as often as possible. Grace hoped that she would be pregnant soon. If Alex was to have to go and fight, at least if she had a child to look after.... she'd still have a part of him. She was being selfish again. On their second anniversary. Alex bought her an emerald and diamond ring. She loved it, putting it on her fourth finger of her left hand immediately. They made love first thing in the morning and when Alex returned from work, they ate out and made love again that night. They had considered a trip to Devon, but work was so busy for Alex.

Christmas 1915 was only the immediate family and a lot less festive than usual. The war had been going on for more than a year already. Elizabeth was worried for her son and son-in-law going off to fight, worried about her daughter and her daughter-in-law and their grandchild. How would they cope with their men gone? Tears, sadness and sorrow had been felt by many mothers and wives throughout the country. She was trying to celebrate Christmas, but the constant reminder of war was always nagging at the back of her mind.

Michael and Alex had met up a few times during April 1916. It was becoming more apparent that married men would soon be called up. Should they pre-empt the compulsory call up or wait? But before they could decide, it became compulsory on 25th May for all men between the age of 18 and 41, married or not to go into military service.

On Tuesday 30th, Alex left work early and met Michael and went to the enlisting office to register. Before leaving, they went for a drink, both having a whisky followed by ale. They had both known it was inevitable, but it was still going to be hard telling their wives. They shook hands as they left the public house and went to their separate ways to give the news to those they loved most, both wishing it hadn't come to this and the war really had only taken till that first Christmas.

Grace hadn't been to the hospital today. She had met her cousin Eloise instead. Eloise had married a little before Grace and was now pregnant. They had shopped for a while then stopped for lunch. Eloise looked radiant, her skin and hair were in beautiful condition and she spoke animatedly about the imminent arrival of her baby.

"I would like a son for Stephen. I think he would like son, too, but he just says he wants a healthy baby."

"Have you thought of names yet?"

"Possibly Jack for a boy, Constance for a girl. They were the names of Stephen's grandparents."

Grace was enjoying the afternoon immensely. She liked to help at the hospital but it was tiring and it made her sad and worried about Alex having to go off to war, this afternoon and been a wonderful distraction. After lunch, Grace saw Eloise home and returned to her own flat to prepare for Alex's return from work. He arrived a little later than normal, but dinner hadn't spoilt. They ate immediately, chatting as normal, well, not quite. Grace sensed Alex had something on his mind. After clearing the dinner things, Grace found Alex in the bedroom. He looked tired.

"You've joined up, haven't you?" Grace asked.

He looked directly at her, "Yes I have. Michael and I signed up, call up was inevitable so we took the bull by the horns. Sorry, Gracey. I know you didn't want to hear this, but Michael and I wanted to feel we had some control of all this. You know that I've felt I should be doing my bit."

He had moved closer to her and took her in his arms. She buried her head in his chest and the tears started to flow; her fears and worries all coming together. She might lose the love of her life. She started to sob and cried harder. Alex guided her to the bed, still holding her and sat beside her.

"Grace, don't worry," he kissed her repeatedly on the top of her head. "I will take care, I'll stay out of trouble wherever possible and I'll come home to you, I promise." He held her tightly for ages. Her sobbing finally ceased and she looked up at him.

"I'll try to believe you. I'll pray that you come back to me soon. I can't live without you. I love you so much."

He kissed her fully on the lips, deep and longing. She needed him now, she wanted him now. All that mattered at this moment was having his body close to hers kissing her, making love to her. As always, he sensed her need and started to undress her. The urgency was incredible, he couldn't wait to take her. She held on to him tightly, even after they climaxed. *God please make me pregnant*, she offered up a prayer.

"I don't suppose Ruth's going to be too happy either," said Grace. "I hope you and Michael will be able to stay together in the same regiment so that you can look out for each other. When will you tell your parents?"

"I thought we could travel up at the weekend. I do want to see them before I'm drafted."

"Then we'll go this weekend."

Not much time had passed since their last coupling, but when he kissed her again, the passion took over and they made love again. A little slower this time, more sensual and just as satisfying. Grace promised herself as she fell asleep, still upset but sexually fulfilled, that she would try not to dwell on the future. Alex would come back from the war and they would carry on with their lives. Who knew? She could be pregnant. She was going to make the most of the next few weeks. They dined with Elizabeth and Frederick the next evening and Alex broke the news to her family. Elizabeth had also had Ruth over that day, telling her about Michael enlisting and had tried to be brave in front of her daughter-in-law, but Alex's news had made her tearful.

"Sorry," she said dabbing her eyes with her handkerchief. "Both of you going are not right. This damn war."

Frederick put his arm around his wife and kissed her cheek. "Our sons will be fine; they'll fight help in the victory and they will be home in no time. Come on my dear, we all have to be brave."

"I know," she sniffed, "it's just that seeing all those wounded soldiers at the hospital brings the horror of it all right to your front door so to speak. I don't want to see either Michael or Alex in one of those beds."

"And they won't," Frederick cuddled his wife.

On Thursday evening, Alex and Grace visited Michael and Ruth. Upon seeing her brother, Grace hugged him tightly and tears sprung to her eyes.

"I promise you, Alex, and I will be back. We've got so much to live for."

Grace kissed his cheek, "I'll keep you to that."

On Friday afternoon, they travelled to Yorkshire to stay with Alex's parents. His mother was upset by the news too. Although the trip had been arranged in a hurry, Alex's parents had called on all the family to be there for Saturday evening. It was good to meet Alex's family again. His cousins were fun and for a short time, she could forget what the future held. The weekend had been a mixture of happiness and sadness, but Alex had been glad to have seen everyone again.

For the next few weeks, they made every day count as if it was the last. When the details of his training arrived, Grace cried again. The ordeal was getting closer and closer. They made love almost every day. They both needed to be close to each other; memorising each touch, taste and scent. Grace refused to go to the hospital during this time. She needed to concentrate all her time and emotion on her husband.

On 26th June, Michael and Ruth arrived at Grace's; Elizabeth and Frederick were already there. Frederick was going to take his sons to the station to join their regiment and start their training. Grace had held Alex all night and had made love twice. She was trying to keep bright and positive. She didn't want to cry on their last night together. Everyone was hugging and saying goodbye to each other. Alex was holding Grace close.

"I love you so much, I'll be back before we go to France. Pray for me."

"I will," Grace kissed him. "I love you too. In no time, you will be back," she smiled her biggest and brightest smile for him.

She was being brave, he thought. "That's my girl," he kissed her again. And then they were gone. The bravery left them and all three women cried and clung to each other for comfort.

Chapter 8

Grace moved back home with her parents. She didn't want to stay at the flat alone. It felt empty and it made her cry more. Alex was only training at the moment, but he would soon be sent to France. Alex wrote letters and Grace responded. She tried to keep cheerful. He was physically tired but fired up and ready to go.

Grace went back to the hospital. She needed to keep active and keep her worries at bay. Speaking to soldiers and sailors about their wives, mothers and families made Grace feel useful. She knew exactly how these men's families would be feeling, so writing letters for them made her at times a little happier. Reports had started to come through from the front lines. At the River Somme, the British Offensive that was aimed at relieving the pressure of the French held at Verdun was going badly. British forces suffered some 57,000 casualties on the first day, more than 19,000 killed.

Frederick tried to keep the mood light every evening, trying to keep war talk to a minimum. He knew that his wife and daughter were worried and the latest news wasn't giving them much to keep up their spirits. He had kept up with the war's development. He had read about the fighting in Anzac and Gallipoli in April 1915 and the losses of many allied soldiers, many Australians. When the Lusitania was sunk on 7th May 1915 by a German U-Boat, he had thought like many others, that as American civilians had died on the ship, the Americans would have joined the war but they hadn't. Each battle and the loses made Frederick realise that Alex and Michael would soon have to be involved. Elizabeth didn't help at the hospital; instead, she visited Ruth two to three times a week to see how she was getting on. Ruth was considering moving back to her parents in Richmond. Elizabeth really hoped she wouldn't as she couldn't see Rachael as much. She also offered that they come and stay with her. Ruth had thanked her and said she would finally decide once Michael had been home on leave.

Michael and Alex arrived home on 23rd July. The family got together on their first full day. Michael and Alex told stories of their training and colleagues. Michael thought that Rachael had already grown, all be it, that he had only been away five weeks.

Alone in their own home, Alex and Grace fell into each other's arms in moments they were making love urgently and passionately.

After, as they lay entwined, Grace said, "I wish we could stay here like this forever. We could forget the war and just enjoy each other and make lots of babies."

"If only that was possible."

He was tired, the training had been hard and reports from the Somme hadn't given him the confidence he needed of what was ahead of him.

"I'll take care, Gracey. I've got everything to come home for. We've got a life time ahead of us, many children and a lot of fun and happiness. Just hold on to that, my love."

"I will try, my love. I will certainly try," and then they slept.

In the next few days, they visited friends, took walks in Hyde Park, shopped and went to the theatre. They were trying to make the most of their time. Whenever alone, they made love. Sometimes quick and frenzied, sometimes for hours. Grace had told Alex how much she wanted a child now and he agreed.

"Let's get on with it then, let's have more sex. I'm definitely up for that," he joked.

Their last night together was romantic and sad. Grace had cooked them a meal and they ate in candlelight. In bed, they made love, slowly taking their time to satisfy each other. Both knowing it would be some time before they would see each other again, let alone enjoy each other this way. She wanted to see him off at the station the next day, but Alex said he would be meeting Michael and they would go alone.

"Please darling, stay here. Let me remember you in our home, just as if we're leaving for work like normal and that I'd be coming back soon."

So she was saying goodbye at the front of the mansion block. Elizabeth and Frederick were going to the station to see Michael so they would see Alex too. They kissed for a long time.

"I love you, Alex. Be safe and come home soon."

"I will, my love."

With that, he picked up his kit bag and walked on, turning twice to wave and then he was out of sight. Grace returned to her flat. She couldn't even cry; there weren't any more tears. She was empty. She sat at the dining table and clasped her hands together.

"Dear God, I know many people are probably asking you to look after their loved ones at this time, but I will still ask you to protect Alex. I need him, I can't live without him. Please keep him safe and my dear brother Michael, please look out for him too. Amen." Then she sank her head into her hands. She felt exhausted.

Grace went back to her parents to live. She hated being alone. It was closer to the hospital anyway.

Ruth did go to her parents in Richmond which upset Elizabeth, but she was determined to still visit them at least once a week. She wasn't going to miss out on her granddaughter, she was the only sunshine in her life.

The more Grace attended the hospital, the more involved she became. Although not official and certain Matrons didn't approve, she had started to help the nurses. They were overwhelmed with the number of casualties and not enough nurses were being trained. On certain shifts, she helped the nurses redress wounds, fetched and carried blankets, clean or soiled. She knew how to sterilise bedpans, instruments and would help with cleaning the wards. Many of the wounded weren't much different in age than herself and Alex. They would tell her about their sweethearts and wives, what they did before the war and what they wanted to do when the war was over. They all had hopes and dreams just like herself and Alex.

This was the pleasant side of her work and she now felt it was a job, not just a voluntary help. There was another side too. Those in pain would cry out, some became abusive or violent. Many nurses had been hit. But it was those who woke up in fright shouting, screaming, still believing they were in the trenches or on the field.

The first few times, it had frightened Grace, chilled her right through to the bone. The stories they had told her became more real when they screamed and shouted. Gradually, she was getting used to these outbursts, well, nearly.

On some occasions, she would help calm them, convince them they were back home being cared for. She always felt sorry for those with more minor injuries, as they would return to barracks and eventually be sent back to France. Those who had lost limbs or injuries were serious enough to stop them returning to the front were the lucky ones, Grace thought. Whatever their disability, it had to be better than facing the horror again.

The wounded who came in and seemed as if they weren't there scared her the most. Their eyes were open, she knew they could see but there was no spark of life. It was as if the lights had been turned off leaving just the shell of man. The nurses explained that they were in shock. Their silence was just as eerie as the shouters and screamers. She couldn't believe how much her life had changed. Blood, lice, wounds, smells she never smelt before were part of everyday, but it was nowhere near as bad as what some of these men had put up with.

The days were long but she felt closer to Alex. Perhaps, she would be able to understand what he was going through so that when he came home, she could understand his experiences. Many evenings passed the same; she would eat, catch up with her parent's events of the day and then go to bed exhausted. Alex sent letters. He wasn't on the frontline yet. He told her he could hear the booms and bangs and occasionally an explosion near the camp, but apart from the uncomfortable sleeping arrangements and mostly cold food, he was fine and she shouldn't worry. Michael was doing fine too and he always sent his love.

If Alex hadn't liked the camp, the life in the trenches was far worse—loads of men all squashed in together, sleeping, eating and fighting. The heat of the summer was at least going as autumn began. The noise was deafening. He had started as a runner giving and receiving information from the officers. He was learning more and more each day. One of the things he learnt was there was a new machine called a tank and the British were going to bring it to the field soon. He tried to see Michael whenever possible, but they were separated more and more. The British had learnt a lot from the start of the battle and were using the knowledge to make an advance.

It was September and his regiment was about to make an offensive. Artillery bombardment created shell cover so that the Germans couldn't see the advancing British so easily. His regiment took the first German trench with ease. Thiepval Chateau was the next offensive. The German machine guns were nonstop. Unknown to Alex, at the start of the advance, Michael had been hit and taken by stretcher-bearers back to camp. Then the tanks had arrived; massive machines, nothing like Alex had seen before. The tanks shot at the German defences; progress could be made. Unfortunately, many tanks ditched in the mud, disabling them and the infantry were once again on their own. The enemy put up a strong fight but the British pushed on and took Thiepval.

Only a week later, Alex was shot in the left shoulder and got shrapnel from a blast in his leg. Now, it was his turn to be stretched to camp. He still didn't know what had happened to Michael. News had reached Ruth at the end of September that Michael was wounded and would be shipped home for treatment. Ruth went straight to Notting Hill to tell Elizabeth. Elizabeth read the telegram and collapsed into a

40

chair. Ruth quietly called Sally to get her some water. Having taken a drink and calmed somewhat, Elizabeth looked at Ruth.

"It doesn't say what has happened or when he will be back. It's awful."

"He's alive though, alive, we can only hope his injuries are not too severe."

Michael was brought back to Charing Cross Hospital. Grace thought that he might come there and had been looking out for him, but Nurse Griffiths had told her he had arrived the previous evening when Grace had started work on 2nd October. The nurse told her where he was and she hurried to his bedside. His eyes were closed. He had a bandage around his head and his abdomen was also bound, but from what she could see, he was intact and had no missing limbs. She knelt by his bed, lightly touching his cheek.

"Michael, it's Gracey. Michael, can you hear me?"

Slowly, he opened his eyes, focused and tried to smile but winced in pain.

"My little sister. It's very good to see you. I'd give you a hug but I can't quite get up."

"Same as ever, my chirpy brother. It's good to see you. None of us knew when or where you'd come back. Once I've done what I have to do today, I'll get Ruth, mother and father here to see you. How do you feel?"

"Like I've been hit by a truck. My head hurts and it hurts all over if I try to move."

She sat with him for a short time and then he fell asleep. She had wanted to ask about Alex but hadn't had the chance before he slept. She wanted to find out how bad her brother's condition was, so she kept a lookout for when doctors did their rounds and found out that his injuries were serious, but a full recovery was hopeful. In between tasks, Grace managed to telephone her mother and tell her about Michael. Elizabeth cried with relief; her son was in London. She promised to contact Frederick and get word to Ruth. At just after 4 o'clock, Elizabeth, Frederick and Ruth were at the reception. Grace having been told of their arrival went to meet them. While on the way to the ward, she filled them in on his condition and recited what the doctor had told her. His eyes were closed when they reached his bed. Ruth did as Grace had done earlier, sank to her knees and touched his cheek.

"It's Ruth, darling. I'm here."

More alert this time, he quickly opened his eyes and smiled at his wife.

"Oh Ruth, it's good to see you. I thought I never would again."

She leant over carefully, trying not to put weight on him and kissed his mouth.

"I've missed you so much and I've been out of my mind with worry," she said, tears starting rolling down her cheeks. "We didn't know when you would be back, it's been awful."

"I don't remember much since I was hit. I had no idea what time had passed. I just wanted to get back to you."

Ruth had taken his hand and held it to her lips.

"You're safe now. You're home and that's all that matters."

Michael realised there were other people at the foot of his bed. He moved his head and tried to focus. His head still hurt. It was his mother and father.

"Good evening, son," said his father. "Good to see you back." He stepped round to the opposite side of the bed to Ruth and took his son's other hand. Michael clasped his father's hand weakly trying to shake it.

"Still got a good grip on you, my boy, "Frederick tried to make his son feel good. Elizabeth moved around to get closer to her son. She had been crying a lot lately and she was trying not to now.

"Hello, mother."

She leant over and kissed the bandages on her son's forehead.

"My darling, I'm so glad you're home."

The conversation was minimal, the family was just glad to be together. They couldn't stay long because of hospital rules, so Grace went back to them after half an hour.

"We'd better leave you to get some rest."

They said their goodbyes, leaving Ruth alone with him for a few moments.

"He doesn't seem too bad," Frederick said. Grace could tell her father wasn't convinced. He didn't let his guard down with regards to his feelings. He was a good father, kind and generous but his feelings were always guarded, typical British stiff upper lip.

"We have to be positive. He's getting all the care possible."

Frederick patted her hand, "You're right, my dear. You have probably seen many men recover from such injuries. Michael will pull through."

She had seen those that had recovered but she'd seen many pass away. *I must stay positive*, she thought. Ruth caught up with them outside the hospital and went home with them. She was going to stay for a few nights so that she could easily visit Michael. Grace spent as much time as she could attending to Michael during the next few days. Some of the soldiers she had sat with had recovered enough to go home. She was sad to see some of them go. She had learnt a lot about them and their families that she felt she knew them all like friends. Private Saunders kissed her hand as he left. She had written letters to his mother and fiancé. He was going home to Norfolk for a few weeks but likely to be back in France not long after.

Finally, after two days, she managed to ask Michael if he'd seen Alex before he himself had been injured.

"I hadn't seen him for about a week. He was tired but otherwise fine. I expect he's still fighting. He will be alright, dear sister."

Michael didn't stay awake for long. His head wound was looking less fierce but the stomach wound wasn't healing as well as they'd hoped. Michael was propped up as far as was possible to help him to eat, but he often said he didn't feel like he wanted to eat. Instead, he would ask for help to lay him back down and instantly fall asleep again. Grace had seen this before—sheer exhaustion, the injuries and even blocking out the horror they had seen made many men sleep. Michael was lucky he wasn't having too many nightmares and she was relieved about that.

By the end of the week, there had been a little improvement in his overall condition. When her family visited, she tried to remain positive, but Grace was becoming quite worried. Michael's strength was depleting and his periods of sleep were increasing. He had woken one time when she had been sitting, reading by his bed and he hadn't known who she was. She felt exhausted from being alert, helping on the ward and whenever possible tending to Michael. Her fear over her brother's health was waning her spirit. She was missing Alex more than ever. There hadn't been any letters for four weeks. Was he alive? Surely, she would know if anything had happened. Therefore, he must be alive. Still, she wished there was some word from him. Grace didn't work over the weekend. Ruth had collected Rachael from her parents on Thursday and had taken her in to the hospital on Friday. Rachael had got upset soon after they arrived, so they left. Grace had agreed to look after her niece on Saturday. The weather wasn't bad so they could go to the park.

She wanted to escape her routine and worries and little adorable Rachael would be light relief. Rachael asked if her daddy would get better. Grace tried to reassure the little girl that her daddy would soon be home and then she and her mummy could look after him. That seemed to please the little girl, thankfully. Grace wasn't sure how she could answer more difficult questions that a three-year-old would understand. They played in the park and then went for tea and cakes. The afternoon passed and Grace thought it was the most pleasant time she had spent in a long time. When they got home, Rachael had a nap, curled up on her grandfather's armchair. When Ruth returned from her visit, she was upset. Michael's temperature had risen and the nurses thought that was a result of an infection. He had hardly been awake and when he was, he was fretful. Grace cuddled her, trying to give as much comfort as she could. This wasn't a good sign. Again, for what seemed the thousandth time, she said a silent prayer. "Try not to worry, he will be well looked after."

Again, on Sunday, Grace looked after Rachael. She was reluctant to go to the hospital because she had an awful feeling of dread. All she wanted to do was play childish games and keep Rachael occupied and keep all her fears firmly in the back of her mind. Other family members had visited over the weekend so she wouldn't be missed. She didn't sleep well over Sunday night and she didn't want to get up on Monday morning. Ruth's parents had visited the day before, to see Michael and then they had taken Rachael back with them. Ruth was still staying to be close to the hospital. Reluctantly, she washed and dressed and went to the hospital. She looked in on Michael and he was clammy and pale. Nurse Griffiths was trying to keep him cool and attend to him.

"The doctors are thinking of putting him in isolation. The fever seems to be getting worse and they're not certain that it's just the wound infection."

Grace got on with her duties, talking to patients and helping with meals. Sister Johnson was on duty today so she could help the nurses with their duties too. Sister Johnson wasn't as stringent on the rules and allowed her volunteers who were capable and learnt certain procedures to assist the nurses. She looked in on Michael again before she left, he was barely awake.

"Gracey," his voice was little more than a whisper. "I feel really tired."

"I know, it's normal with your type of injury. Sleep as much as you like. Sleep helps you recover your strength." She stoked his cheek; it was wet and cold.

"Tell Ruth I love her and my baby," he paused to catch his breath, "I love you all."

"Of course, I'll tell Ruth. I love you too, big brother. Rest now and gain your strength and I'll be back in the morning."

She kissed him lightly on the lips and left quickly. He might not be alert enough to see but she wanted to make sure he didn't see her cry. Once outside the hospital, she leant against the wall and sobbed into her hands. Nurse Jackson was leaving and saw Grace crying.

"Grace, can I help?"

Trying to stop crying, she replied, "No, Maggie. I'm fine really, just tired, I'd better get home."

43

"If you're sure or I could walk back with you," she had put a hand on Grace's shoulder.

"No really, I am fine. You better get home and have some rest, your next shift will some come around and you will be exhausted. Thank you, Maggie."

Maggie patted her shoulder, smiled and turned to go home. For a volunteer, Grace worked hard and she had her brother to think about. *She's probably exhausted herself,* thought Maggie.

Unknown to Grace, not long after she left, Michael's breathing became laboured and he became unconscious. By the next morning, Michael had passed away.

Chapter 9

Not following the strict protocol of the hospital but making allowances as Grace and her mother helped out so much, Maggie Johnson asked if she could go to their home to deliver the news of Michael's death. Grace was just finishing breakfast when Maggie arrived. George had shown her into the sitting room and then went to get Grace. When George announced, Maggie was there. She expected the worst. Already shaking, she joined Maggie and one look at the nurse's face confirmed her fears and her eyes filled with tears. Maggie moved towards Grace, "I'm so sorry."

"Thank you for coming, when did it happen?" tears were streaming down her cheeks.

"About 4 o'clock this morning. He was unconscious, he didn't know anything about it. It was just as if he'd fallen asleep."

"Was it the infection?"

"The doctors think it was septicaemia," Maggie put her arms around Grace, the poor girl looked like she might faint. "Is Ruth staying with you?"

"Yes, she's upstairs. I will tell her and mother in a moment," she gently pulled away from Maggie. "I'd better compose myself first."

"Would you like me to stay?"

"No, thank you. You've been so kind already; it was good of you to come. You had better get back. They will be missing you."

The women hugged again. "If you want to come in to see Michael, just let me know."

"Yes, thank you."

"I don't think anyone will be expecting you to work for the next few days, so if you want or need anything, help with the funeral directors, anything, just let me know." She really did want to help Grace. Maggie had grown rather fond of Grace. She was always so helpful and cheered up so many of the patients. She wanted to show some of that support to her.

"Thank you, Maggie."

When Maggie left, Grace climbed the stairs to relay the awful news. She would tell her mother first, then they would both tell Ruth. Elizabeth wept silently. She had lost another child; how could she bear another loss? They both sat on Elizabeth's bed for some time mostly in silence, holding each other and occasionally remembering small things about Michael—his beautiful golden hair, his smile and his zest for life. Then they heard Ruth outside on the landing about to descend the stairs.

Elizabeth wiped her eyes and said, almost in a whisper, "You'd better bring her in here."

Grace caught Ruth as she started down the stairs. Hearing the door open, Ruth turned to see Grace. She had been crying.

"What's wrong?" she enquired.

"Come in with mother and me," Grace nodded towards her mother's room.

Fear clutched at Ruth's heart, "No, Grace, no...it's Michael isn't it? What happened?"

Grace took Ruth's hand and guided her into the bedroom. One look at her mother-in-law's face, gave her the terrible truth and Elizabeth said, "I'm sorry, Ruth. Michael passed away this morning in his sleep."

An awful sound escaped from deep within Ruth and she began to fall to the floor. The two women caught her and guided her to the bed. They got her to lie down. Her sobs racked her body and she kept saying, "He can't be dead. He can't be dead."

"Grace, I think we had better call the doctor and then get your father home. Are you up to that?"

"Yes," she grabbed her mother's hand. "Yes, of course. Just look after Ruth."

She wanted to just fall apart and cry for her beloved brother and now, she was even more scared for Alex than ever. She wished he was here. Where was he? There still had been no word. He would be upset too; Michael and he had been friends for years. *God, please stop this horrible war before any more men die.* She telephoned the doctorand then her father. Frederick got back just after the doctor had arrived. Grace hugged her father. Tears were in his eyes and he was still trying to keep a check of his emotions.

"I'll get mother, she has stayed with Ruth all the time. I'll take over and you and she can..."

The words failed her.

Back upstairs, the doctor was giving Ruth a sedative.

"Mother, Father's home, I'll stay with Ruth."

Elizabeth got up from the chair beside the bed, hugged her daughter and hurried down to her husband.

"Let me know how she is later in the day. I will call in anyway, but I think it's better to keep her sedated for a while," the doctor explained. "Does her family know yet?"

Grace shook her head, "No, they are looking after Michael's daughter." Tears filled her eyes again. *Oh, dear God, Rachael will never know her father.* Grace had taken the seat by the bed. The doctor checked Ruth's pulse and then came around to Grace. He had known her family a long time. He'd seen Michael and Grace grow up. The family had already lost one member at a young age not that many years ago and now this, it was awful for them.

He put his hand on Grace's shoulder, "My prayers are with you all. You must take care of yourself too, Grace. Michael has left you all far too soon, but we all have our memories and he left his daughter and she will need all the love your family can give her and help her to remember her father."

Grace was trying hard to control her tears, "I know, Doctor, but the pain is so hard to bear. I thought I'd seen so much death during my volunteering, but nothing hurts as much as when it's one of your loved ones."

He patted her shoulder, "I do know, my dear." He looked at Ruth, "She will be asleep for a while now, keep looking out for her but it would be better for you to be with your mother and father. Give me Ruth's parent's telephone number and I'll contact them."

"Thank you, I don't think I'm up to that now."

She gave the number to the doctor, said goodbye and let him out of the house. She found her parents cuddled up together in silence. Perhaps, she should leave them alone for now. She would tell Sally and the rest of the staff. She really wished Alex was here. She needed his strength. *I just hope you are all right my love*, she thought.

By 3 o'clock, most of the family had been contacted. Ruth's parents had arrived and they were sitting upstairs with her; she was semi-conscious. Grace kept Rachael with her, playing games in the dining room. Sally made tea every hour. Elizabeth, Frederick and Grace kept consoling each other, trying not to cry in front of Rachael. While Rachael napped, the three of them sat at the dining table.

"I'll start with the funeral arrangements tomorrow," Frederick said.

"Had we better not ask Ruth if there is anything she wants regarding arrangements?" Grace asked. "They may have talked on these things what with the war and going to fight."

"I don't think she is going to be in any state to ask, unfortunately. I'll speak to the vicar at All Saint's and arrange a day. Hymns and the like can be looked at later. Hopefully, Ruth will be a little better in a couple of days and then we can ask her."

Ruth didn't improve much. She listened as the arrangements were told to her and just nodded in agreement. Ruth's parents stayed all week, which greatly relieved Grace as she didn't think they would have coped with their grief and Ruth's sorrow without help. She helped her father with the funeral details and contacted family and friends to tell them that the funeral would be on the 17th October. Every evening, she heard her mother cry and she too would cry as she fell asleep, dreaming of her brother as he had been in their childhood.

Everyone dressed in the customary black the whole time. Ruth seemed ghost-like. She hardly ate and moved about in a daze. Margaret and George, Ruth's parents, were always willing to help with anything, trying to ease the family's pain.

At ten in the morning, the family and friends of Michael Richardson crammed into All Saints Church. Maggie Johnson and their doctor who had attended to Ruth were at the service too. Prayers said, a reading by her father and then everyone sang Jerusalem. Then at the graveside, the service concluded and her brother was laid to rest. Tears rolled down Grace's cheeks as she threw some earth into his grave. Ruth could barely stand; Margaret and George either side of her trying to keep her on her feet. Frederick was trying to look after Elizabeth and Grace and battle with his feelings, but as his son was lowered into the ground, he too couldn't stop his tears.

Most of the gathering came back to the house. Maggie said she had to get back to the hospital, but Grace was still to say if she wanted her to do anything at all. Once everyone had paid their respects and left, George suggested that he and Margaret take Ruth and Rachael back with them to Richmond. Elizabeth clung to Rachael when saying goodbye. She was all that was left of her son.

"Come and visit anytime," said Margaret.

Grace hugged Ruth, "I'll see you soon, look after yourself." She kissed Ruth's cheek.

Ruth tried to smile, "Come soon, we will remember Michael together."

"We definitely will."

By 4 o'clock, the house was quiet, more quiet than it had been during the week of mourning. There had always been someone calling to offer help or pay their respects. Elizabeth had gone to lie down, Frederick sat by the fireside and Grace sat on a stool by his side. They were reminiscing.

After a while, Frederick said he had better check on Elizabeth and as he got up, he said, "Alex will be fine, Gracey. He's got to be now we've lost Michael."

She only hoped he was right. Two days later, she had an answer. The morning post brought a telegram. Her hands shook as she opened the item for Mrs Alexander Whitfield. Alex had been injured in action, was alive and would be shipped back to England.

"Oh mother, not again, it's just like Michael."

"No, darling, he's alive. He's not going to die. He can't. He's going to live we have got to believe that. Soon, he will be back home and he will be well," they hugged.

"He will be fine, I know he will," said Grace. "I just want to see him."

Chapter 10

They didn't have to wait too long after, the letter arrived five days later, to inform Grace that Alex was in The Royal Hospital Haslar in Gosport Hampshire. Frederick was going to take a couple of days off from work. Grace still hadn't returned to Charing Cross Hospital, but had got word to Maggie so that she could tell everyone what was happening and why she wouldn't be in for a while. She had sent a note to Ruth too, to let her know about Alex. Two days after, the letter came and the family made their way to Gosport by train. They hailed a cab at the station and went to the military hospital. Frederick took charge at reception and soon they were shown to the block where Alex was being cared for. The doctor on duty explained what treatment Alex had received and said that the physical injuries should improve. He said Alex had wanted some fresh air and one of the nurses had taken him out to the grounds near the chapel. The doctor gave directions to where Alex could be found and where to get some refreshments and the room designated for visitors was usually a storeroom, but since the war, the hospital had been inundated with relatives of patients.

"Best you go and see Alex on your own," Frederick said.

Grace nodded. She was frightened, of what she wasn't sure. She had wanted to see Alex for so long but now; here, she wasn't so sure. What if he wasn't the same? She would just cry and what good would that do.

"That is if you feel up to it," Frederick added.

"You are right, Dad," half smiling, half wanting to cry, she left the ward and made her way towards the chapel.

There were servicemen and nurses everywhere she looked. The weather was fair today and it appeared that everyone was making the most of it. Nurses were assisting men to walk, aided with sticks or crutches. Some men were without limbs. As she looked around, she spotted a man in a wheelchair. He appeared to be watching the others attempting to walk. Grace moved slowly towards the man, her fear growing with each step. She was now alongside of the chair, then she moved around to stand in front of the man; her breathing was heavy. It was Alex in front of her. Her heart leapt to her throat. It was really Alex; no visible disabilities, thinner, tired-looking but it was Alex. Her whole body flooded with the relief of what she saw. He hadn't looked at her though.

She could barely speak but in a quiet soft voice she said, "Alex darling, it's Gracey."

He turned his head and looked up at her. At first, it was as if he didn't know her, but then the light seemed to come back into his eyes as he lost that faraway look.

"Gracey, is it really you?" he started to smile and tears were in his eyes.

Grace sank to her knees, "It's me Alex. It is so good to see you; I was so worried about you."

She leant towards him and put her arms around him. He laid his head on her chest. They stayed like that for what seemed an eternity. Alex wept. She had never seen him cry before and it made her want to hold him more and take care of him and protect him from everything. When he calmed, she moved away a little, still resting her arms on his lap. She took a handkerchief from her bag.

"Sorry, my love, you shouldn't see me cry; not the way a man should behave."

"Never mind that, you've been through so much. You're entitled and anyway, they are tears of joy as you are so pleased to see me," she tried to lessen his discomfort.

"I thought I'd never see you again," he paused, then carried on, "I thought of you all the time. Even before I went to the trenches; the days were long and tiring. You'd see all the injured brought back from the fighting. It didn't give you much confidence of what was to come. Then once you are there, you know you have reached hell. I knew why I was there; I knew what my job was but beyond that, I had to switch off as much as I could. The horror, Gracey, I could never have imagined such devastation and waste of life," he paused again. He was looking at her intently and a haunted look took hold on his face. His beautiful green eyes, as Grace thought, are dull and there is pain. He looked tired, he'd shaved but not well and he looked older. Her fear grew again. She had seen so many soldiers with this same look. He was home, here in body, but would her Alex ever be the same again? He was watching her, "I thought of you, our life together, making love to you, hoping that one day, the fighting would be over and I could come home."

Grace looked deep into his eyes, seeking the man she married. She would help him and he would get better.

"You are back now and you'll be back in our home soon. We've got our life together for many years to come. I've got your back and I'm not letting you go anywhere again. I love you, Alex," she leaned further forward and kissed his lips, he returned her kiss with as much energy as he could muster.

As she moved away, he whispered, "I love you, Grace." Then looking straight at her, "I never thought I'd see you again." He raised his right hand and touched her cheek. "You're like an angel, you are really here, my love. It is you, isn't it?" she kissed him again.

"I'm really here, really and truly."

"I'm feeling quite tired now. Do you think you could take me back to the ward?"

"Of course, mother and father are here too. Are you up to seeing them before you sleep?"

"Yes, seeing them too will help me to believe I'm really home."

They didn't speak again on their way to the ward; each lost in their own thoughts. Grace was relieved but still concerned. Alex was suffering with shock as well as his physical wounds. She had learnt about how shock affected people from her experiences at Charing Cross. It wasn't going to be easy but she would nurse Alex back to health. Once back in his bed, Grace found her parents and went back to his bedside. Alex looked dazed. A cold feeling ran through Grace, it was like seeing Michael all over again.

Sensing the closeness of people, Alex focused on reality and tried to smile, "Frederick, Elizabeth, it's good to see you."

"You too, son," Frederick said. "You are looking well, be back on your feet in no time."

"I hope so."

Elizabeth took hold of his hand, "We'll have you home soon and look after you, pamper you."

Alex smiled weakly again, "That sounds good, I'll take you up on that."

They spoke a little longer but Alex was tired. They only stayed for a few minutes and then said their goodbyes. Alex clung to Grace's hand.

"You will be back, won't you?" that haunted look was back in his eyes.

"Of course, darling. I'll be back tomorrow and the next day and the next. I made a promise to you. I'm never going to let you be out of my sight for too long ever again," she kissed him, made sure he had settled and then left.

They had organised to stay at the Anglesey Hotel, Stokes Bay. The buildings were very like their own home—a Georgian terrace with gardens just across from the properties. Grace was glad to be able to rest and fell onto the bed in her room. Did she ever feel awake and refreshed these days? She truly didn't think so. What mattered was that Alex was home and physically not too bad. The wound in his left shoulder had affected his muscles and he would need to exercise to get that back to normal, but it may never be as strong again. His leg was in a cast as the shrapnel had splintered the bone. Again, it should heal but he could be left with a limp. At least, these injuries would stop Alex having to go back to the front. It was going to be hard, but their life could start again now. She hadn't told Alex's family of his injuries yet. She had wanted to see him first for herself so she could tell them accurately. *I'd better call them;* she thought and went back to the reception and asked to use the telephone.

The mill had a telephone and she hoped her father-in-law would be there. He didn't answer but after being called for, he answered and Grace explained about Alex's condition. James listened intently and then asked questions. He said they were so busy as they were making uniforms for the services but they would come and see Alex in the next couple of weeks. James was just relieved that his only child was safe and well. Grace promised to keep in touch and let them know of his progress and as to when he would be able to go home.

When she got to the hospital the next day, the doctor wanted to speak to her before she visited Alex.

"He had a bad night," said Doctor Gregson, himself a naval serviceman, as well as a doctor. "We have been concerned about his lapses into silence. The report from the field hospital said he hadn't had nightmares but he had been very withdrawn. I'm really not concerned about his physical injuries. He's a strong young man and he is healing, but his mental state is a problem."

Grace explained about her voluntary work at the London hospital and what she had experienced in caring for the poor soldiers.

"Your arrival has opened up a new can of worms. Please don't look so worried, Mrs Whitfield. It's got to happen; Alex has got to confront his fears, experiences. His withdrawal is not healthy. He screamed out for you last night. He's more irritable today and anxious that you won't be back or that you really weren't here at all."

Grace thanked the doctor and went with a heavy heart to the ward and to Alex's bed. He was awake and smiled at her as she approached.

"I thought I'd dreamt yesterday. I was convinced you had been a dream."

Grace leant over and kissed his mouth.

"I am here as promised and I am real, darling."

He touched her face to reassure himself of her presence. They talked and then he got tired. After a short nap, she wheeled him out for some air, but it was a little colder so they didn't stay out long. When his meal arrived, she helped him to eat but he couldn't take much food. When she left that day, she wasn't sure if she was helping him and she wasn't happy at all about his condition. The family had only booked to stay till Monday, but Frederick suggested that she might want to stay on for another week. Grace thought it was a good idea, so Frederick spoke to the proprietor and the husband and wife team said they would take care of Grace. So the arrangements were made, Frederick and Elizabeth returned to London and Grace remained in Gosport.

Some visits were easier than the others. Some days, Alex was like his old self, but on others, she hardly recognised him. At times, he was loving, speaking of their past and their future and then his mood could turn. He would become withdrawn and whatever she said could not penetrate those moods. She hadn't mentioned Michael and he hadn't asked, but on Wednesday, they had been talking quite normally and then he asked after Michael.

"Is he still in France or has he managed to get leave?"

Grace paused, not sure what to say. She looked directly at Alex. She was worried how he was going to take the bad news. Before she could say anything, Alex said, "What's happened to Michael?"

"Michael was injured and brought back to Charing Cross Hospital earlier this month. He had been hit in the head and the stomach. Alex, he died two weeks ago." She watched his face. He was fighting back the tears.

Finally, he said, "I'm sorry, I had no idea. We hadn't seen each other once we got to the trenches."

He fell silent for a long while with tears in his eyes. Then he broke the silence, "I know he was your brother and you grew up together and it must have hurt losing him, but he was like a brother to me too. We made a pact to look out for each other but it didn't work, did it?"

"It's not your fault you couldn't have helped him. If you want to blame anything, blame this bloody war; what use is it to anyone? Nothing is being achieved but heartache and loss."

"He made me feel I belonged when we were at university. Many of the boys were from well-off families, obviously I wasn't, so I was left out of social and curricular activities. Michael wasn't going to let that happen and because of his care, we became firm friends. I will miss him."

The next day was his worst yet. He had hardly slept due to nightmares. He was angry and for the first time, he was violent. There was little conversation during her visit and she left exhausted and scared. Friday wasn't as bad. When he started to get angry over the food he had been given, Grace got angry herself.

"The nurses have enough to do. They don't need this sort of behaviour from you," she shouted. Some of the nurses turned around, surprised by her outburst. Alex seemed shocked too. Before she lost her confidence, she added, "The nurses are busy, they don't need your tantrums over the food. Eat or don't eat but don't give them your childish attitude."

Had she gone too far? Alex was startled into the submission. She knew she shouldn't disrespect her husband and was this the right way to deal with his condition. She would just have to wait and see. She had surprised herself at her aggressiveness.

He ate a little more, then laid back, "That suit you!" he said sarcastically.

Grace just glared at him and cleared away the tray. She needed some air and wanted to get out of the ward. Doctor Gregson found her under the veranda of the ward block, watching the rain. She had been crying.

"Mrs Whitfield."

Grace turned, "Afternoon, Doctor, wonderful weather!"

"Suits many a mood in this hospital, don't you think?"

"It does."

"I heard what happened. Don't worry Mrs Whitfield, Alex needs to know when his behaviour is unacceptable. Yes, he has had a hard time. We need to give him time to heal physically and mentally, but he also has to live in this world again. You have to be firm at times. Make acceptable boundaries of behaviour in your normal life. He's going to be like a child again for a while. He's been following orders, orders that have led to death, not only of the enemy but of his friends. It will take time for him to adjust to your life from before. With your help, guidance and love, he will get better but it won't be easy and you will have to be strong. I've never killed anyone in battle. I'm trained, but I've only treated the wounded, never inflicted the pain. Well, most of my patients think I don't inflict pain," he smiled, making the moment a little lighter.

Grace smiled, "Thank you, I was worried I could have set him back and please, call me Grace."

"Grace, I'm John" They shook hands. "Alex is doing well Grace, try not to worry. You need to take care of yourself too."

The rest of her visits that week weren't so bad. Frederick returned on Sunday, ready to accompany Grace back to London. Alex said Goodbye reluctantly to Grace and made her promise to be back soon.

She said she would write every day and he had to reply as often. She remembered to tell him his father had called the hotel and he would be down to visit very soon. She was back home only a few days when there was news that her cousin Eloise had given birth to a baby boy on 2nd November and they were naming him Jack Frederick. Eloise's husband had not been able to join up due to weak lungs. This was due to childhood illness and he had been deemed unfit to fight. He had been disappointed but Eloise had confided in Grace that she was relieved he couldn't go. Eloise knew she was lucky to have her man at home. Adam had a job in local government which he didn't talk about much, so it appeared to the family he was doing his bit for the country. They visited Eloise and Grace, thought Jack was the most handsome baby boy she had ever seen. Again, her heart ached for a child of her own. They also visited Ruth and Rachael. Ruth was glad to see them and heard news of Alex, but Ruth's grief was so raw. She found it hard to be around with them all without Michael being there too. She wept when she was told Eloise's son had Michael's second name and Grace tried to console her.

Once back home, Grace received a call from James at the hotel to say they would be staying in Gosport till the following week. They were more than pleased with Alex's progress and to say that Alex was forever asking after her. Grace was writing to him every day, telling him whatever news she could. With his mother's help, she was getting replies; each letter ending 'I miss you, come soon, love Alex'. She visited Charing Cross Hospital mainly to see Maggie and fill her in on Alex. She apologised many times that she wouldn't be back for a while, but promised that once Alex was home, she would be back. Maggie's brother was home for a couple of weeks and she was trying to see him as much as possible before he went back and to fight again. They hugged and said goodbye, promising to keep in touch. Grace had really grown to care for Maggie and thought she had made a good friend in this caring nurse. She hoped nothing would happen to her brother and at least her family would come out of the war unscathed.

The weather was getting much colder, so she wrapped up warmly for her trip to Gosport on Monday, 13th November. The hotel owners were pleased to see her again and gave her the same room as before. She was relieved to be in the warm again. Her visits during that week were good. Doctor Gregson said Alex's wounds were healing well. His moods were still up and down and there were still many disturbed nights, but Alex's parents had been a great help chatting about his childhood and happier times. Alex greeted her with more energy than before. He was trying to walk but the cast made it awkward and having only one strong arm to use the crutches, made his balance uneven. She was only going to stay a week but Alex's improvement had given her hope and cheered her so she decided to stay longer.

It was in the second week of her stay when reports reached the rest of the country that there had been aeroplane bombing raids in London. *What else is going to happen before this war will be over?* She thought. The morning of 24th November, Grace rang home and was pleased to hear her mother's voice and to know that her family had not been affected by the bombing. She left Gosport the following Sunday with the hope that Alex would soon be home and that her cousins, aunts and uncles hadn't been hurt in the bombings too.

Grace's 22nd birthday was a quite affair. She had greeting cards from family members and her parents had bought her a couple of small presents. Maggie had sent a card. A letter from Alex arrived sending birthday wishes and love. He apologised that he hadn't been able to get her gift, but presents were in short supply in a military hospital.

She visited again the weekend of 9th and 10th of December. They were going to remove the cast this week and see if his leg was healing. The wound in his shoulder was almost healed and if Grace continued to keep it clean and change the dressings, it wouldn't be too long before it would be as right as rain. He would have to build up the muscles again, but that would take time. The leg was doing well but still needed a further cast, but the best news was Alex could be home for Christmas. Alex wrote with news and asked Grace to come for him.

Frederick and Grace travelled down on 20th December and on the 21st Alex left Haslar. Grace thanked the nursing staff. Doctor Gregson was there to say goodbye.

"Thank you, John. You've been wonderful, a great help to Alex and I."

"You're welcome. If you ever want to ask anything regarding Alex's recovery, just get in touch. Alex hasn't been discharged from the army yet. I'll pass his notes onto the medical services at his barracks in London. He will have to go for check-ups and have the cast removed, but if you want any information, please call me."

"Thank you," she wasn't sure if it was the right thing to do but she hugged the doctor anyway. "Sorry," she said as she let go. "It's just that I couldn't have done this without you, you have given me the confidence to cope."

"Don't belittle yourself, Grace. You are a very strong woman. Alex is lucky to have you." Grace smiled and said goodbye.

They travelled back by train. Grace and Alex were going to stay with her parents for a while on Elizabeth's insistence. She was trying to bring what was left of her family back together again. Alex was pleased to be home. The cast made the stairs awkward to climb, so Grace and him spent most of their time in her old room, reading, having their meals, talking and relaxing. There was no big Christmas party this year since no one felt like it. Eloise, Stephan and baby Jack stayed for a couple of days, but Ruth didn't take up the invitation, preferring to stay with her own family.

For the New Year, Alex's family came to stay. As they toasted in the New Year of 1917, Grace thought back to the Christmas of 1912 to the New Year of 1913 and her first festive time with Alex. She had been so hopeful of the future, starry eyed and optimistic. In just a short time, life had changed so much. They had lost Michael, Alex had escaped death, but he had a long way to go to full health yet. Elizabeth had down days when no one could help or console her. Grace could only hope that the war would soon be over. Alex would be fully fit again and they could look forward to the future. She felt older, certainly more knowledgeable of what the world was like. It was a strange but a good feeling. As she kissed both her and Alex's family and then Alex, she wished that 1917 would be a better year.

Chapter 11

The winter was cold. It made it hard for Alex to get around with the cast on his leg, especially in the snow. He was getting bored and then his temper would take over. The nightmares were few and far between during his first few months at home. A combination of being glad to be home and being glad to be alive to live his old life again, but he would be glad to rid himself of the second damn cast and be mobile again.

Elizabeth went through periods of depression. The ups and downs of her grief over losing her second son were having a bad effect on all their lives. She couldn't even see her granddaughter as much as she would like.

Frederick tried to be at home more to comfort Elizabeth, but this also helped with caring for Alex. The two men would have many quiet chats, Grace wasn't sure what those were about but she was grateful for the distraction and would use some of these times to go off to the hospital. She felt more compelled than ever to help. The life with Alex had not returned to normal yet, but at least, he was home safe. She missed Michael enormously but felt she couldn't talk about him much at home as it would upset her mother. Frederick was the rock for them all and Grace knew they couldn't get through without his strength. Every evening, she tried to catch him alone for a few minutes to check up on and ensure that he was holding up under the pressures of the family and his own grief.

It was good to see Maggie again as they caught up on their respective lives as Maggie went about her duties and Grace following her orders. Ruth's absence in her life now made Grace gravitate to Maggie for female company and although they were from very different backgrounds, they were close due to their current roles in wartime.

It was Easter and the United States declared war on Germany in April. By now, Alex had his cast removed and Doctor Gregson had been right; Alex did have a limp. He used a cane to aid his getting about. He was gaining strength in his left arm and shoulder, but there were many accidents when he miscalculated his strength and he'd drop cups, glasses and other items, and this annoyed him. The army had called him for his physical examination and because of his injuries he was discharged from the service. Just before Easter, he had approached his former employer and inquired as to whether he could return. They jumped at the chance and by mid-April, he was back at the law office.

Elizabeth seemed to be improving with the spring weather. She could more easily visit Ruth and Rachael, which lightened her mood. The bombing raids had started again. One of the largest was on 2nd May 1917, where 24 bombers dropped bombs over the south east of the country; killing nearly 100 civilians. The war was hitting home now. On 13th June, London was heavily bombed and underground stations were hit where the people sheltered. Not only soldiers were hurt in the conflict, civilians were also being treated in the hospitals now.

Alex had been back to work for a couple of months. In some ways, this improved his mood, giving him something else to concentrate on but he became tired easily and was slipping further from Grace. His nightmares returned when he was stressed with work. He was attentive towards Grace to some degree but although they shared a bed, Alex would kiss Grace goodnight then turn away from her. The only time he wanted her close was when he woke startled and frightened from another nightmare, then he would cling to her for dear life. Physically, he was improving. He walked unaided and his arm gained strength all the time. Grace was pleased at the improvement, but she wanted him to love her as he had before. She was tired of being understanding, she needed her husband back.

The whole family went to Ruth's family's home the weekend before Rachael's fourth birthday in July. Grace thought it was the best day they had all had in a long time. Rachael was a beautiful little girl, happy and smiling all the time. She looked a lot like Michael with her beautiful blond hair, which was a lovely reminder of her dear brother but it also made her sad. If only Michael could be here to see his lovely daughter celebrating her birthday and entertaining everyone. Her own longing for a child was getting worse. She tried to initiate sex but Alex didn't seem to want to have that closeness still. She could only pray that time would bring back that part of their lives.

For their fourth anniversary, Grace suggested they go back to Devon but Alex said he was far too busy at work. They did move back to their own apartment. On the first night back, Grace prepared a meal and tried to make the evening romantic. Her sexual advances started well, but Alex then said he was tired and turned over. She felt alone and dejected and cried silently so as not to disturb Alex. She would have to stop worrying and let nature and time take its course.

On 31st July, the third battle of Ypres, later to be known as the Battle of Passchendaele, began. The German defence coupled with appalling weather and ground conditions, made advancement almost impossible. Many casualties from shells and poison gases arrived at hospitals in pain, with only aspirin or morphine that had started in tablet form that had been dissolved and then sucked up and administered by a needle. The soldiers were dirty, many had boils, amputations, still dressed in what they had been in in the trenches. Grace tried to help as much as she could at the hospital. Again, she was offered nursing training, but she was still unsure what to do. How long would the war go on for? Maybe it would be a good career if she wasn't going to be a mother. She learnt more as the days passed. More and more injured soldiers arrived, more and more work for the nurses and the doctors, so she felt compelled to work harder to help. The offensive at Ypres lasted till November. It had been a costly advance and morale was low. Bombing raids continued. Many nights were spent in the basement of the mansion block or in her parent's basement.

Elizabeth had broached the subject of Christmas and a party. It was agreed that a small affair would be a good idea. Grace hadn't made much fuss leading to her birthday. She was just relieved that Alex was more relaxed of late. They had visited his family at the end of November and the trip appeared to have done him good. He had kissed her passionately the morning of her birthday and presented her with a gold bracelet as a present. Having got on with her work and letting life take its course, had left her less tense about the areas of their life that weren't so good, but perhaps now, they were turning a corner.

Alex had more energy now, although long days at the hospital left her drained. He had started to take more notice of her and her needs by running a bath for her when she came home tired or massaging her feet.

As Christmas drew closer, Grace helped Elizabeth. It wasn't going to be a big affair but it would be good to enjoy oneself for a change as the war was still going on. Maggie was coming with Doctor Arthur Smith. He was relatively new at the hospital but he and Maggie hit it off immediately. Although due to hospital protocol, they needed to keep their blossoming romance a secret; doctors and nurses were not supposed to mix. Maggie was smitten and Grace was pleased that her friend had found someone special. Maggie had often joked that there were so few men around and that the only ones she met were the ones she treated.

Some of Alex's colleagues had been invited, as well as family and Frederick's colleagues. The meal, although smaller than in previous years, still went down well. The group just seemed to be pleased to relax and enjoyed themselves. Ruth, her parents and Rachael, only stayed for the meal and then left. Maggie and Arthur also left as they were both on duty early the next day.

Grace had brought a new dress to wear. Fashions had begun to change; this dress was calf-length and the waist was high. The silver chiffon and silk flowed over her slim figure. There were no sleeves, just chiffon covering the tops of her arms. She had matching silver shoes and her fair hair was pulled up into a bun. No rigid corset underneath either; she had found a beautiful silk chemise which suited the style of the dress and there was definitely more freedom of movement. When Alex first saw her in her new outfit, he said she looked beautiful and it had taken him back to the Christmas four years ago. She chatted to friends and family during the evening as they asked her about her volunteering mostly.

Once the meal was over, the music started and Elizabeth and Frederick were the first to dance. Grace thought her mother looked better today than she had all year. Her health and spirit had suffered much these past few months. Grace was trying to manoeuvre around the groups of guests when a rather merry colleague of Alex grabbed her arm. He had recently divorced and had come alone. She remembered Alex feeling a bit sorry for him. She tried to be polite and excused herself, but the man wasn't taking the hint and was making Grace dance with him. Just as she thought, she might have to give in and dance with the dreadful man. Alex was there by her pushing the man away.

"You are a guest in my family's home, Harry. Behave like a gentleman or leave and leave my wife alone. It's clear she wants nothing to do with you," and he lent forward and quietly in his ear, "I suggest you leave, man, before you make more of a fool of yourself." Alex took hold of Grace's hand and moved her away.

"I think it's time we danced," he said.

Grace looked up into his face. He had been angry at Harry's behaviour and she worried when his temper flared, but to her relief, his anger was subsiding. She had been relieved at his intervention. She felt inept in dealing with him. She laughed to herself. *I don't know why after all the men I deal with at the hospital.* She looked up at Alex and found him smiling at her. For a split second, she caught her breath. His eyes, those beautiful magical green eyes were sparkling. She was taken back to their first dance together, the Christmas they had first met. She felt the same heady excitement of that evening. He was holding her close, very close, moving slowly to the waltz rhythm. Her heart was beating fast and she felt as if they were the only people in the room. Alex's hand was at the base of her back, holding her firmly against him.

He whispered in her ear, "I want you."

Again, she caught her breath. She couldn't believe the change in him. She moved away from him, just a little and looked up into his face. This man in front of her was her Alex, the man she fell in love with.

"I'd like to leave now," he said.

"What, go home?"

"I don't think I could wait that long."

Grace smiled, "Let's go then, I'm sure no one will miss us."

He released Grace from their dance and they made their way out of the sitting room, up the two flights of stairs and into Grace's old room. Grace went in first, closely followed by Alex who locked the door. He took of his jacket and tie and let them fall to the floor. They stared at each other. They both kicked off their shoes, still with their eyes locked on the other. Then they were together, kissing, touching, getting undressed as they went. It was a frenzy of unbuttoning and removing the unwanted clothes and in a moment, they were naked. They all but fell on to the bed. The party, the guests, were long forgotten. Their kisses became more urgent and passionate. Alex's hands were all over her body setting her alight. She felt like she would explode. She so desperately wanted him. She had missed him so much. Of course, she had been relieved and glad he was home with her, but she felt that something had died within him on that battlefield, but she was so wrong. This was truly the Alex of before and she wanted him more than ever. They climaxed together and stayed entwined, not wanting to let go of each other.

"I love you, Grace."

"I love you, Alex. I've missed you, this, I've so wanted to make you happy."

"I know, I'm sorry. I just couldn't, no excuses, I just couldn't. I'd seen too much horror. I felt guilty of having escaped with my life and I felt wrong in enjoying myself. I took that out on you. I'm so sorry."

"Don't be sorry, I can never imagine what you went through. I've seen enough of the aftermath but I will never feel what you went through. I've got your back now and that's all that matters."

They kissed again.

"I think we'd better get dressed," Alex said, "and I'd rather leave now and go home, by then I'll want to do this all over again."

They dressed quickly and said goodbye to her parents before leaving. Once back in their own home, they made love again, rested a while then again till the early hours of the morning. Grace lay her head on Alex's chest; their bodies entwined and fell asleep happier than she could have thought possible.

Chapter 12

The next morning, she woke still in the same position. Gently, she levered herself up and gazed down upon her husband. He hadn't moved or murmured the whole night. It must have been the best nights rest he'd had in over a year. Love flowed through her, so overwhelming it brought tears to her eyes. She thanked God so many times that Alex was safe and home with her. She mourned for her dead brother and missed his family's presence in her life. She saw Ruth and Rachael as often as she could, but it wasn't the same, Ruth wasn't the same. Still gazing at Alex, she felt the need to love him again. She gently stroked the wound on his shoulder and then kissed the same place. With feather-like kisses she kissed his chest and let her tongue linger. He began to stir. She traced her tongue from his chest to his Adam's apple, her hands stroking his body. Awake now and aroused, he stroked Grace's hair that fell on him. She pulled herself up to look at him.

"My wife is insatiable and I love her."

She kissed him. They were together again, lost in the rhythm of their lovemaking. She didn't want this to end, the pleasure so immense, they both cried out in ecstasy as they came together. Later, he explained that last night, he was jealous when Harry was flirting with her and suddenly, he realised how much he wanted her. His anger had brought back his passion.

The rest of Christmas and New Year was bitter sweet. The whole family tried to celebrate as best they could, but Michael's absence left a gaping hole. All were thankful that no one else was hurt or lost to them and hoped that this war would be over.

1918 saw ever more changes. On New Year's Day, rationing of food items such as tea, margarine, bacon, cheese and butter started. Ships were being sunk by Germans and items were getting harder to get into the country. Bombing raids continued through January and February, but Britain was also bombing Germany. There still seemed no end to this bloody war.

Grace and Alex had settled more into their old routine. Alex was now more relaxed and was having less nightmares. He had even shared some of his experiences trying not to be too graphic and he felt the benefit of being able to talk about it all. They were like newlyweds again, spending much of their time alone. It was as if they were getting to know each other again. He was doing well at work; home life was good and this helped to keep the horrors of the trenches at bay.

During the middle of March, Grace had risen and then started to feel queasy on a couple of mornings. She hadn't taken much notice of it, carried on as normal but when helping at the hospital on one of these days, she had become very ill. There were always smells at the hospital—rotten flesh, vomit, cleaning fluids and Grace had grown used to their unpleasantness, but on this particular day, the bloody bandages, these smells were making her nauseous and she felt hot. She had been helping one of the new patients compose a letter to his mother when she had to rush to the toilet. Maggie wasn't on duty but Nurse Griffiths was and followed her to the toilets. She found Grace taking a sip of water, having been sick.

"How are you feeling?"

"Better, sorry about that, how embarrassing."

"It would be a good idea if we get one of the doctors to check you over."

"No, I am fine really. Perhaps, I'd better go home. It would be best in case I've caught something."

The women agreed and Grace got her things and set off for home. It was on her way, it suddenly occurred to her what might be upsetting her. Excitement rushed through her as she tried to recall when she'd had her last menses. It must have been late January. Was it possible? She was finally pregnant. She stopped off at her parent's home and called the family doctor. Yes, he could call on her that afternoon. She confided in Elizabeth and the pair waited for the doctor. That afternoon, he examined her and confirmed she was indeed pregnant.

"From the smile on your face, Grace, you are obviously happy about your condition!"

"Yes, Doctor. I've wanted a child for sometimes and Alex will be pleased too."

The doctor had said his goodbyes and left, Elizabeth cuddled with her daughter, "You'll have to look after yourself now, my dear. I'm so happy for you and a new life is what we all need to bring joy back into our family."

Grace hugged her mother. They were both thinking of Michael. Elizabeth insisted Grace take a cab home so she did. At first, she couldn't wait for Alex to get home. She was so excited about her news but as the evening drew to a close, she was getting nervous. She had desperately wanted a child for so long, but Alex hadn't spoken about it much at all. With his fighting experiences and his recovery and then finding his feet at work again, Alex hadn't given much thought to a family. It had been a long-haul to where they were now and Grace wondered if it was the right time after all. Alex got home at the normal time and found Grace in the kitchen, they kissed as always and she handed him a cup of tea. She was really nervous now and Alex sensed it.

"What's wrong?"

"I wasn't well today when I was helping at the hospital."

"Best place to be when you don't feel well," he smiled. "Are you all right? You look as gorgeous as ever."

"I'm pregnant. I've seen Doctor Robinson and he has confirmed it."

Silence fell in the room, Alex put his cup down and moved to stand in front of his wife. He cupped her face in his hands and gently kissed her on the lips. She closed her eyes and savoured the kiss. When she opened her eyes, he was smiling.

"Well done you, well done us."

He cuddled her then picked her up and swung her around then thought better of it.

"Best not do that, my arm still isn't that good and we'll have to take extra special care of you now. Come, let's sit down."

Sitting side by side on the sofa Grace said, "You are pleased, then Alex. I wasn't sure if now was the right time."

"Now is the perfect time. We've had so much unpleasantness and heartache to deal with, but a baby will be a breath of fresh air, a new beginning. I love you Grace and I would like a large family with you. When do we expect our arrival?"

"November."

"In time for Christmas. Your parents know I take it."

"Mother was there and I expect she's told Father by now. She was so pleased."

"I'll telephone Mum and Dad tomorrow. I think they will be thrilled too. Oh, Grace, let's hope this war is over soon and we can bring our son or daughter into a better world."

At Easter, they visited Alex's family. Grace was still struggling with morning sickness but was otherwise fine. She still helped out at the hospital but a lot less now than before. Alex was worried about her catching anything, as he didn't want her or the baby harmed. She agreed with him but was also sad at not being able to help as much with the soldiers. She had grown fond of many of them over the years. She understood their pain, their fears, their hopes. Some had been so young and took their place to go and fight for the country. Life would never be the same again for many of them. They had all been brave in Grace's eyes. No one should have to suffer as these men had.

She had written and told Ruth her news and had received a reply. Grace understood that Ruth had to start trying to build a new life, but hoped that she and her family would always consider Grace's family as part of her life, but they were growing apart.

Maggie was thrilled with the news of the baby. She said she would start knitting a shawl and some clothes for the impending arrival. On her day off, Maggie would visit and the two women would gossip about the hospital, doctors and nurses and catch up on all the news. Maggie was only a year older than Grace, but seemed older than her years. She took her nursing seriously and was good at her job. Her family weren't that well-off and at times, life had been hard, but Maggie hadn't been affected by this. She had a big heart and dealt with whatever life threw at her. She had letters from her brother; he was still alive and still fighting. Arthur Smith was becoming more important to her. When she spoke of him, her face would soften and become a little flushed. It wasn't deemed appropriate for doctors and nurses to fraternise, so they were keeping their friendship a secret. Arthur's family were originally from Dorset, but he and they had lived in London for some time now as most of Arthur's training and practise had been in the capital's hospitals.

"We went to the theatre last weekend," Maggie said," got there early so we could sit before anyone else, you know, us keeping a low profile and all," she laughed. "It's silly that we have to behave like this. So much has changed because of the war. Why should we stick to such stuffy rules?"

"I agree," Grace said, "but for now, it's probably best if you keep your secret. If you were found out, you could lose your job and you wouldn't want that."

"No, couldn't afford to. I think I love him, Grace. I've never had any real relationships before. Went out with a couple of boys from school but nothing serious. Then when the war started, I just threw myself more into the nursing and the only men I saw then were injured or dying. He's so kind, a great doctor, he's thoughtful and I can't wait to go to work most of the time so that I can see him."

"Sounds like love to me. I remember when I first met Alex, my world changed. It just centred around him. Every thought, every decision, what would Alex think about that?"

"How do you know that he's the one?" Maggie asked.

Grace smiled remembering her conversation with Ruth, "You just do, instinct, I suppose. I couldn't think of a life without Alex in it. That was when I realised he was in my heart for good."

Maggie nodded; it was love alright.

By July, Grace was showing a lot. She hadn't put on much weight but her bump was quite big for five months. Rationing was taking a grip on everyday life. Coupon books were introduced for meat, fats, sugar and lard. Elizabeth fussed as she wanted to ensure that Grace ate correctly throughout her pregnancy. Grace didn't go to the hospital at all now. There was a flu epidemic sweeping the continent and Grace and Alex thought it best that she didn't work; best not to risk her health and the baby's. Many soldiers and civilians were dying of the flu, so it was wise to limit the risk.

Between July and August, it was the last offensive of the western front and the battle of Amiens during August and September was the real turning point.

Grace and Alex had gone to Devon for their fifth wedding anniversary but not to Torquay, but to Ilfracombe, in the north of the county. The train took them from Exeter via Barnstaple to Ilfracombe. Their hotel, the same name as the town, was along the pavilion. It was close to the tunnels that lead to the beach and the pavilion held entertainment daily. They walked to the harbour and watched boats going out to fish and pleasure trips to Lundy. The town was very hilly, which Grace found a little difficult in her condition along with the hot weather, but she could relax in the comfort and luxury of the hotel. She had liked Torquay but Ilfracombe was more intimate.

She said, "We'll definitely come back here for holidays, Alex. It will be great for the baby next year."

Alex was fascinated when Grace felt the baby kicking from the first time. If he was around, he told Grace to tell him when it happened so that he could touch her belly and feel the baby moving. He would lay his head on her many evenings in bed, speaking to their unborn child. *He is going to be a good father,* Grace thought. She felt good and looked well. The early sickness bouts hadn't lasted and apart from the extra weight and the summer heat, which made her tired, she was enjoying her pregnancy.

In September, the battle of St Michael was the first great American triumph of the war. Sixteen US Divisions supported by the French attacked and the Germans had to fall back in that sector. By 4th October, British, Canadian and French forces held the entire German defensive position and by 31st, the Germans had been driven back over the Scheldt River. The day before Turkey surrendered and signed an armistice, everyone was hopeful the war would be at an end. On 3rd November, Austria and Hungary signed an armistice.

As the Kaiser, the German leader was abdicating, Grace went into labour. Pain had woken her in the early hours of 9th November. She woke Alex and he started to get dressed and help her dress. Her bag of necessities had been ready for days. He made a telephone call to Elizabeth and she said they would meet them at the hospital. She wasn't in the hospital long, when her waters broke. By the evening, everyone was tired and anxious. Grace was exhausted. The pains had been intense and had then stopped.

In the early hours on 10th November, when the doctors were considering a Caesarean, Grace gave birth to a boy weighing in at 6lbs 2ozs. Mother and baby were settled into a bed on a ward and Alex, Elizabeth and Frederick went into visit briefly. Alex was alarmed at how tired and grey Grace looked. He leant over and kissed her.

"Well done, darling," he stroked her cheek.

"Thank you. I never thought it was ever going to end." The nurse brought the baby into see his father and grandparents.

"Take a look at your son," Grace said.

"Would you like to hold him, Mr Whitfield?" the nurse asked.

Alex couldn't get there quick enough. The nurse laid his son in his arms and he was hypnotised. This small bundle is his son. He had dark hair, much the colour of his own. Love and feelings of protection flooded through him. The look on his face brought tears to Grace's eyes and she would never forget that moment. Elizabeth had moved closer to her daughter and kissed her forehead.

"We won't stay long; we have got to let you rest. Well done darling, you have a beautiful son."

Memories of holding her own dear sons had flooded back. She wanted to hold her grandson and Alex reluctantly handed her his son. He moved back to be close to Grace.

"He's gorgeous, Gracey. You are wonderful and so brave and clever."

"I don't feel it at the moment."

Together, they watched the proud grandparents looking and cooing over their grandchild.

Grace said, "We are going to call him Michael James."

It was obvious to the group that Michael was in honour of their lost son and brother and James was Alex's father's name and Frederick's second Christian Name.

"Two grand names for a grand boy," Frederick said proudly. "You'll want for nothing my boy. You have a lot of family to look after you."

The nurse was back now to take baby Michael back to the nursery.

"Time to go then," Frederick said. Elizabeth kissed Grace and left with Frederick so that Alex could say goodbye.

"I'll telephone my parents and tell them about Michael. You rest now, my love and I'll be back this evening. You've been so brave and I love you so much."

"I love you too."

They kissed and Alex left. She was exhausted and she needed to sleep, but she was happy. Finally, she had the baby she had longed for and Michael was perfect. It was time for sleep. Alex came back that evening. She had felt refreshed after her sleep and the nurse had helped her freshen up for Alex's visit. She had fed Michael and he was sleeping in her arms when Alex arrived. This little group, their family, felt very content and happy.

The next day on 11th November, the Germans signed the armistice in a railway carriage in the Forte de Compiegne. The Kaiser had fled to neutral Holland. The war was over. Great Britain, her dominions and empire had lost 908,371 servicemen, 2,080,212 wounded, 191,652 captured or missing and 3,190,235casualties. More than 700,000 of the dead were from the United Kingdom. The cost of human life was immense. But in a London hospital was a new mother hoping that the world would now be a better and safer place for her new born son and that he would never have to fight like his father, uncle and so many other men had had to do.

Chapter 13

Joy and sadness described the end of the war. Of course, everyone was relieved that the fighting was over, but so many had lost sons, husbands, uncles and brothers; so much loss. Another flu epidemic was sweeping the country, so it was suggested that Grace may want to go home as it may reduce the risk of her catching the flu. She wanted to but she still felt so tired and had little energy. She was trying to feed Michael, but was always exhausted immediately after. She had told the nurses that she was in pain about an hour after the feeds but they didn't seem too concerned. When she tried to walk, pain shot through her body, surely this was not right. Alex had tried to talk to the doctor but he said she'd had a difficult delivery and it would take time for her to recover. Unhappy with the way she was feeling, but was consoled by having her son Michael in her arms, more than made up for the discomfort.

He had dark hair like his father and blue eyes that stared at her intently. He didn't cry much and seemed to want to sleep as much as she did. She agreed it would be better to go home maybe in her parent's home, so she would recover quicker. She was dressing, preparing to leave, when the pain returned to such a degree that she doubled up. The cry of pain alerted a nurse who came rushing to her aid. She could barely get back onto the bed. Alex was just arriving at the ward when he heard Grace cry out. He started to run what on earth could be wrong.

"Grace, what's wrong?" he was leaning over the bed. She was partly dressed and crunched up in the foetal position.

"Alex, it hurts. The pain is unbearable. I tried to get up but I can't," she paused for breath, "I'm scared Alex, something is wrong."

The nurse returned with the doctor. Grace was asked to straighten and lay on her back, but as soon as the doctor touched her tummy, she doubled up again. The nurse pulled screens around the bed. Grace was bleeding more now than before.

"Close your eyes and concentrate on my voice. Try and stay calm while he examines you."

She tried but every time he touched her; the pain soured through her body. The nurse returned with some morphine.

"This will help the pain, Mrs Whitfield," said the doctor while he administered the morphine. "Can I speak to you for a moment, Mr Whitfield?"

"Don't go, Alex, please."

"The nurse will stay with you, darling. I'll be back in a moment."

Just outside the ward, the doctor was waiting for him. Alex was nervous what was he going to be told.

"Mr Whitfield, I'm sorry to say your wife is going to need surgery. I believe she has a prolapsed uterus. We may be able to save her uterus, but she had a difficult delivery and I suspect that I will have to result to a hysterectomy. Do you understand what that would mean?"

"Yes, I do," Alex was stunned. Grace had wanted a big family, they both had. But not only that, she needed an operation and that was dangerous in itself.

"I suggest you talk to your wife. It would be better coming from you. It is usually hard for women to take that they will not be able to have other children. I will stay close by if you need help explaining, but time is of the essence. She is losing a lot of blood."

Alex leant against the corridor wall. God, how was he going to tell her? She had been overjoyed when she found out about the pregnancy. The war hadn't ended but she had started to hope that the future would bring good things. Their celebration at Michael's birth and Armistice Day seemed a million miles away now and yet it was only a week. He thought of Michael, at least they had a healthy son, they had each other. They were a family. He was shocked she was bleeding; time was of the essence, she needed surgery. He could lose her, she could die. He put his head in his hands. He couldn't lose her. She was his life. She had gone through so much helping him back to health after his injuries. He loved her more than anything. He had to pull himself together, make her understand. Alex turned back towards the ward. Behind the screen, Grace had calmed a little; the morphine was helping. He sat on the edge of the bed and took her hand in his. Her eyes still glistened from tears.

"What did he say?"

"You are not well, Gracey. You are going to need an operation."

"Just tell me exactly what's wrong. I've been around sick and injured people and hospitals. You don't have to hide anything from me."

"I know, darling. You've been so brave throughout your time at Charing Cross and the help you gave all those servicemen. I'm so proud of you."

"Alex, just tell me."

"You have a prolapsed uterus. It may be able to be repaired but it's likely you will have to have a hysterectomy."

Her face changed, as if all the pain she felt had strangely disappeared along with her soul and left a ghostly shell. All she could say was, "No."

Alex waited a few moments before continuing, "You are bleeding more than before. They need to operate soon."

"No, Alex. I can't let them do it. Do you realise we could never have any more children?"

"I know Grace, but we have Michael. We are a family."

"I wanted more children. I can't go through with this. There has to be another way," she closed her eyes to blank out the world.

"Grace, you need this operation," he stopped. Should he be blunt? He didn't want to be, he didn't want to hurt her any more than she was already, but time was running out.

"I can't lose you, Grace. What would I do without you? Look how you nursed me back to health when I could so easily give up. Look at our life together. We have so much to look forward to," he stopped. Was he getting through to her? He wasn't sure. She wasn't moving, her eyes were still closed.

"Michael needs his mother. Who would care for him the way you will care for him? If we want more children, we could adopt. There must be many children who have lost parents because of the war. We could care and love an adopted child.

Without opening her eyes, she said flatly, "It wouldn't be the same, Alex. It wouldn't be ours."

"I know, my love, but we could still love a child, give it a good home and family life, make it one of ours. Please, Gracey, take the doctor's advice, have the operation. I need you," he was desperate. His voice had started to crack as he finished pleading. He was taken back to the trenches at that moment. Thinking of the last moments before he was shot, he had been thinking of Grace, her beauty, their lovemaking, their whole life together. Back to now, he knew he couldn't go on without her. "Please Grace, I need you. Please don't leave me," tears were in his eyes.

Slowly, she opened her eyes and looked at Alex. She had little energy left. She knew she was very ill. Looking at Alex, her resolve was melting. She did have Michael, her lovely son. They could adopt and Alex needed her. Damn Alex and those eyes, they always melted her and they radiated with so much love at this moment.

"Alright, you win."

"I know it's hard to take in now, but it will be for the best. I promise you now Grace, we will have a lovely family. Me, you and Michael and that's all we will need."

He leant over and kissed her lips.

"I will keep you to that," Grace said.

The nurse had left to tell the doctor that the operation was to go ahead. Both Alex and Grace knew there were risks, but as she laid in the bed, with Alex as close as he could get to her, they gave each other confidence, hope for the future, their future.

"Get mother to take Michael home. She can take better care of him there and there will be less chance of him catching influenza."

Alex responded, "As soon as you go to surgery, I will get Frederick and Elizabeth here. We will stay and we will be here when you wake, I promise."

"I love you, Alexander Whitfield."

"I love you more than anything. We three will be happy, I know we will."

"Would you adopt?" Grace asked.

"I would if that was what you wanted."

"That's not what I asked."

"Yes, I would. We could give a loving home to another child. We have Michael and we may never have more, but if we ever want to, we will look into it. But more important now, we get you better and you, me and Michael can get on with our lives."

The doctor was soon back and Grace was wheeled to theatre. Alex left the hospital to go fetch Elizabeth and Frederick, but had stopped at the entrance steps and suddenly wept. It wasn't what a man should do but he couldn't help his feelings. He was so worried about her. Even if she got through the surgery, how would she be afterwards? She had desperately wanted a large family. He was scared for her at this moment but also for what the future might hold. He took out his handkerchief and wiped his eyes and blew his nose. One thing was for sure, he had to be strong just as Grace had been for him and he wouldn't let her down. He needed to get her parents back to the hospital first. He would not break his promise to her. They would all be there when she woke. He took a deep breath and hurried on his way to his in-laws' home.

Chapter 14

It was as bad as the doctor had expected and Grace had to have a hysterectomy, but fortunately, the operation had gone well and she was expected to fully recover. She felt like she had been sleeping for a long time and was fighting to wake. Gradually, she fought through the fog and could open her eyes. Where was she? She felt pain; she didn't think she could move.

"Grace, it's me," Alex said softly. "You're finally awake…can you hear me?"

She turned her head, more fog. What was wrong with her? Seeing Alex made her smile.

"Your mother and father are here too."

She looked towards the bottom of the bed and there they were, smiling back at her. Slowly, everything was coming back. The hospital, the pain, the bleeding, no more children. She closed her eyes again. She was hurting from the operation but also from her loss. Tears started to flow and escaped from her tightly shut lids, trying to keep out the pain.

"Don't cry, darling. You have been through a big operation and the doctors are pleased with you. We'll have you home in no time."

Without opening her eyes she asked, "Where's Michael?"

Elizabeth moved to the opposite side of the bed from Alex and took her daughter's hand.

"Eloise has come to our house and she is looking after him. Don't worry about Michael, he will be fine with all of us taking care of him. It is you who we need to help to get better, so try not to think of anything but your own recovery. We were so worried about you when Alex came with the news," she paused. "My little girl is in so much pain, I didn't want to believe what you were going through. I was scared Grace, but I know you are strong and you will fight and get through this."

Grace opened her eyes and looked directly upon her mother's concerned face. "I'll never be able to have any more children."

Elizabeth's heart went out to her daughter. She had suffered the loss of two of her children, so she knew the sense of loss Grace was feeling; at least she had had three children.

Tears came to her eyes. "I know, my sweet girl. It will be hard for you but you do have Michael. He's a strong little boy and he will bring joy and love to your life. I promise you; you will get through this. We are all here to help you and there are other ways to have children."

"Does Eloise know what has happened to me?"

"No, we said there had been complications."

"Please, don't tell anyone. I couldn't bear it."

"There's no reason to tell anyone exactly what has happened. The family are just going to want you to get better," Elizabeth hoped her words were helping Grace.

Grace did feel a little better. She knew some people may view her as a failure, not being able to have more children.

She had to stay in hospital a further three and a half weeks. Alex and Elizabeth visited every day. Sometimes, even if it's against the hospital regulations, they brought Michael, who seemed to be growing by the day. Frederick and Eloise came to visit too. Ruth had made a special trip to see Michael and also to see Grace. Grace was so pleased to see Ruth, but they didn't chat in the same way as they had in the past. Grace didn't feel it was as sisterly as it once was.

Rachael had drawn her auntie a picture of bright flowers. Rachael was now five years old and Ruth said, "She looks more and more like her father."

"When you are out of hospital, I will come back with Rachael so you can see her."

"That would be nice, Ruth. Thank you."

"Michael is gorgeous, he's going to take after Alex."

"Yes, he has his father's colouring. I miss him. I feel like I am missing out on so much of his early days and I will never get them back."

"You will be home soon and you can make up for the lost time."

It had been good to see Ruth, but it was her visits from Maggie that made her feel like her old self.

"I will have to be careful," Maggie said. "This flu is getting worse. I wouldn't want to bring it to you."

Maggie would tell her stories of her patients. There were still so many soldiers returning who needed treatment.

"I have spoken with Alex and he told me that you don't want anyone to know about the hysterectomy, but Grace, I guessed."

"It is fine Maggie. You are a nurse. I thought you would know. It is just that I feel such a failure. I can't even have a baby without massive complications."

"It wasn't your fault. Just one of those things, no rhyme or reason, not even God's will. You'll do just fine, you are a tough old bird, that's what my mum would say. Anyway, I've seen you with them soldiers. You've seen some sights for a rich girl. I didn't think you would stick it out when you first came to volunteer but you proved me wrong. I think you would make a damn good nurse. So, you can't have any more children, so what? You've got lovely Michael and a handsome husband, what more could you want?"

Grace laughed. Maggie was so direct but whatever she said or did was heartfelt. Her friend's visits lifted her and gave her hope.

"What of Doctor Arthur?" Grace asked. "Is the romance progressing?"

"Shush, keep it quite Grace, you'll get me fired. You know I wouldn't fraternise with a doctor," she said jokingly for the sake of any passer-by who may be listening in. She lowered her voice, "I think he's going to propose."

"Really?" Grace was delighted. "When do you think he will ask?"

"I think it will be at Christmas," Maggie didn't seem as excited as Grace thought she would be.

"You do love him Maggie, don't you?"

"Of course, very much. It's just that I like my job too and when I marry, I'll have to give it up. It's so unfair."

"Surely, they would still like you to volunteer."

"I don't think there will be so much of that, now that the war's over. I know it's selfish, but I'd like to marry Arthur and keep my job. I think if this war has taught us all something, it's that life is too short not to have what you want."

Grace was in full agreement with her friend. If it hadn't been for the war, Grace and Maggie would never have met. Moving in different circles, their paths would never have crossed but Grace was glad they had. Maggie's down to earth approach to life was liberating to Grace's upper class but sometimes stiff lifestyle. She thought she had an insight to life of other classes, not in a condescending way.

Rich, poor, upper class or lower class, they had all lost someone because of the war and everyone was rebuilding their lives.

"Oh, I nearly forgot. That is bad of me, he'd never forgive me, my brother will be home next week."

"That's good news too, Maggie. He must have had a guardian angel to get through four years of war and come home in one piece."

"He's always been lucky," she joked. "But I'm really glad he's coming back."

Grace finally left hospital on 12th December. Frederick had got a cold the week before and they'd all been worried it might be the flu, but fortunately, it wasn't and by the time Grace came to stay, he was better. Alex's mother arrived on Saturday. It was the first chance she'd got to see her grandson and she wanted to help care for Grace. She also wanted to shop in London for some Christmas presents. She wanted to spoil her son's family.

Grace was glad to be home. It meant she was finally getting time with Michael and be a proper mother. He had taken to bottle feeding in her absence; another failure she felt. He was a happy child though and she couldn't help the overwhelming feelings of love towards him. At a month old, he was alert and lively when awake. Then once fed and changed, he would sleep at regular times. He was truly a model baby. Alex was there every evening to bath and put Michael in his crib. Neither Alex nor Grace had said anything to each other, but they both felt they needed to make the most of every moment in Michael's young life as they would never experience it again.

Helen was infatuated with her grandson. Two grandmothers in the same household were almost explosive, each trying to outdo the other. James, Alex's father joined them the following week. They were both going to stay at Alex and Grace's home then join everyone for the Christmas festivities. There wasn't a big party, both sets of grandparents and Alex and Grace. It was an intimate family gathering. Ruth visited with Rachael, and Maggie and Arthur came to tell them of their engagement. Then on New Year's Eve, Eloise, Stephan and Jack came for dinner and to ring in the New Year.

In the early hours of 1st January 1919, Grace lay in bed with Alex.

"How do you feel? How's your Abdomen?" he said, laying his hand gently on her.

"It's not so bad, I'm mending but I'm going to have a big scar and I'm not happy about that."

"It will be a lovely scar and I will love it," he propped himself up on his elbow so he could look at her.

"Thank you," she said softly.

"For what?"

"Being you. Looking after me, taking care of Michael when I wasn't around."

"Why wouldn't I? I'm your husband, Michael's father and besides, look at what you did for me. I might not have recovered if it wasn't for you. You saved me, Grace. I would have still been locked in the horrors of the trenches if you hadn't helped me back to reality. We have a lot to be thankful for and I am. From the first night I met you over six years ago, I knew I had met the girl I wanted to spend the rest of my life with and that's what I intend to do. We've had some pretty hard times thrown at us already, but we have survived. We have a handsome and healthy son; you are feeling better and stronger each day and the best thing of all is we love each other. What more could anyone want?" he laid back and she snuggled up to him.

"You are so right."

The years had moved on from their first meeting. She was now 24 years old, a wife and a mother. She'd seen so much, she felt older and wiser and Alex was right. They had come through so much and they did love each other. 1919 was a fresh year, a fresh start for them and countless others and she was counting her blessings.

"Goodnight, my love," she said happy and sleepy.

"Goodnight, Gracey."

Chapter 15

1919, the country was trying to recover from the war and Grace was recovering from her operation. She was healing but it seemed a slow process to her. It hurt to feed Michael at times. She couldn't rest him anywhere near her abdomen or pick him up unless she herself was seated. She did enjoy motherhood though and it took up most of the day. She enjoyed bathing him and dressing him in his tiny clothes. As spring arrived, she would put him in the perambulator and take him on walks to the park. Ruth had met her on a couple of occasions, bringing Rachael with her. Her niece was a beautiful little girl and was the image of her father. Rachael liked to play with Michael, all be it that she had to be careful because he was only a baby.

Alex was working hard again. As a family, they were trying to live a normal routine. The hysterectomy had upset both of them but Alex had been more scared of losing Grace than anything. He understood what she must have gone through, when he went off to fight not knowing if he would come back and then on his return, was injured and disturbed by the whole thing. Then Michael's birth and the operation. They had been through much but they were both alive, healthy and building their future. His workload was increasing. He was doing more in-depth work and he was enjoying it. He didn't want to think about the war; the future was more important and that meant his family's security.

At home, he would help with Michael as much as he could. He knew it helped Grace and he was also aware that it was going to be his only child and he didn't want to miss out on his childhood. He missed his sex life though. He wanted to make love to Grace, but it was not advised. He would hold her, cuddle up to her in bed, kiss her but would stop before it went too far. He had to admit he was worried that that part of their lives would never be the same again. He felt guilty at these thoughts and scolded himself.

In May, Maggie and Arthur married. It wasn't a big affair with their immediate families and a few friends. Alex and Grace attended. After the church service, they had a wedding breakfast at Arthur's parent's home in Turnham Green. Maggie wore a cream dress and a hat and looked extremely happy. They were keeping their marriage a secret so Maggie could still work. She was transferring to Queen Charlotte's Hospital in Hammersmith next month, so that for a while, she could still work. Well, that was the plan. Maggie and Arthur took a few days on the Isle of Wight for their honeymoon.

In July, Alex suggested that they have a holiday the following month. Going to Europe was still not advised, so they decided to go to Devon again. Elizabeth had suggested they go alone and spend time together. At first, they said no. Grace wanted Michael to see the sea and play on the beach but as the holiday drew near, she increasingly thought it was a good idea.

Alex had been great since Michael's birth and then the complications. He had been attentive and kind and although she knew he had wanted more from her sexually, he hadn't made any demands of her and was never down or despondent when she stopped his advances. She knew she was lucky; a lesser man may have gone elsewhere for satisfaction. Her last check up with the doctors had confirmed that she had healed and sexual activity was now down to what she felt comfortable and capable of. She was nervous, but she had missed their closeness too. He had kissed her scar many times, reassuring her that it didn't change how he felt about her and she was still beautiful, but she didn't feel the same. She didn't feel desirable or attractive. Perhaps, it was a good idea for them to go alone just like their honeymoon, hopefully.

So, in August, Alex and Grace left for Ilfracombe. This time, they stayed at the Belgrave Hotel. *It was good to be alone again,* she thought and she had already made the decision that they would return to their own home after the holiday. *I'm fit again and I need to be more independent in looking after Michael.* They settled into their room and then went down for dinner. Both were tired so they returned to their room and slept peacefully. After breakfast the next day, they took a stroll to the town's shops. Grace loved this town, although it was very hilly. They sat and listened to the band performing at the bandstand after lunch and then went through the tunnels to the beach. It was relaxing; neither felt the need for conversation. It was a beautiful day and they were enjoying each other's company. Many were bathing and Grace commented that if it was as hot in the next few days, she would definitely be taking dip.

After dinner, they returned to their room. Instead of being nervous of what might happen, Grace was excited. The relaxing day and the warmth of the sun had made her feel young and carefree, like on their honeymoon. She stole glances of Alex when he wasn't aware during the day and couldn't believe what they had gone through. The holiday feeling had stripped away the years and she was seeing her husband as she had in their early years. The war and her operation had made her forget who they were. How they had been before his recovery and nightmares and then their disappointment of the future without more children. He was very handsome, strong and she wanted him.

When they got to the room, she took her sheer nightdress from the chest of drawers and excused herself. In the bathroom, she undressed, cleaned her teeth, brushed her hair and sprayed some scent over her body. She was tingling with excitement and for the first time in a long time, she felt desirable. When she stepped back into the bedroom, Alex was almost undressed. He turned to look at her. She looked more beautiful than ever. The silk nightdress clung to her slim body and her scent wafted through the room. He caught his breath. He had sensed a change in her during the day but had tried to play his hopes down. He wanted her so bad but he wanted her to be ready and not nervous. Now, she was right in front of him. He kissed her hard and strong. She responded just as urgently. He slipped the straps of her nightdress from her shoulders and the silk slid down her body to the floor. His hands slowly stroked her breasts then continued down feeling the curve of her waist.

"Are you sure you are ready?" he asked almost whispering.

"Yes."

"I'll be gentle. Stop me if you need to."

They were kissing again. They fell onto the bed. It felt good, his body was firm and muscular; she felt safe and excited. She had missed this closeness. He sensed her fear and kissed the scar on her tummy, hoping she would be reassured and she relaxed completely and he continued to excite her.

She couldn't wait any longer, she touched his face and he looked at her. She smiled at him and he moved nearer to kiss her. Their kisses were deep and intense. He was excited as her. All her fear was gone. She was making love to Alex and it was as natural and as wonderful as ever. She moved down to kiss him and they moved in unison, savouring each other.

"I love you, Grace."

Before she could say anything, their orgasm exploded and they were both caught up in the ecstasy of the moment. It hadn't taken long but neither was disappointed. They clung to each other for hours. Both lost in their enjoyment and relieved that their passion for each other had not disappeared or been impeded. Early the next morning, they made love again; slower and taking their time to please each other. It felt wonderful and they didn't want to stop.

After breakfast, they took an organised trip to Woolacombe. It was another beautiful day and Alex had heard that the beach was sandy and stretched for miles so they could relax in the sun. He wasn't wrong. The beach was long, sandy and the view as they made their way down to the bay was breath-taking. The driver pointed out Lundy Island on the horizon. There were a few shops in the small town and an impressive hotel almost on the beach, but it was the view that impressed the couple most. The driver informed that the hotel would serve a light lunch for them at 12:30 and the return journey would leave at 3 o'clock from the hotel. They looked in the shops and then made their way to the beach. Alex hired two deck chairs and they walked little way up the beach and set up the chairs. The tide was coming in and there were many families enjoying the summer's day.

"I think Michael would like this," Grace said.

"Next year, we'll bring him and we'll stay in this hotel. We can walk in the fields or take trips to other places and yet being this close to the beach would give him room to play," Alex answered.

As the tide came in, more people were going in for a swim. Grace couldn't wait any longer. She took off her shoes and stockings.

"You coming in for a cool down, Alex?"

He had been laying back in his deckchair with his eyes closed. As he looked up, there was Grace standing barefoot and holding up her dress, showing her ankles and calves. He smiled, she looked like an excited schoolgirl.

He found her enthusiasm infectious, "Yes, just a moment."

He took off his shoes and socks and rolled up his trousers. He looked ridiculous, he thought, but still he followed her to the water's edge. The water felt cold on his feet but it did cool him down. The waves rippled in to the bay and the sand was soft beneath his feet. He'd never swam in the sea before. For a moment, he was lost in his thoughts. As his feet sank in the sand, it reminded him of the trenches and the mud. He suddenly tensed and felt his head spin. Grace had been splashing around and had been speaking to a little girl who had run in her direction chasing a ball. She turned and focused on Alex. She smiled but the smile faded into a frown. She waded towards him.

"Alex, what's wrong?"

He didn't respond. She grasped both of his arms and gently shook him. He looked grey and lost and then suddenly he was back. He blinked several times, taking in where he was.

"Are you all right?" Grace touched his face. "You scared me, whatever came over you, what were you thinking of?"

"Sorry, Grace, the sinking sand…. I just thought of…" he trailed off. "Never mind, sorry I alarmed you. Do you mind if we sit back down again?"

"Of course not."

She took his hand and they made their way back up the beach to their deckchairs. She assumed it must have been memories of the war, but she couldn't be sure. She had lived through his nightmares. They had been rare in the last year and she hoped that whatever had stirred up these memories, if that was truly the problem, that they would just as quickly go away. She knew she was selfish, but she felt that the last few days had got them back to where they had been before the war, loving and laughing as they had on their honeymoon. Now back in the chair, settled and more relaxed, he was calming down.

"Sorry, Grace. I didn't mean to scare you; I was lost there for a while but I'm fine now. "

She took his hand, brought it to her lips and kissed it.

"No need to be sorry, I don't like to see you upset and remembering those awful times. We've just got each other back I don't want to lose the good feelings again. We deserve good times together, don't we?"

"We do. I promise you, I'm fine and it will not spoil our holiday."

They relaxed and chatted occasionally. The sun had dried their feet, which made it easy to put their shoes back on and go for lunch back at the hotel. Grace used the powder room to put on her stockings and made herself more presentable for dining. During the meal, they chatted with others of their outing group and Grace was pleased to see him happy and engaging with the others. They took a walk around the bay after lunch, then returned to the hotel ready for their journey back. In the evening after dinner, there was dancing in the ballroom of their hotel. Grace and Alex joined another couple for the evening.

They were a little younger than them and came from Wales. Gareth had fought in the war too and since returning, he had gone back to his family's farm and worked the land as before. His wife, Anne, had helped Gareth's parents with the upkeep of the farm during the war and was now relieved that Gareth was back. Alex and Grace danced almost every dance. Grace was relieved that Alex's earlier episode had not lingered and he appeared to be enjoying himself as much as her. After the excursion of the dancing, they were a little tired for lovemaking that night so they cuddled up and slept. In the early hours, Alex became restless. He was mumbling and suddenly, he cried out and sat up in bed. Grace had been awake, listening to Alex's mumbling. She put her hand on his back and gently stroked him.

"Alright now?"

"Yes, thank you," he put his head in his hands. "I thought the dreams were over," he said his voice as cold as ice.

"It was likely to happen with what you experienced today. It won't keep on happening. I'm sure, it's just a hiccup. Come on, lay back down. You are sweating, you need to cool down."

He laid back. She turned on her side so she could watch him. She held on to his hand. He was gradually calming. Once the nightmare passed, he explained that the sinking sand had made him think of the mud in the trenches. He had been transported back and couldn't make out why he was sinking in the mud when it was so hot. In this dream, he was with Michael, his brother-in-law and was trying to save him during a battle. Grace held him close while he talked. When he finished, she ran a bath and together they bathed. He kissed her neck.

"I'd never have got through this without you. You are always there to listen, helping and guiding me through all the bad times," he soaked her back with a sponge as he spoke softly to her. "You helped me to recover. You convinced me to have the operation when I was being awkward. We're in this together, for better, for worse. Good times are ahead of us."

Soon, the nightmare was forgotten and their passion took over and they made love. Over the next few days, they took a trip to Barnstaple, the county town. Here, there were a lot of shops and a busy market. They sat by the river and enjoyed another sunny day. She had brought presents for her parents and something for Maggie. She had got Michael a new outfit and a new dress for herself.

"It's lovely here in Devon. I'm growing quite fond of it. Everywhere is more open and picturesque."

"Growing tired of London?" Alex asked.

"I don't know, really. I've never lived anywhere else. I suppose it would be interesting to see what it would be like to live somewhere like this."

"I have, London is different to Yorkshire and both are different to Devon. I don't think I would have the chance of such a good career here though."

"I know, it's just a thought. Anyway, we can always come back for more holidays."

They relaxed for a couple of days but on the last full day of the holiday, they went back to Woolacombe and Grace convinced Alex to swim in the sea. She wanted him to lose the ghosts of earlier in the week. He wasn't a strong swimmer and his memory of a few days ago made him apprehensive, but Grace was persuasive and given that the day was the hottest, yet he gave in. The water was a cooling relief and they had a great day enjoying the freedom and relaxation. They had enjoyed the pleasure of lovemaking most nights and felt that the holiday had been revitalising, as well as calming. As they boarded the train, they weren't unhappy that it was over but they were going back to their own home and with Michael, they were ready to start a fresh. Next year, they would be back and bring their son to enjoy the Devon summer.

Chapter 16

In the time, since Alex had been injured and the end of the war, few of his comrades had been in touch, but since peace had been declared and the summer of 1919, Alex had received a couple of letters from the war department from soldiers he had fought with. At first, he hadn't wanted to reply, but Grace had talked him into responding.

"If they have been good enough to put pen to paper, then you should do the decent thing and reply."

His reluctance had been because he didn't want to relive that awful time but Grace was right. These men had experienced the same as he had and maybe they needed to see each other to then be able to move on.

George Talbot was from Surrey and William Castle was from Sussex. Both had fought in the Somme. George had been injured just four weeks after Alex, but William had carried on with the regiment to the end. Both were married with children. They arranged to meet the first weekend in October. They met and had drinks and meal together in the city. In spite of his reticence, Alex couldn't help but enjoy himself. They had reminisced, but the conversation was more about what life was like for them now and what they hoped for the future. Unlike Alex, neither of the other men had found it easy to find work on their return. Times were difficult but at least they had come home unlike many of their friends. There was to be a two-minute silence on 11th November, to honour those that had given their lives in war. All three men were going to be at the parade; that decision was unanimous.

On Sunday, 9th November the eve of Michael's first birthday. Grace threw a small party at her parent's home. Little Michael obviously didn't understand the reason for the party but he tore at this presents and adored the attention. Both sets of grandparents were present, as was Ruth and Rachael, Maggie and Arthur and Eloise, Stephan and Jack. George and his wife, Irene, were up from Surrey for the remembrance on 11th, so Alex invited them too. It wasn't for the first time when Grace had thought what a different crowd of people were in her family's home. In the past, it had only been upper-class colleagues and friends of her parents and of course family, but now, for her son's birthday, there were such a mixture of backgrounds and as unlikely as it would have once occurred to her, everyone was getting on well and enjoying the afternoon.

The war had really changed people. Everyone had been so affected and lives were still changing even now a year later. *Was this for the best?* Grace thought it might be. The two-minute silence took place and was to be done every year to honour the dead. Alex made a fuss of Grace's 25th birthday, as her last one had been spent in hospital. They went to the theatre and with Michael with Grace's parents for the night, they were free to have a night of passion.

Christmas again was low key with just the immediate family.1920 started and normal life was in full swing for Grace and her family. Alex was working hard and

Michael was growing up fast. By March, he was taking his first steps and was ensuring that everyone else around him were on their toes. Grace was beginning to find the apartment too small and awkward, now that Michael was on the move. She and Alex discussed the possibility of getting a house in the area so they started to look for a new home.

Maggie announced she was pregnant in April and although she was pleased to be having a child, she was upset that she would have to give up nursing. She had successfully covered up her married status up to now, but that was growing increasingly hard to cover up. Having ranted about how unfair it was that married women were supposed to stay at home and not work, Maggie then realised how ignorant of Grace's feelings she had been. She knew Grace would have loved another child.

"Oh Grace, I am sorry. I just shoot my mouth off without thinking sometimes. Will you forgive me?"

"Of course," she hugged her friend. "I know how much your work means to you and I agree it is unfair, but you will have your hands full when you've got that little one," she said, patting Maggie's tummy affectionately.

Eloise and Jack were also constant companions for days out. Although Jack was two years older than Michael, he would look after him like he was his older brother and made up games to fit his younger cousin. Grace hoped their friendship would last as Michael would never have any siblings.

The summer was here and on their seventh wedding anniversary, they went to Devon for their holiday. They were tempted to have the time alone again as they had enjoyed it so much last year, but Grace thought Michael needed new experiences, like playing in the sand and splashing in the sea. Alex had picked Woolacombe as their destination and the hotel they had stopped for lunch at last year would be their home for the holiday. The weather was good and Michael did enjoy the beach. No repercussions of Alex's beach flashbacks, thankfully, just father and son enjoying themselves, engrossed in building sandcastles and playing in the sea. It was a wonderful time. They were happy as a family. Michael was so worn out with the day's activities and the fresh air that he slept soundly each night. Grace and Alex enjoyed themselves and used their time making love and planning for their future. The year so far had been better than some before and they hoped it would continue to do so.

When they returned from the holiday, they found that the offer they had put on a house in Notting Hill had been accepted and they would be moving fairly soon. Making arrangements for the move now took up most of Grace's time along with caring for Michael.

By November, they were in their new home. Grace was relieved that she now didn't have to climb several flights of stairs every time she left or returned home, carrying Michael or shopping. The property had a small garden but enough for Michael to play in next spring. She wanted to make the property feel more like their home by decorating, but she didn't have time for that now.

On 3rd December, Maggie gave birth to a baby girl they named Mary Grace. Alex and Grace were to be one set of godparents and the christening took place on Sunday 19th December. Maggie had had an easy delivery and was fit and raring to celebrate Christmas. Grace admired Maggie's energy but was also jealous. Why hadn't it been this easy for her? Maggie would probably have another child in the future but she would never be able to. She was happy for Maggie and baby Mary was beautiful and she was her godmother. She could spoil and make every effort to be there for this little girl. She would always hide her unhappiness of her barren state from her friend; after all, it wasn't her fault. The bitterness was slowly eating away at her and her failure in not being able to have more children.

Alex had observed the changes in Grace and he was constantly worried about her. She kept herself busy with friends and family and Mary's arrival had been a joyful time as Grace had made a big fuss of both mother and baby, but he knew she was hurting and he wanted to help her.

Michael got measles in February 1921. All other concerns were forgotten. Grace became the overprotective mother. He was going to get better. She isolated him from everyone except herself and Alex. She was so worried about him, she hardly slept but he did get over it, but Grace was ill with exhaustion and worry. Elizabeth came to stay. She looked after Michael during the day so that Grace could rest. The doctor had instructed that Grace take care of herself more and not to worry about Michael. He was a strong, healthy boy. She had cried so many times when her son was ill. She was so scared she would lose her only child. She prayed so much for his recovery. Her prayers had been answered and he was fine.

Once the spring arrived, Grace was feeling much better and more hopeful. Michael was truly fit and getting up to all sorts again. When he played in the garden, she would watch him for hours. Maggie visited often with Mary and Grace would cuddle the little girl and talk and play with her. Alex wasn't sure that this was good for her but Maggie was the only one who knew about the hysterectomy outside their immediate family; Grace would talk to her and confide in her. They were good friends and Grace really needed that.

Knowing Grace was feeling stronger, Alex broached the subject he had been mulling over for some time; an adoption. He wasn't sure it would help but he knew his wife was so desperate to have more children and this was their only option. When they were alone one evening in June, Michael was staying with Eloise and Stephen as it was Jack's birthday. They made love and Grace was snuggled close to Alex. They were relaxed and started chatting. He brought in about adoption and she went deathly quiet.

After a while, he said, "I think it is something we should consider. It would be good for Michael to have a brother or sister and you are such a wonderful mother. You could give so much to a new baby."

She rolled away from him and turned over so that her back was towards him. He had failed, he thought. He tenderly stroked her back. It was unfair, why shouldn't they be able to have more children? He just wanted to take her in his arms and help her forget all the hurt she felt. He felt it too, but it was worse for her.

Quietly, she said, "Would you really think of it as your own?"

"Yes, I believe I would."

"I'm not so sure," she turned and rolled back to face him. "I'd want it to be the same, but I'm not sure I would feel the same as I do about Michael. Is that wrong?"

"I don't think there are any rights or wrongs where this is concerned darling and I don't think we would really know how we feel unless we make enquiries. I'm sure you would love and take care of any child that we adopt. Look at how you care for Mary. However bad you feel about our situation and babies, you shower Mary with love. I think it probably wouldn't feel the same. It would be different but that difference would be special in its own way," he stopped. A single tear slipped from Grace's eye onto her cheek. He softly wiped it away.

"I love you, Alex, so much and I'm sorry that I have been unable to provide you with more children. I know it hurts you as much as it hurts me," she paused. "I would like to make enquires just to see what happens and what's involved. You are right. Michael should have a brother or sister."

He kissed her and smiled down at her.

"I'll look into it as you say just to see what's involved. I think you are one of the bravest and strongest people I have ever known and I'm so proud to be your husband. And no more apologies, you gave me more than I could ever want and more."

She snuggled up to him again. *It hadn't gone that bad after all,* he thought. I think this is what she needs. He did start to make enquires but slowly, as he didn't want to push too much too soon. It was better that Grace got used to the idea. Gradually, the thought of adopting a new baby was becoming more appealing to Grace. Michael would be three this year and was already showing signs of not needing her as much.

They holidayed in Devon again in early August, stayed in Woolacombe but travelling around to Barnstaple, Bideford and Westward Ho. Grace was adamant that she wanted to learn to drive, as it would make it easier to get around. Alex had to be back to work promptly on their return. There was an important case about to start over fraud and some very high-profile people were involved. Alex had spent a lot of time helping build the case for the prosecution and would have to be in court during the trial. This was a big deal for him and advancement was sure to come if the verdict went in his firm's favour.

The trial started on 5th September 1921. As expected, Alex was deeply involved so Grace tried to keep home life as simple as possible. She knew how important this was to Alex and his career, so she was being as supportive as she could. The trial was about to start its third week. Alex was hopeful of a guilty verdict and was starting to feel that the pressure was decreasing. He had kissed her goodbye as normal on that Monday morning and gone off with a spring in his step. Grace was happy that this would all be at an end soon. It was all consuming for Alex. She was proud of him and wanted every success for him but she did want her husband's attention back with her and their son.

It was warm for an autumn day. Well, it had started out that way. She had bundled up the washing for the laundry and had also hand washed some of their frequently needed items and hung them out to dry. Michael was playing some game as usual. They had a bite to eat at lunchtime and then they were going with Grandmother Elizabeth to Holland Park in the afternoon. About 1:00 pm, the clouds moved in and it started to rain. Grace rushed to get the washing in and found places to hang up the wet clothes.

"That has put pay to the park. Grandma Elizabeth will be upset; we will still go and see her though."

She had finished tidying their lunch things and was getting Michael's coat on when there was a knock at the door. Standing on her doorstep was a policeman.

"Mrs Whitfield?"

"Yes, I am. What can I do for you?"

"May I come in, Mrs Whitfield?"

"Yes, of course," she stood aside and in walked the constable. She showed him into the living room.

"Please take a seat."

He sat on a chair and Grace scooped up Michael and sat him with her on the settee.

"There's been an incident outside the courthouse in the Strand."

Grace was suddenly very frightened and she couldn't speak to ask any questions.

The policeman continued, "I am sorry to say that your husband, Mr Alexander Whitfield, was hurt during an altercation outside the court."

"Hurt?" Grace blurted out; she was shaking now. "Hurt? What do you mean hurt?"

"I'm afraid Mr Whitfield has been stabbed. He is alive, Mrs Whitfield and has been taken to Charing Cross Hospital."

"Oh my God," Grace started to cry.

"Mummy…Mummy…why you crying? What's happened to Daddy?" Grace cuddled her son.

Still crying and between her sobs, she asked, "Is he going to be all right?"

"It's probably best if I get you to the hospital, then the doctors can let you know. Is there anyone you would like to contact that can go with you?"

"I'll need to contact my parents. Michael, stay with the policeman. I need to call grandma and grandpa."

"No, mummy. I want to come with you," Michael was clinging to her. She carried him out to the hall and telephoned her parents. Frederick was at home more now. He did fewer days at the bank. Grace was glad he had taken the call; he'd know what to do.

"Go with the officer and mother and I will meet you at the hospital. Try not to worry, my dear, he's a strong one. Alex will get through this."

She replaced the receiver and took Michael back into the living room.

"We'd better go."

She got her coat and bag and they left. In the carriage on the way to the hospital, she thought back to the time when the news had come through, saying Alex had been hurt in the war. She had been terrified then and she was again. What was happening to them again? Were their lives always to be plagued with upset and heartache? And then she really did get scared. What would happen if he didn't get through this? What if he died? *Oh Alex, please hold on for all our sakes. I love you so much. We couldn't live without you*, she thought and held on tightly to Michael, who wasn't really sure what was happening. Grace just wanted to see Alex and make sure he was all right. *God, I know I've asked you to help him before, but please don't let him die.*

Chapter 17

Apparently, the fight had already broken out before Alex had become involved. The case he was working on had created a great deal of publicity and therefore a lot of the public were more aware of what was happening. The court session had finished for the morning and seemed unlikely to continue into the afternoon, as new evidence had come to light and the defence had asked for a recess to look into this new information. As two of the jurors had left two or three other men, no one was sure how many had started it, were waiting for them outside. These men had been in court listening to the proceedings and were on payload of the defendant. The police suggested that they had been trying to bribe the jurors and a struggle had started. Passers-by had either moved away from the trouble, but some had stopped to try and break up the argument. The court's usher had noticed the huddle and heard shouting and tried to calm the situation. By the time Alex emerged from the court, there was quite a group brawling. The police had been called. Alex had checked that before he left the safety of the building. People were getting shoved about and some were hurt. Alex had broken up one group of on lookers and turned to try with the next group when he came face to face with one of the instigators.

"Well what have I got 'er, a fancy lawyer who thinks he can fight."

The man went to hit Alex, but Alex dodged and went to push his attacker over. Alex hadn't realised the man had a knife and as he lunged forward, he felt a sudden surge of pain cut through his body.

As he backed off he looked down and saw the knife in his stomach and blood had started to trickle from the wound; deep red on his white shirt. The attacker pushed Alex out of the way and took off. Alex stumbled back to the pavement. One of the ushers saw him collapse and rushed towards him.

"Mr Whitfield, you've been stabbed." He turned to another man and said, "Mr Thompson, Mr Whitfield is hurt. Can you help me carry him inside?"

Thompson was one of Alex's colleagues.

"How are you feeling, Alex?" asked Thompson.

"Cold, Jeffrey, I need help. You need to contact Grace for me."

"Don't worry, we'll get you sorted," said Charlie, the usher.

Once inside the entrance hall, Charlie left to get help. Outside, the police had arrived and were quelling the violence and the crowd was dispersing. Many were arrested. Charlie caught sight of an officer who was leaving the scene.

"Sir, we need help. One of our colleagues has been stabbed, we've taken him inside."

"I'll get an ambulance and meet you inside, sir," replied the officer.

Charlie hadn't been back that long when the officer arrived with help.

"What's your name, sir?"

"Alex."

"Well Alex, try to stay awake and we'll get you to the hospital." The ambulance men lifted him on to a stretcher and took him off.

"Is the gentleman married?" asked the officer.

"Yes. He asked me to contact her. Her name is Grace."

"We'll do that, sir. Do you have an address?"

Jeffrey told the man the address.

"Yes, you can leave that to me Mr?"

"Thompson. Jeffrey Thompson."

"Mr Thompson, if you could wait here, I'll get another officer to come and take a statement from you. I'd better go and advice the victim's wife. What's their surname?"

"Whitfield."

"Thank you, Mr Thompson," and then he was gone and he was the officer who had arrived at Grace's door with the news.

He'd hadn't had much time to fill her in, but he didn't know that much, he'd arrived late to the incident. Anyway, Mrs Whitfield didn't look much like she wanted to talk. In fact, she looked deathly pale and he thought she might pass out. He helped her and her son out of the carriage and followed her into the hospital. He made the enquires as to where Alex could be found. He was informed they had taken Alex straight to the theatre. A doctor came to see Grace and explained that although serious, the knife didn't appear to have hit any major organs. He was being operated on now and he would bring further news to her as soon as possible. The police officer and Grace were shown to a small room off of the ward where Alex would be brought to. When Elizabeth and Frederick arrived, the officer stepped outside the room, leaving the family together.

On the sight of her parents, Grace broke down in tears. Michael ran to his grandfather and Frederick scooped the boy up into his arms. Elizabeth rushed to her daughter's side and cuddled her into her arms. There had been so much heartache in her daughter's life in the recent years and she so wanted to be able to protect her and take away the pain. Grace told them what the doctor had said.

"Hush, my darling. Alex is strong, he'll do just fine. You wait and see."

"I hope so, Mother, I really hope so. I feel like I'm in a nightmare that never ends. We lurch from one disaster to another."

"I know it seems that way Grace and you have had your share of bad luck, but Alex will live and we will all be here to help him recover."

Frederick had taken Michael out for a walk. Michael had questions and Frederick tried to explain so that he might understand. Frederick was just returning as another doctor was coming to update Grace. Grace looked up and recognised the man.

"Doctor Gregson."

"Grace Whitfield, I hoped I'd never see you again in the nicest possible way, of course."

"Have you been treating Alex?"

He pulled up a chair and sat directly in front of the women. "Yes, well, assisting. I've been here for a couple of weeks teaching and seeing new techniques of the hospital. I'm so glad I was here so I could assist with Alex's operation."

"How is he, doctor?" asked Elizabeth.

"He's doing very well; the surgery was quite straightforward. The wound wasn't deep and no major organs were affected. He's lost a lot of blood and will be weak, but we'll keep the wound clean and stop any infection and we hope he will be back on his feet in no time."

"When can I see him?"

"He will be brought to the ward soon and you can see him briefly, but it would be better for you and him to get some rest and come back later when he's awake. He's going to want to see you then."

"Thank you, Doctor Gregson. I'm glad you were here. Did he know you were helping him?"

"Yes, he recognised me. I do believe he thought he would get through the surgery then, he had confidence in me. He was asking if you knew about the fight. Obviously, I didn't know if you had been told, but I reassured him you would be here when he came around."

"So, all being well, Alex will be all right."

"We've done all we can and will continue to take care of him during his recovery. I am confident that as Alex got through his war injuries, this is nothing in comparison and you will be there to help him again, strong and compassionate Grace," he smiled.

"Thank you, I feel better now."

They all shook hands and the doctor left. They all felt more at ease now. Just a short while, after a nurse came in to advise that Alex was on the ward and they could see him. Grace and Elizabeth went first. He was still asleep. He looked pale but otherwise, it was just as if he was resting in his own bed. Elizabeth tightened her arm around Grace.

"He looks fine, Gracey. He's going to be up and about soon enough."

"I know, Mother."

Elizabeth left so that Frederick could bring Michael in quickly, to see that his father was all right. Frederick lifted up the boy so that he could see that his daddy was alive and sleeping and then took him back outside. Memories flooded back in a rush to Grace. She had been in this situation before. She was again kneeling by his bed, praying he would recover. Tears filled her eyes.

"If you can hear me darling, I just want to say that I am so angry at you for trying to be a hero. You are my hero, my rock, my love and I need you more than anyone does. You had better recover or I'll knock you into next week," she smiled. "See what you've done. I'm quoting Maggie's crazy sayings. I'm going home now, but I will be back tomorrow. Promise me, you will be awake tomorrow and will feel better. I love you, Alex, I need you," she leant over and kissed his lips. "I'll be back tomorrow. Goodnight, darling."

She didn't want to leave but she needed to rest. He'll need her strength tomorrow and the next day and the next. They left the hospital having told the nurses on duty that Grace could be contacted at her parent's home. Back in Royal Crescent, Elizabeth settled the exhausted Michael into his room. Sally and George wanted to know how Alex was and Frederick told them the whole story. Sally made a light meal and hot drinks for them all. They hardly spoke, all three were worried and exhausted.

"I'd better go to bed," said Grace. "Thank you both for your help today. I couldn't have done it without you."

"We will always be there for you, you know that," Frederick took hold of Grace's hand across the dining table. "You, Alex and Michael are all we've got, we are family and we'll always be there to help each other."

Grace kissed both her parents and went to her room. She was tired and she hoped she would sleep, but thought she probably wouldn't as she was worried about Alex. Her head hit the pillow and she yawned.

"I'm asking again dear Lord, please look after my husband. Keep him safe tonight and give him the strength and courage to recover soon," and then she fell asleep.

Chapter 18

Alex was confused. He didn't know where he was or why he was hurting. He was confused and felt cold. He looked down at his feet and there was mud or sand all around, he wasn't sure which. He was in his uniform, his service uniform from the war. *Oh God, not the trenches,* he thought. It was odd though, the trenches were noisy; bangs, shouts, shells flying around and yet it was almost silent here. He called out, "anyone there?" no one replied. He tried to move but nothing happened, why was that? He looked down again, no mud, no sand but someone was shouting now. What were they saying? He couldn't tell. I have got to see what's happening. It sounds like an argument but who was arguing? Other soldiers? Had they come across the enemy? He would have to look. He looked around for one of the lookouts, none were to be seen. Then Doctor Gregson was there explaining that he needed surgery. Gregson hadn't been at the front so he must be back home in England. So, why did it feel like he was in the trenches? Grace had been there too. She sounded worried, what was wrong? *I'd got over my injuries from the war, the time had moved on, hadn't it?* They had a son now, even if that was the only reason he couldn't possibly be back on the front. He looked around again and it was dark, silent again and he was wearing a suit like he would wear for work. *It's too confusing, and I'm tired,* he thought, *I'll lie down and sleep awhile. It will be clearer in the morning.*

The nurse on duty during the night kept an eye on her restless patient. He had tossed and turned so much; she had kept adjusting the bed covers. He was mumbling a lot and seemed to be getting a temperature but finally, in the early hours of the morning, he had calmed and was finally in a comfortable sleep.

Doctor Gregson checked on him in the morning. Alex was a little hot but his temperature wasn't that high. His previous injuries had been worse and he had recovered, so he was sure Alex would pull through. His wife, Grace, would do everything she could to help, he was sure of that. She had been a great help with Alex's recovery before. He left his patient asleep. Sleep was always a great healer.

His mind wasn't as foggy this time, Alex thought, but he still wasn't sure where he was. He felt hot and shaky. He wasn't in his uniform or his suit. He was on a beach, wearing his swimming attire. Grace said he was too hot and he should go and have a swim. He looked around again but there was no sea, but before he could say anything to Grace, the argument had started again. The same voices as before but louder. He was back in his suit now and when he looked around, he saw a crowd fighting. Grace was in the group; she'd been right here with him just now. He had to find out. His movement was slow like he was walking through treacle. He tried to shout, but nothing came out. As he drew closer, he recognised one of the men who was now coming towards him. The court, this man looked like someone from the fraud case. He had been told to stop heckling during the proceedings earlier today. What did he have in his hand? Alex felt cold now, there was something cold in his stomach. He looked down and saw the knife His knees gave way, he'd been stabbed. Where was Grace? Was she hurt too? No, she couldn't be. She had been here earlier, hadn't she? She had been talking to him. She was worried, it must have been because of the stabbing. Exhaustion consumed him again and he was soon asleep but felt calmer. He could now remember what had happened. He would rest and then he would wake up, he was sure.

Alex was still sleeping when Grace arrived that evening. She checked on Alex's progress and the nurses seemed pleased with the way things were going. She had come prepared. She had sat by his bed before when he slept, so she had brought a book to read. He stirred a few times but didn't fully wake. The nurse said it was unusual that he hadn't woken up as it had been some time since the surgery, but sometimes, the shock of such an incident made patients sleep a lot. She felt a little upset that he hadn't opened his eyes.

Alex could sense sunlight. He should wake up. He wasn't sure how long he had been asleep, but it did seem quite a while. It was an effort but finally, his eyes opened. He was in the hospital. *That's right,* he thought, *I've been stabbed, I've had an operation and I've been asleep along time.* He tried to sit up slightly, but he was stiff and he had pain. He spotted a nurse and called to her.

"Mr Whitfield, finally you've decided to join us. Don't move for a moment. Let me help you," she called to another nurse and they both came to his bed.

"Nurse Turner will help you sit up while I adjust your pillows. That will make you feel more comfortable," as the nurse helped him, he felt the pain again and winced. It was a relief when he was able to lay back on the pillows again. Now, he was more upright. Nurse Turner returned to her duties.

"How long have I been asleep?" Alex asked.

"You came in on Monday and it is now Wednesday," she checked the clock on the wall, "11:33 in the morning to be precise. How do you feel?"

"I have pain but it's not so bad if I don't move. I am hungry though."

"Well that's good, lunch will be around soon and I'll speak to the doctor about the pain and see if he can give you something for it. You know why you're here, Mr Whitfield?"

He nodded.

"You remember the accident?"

"Yes, I was stabbed."

"You were incredibly lucky. The knife didn't hit any vital organs so the operation was a little easier. You've a dressing on the wound which we have changed twice already and will change again tomorrow. The doctor believes you will make a complete recovery. You will be a little weak for a while, but it's good you have an appetite. Eating will bring you back to full strength sooner."

"My wife, has she been here?"

"Yes, she was here when you came out of surgery with other members of your family and she came yesterday evening and sat with you. She said she would be back today. She was really concerned about you."

"What's your name?" Alex asked

"I'm Nurse Bruce."

"Thank you, Nurse Bruce, for updating me on my recent life. Could I possibly ask one more favour?"

"What is that, Mr Whitfield?"

"Could I freshen up? I'd like to look clean and tidy when my wife arrives."

"Yes, I can do that for you."

Once he'd had a small wash and a shave, which he had tried to do himself and then had to have Nurse Bruce's assistance, lunch arrived. It was a stew and Alex couldn't remember when anything tasted so good. He was feeling a little tired again. So he took a nap. He really wanted to be awake when Grace arrived. When visiting started, there was Grace. Once she saw that he was awake, she smiled a smile so bright, it made Alex's heart leap. He had given her so much worry. She kissed him, took his face in her hands and told him she loved him and was glad to see he was awake.

He apologised for worrying her and she just waved it away, saying she was pleased that he was feeling better and that he really did look brighter than yesterday. They talked for ages. She told him that his parents would be down at the weekend and that the rest of the family wanted to visit now that he was feeling better. Michael was missing his daddy and wanted him home. He was tired after all the chatting and once Grace left, he settled down to sleep. For the first time in a couple of weeks, he felt relaxed and happy. The case he'd been a part of had really made him tired and then the stabbing. His dreams had been confusing and exhausting, but tonight he knew what had happened. He was feeling better and Grace had been here. His Grace, his wonderful wife, was being brave for him again. When he got home, he would really make it up to her. She deserved the best of everything. He slept soundly all night.

A stream of visitors came. By the weekend, as promised, his parents arrived. The stitches on his wound were beginning to itch and the doctor had said he would soon have them removed; he was healing quickly. Alex had enquired about Doctor Gregson and was told he had returned to his hospital in Hampshire. He would write to him and thank him for saving his life for a second time. At the end of his second week in the hospital, Alex was discharged.

It felt so good to be home. Michael had quickly cuddled his father and told him he needed a lot of sleep time. At his first night at home, Grace and Alex were in bed.

"We are a pair, aren't we?" Grace exclaimed.

"What do you mean?"

"We're like a patchwork quilt of doctor's needlework. We have so many scars between us now."

Alex laughed, "I have more than you."

"Just make sure there's never anymore."

"I promise."

She cuddled up to him, it felt really good.

"Alex, you remember we spoke about adopting before."

"Yes."

"Well, I was thinking while you've been in the hospital that one never knows what the new day brings, good or bad, "she leant on her elbow so that she could look at him. "You know I've always wanted to have a big family and adopting is our only way. We could give a child a good home and love it as our own. It would be good for Michael," she stopped. "I was scared I was going to lose you and now more than ever, I want to spend as much time as we can as a family and another child would make it even better."

"You've thought a lot about this."

"Yes, even before the accident but as a result of it, I want us to be a bigger family and enjoy our home life."

"Then I'll look into it. I agree it would be good for Michael and if you are sure it is what you want, then it is what I want."

She curled into his arm again, "It really is, Alex. I truly want another child."

Chapter 19

Alex was glad to be home, but he was plagued by nightmares once again. Some were of the war, some from the stabbing. He didn't want to admit it to anyone, but his confidence had taken a knock and he felt vulnerable. He woke from traumatised sleep with his heart racing and sweating profusely many times. He woke Grace on many occasions, especially when he shouted out. She always comforted him and calmed him down. Was it survivor guilt? So many soldiers that had fought alongside him had died, including his brother-in-law. Michael had changed his life, introduced him to another world, a different class of people. Yes, he had made it to college as a result of his own intelligence but Michael had accepted him into his circle and things had changed. Without Michael, there would never have been Grace. He had come close to death twice, how long would his luck last? He no longer felt strong, he didn't feel like a man.

He wrote to Doctor Gregson to thank him for saving his life. He also wrote of his concerns regarding the nightmares and his fears for the future. The doctor replied, offering his advice and help. Maggie, Arthur and Mary were constant visitors to the Whitfield's home. Alex was grateful for Arthur's company and Arthur's skills through his medical knowledge and as a friend was also able to give advice too. Alex also commandeered Arthur to help regarding the adoption.

Arthur was sworn to secrecy, "No one other than the immediate family and of course Maggie knew of Grace and my situation and we would like to keep it that way."

"Not a problem, Alex. Anyhow, reputable adoption organisations are the height of discretion and I would never divulge anything you didn't want anyone to know."

"Thank you, Arthur. As you know, I have a great deal on my mind at present and I do appreciate your help and your integrity is never in question."

"What are friends for if not to help?"

For Michael's third birthday, there was a small family gathering with Eloise, Stephan and Jack. Alex's parents couldn't make it but Elizabeth and Frederick were there, as were Maggie, Arthur and Mary. Ruth had been invited but Grace wasn't sure she would attend, but she and Rachael did come.

Rachael was now eight years old. She was a beautiful girl with excellent manners. She was good at lessons and was excelling in her studies. Grace kissed her niece when she arrived; still struck by how much like Michael she was with her blond hair and blue eyes. Rachael's smile was so like her dear brother's had been. Michael and Jack played while Rachael wanted to help look after baby Mary.

Once the party was over, Ruth seemed reluctant to leave. Grace had been glad she had come and had realised Ruth seemed nervous. Alex said it was so nice to have them over and asked if they could stay for the night. Ruth accepted. Once the children were settled for the night, Frederick and Elizabeth had left the three some, sat, finally relaxing after the excitement. Alex had made some cocoa and they sat peacefully.

"I wanted to get you alone to tell you something," Ruth said nervously. "But before I tell you Grace, Alex, please remember that I loved Michael very much and I will always love him. There isn't a day that goes by that I don't think of him, our life together and the sorrow of losing him so soon," she paused and sipped her cocoa.

"We know you loved him Ruth, dear, you were perfect for each other and he loved you very much," said Alex.

"Thank you, you are very kind."

"Not at all, Ruth," said Grace. "You are family, you always will be and Michael is always in our thoughts and memories and he left a wonderful legacy in the beautiful and clever Rachael."

"She is so like him," Ruth agreed.

"She has the same sensitive and kind disposition, as well as his looks."

Ruth paused again and looked down.

"Have you met someone, Ruth?" Grace asked.

Ruth looked up with tears in her eyes she was a little surprised that Grace could still read her so well. "Yes, I have. I wasn't sure how to tell you all. Not sure how you would all feel about it."

Although she had realised what had been troubling Ruth, it still hit Grace with a feeling of hurt.

"I wanted to tell you, Grace, tell the family, but I was worried what you might think. As I said, I still love Michael always will and I have Rachael as a reminder of that love. His name is Robert Jarvis. I've known him most of my life. He grew up near to my parent's home. He fought in the war and when he got back, his wife had left him. He was very hurt. He's in banking and has a house near to my parents. He's the same age as Michael would have been. He has been a dear friend over the last couple of years and I enjoy his company and he's very good with Rachael. He isn't Michael and it will never be the same, but I do care for him very much and in my own way, I do love him. He has asked me to marry him and I have accepted. I hope I haven't upset you too much, Grace, Alex. I really don't want to do that and I hope that whatever happens, we can still all remain friends, as Rachael still needs to see her family and remember her father and if you would, I would like to introduce you to Robert, so you can see that he is a decent man."

Tears were still in Ruth's eyes. She was quite pale and really worried about what their reaction might be. Grace's heart went out to this nervous woman she had so long thought of as a sister. Grace left her chair and sat beside Ruth on the sofa.

She took Ruth's hand in hers and said, "Ruth, you deserve a life of your own, you deserve happiness. Who are we to deny you of that? We all miss Michael and yes, it is a little bit of a shock but life does go on. We'll never lose Michael as long as we remember him and Rachael and you are those links and we want you to always feel that we are your family too. "Tears were now streaming down Ruth's cheeks; Grace gave her a handkerchief. "You shouldn't be upset Ruthie; a wedding is a time to be happy. You do love him, Ruth, really want this, it isn't just to fill...," she stopped not sure what to say.

"Michael was the man of my dreams. He set my heart on fire. I never imagined that marriage could be so good. His death left me lost and adrift. Everyone was so kind but I didn't know what life would be without the man I loved so much. Rachael kept me going but I felt that the future only left empty years just tending to my child's needs. It had to be enough, I thought. Robert has suffered too. His divorce hit him hard especially coming back after fighting. He had been looking forward to seeing his wife. He is a kind man and handsome, different from Michaels looks, but still nice. At first, he just called in for tea and conversation. Then he would ask if Rachael and I would like to go to the park for a walk.

"Gradually, I brightened from my sorrowful life. He let me talk about Michael and he talked about his ex-wife. I started to look forward to his visits as he brought some light into my life. I hadn't realised that I cared so much about him till you told me about Alex's accident and I suddenly thought about how I would feel if that had happened to Robert. I was surprised when I realised that it would really hurt if I lost him. When I told Robert about the stabbing and how that had made me feel, he just smiled, cuddled me and said that I was now ready for the question he had wanted to ask me for some time and then he asked me to marry him. He hadn't wanted to say anything, as he felt I had still been mourning Michael, but he now felt that I cared for him as he cared for me and he wanted me to be his wife," she felt herself relaxing and her tears slowed then stopped.

"I am pleased for you Ruth, do not be sad. I'm sure Michael wouldn't want you to give up on life. If Robert makes you happy, then that's good enough for me. Don't you agree, Alex?"

Michael had been in his thoughts a lot lately and he missed him terribly, but Ruth did deserve a life and happiness.

"Of course, Ruth, you have our blessing. We will have to meet this Robert now."

"Yes, yes. I'll arrange that soon. Thank you both for understanding. You two are so dear to me and I really wouldn't want anything to change that."

Grace gave Ruth a hug. "Let me tell Mother and Father. I'm sure they'll be all right, but it may disturb mother a little."

"Thank you, I was afraid of telling your parents. I'm being a coward."

"No, you're not. I'm just glad you came to let us know. I've missed your friendship and I hope now you will feel more comfortable visiting us and still be part of our family."

The trio carried on talking late into the evening, laughing and reminiscing. Talking and remembering Michael was good for all of them. The conversation and laughter reinforced the friendship and love that had once been when Michael had been alive.

After the weekend, Alex received a visit from a colleague to inform him that the trial of his attacker was scheduled for January. The fraud case Alex had worked on prior to the stabbing had been won by his prosecuting team a couple of weeks earlier. He didn't take the news of his impending trial well. He was slowly gaining his confidence, but he still felt nervous around large crowds. His colleague said he wasn't expected back at work till after he gave evidence. The firm wanted him to take his time to recover, they were in no hurry for him to return. He was pleased about that as his priority now was to spend time with Grace and Michael. Their time together was more precious than ever and Grace made him feel more confident and at ease.

Grace told her parents of Ruth's news. As predicted, Elizabeth was a bit upset but once Grace explained the whole story and how distressed Ruth had been in telling them, Elizabeth relented.

"I hope she will be happy. I am pleased for her, really. It just upsets me; the loss of Michael and the life he and Ruth had together."

"Ruth doesn't want to forget her life from before and her link to our family. She wants to ensure that you see your granddaughter as much as you like."

"She's a dear girl," Elizabeth said. "Do we get to meet Mr Jarvis?"

"I'll contact Ruth and suggest we all have dinner together before Christmas, if you agree."

"That would be a good idea."

Grace celebrated her 26th birthday a day late, to celebrate with Mary Grace's 1st birthday. On 3rd December, Arthur changed his shift so that he could be at home all day on the Saturday. Both couples and their children met at Maggie and Arthur's cottage in Chiswick. Once Mary, with Maggie's help, had opened her presents, they blew out the one candle on the cake and then ate the tea they prepared. Other family members popped in and out during the afternoon but by the evening, it was just the four of them again. They laughed and joked and played Bridge. Grace helped Maggie tidy up the kitchen and cut up cake to have with tea, while Arthur and Alex talked. Alex found Arthur's company agreeable. Arthur's advice since the stabbing had helped Alex and he knew he could always rely on him. It wasn't the same as his friendship with Michael but Arthur was a clever doctor and a wise and decent friend. Arthur had also confirmed that he was looking into the adoption for them. Before the evening ended, they confirmed arrangements for the Christmas and New Year festivities.

The following weekend was the date arranged for the family to meet Robert Jarvis. Grace had arranged dinner for the Saturday evening. Sally had offered her services and came to Grace's home to cook a special meal. At 6 o'clock, Ruth, Rachael and Robert arrived. After introductions, they sat chatting amicably for a while before dinner.

Grace studied Robert. He was good looking, not as tall as Michael and Alex, but had a strong muscular physique. He had brown hair and brown eyes. He was polite and particularly gracious towards Elizabeth. Rachael was obviously used to his company and he was affectionate towards her. Once they finished eating, the women left the men at the table and relaxed in the drawing room. At the beginning of the evening, Ruth had been anxious but as the evening progressed, she relaxed and was pleased Elizabeth was behaving fondly towards Robert. Alex told Grace later that he found Robert quite agreeable and he would make a good husband for Ruth. Frederick and Robert had talked with ease about banking and his career. Everyone agreed that the whole evening had been a great success. Grace truly hoped that Ruth would become a close friend again.

Christmas and New Year was full of friends and family and the joy that children bring to the festive time. Ruth, Robert and Rachael accepted an invitation to Elizabeth's during the festivities and announced that their wedding was to be on Saturday, 4th March next year. She wanted Grace to be Matron of Honour and Michael to be a page boy, along with Rachael as a bridesmaid. Grace accepted with pleasure.

Alex and Grace made love in the early hours of 1st January 1922. They had partied with family and friends at her parent's home and were glad to finally be at home alone. The parties had been fun but exhausting. They took their time enjoying each other slowly and sensuously. Alex had enjoyed his time away from work and was reluctant to go back. As he made love to Grace, he felt at ease and safe and that was the best feeling. He liked to please her. And he did please her as they climaxed, she cried out in ecstasy. She clung to him for a long time after, neither wanting to part.

Alex was the first to speak, "That was fantastic."

"It really was, if I wasn't tired before, I really am now but that was one of the best."

"Every time is great with you. You do know how much I love you!"

"I can always be reminded."

"I love you more than anything."

"I love you too."

They were soon kissing and caressing again, sleepy but aroused again.

He smiled at her. "Are you ready for more, Mrs Whitfield?"

"For you, Mr Whitfield, I'm always ready."

Chapter 20

On the day of the trial of Alex's attacker, Alex arrived at court to find out the accused had admitted his guilt. Alex hadn't been looking forward to the experience and was relieved that the matter had been taken out of his hands. He had been popping in and out of work since the New Year trying to get back into the routine, but the work wasn't holding his interest in the way it had before. He was enjoying his home life and time spent with Grace and Michael. A lot of his attention was taken up with their adoption plans. Arthur was on the case and so was Doctor Gregson. He still corresponded with the doctor regarding his recovery and he had also found himself asking for advice on adoption. Grace seemed to be calming down too. Their time together had soothed her worries over the stabbing. They had spent a lot of time in bed making love the last couple of weeks, making up for the time when Alex's wounds had stopped them. It reminded him of their early years together. He told her what he was doing about the adoption and she was pleased and a little excited. Another child in their home would be good for them, he thought. Grace was a good mother and a big family was what she wanted. Her renewed friendship with Ruth was also doing her good. They had been like sisters in the past, he hoped it was going that way again. Maybe not exactly the same but they still shared the same interests and memories, and Grace's other true friend, Maggie, liked Ruth too, so Grace was happy.

It was strange seeing Ruth getting a wedding outfit again, thought Grace. She had been with her when she was trying dresses for the marriage to her brother years before. Ruth wasn't going for the same flowing gown; more of a dress and coat, but still Grace had to keep the sadness to herself. *Michael would have wanted Ruth to be happy,* she thought. Ruth chose a cream suit, hat and shoes. Grace chose a similar outfit but in powder blue and Michael was to wear a suit. They had spent a number of days checking all the stores in the city for just what they wanted. Maggie and baby Mary came too, to give their opinion.

It was a crisp Saturday morning in early March. Everyone travelled early in the morning to Richmond to Ruth's parent's home. Once the bride and her attendants were dressed, photographs were taken. Elizabeth kissed Ruth as she left to go the church.

"Thank you, Elizabeth. It must be a hard day for you today," said Ruth.

"It is a little, my dear, but I'm glad you've found someone who makes you happy. He is a very lucky man as was my son. You look beautiful and you will have a wonderful day and a good life with Robert."

Ruth kissed the woman she once called mother with tears in her eyes. "Michael is always with me and he always will be."

"I know, my dear."

Elizabeth and Frederick left for the church with Alex. The first car took Grace, Michael and Rachael. Michael looked so adorable in his suit thought Grace and Rachael looked pretty in her powder blue dress. Grace's heart was full of pride watching her son and niece on their best behaviour for such an important day of their young lives.

Ruth arrived at the church with her father. She was radiant with happiness. Grace and the children followed them up the aisle and the ceremony began. The reception was in the church hall next to the church. It was a happy occasion and Grace was grateful that Ruth had wanted her to be such a part of her day. Rachael was going to stay with Elizabeth and Frederick for a few days, which she was excited about so that her mother and Robert could take a honeymoon in the Lake District. The day had gone well and everyone was happy for the newly married couple.

Alex was getting back to the daily grind at work. He still wasn't that active in court cases and he was considering another area of law rather than criminal. He was taking his time weighing up his options. His colleagues and peers were supporting him and were allowing him the time to figure out what he wanted to do.

During Easter, Alex took Grace, Michael and Jack to Devon. It wasn't exactly beach weather so they chose the Royal Hotel in Bideford. It was easy travelling as the train station stopped at the back of the hotel. You got off the train and entered the hotel from the platform which with two excitable young boys in tow, it certainly made the journey much easier. While they were holidaying, Grace said again that she should learn to drive. The area always gave her renewed feeling for adventure and being able to drive and explore the countryside excited her. Alex said she should do it when they returned. Once Grace got a bee in her bonnet, it was best to let her get on with it. The boys liked riding on the trains to different places and playing football on the beach. So most evenings, they were tired and went to bed early, giving Grace and Alex time for themselves. It turned out to be a good break for all.

An adoption agency in the city had been trying to get in touch with Alex while he was away. Arthur had recommended it so Alex was hopeful. He called and made an appointment and him and Grace attended in early May. They told them there were a lot of children orphaned during the war. Many had found families; it was mostly the older children that hadn't been housed. Grace felt awful and sad for those children but she had always hoped it would be a baby they could have. Carefully choosing her words, she explained this to Mr Williams, the agency manager. He understood and said he would keep them informed with any developments and wished them luck.

At the end of June, Grace was packing to go on holiday. Doctor Gregson had a friend in the navy who had a townhouse in Bideford that he wanted to rent out for the summer. Alex said they would take it for six weeks starting in July. He wouldn't be able to stay for the whole time, but Elizabeth and Frederick could come for some of the time, as could Eloise, Stephan and Jack. He could commute by train at the weekends to be with the family. Grace wanted him there all the time but she knew it wasn't possible and at least, the summer in Devon would be more pleasant than in London. She had taken driving tuition from her father and now had a licence. She would hire a car and drive and explore at least a small part of the countryside.

Just as they were about to leave for the holiday, the adoption agency contacted Alex at his office. He went on his lunchbreak to the children's wing of the local hospital. Mr Williams met him and they were taken into a small room, wherein a crib was a small baby girl sleeping peacefully. Mr Williams explained that her mother had died a day after her birth. Her mother had been weak before the birth. It was a sad story; the baby's mother had been from a well-connected rich family. She had fallen in love with an army officer, not of her station. She married him against her families wishes. As a result, her family had disowned her. She had had poor health throughout her pregnancy and with her husband away a lot, she had felt very much alone. Nearing her due date, her husband was on leave in preparation for the arrival of their child, but tragedy struck just a day after the baby came into the world. Alex was struck at how things could have been just like this for him. Obviously, not the part of being disowned, but he could have been left alone with a child. He couldn't take his eyes off the bundle in the crib all the time Williams talked to him.

"The child's father, does he really not want to look after her? After all, she's all he has left," Alex queried.

"He's a career soldier, quite high up. He's thought long and hard and although he's distraught over the death of his wife, he can't bear to keep the child and it is impossible with his job."

"It must be a difficult time for him."

"I have told him about you and your wife and he thinks you would be able to give Elizabeth a good life. Oh…that's the one condition, he would really like her to keep the name Elizabeth after his late wife."

"That wouldn't be a problem."

The nurse who had shown them to the room had returned with a small bottle for the baby. "Time for a feed little one," she leant over and picked up Elizabeth.

The tiny baby stirred and opened her eyes. Her eyes weren't totally blue. There was a hint of green and her fair hair was fair with flecks of auburn. It suddenly struck Alex, how much like Grace this baby looked. His heart skipped a beat. This baby was the one they had hoped for. Her name was the same as his mother-in-law's and she looked uncannily like Grace.

"Mr Williams, I need my wife to meet Elizabeth, but I'm sure she will want her. She is absolutely lovely. If I bring Mrs Whitfield back this afternoon, how soon could we take the baby home?"

"Elizabeth's father has signed over custody to us already. He just wants to know that she gets a good home and family. If you agree today, we can get all the legal papers completed in two days."

"Set things in motion, Mr Williams, I'll be back soon."

He returned to work, cleared the last of his work and left; everyone wishing him a good break. He called at his in-laws first and asked Elizabeth to come home with him.

"What for?" Elizabeth asked.

"Just come, mother, it's a surprise. Hurry, I need to get home quickly and I need your help."

Grace was surprised to see Alex home earlier than usual and with her mother too.

"Grace, darling, how do you feel about becoming a mother again?" Alex asked excitedly. Grace looked at her mother who was looking surprised too and then she realised what he must be referring too.

"The agency," she said "They've been in touch, have they?"

Alex was smiling as he took her in his arms. "Grace, there's a beautiful little girl who looks just like you who needs loving parents. She's only a week old and she could be ours in two days."

"Then we must go and see her. Obviously, you already have," she paused and looked deep into his eyes. He was smitten he wanted this baby. "Is she lovely?"

"She's adorable and she looks like you."

They hadn't said too much about adoption to Elizabeth and Frederick, but Elizabeth knew her daughter desperately wanted more children.

"Go you two, go see the baby. I'm here for Michael. Go quickly," Elizabeth sensed the urgency in Alex.

Grace kissed her mother and Elizabeth hugged Grace. "Don't worry about Michael, just go."

They got a taxi and within minutes, they were at the hospital. On the way Alex had got Grace up to speed on the baby's background. Grace was nervous entering the ward and Alex seemed so taken with the child. What if she didn't feel anything for her? She needn't have had any anxiety over their meeting because she fell in love with her instantly.

Elizabeth was awake and the nurse encouraged Grace to hold the baby. Once in her arms, Grace felt the same as she had with Michael. Her heart leapt with joy and tears sprung into her eyes. Alex was right, she did look like her. For the longest time, the couple didn't speak. They were mesmerised, Grace holding the little girl and Alex protectively watching them both. Mr Williams appeared.

"Mr Whitfield, Mrs Whitfield, the nurses said you were here… Everything all right?"

"Yes," replied Alex.

Grace looked up and said to Williams, "My husband said that all the formalities could be dealt with quickly."

"That's correct, Mrs Whitfield. I've already started the process by bringing papers with me if you wish to sign right now."

Alex had been watching Grace intently. He wanted this child but Grace needed to make up her own mind. She looked directly at him, smiled an incredible smile that lit up the room and then turned back to Mr Williams.

"I do believe we are ready to sign right away. We want Elizabeth very much."

Alex took the document, read it completely and then signed. Grace handed the baby to him so that she too could read and sign. She looked at Alex holding his daughter and those tears that had sprung to her eyes now fell down her cheeks. It was such a picture of love that she would hold in her memory forever. She hadn't given birth to Elizabeth, but this was special in its way, different but almost as good. Mr Williams shook hands with them and left as the nurse brought in another feed. Grace sat in the chair by the crib. Alex placed Elizabeth in her arms and she fed their daughter for the first time. Alex knelt in front of them to watch and feel close to his family.

"How do you think Michael will react?" he asked.

"I'm not sure, but we will tell him he will have to help us look after his baby sister and he can protect them forever."

Alex was filled with love for his wife. He'd known she would want Elizabeth as much as he did. Grace finished the feed, winded her and changed her nappy, then cuddled her up as the baby fell asleep. They laid her in the crib and told her that her mummy and daddy would be back soon. Arm in arm, they left the hospital. Just outside, Alex turned to Grace.

"Happy?" he asked.

"Deliriously, we have a beautiful baby daughter."

"Yes, we really do."

Chapter 21

The next two days were busy and full of excitement and nervousness. When Alex and Grace returned to their home and told Elizabeth about the baby, the completion of the adoption and that their daughter would be home with them in two days, Elizabeth and Grace danced around the room, crying and hugging. Frederick's reaction was of joy too. He missed not having Rachael around as much as in the early times before his son had died. He was proud of his grandson, but a granddaughter was special and she was going to be called Elizabeth as if after his adorable wife. He would soon be retiring and apart from spending time with his wife, he wanted to enjoy time with his grandchildren. Their holiday postponed for a couple of days, Alex and Grace went shopping for clothes and items for a baby girl. They hadn't given away the crib and the perambulator they'd had for Michael as both were suitable for use at home and once they got to Devon, they would buy a crib for their time there. They visited Elizabeth in the hospital both days and made certain with the agency that the adoption would truly go through without hassle by Wednesday.

Their plan had worked. They kept everything low key from family and friends, pretending they had already left for the holiday. Elizabeth and Frederick decided to go to Devon immediately due to the new arrival and as Elizabeth said, "You've two children to take care of now, "she explained to Grace. "You'll need my help."

Explaining the baby's arrival to Michael was difficult. Alex wasn't sure how much Michael understood but Michael made it quite clear he would have liked a brother, like his cousin Jack. Alex said it would be up to Michael to look after his sister, as she was much younger and would need help from her big brother as she got older. That seemed to make Michael a bit happier with the prospect of the intruder.

All packed and ready for the off, Elizabeth, Frederick and Michael went to the station with the luggage. Grace and Alex went to the adoption agency to collect Elizabeth. The family solicitor had been immediately contacted after they had first seen the baby and he was at the agency too when they arrived. They had left an outfit for the nurses to dress Elizabeth in and there, she was in the pale pink dress and white shawl. Alex checked all the legal papers; Grace eagerly rushed to the nurse for her daughter.

The last few days had been wonderful but also worrying. Between periods of pure joy at getting her greatest wish, were moments where she got anxious that the baby's natural father would come back and say he had changed his mind. Alex had tried to calm her but he too was fraught with worry. She still couldn't believe Alex's reaction towards Elizabeth. She'd known he was committed to them having another child and obviously, this was the only way, but he had been so eager that they had Elizabeth. It had amazed her. He had been ecstatic at the arrival of Michael but the joy had been short lived when she became ill and had to go through with the operation. He was now making Elizabeth's arrival just the same as Michael's, as if

Grace had just given birth and he wanted to ensure wife and child were home safe with him with no complications. Holding their daughter, she glanced at the men checking the paperwork and then shaking hands when the proceedings had been completed, she looked at Alex and thanked God that she had married such a wonderful man with the capacity to love her, their children and deal with whatever was thrown at them. He came over to his wife and daughter and thanked the nurse for all her care and having said goodbye to Williams and the solicitor, they left.

They hardly spoke, Alex had the legal papers and Elizabeth's birth certificate. He had also left details of the baby's new name that would be legally changed while they were away. At the station, Frederick, Elizabeth and Michael were already on the train. Frederick had paid for first class so they could relax for their journey. Grace handed Elizabeth Helen Whitfield to her grandmother. Elizabeth cooed and chatted to the baby. Michael climbed up beside his grandmother so that he could see.

"She's so small."

"You were small like that once!" said his grandfather.

Michael looked confused, not really understanding.

"She's beautiful," said Frederick. "She looks a lot like you did, Grace, when you were born. It's incredible. No one would guess she was adopted."

That pleased Grace. Only her immediate family knew the truth and she wanted to keep it that way. If Elizabeth grew up to look like her, her deception would work as she could tell everyone that such a troubled delivery the first time had made her keep quite this time and she had kept the pregnancy a secret. Elizabeth was passed around them all during the journey. Some of the time, she slept. Sometimes, she was awake, looking around with eyes of wonder at what was happening to her. Even Michael spoke to her, telling her they were going to a new house for a holiday.

The train pulled into Bideford Station. Alex said it wasn't far to walk. So, having packed Elizabeth, Frederick and the luggage into a cab, the new family walked across the bridge over the River Torridge, along the Quay and passed Victoria Park and turned into the Strand.

The Georgian terrace, much like her parent's home, was on the edge of the town. The front door was open, awaiting their arrival. There was a basement and three floors to the house; more than enough room for all of them. The decoration was a little tired but every room was clean, tidy and comfortable. The housekeeper who was called Millie Dean, who wanted to be known to everyone as Millie, had ensured everywhere was ready for the family. Alex had contacted her and said they had a new baby and Millie had told him that the owner had a crib in the loft and also a small baby carrier. Neither were that grand, but she would get her husband into the loft to check their condition. She had been as good as her word. When she showed Alex and Grace their room, by the bed was a small crib made up with crisp white linens and blanket.

"Oh Millie, this is just lovely. Thank you for taking so much trouble to help us."

"No trouble, Mrs Whitfield. The new baby needs a clean and comfortable place to sleep."

"They surely do and this is just fine and please call me Grace."

"Grace it is. I've explained to your mother what I usually do around the house. If there is anything you want me to do or not to do, let me know. I've prepared salad and potatoes and a flan for a meal for this evening. I'll leave you to settle in and I will be back in the morning. I only live a few streets away, so whatever you want, let me know."

She gave directions to Alex as to where she lived.

"Thank you, Millie. I'm sure we will be fine and we will see you tomorrow."

"You have a beautiful daughter and your son is handsome and very excited about his home for the holiday. I hope you enjoy your time here," Millie said then left.

There was a small room just next door to the room Grace and Alex were and Michael wanted that room. On the next floor were a further three rooms. The biggest of them all, Frederick picked. The journey and the excitement of Elizabeth's arrival had exhausted them all. Millie's prepared meal went down a treat. Grace bathed with Elizabeth. Alex then wrapped Elizabeth in a towel while Grace dried off and then Michael wanted a bath. As he splashed about, he said he wanted to go to the beach tomorrow and play in the sand and splash about 'like this', he demonstrated.

"We'll have to see what the weather's like and we've got to take a trip into town to get some shopping first, but I am sure we will find time for the beach," Grace explained.

Alex took Michael to his room and read to him till he slept. When he returned to their room, his heart skipped a beat at the sight of Grace cuddling Elizabeth and singing a lullaby softly. What a picture. For the first time since the stabbing, he felt completely at peace. Everything had worked out well with the adoption and so quickly as it turned out and they were both smitten with their darling daughter. Alex took Elizabeth and settled her in the crib, tucking her in gently.

"How did she feed?"

"Very well, she seemed hungry. Perhaps, the trip tired her too."

They both stood watching her sleep.

"Unsettled nights again," Alex said smiling.

"Yes, I expect there will be but I don't care. I would stay up all night if she needed me," Grace stated.

Alex kissed her neck. "Stay up with me tonight." His hands had moved from her waist and were stroking her hips. She hadn't dressed from her bath and only had a robe around her.

"I'm a little tired and we're not sure how long Elizabeth will sleep," but her resolve had surrendered before she finished the sentence. He never ceased to excite her and soon, he too was undressed and then he took her. All thoughts of tiredness gone. She wanted their bodies to be close and enjoy the passion. They fell asleep entwined. As for little Elizabeth, she slept peacefully till nearly five the next morning. What life had already dealt her, she had no knowledge of and it appeared that she was content.

Chapter 22

The next day was just as busy. Elizabeth and Grace talked with Millie when she arrived at 10 o'clock. Millie was happy to clean and cook as she always did when the resident family were here. Elizabeth assured Millie that whatever was normal practice for her, they wished her to continue. Millie was relieved. She liked these people and their stay wasn't going to be that difficult after all. Once the routine of the household was settled, the two women made up the pram as best they could. They would buy another mattress and blankets in town. They walked to the shops in Bideford. It was so different from London; more small local shops, not department stores. There were butchers, grocery shops, silversmiths and there were Braddicks, the furnishers who were cabinet makers and upholsters. Many items would suit the house, the women agreed. Villacott, Trapnell and Merifield they were to discover were the oldest drapery business in the area. They stopped for tea and to rest with their goods before returning to the house.

Elizabeth had been an ideal baby. After her feed that morning, she had settled into her pram and had hardly stirred all the time they were out. Once at the house, probably as the motion of the pram had ceased, she woke up immediately. She needed changing, so Grace took her upstairs while her grandmother made her next feed. Millie was finishing the evening meal preparations and wanted to hear about the women's shopping trip. Elizabeth, while making the bottle, told her all about it.

"It must seem quiet, compared to London shopping."

"It is different, but we found everything we wanted and everyone was most agreeable and friendly."

"That's good, you'll find most are friendly here, Mrs Richardson."

Millie finished her chores, left instructions for the cooking of dinner and left with a cheery goodbye. After feeding Elizabeth, the women left the house again and walked to the station. Alex and Frederick had taken Michael to the park initially. Michael had run around and was soon tired. So, they walked him along the quay to the station. They boarded a train and went to the next village of Instow, a small village on the estuary of the River Torridge that led to the sea. *There was a small beach which would suffice for today,* thought Alex. He sensed Michael was already tired, so they could all relax here. Lovely little houses and Georgian terraces lined the seafront. Millie had heard the men talking and had prepared sandwiches, cake and some lemonade.

The tide was coming in when they arrived and Michael was instantly rejuvenated and ready to play again. Frederick laid out the blanket from the hamper and settled to take a rest. Michael took his shoes and socks off. Michael in shorts was fine for paddling, but Alex had to roll up his trousers. Michael took off running to the water's edge. The water touched cold but he wasn't bothered and soon, he splashed around in the incoming tide. Alex followed, watching the delight on his son's face.

All felt good to Alex today. He would contact work and tell them his wife had given birth and he wanted to extend his time away. He wasn't sure how this would be received but for now, he wanted peace, this haven, his family altogether. He would also contact his parents to tell them of Elizabeth. The water was cool at first, but soon a relief to the heat of the midday sun. They looked for shells and threw stones in the water. Alex wished he had brought his swimming costume now. Perhaps, tomorrow and the destination would be Westward Ho! beach. Another little boy named Peter had joined in their search for shells. His family were sitting a little further up the beach and his father had come along to see if Peter was disturbing them.

"No, he seems to be enjoying himself and he's no bother. He's about the same age as my son. Four?"

"Yes, he is. I'm Dennis, Peter, you have met and my wife Helen is just up the beach."

"Alex," the men shook hands.

"Are you on holiday?" Dennis asked.

"Yes, we have rented a house in Bideford. My wife hasn't long given birth to our second child and we thought it would be a pleasant break for us and the wife's parents."

"Congratulations! Boy or girl?"

"A girl, Elizabeth," the lie had rolled off his tongue so easily but it was only a little white lie. Elizabeth was his daughter and she had captured his heart as much as Michael had on sight. She was his own daughter. They chatted, keeping an eye on the boys. Dennis and his family were from Manchester and he was a foreman at a factory. They were staying at the Royal Hotel for a week. Helen then called them back for lunch. Dennis called Peter and the men shook hands again. Alex was hungry now, so he called Michael back and they made their way to where Frederick was sitting. Frederick had started to read the newspaper and had fallen asleep. He stirred as Alex and Michael sat and started to empty the hamper and hungrily tucked into the food.

When Elizabeth and Grace and the baby arrived, only Alex, was awake. The ladies had some lemonade and sat down on the sand to relax. Baby Elizabeth had promptly fallen asleep on their trip to the beach. Dennis and his family came over to say goodbye and admired Elizabeth sleeping soundly. Upon waking, Michael had wanted to paddle again, so Alex took him back to the water's edge. As the afternoon drew to a close and tea time approached, the family packed up their things and got the train back to Bideford.

Over dinner, Alex suggested that if the weather was fine the next day, he thought a trip to Westward Ho! would be good, as he wanted to swim and teach Michael to. Frederick suggested that he and Elizabeth would look after their granddaughter so that the three of them could enjoy the beach. Grace was sceptical at first. It was only her third day with her daughter, she wasn't sure if she wanted her out of her sight yet.

Elizabeth realised this and said, "Go for the morning only, Grace. You enjoy swimming and it would be good for Michael if you are both there while you're teaching him to swim." She leant closer to her daughter and spoke quietly so that Michael wouldn't be able to hear, "Michael needs you just as much now, if not more. I'll be fine with Elizabeth, try not to fret."

She smiled, "You're right, Mother. Thank you."

Turning back to Alex, she said, "Then we'll go swimming tomorrow."

The fresh air was making both children sleepy. Grace looked in on Michael who was fast asleep and checked that Elizabeth was settled. It was Grace that initiated sex this time. She felt relaxed and happy. Her children were beautiful and Alex was like a man revived. She couldn't wait to be free of her clothes and close to Alex.

The next day, they went to Westward Ho! Michael showed an aptitude to swimming and had no fear of the water. Upon returning home, the whole family walked to Victoria Park to spend a peaceful afternoon.

Alex contacted his office and extended his leave on mentioning that his wife had not long given birth. Grace wrote to Eloise, telling her about Elizabeth. Of course, she didn't know the truth about the hysterectomy, so she carried on the lie that she had covered up her pregnancy due to the difficulties last time; also writing to check if they were still coming to Devon in August. She received a letter back full of excitement and well wishes and that Eloise, Stephan and Jack couldn't wait to see the baby but unfortunately, they weren't able to come, as unknown to her, Stephan had arranged a holiday to Morecombe. Grace was a little disappointed. She wrote to Maggie then to tell her about the adoption and Maggie replied with well wishes and also asked if she, Arthur and Mary could come down in early August. Grace quickly replied saying yes to her request. It would be good to have Maggie around when Alex and her father returned to London.

The next couple of weeks were spent walking, swimming and taking the train to Barnstaple, where there were more shops and the town was busy especially on market days. By train, they also visited Ilfracombe again. Sometimes, the whole family went on a trip, other times just Alex, Grace and the children. Elizabeth and Frederick left to the own devises would go for walk, or visit the cinema or just relax in the park or on a beach. Both really enjoyed the change from London and the restful days. Sometimes, the grandparents looked after the little ones so that Grace and Alex could go to the theatre or cinema. Elizabeth was pleased that her husband was enjoying the break. He was hardly working now and he seemed more tired lately. The holiday had come at the right time and he seemed to be relaxed and more like his old self. She was happier too. The new baby's arrival had a good effect on everyone. Grace especially seemed calmer and more positive. Her daughter had had a lot to deal with in the last few years and Elizabeth was relieved that Grace at last seemed content. Elizabeth herself would have been heartbroken if she had not been able to have children. She had lost two sons, which had been devastating, but she had given birth to them and had their love all be it for a shorter time than she would have liked.

Alex truly relaxed and enjoyed every day. He delighted in the time with his family walking in the park, playing games with Michael and wonderful love-filled nights with Grace. On one occasion, Alex hadn't heard the baby crying when she was in her crib.

Michael came running quite concerned to find him and said, "Lizzie's crying papa, come and see. She's not very happy." Michael grabbed his hand and took Alex to the crib.

"Well done, Michael. It was good that you came and found me. Elizabeth could have been in trouble and you were being a clever big brother and looking out for your sister."

Michael was pleased with the praise, maybe having a sister wasn't going to be as bad and he could help look after her. Later, Alex retold the story to the family.

"He seems to have adjusted well and in a short time," Frederick observed. "You're lucky, he's not had the build up to a new arrival but you've done the right thing coming here to start your time with Elizabeth. He is getting as much attention as the baby. I also think Lizzie is a brilliant name for our little bundle. At least, Michael can say it."

They all agreed. "Lizzie it is then," Frederick said.

When the time came for Alex to return to London, Grace was unsure she wanted to stay in Devon. They had made love most nights. Each evening, they sought out each other, hungrier and more passionate than the night before. Grace felt she really had got her husband back. He promised that he would be back the following weekend, "And anyway, Maggie and her family will be here soon and you'll have fun," he said.

Maggie couldn't wait to hold Lizzie. "She looks so much like you Grace. It's amazing. How's she been?"

"Like a dream, she feeds, sleeps almost all night. She's such a happy baby, so calm, she hardly cries."

"How's Michael been with her?"

"Good. He's changed her name to Lizzie, because that's all he could manage of Elizabeth. He's playing the big brother helping when he can. We've spent some time alone with him too, to make sure he knows we still love him, to hopefully stop the sibling rivalry."

"Can I feed her?"

"Of course, you getting broody, Maggie?"

"Yes I am. I knew I wanted children but hadn't realised how much till I had Mary and I don't want to wait for too long or I'll be getting too blooming old."

"Maggie, I could never imagine you old. You've so much energy for starters."

Arthur took his family out on trips and other days, both families went out together. Mary adored Michael and would follow him anywhere, which was a little dangerous on the beach. Michael was now more confident at swimming and would take off to the water's edge alone. Arthur was a strong swimmer, so he took charge, keeping a watchful eye on Michael and getting Mary used to the sea.

As promised, Alex returned late the following Friday night. On Saturday, the men went for a drink and the ladies went to the park. The children played games and ran around, while the ladies had a refined afternoon with tea and cake. It was a wonderful time spent with friends and family.

After their two weeks, Maggie, Arthur and Mary left with Alex to return to London. They had enjoyed their time together and were reluctant to go home. At the station, Grace and Maggie hugged, "Come and visit as soon as you get home," Maggie said. "Promise me."

"Promise."

"No one will ever know that you are not Lizzie's biological mother, Grace. She is so much like you and I think she is going to have your calm temperament and loving ways too."

"You are so kind, Maggie," she hugged her friend tightly. "She truly is a gift from heaven and I am blessed. I will visit soon as I get back and you can help me plan the christening. Lizzie is going to need godparents."

"I'd be honoured and so would Arthur. Thank you. "They hugged again and then they boarded the train. Alex and Grace embraced and kissed.

"Till next weekend then."

"I'll look forward to it," Grace replied. Then she waved goodbye as her husband and friends left for the city.

Alex was able to get a couple of extra days for holiday towards the end of August to help them all return to London. He had managed to change direction with his career and instead of criminal law and trails of murder and fraud, he would be dealing with property and business law. He would be happier now, he told Grace and it would probably mean more regular hours so that he could be with his family more.

This summer had been the best ever, they agreed. Their family was complete now with Lizzie. They had spent so much time together and Devon had proved a haven of happiness again. Saying goodbye to Millie had been emotional. Millie had grown to like the family in the short time they had stayed at her employer's home and she hoped they would come back again. Grace and Elizabeth had bought her flowers and a shawl to say thank you for all the wonderful meals she had cooked and all the looking after she had done for them all. There were tears all around. As the train left the Devon county, her children both sound asleep, Grace leaned towards her husband and rested her head on his shoulder. She was the luckiest woman in the world.

Chapter 23

As autumn began, there was a whirlwind of visitors and well wishes who wanted to see Elizabeth. The shortening of her name to Lizzie stuck mainly, because Michael could pronounce it and it did suit her. She continued to be a good baby, rarely waking at night and good natured when awake. Normal routine for Lizzie was to be fed, changed and then back to sleep. Michael had enjoyed Devon and was finding home not so easy, not so much fun. Grace had things to do in the house and care for Lizzie and grandma and grandpa weren't with them all the time as they were back in their own home. Helen came very soon after their return. James couldn't get away from the business but promised he would get to see his new granddaughter at Christmas. Grace explained they hadn't said anything before wanting the delivery over with after last time's problems. Helen said she understood and was just pleased that both mother and baby were well. Michael was back in his element, Grandma Helen would play with him and read stories. She said he was a grown-up boy and a big brother and he liked that too. Eloise visited several times and Grace asked her if Stephan would like to be Lizzie's other godparent. Eloise asked Stephan and he accepted. Ruth, Rachael and Robert came the second weekend they were home. Ruth made a fuss of both Michael and Lizzie. She was excited and wanted to get Grace alone. While the men chatted and the children played, Ruth joined Grace in the kitchen to make tea.

"Grace, I have something to tell you."

"What is it Ruth dear? You seem very excitable."

"I'm pregnant."

"Really? You are obviously happy about it. Are you feeling all right?"

"Yes, I'm really happy. I never dreamed I would have any more children but I am. It's early days yet and Robert is so pleased too. Rachael hopes it's a little girl so that she can share some of her baby things. Do you think Frederick and Elizabeth will be all right about it?"

"Of course, they will. They want you to be happy and you know how they adore children. Father is totally smitten with Lizzie. I expect they will treat your new baby as one of the family."

"I do hope so. I do love you all very much and I know my absence from your lives was more my fault than anything, but I'm so pleased you've all taken to Robert and now my family is growing just like yours. A girl as beautiful as Lizzie would be nice, but I wouldn't mind a boy either."

Grace was genuinely happy for Ruth. There had been a small pang of jealousy at Ruth's ability to conceive, but it was momentary and soon passed. She had Michael and Lizzie and her marriage to Alex had reached an even better place. The holiday had given him new energy. Lizzie's arrival had brought sparkle to both of them.

They rarely had a night they didn't make love. He hadn't had nightmares for a few months now. He slept more peacefully and was happier at work.

Lizzie's christening was on 29th October 1922. Maggie, Arthur and Stephan were proud godparents and Lizzie behaved as wonderful as ever. As the vicar made the sign of the cross on her forehead, Lizzie gurgled and then smiled. All the family and guests had tea at Grace's parent's house and made plans for the forthcoming Christmas.

The family and circle of friends were growing and there were more children. Sally said she needed more help and Cassie, one of the housemaids, had shown an aptitude in the kitchen learning to cook. Elizabeth agreed with the change to Cassie's duties when there was to be a party or celebration. The meal for Christmas was a great success and Cassie's contribution was as good as any dish Sally had produced. Frederick ordered the dancing to start as he had many times in the past. Now retired, he took pleasure in being with his grandchildren and had Rachael dancing with him straight away. The news of Ruth's pregnancy had been greeted with warmth and as Grace predicted, the baby would be an honouree grandchild. Grace and Alex danced many times. Lizzie was asleep and as each child tired, they were all accommodated in the next room and in turn, each set of parents checked on them all.

"I remember the first time we danced at a Christmas party in this house," Alex whispered in Grace's ear and then he kissed her neck.

"I remember too. I wondered if you liked me enough to ask me to dance and then when you did, I didn't want the night to end."

Alex was looking deep into her eyes with warmth and love. His green eyes still sparkled so bright. It was his eyes that she had fallen for first. The way he'd looked at her had excited her and made her feel desirable. She melted in those eyes.

"I fell in love with you that night and I knew that you would be my wife."

"How could you have been so sure? I had been so worried that you wouldn't ask to see me again."

"I was sure because I'd never met a woman that was as beautiful as you and could dance without stepping on my feet." He smiled at her.

She laughed and he held her tightly. He couldn't wait to get her home. The fragrance she was wearing was intoxicating and holding her slim sexy body made him want her all the more.

On New Year's Day, Arthur and Maggie invited them over to theirs. Maggie also wanted to share the news that she was pregnant. Grace congratulated her friend. She knew that Maggie had wanted another child before she was much older. Their circle was certainly growing. A whole generation was blooming. Would they all remain together? Grace hoped they would.

1923 was flying by. Ruth gave birth to a son she named Matthew on 2nd April. He looked a lot like Ruth in his colouring and features. Both mother and baby were doing well and Robert was a proud father.

It was June and Lizzie's first birthday came. They had a party in the garden for her. Aided, she was able to walk a little. Michael thought she looked funny trying to walk, but he was already becoming a protective older brother because he was always there to help if she fell. Michael was to start school in September and Grace and Alex were introducing the idea, telling him how much fun it would be and that it was the same school that his uncle had taught at. It seemed to be going down well because

Michael was telling everyone that he would soon be going to school with older children and wasn't alarmed by it.

They hired the house in Bideford again for July. Millie was pleased to see them. She had become a grandmother earlier that year. Her daughter had given birth to a boy, she'd named Paul. Millie was surprised at how much Michael and Lizzie had grown and made a fuss of them. She looked after them all and spent a lot of time talking to Elizabeth about grandchildren. One morning, she brought Jane and Paul to meet everyone. Devon was as good a holiday as ever. They had hired a car from the garage and Grace drove them to Westward Ho! Clovelly and to Barnstaple, but Michael said he preferred the train. Frederick and Elizabeth left after three weeks to let the family have some time alone. The beach outings were always the favourite. Michael loved to swim and would race to the water a soon as they reached any resort.

"I once promised I'd take you to Paris or anywhere else abroad you wanted to go to and I know we haven't travelled yet. Do you still want to go abroad?" Alex asked while they relaxed on the beach at Instow.

"I suppose I would like to sometime, but I'm happy here in Devon now and all of the holidays we've had so far. So long as we have time together as a family, we could be anywhere and I'll be happy."

They returned to London just in time as Maggie gave birth to a girl on 3rd August. They named her Jessica Margaret. Alex and Grace were godparents at her Christening in September. *This generation was certainly growing,* thought Grace. There was Rachael, Jack, Michael, Mary, Lizzie, Matthew and now Jessica. Friends and family, all these children. Grace thought she might only have one child. She now had two and was godparent to many more. She was in her element.

Chapter 24

Michael enjoyed school and excelled from the start. He was more occupied during the day and that made him easier to occupy in the evenings. Lizzie always got excited when he got home and Michael paid her attention telling her about school, although she couldn't really understand. He had a thirst for knowledge and was constantly asking questions. Grace could see traits of her brother all the time in her son and that made her happy. Lizzie was growing up quickly. By Christmas 1923, she was toddling around, getting into everything. She was the apple of her grandfather's eye and he spent a lot of time with her.

Over the next year, it was a whirl of parties and celebrations as each child reached a birthday. Grace's home was always full of family and friends. Each couple took turns to look after the children so that the adults could go out alone. Devon was the holiday destination again. They had been able to rent the house in Bideford again and family and friends visited throughout the summer. Alex was enjoying his work and he was also managing to spend more time at home too.

Times had changed and so had the way women dressed. Clothes were less restrictive and simpler in design. Grace loved the simple lines of the dresses and the hemlines had risen too. It felt very feminine and no more boned corsets if you chose not to. Under garments were softer and prettier. She had considered cutting her hair to follow the fashion of shorter hair but Alex had objected. Maggie had hers done and it looked fabulous but Alex was adamant. He loved her long hair and his answer was, "You can always wear it up!"

At 32, Alex was more handsome than ever. He played a lot of sport and become even more muscular and strong. He had kept his hair short as he had in the army. He still excited her and she ensured they had time for each other—special time to dine out, go to the theatre, take walks and make love as often as possible. Grace no longer worried about her hysterectomy scar. She was still slim and Alex adored her. Having Michael and Lizzie demanding of her time kept her busy, as did all friends and their children at times. She was just relieved that life had settled down not too many upsets or surprises. There had been such tragedies for some years. It was lovely to enjoy the calm with her family.

Things were to change for the family again in 1925, not in a bad way though. Early April, Alex received a telephone call from Doctor Gregson. Alex wasn't sure what to think about the contents of the call but one thing was for sure: he was interested. He got home quickly that evening and as soon as possible got Grace alone and sat comfortably in the lounge. Grace could tell something was on his mind and was a little apprehensive.

"Don't look so worried, Gracey. It's nothing awful, I promise. Doctor Gregson called me today. Evidently, someone they know works at the Queen Alexandra Hospital in Portsmouth. A couple of days ago, a young woman gave birth to twins.

Already well into her labour, they couldn't turn her away to go to the maternity hospital. The babies were born and while nurses attended the twins, the girl disappeared. The hospital and the police have tried to track down the mother but have not succeeded. The twin girls are probably going to be put into a children's home, unless anyone can be found to adopt them," he paused for a moment, he wanted to gauge her reaction. He'd had time to mull over the news and was sure how he felt about it.

"John obviously knows that as a family, we are happy, but just thought we may want to know about the babies. Irene had been talking to her friend from the hospital and thought straight away about us," again, he stopped. He wasn't sure what was going through her mind. "Evidently, they are healthy and tiny, both only weighing about 5lbs each but doing well. You're not saying anything…"

"I know," was all she said. Her mind was racing. Two more children, two little girls. Two tiny lives that needed her help. "We would never be able to pretend I gave birth this time."

"No".

"Everyone would know they were adopted."

"Yes."

She was silent again.

Four children, would she be able to cope? How would Michael and Lizzie take two tiny babies? Would they have enough room in the house? Millions of thoughts, problems, worries rushed through her mind.

Then she suddenly blurted out, "I think we should go and see them Alex," she stopped and then started again, "just to see. We should consider these two little lives and what futures do they have at the moment. "She looked at Alex who was smiling from ear to ear.

"I hoped you'd say that." He had been standing, leaning on the mantel by the fire close to where Grace was sitting. He knelt down and took her hands that were lying in her lap. "I know there's a lot to think about but I've had a little longer to think about this and I believe it is fate. We've always wanted a big family. Michael and Lizzie would be enough, they are wonderful children. I know that adopting Lizzie helped you tremendously and getting John's call now seems so right. I'm trying not to get too excited, we may see these little girls and not feel anything, but I can't help remembering how we both felt about Lizzie on first sight. I fell in love with her instantly and everyone has believed she's ours in the same way as Michael. This would be different, I know, but I'm sure if we feel the same about them as Lizzie. We'll be good parents for these poor little things."

Her heart went out to her husband. He was such a softy when it came to their children. He loved to play with them, show them how to draw, make things. Although he'd been through the war and the stabbing, she was lucky. He was still Alex; loving and kind. She kissed him lightly on the lips.

"I'll speak to Mother and Father tomorrow. We will be visiting them anyway and Ruth will be there too. I'll ask them to look after Michael and Lizzie for the weekend and we'll go to Portsmouth. If Ruth is there, it will be good to see how other people will react but then Ruth is family and she'll think it's a good idea."

"I'll telephone John straight away. I'll tell him we will be down on Saturday. He said we could stay with him and Irene for however long we want. I do believe we are meant to have these children, Grace. "He kissed her. "I love you very much.""

"I love you, too. Go and make the call before I panic and change my mind."

After speaking to John, Alex relayed the conversation to Grace. Irene would tell her friend when they would be arriving so that the hospital would hopefully hold on to the twins instead of sending them to the orphanage. Irene and John would be pleased for them to stay with them and if we went to Fareham train station, John would meet them and take them to the hospital. The plan was coming together. Throughout the evening, they talked about other subjects but the twins kept popping up in conversation. Did they really have the room for more children?

The next day, having got Michael to school, Grace made her way to her parents' home. She was confused, excited and nervous. Was this a good idea at all? They had passed Lizzie off as their own, but everyone knowing about adoption, what would they think? Ruth had already arrived. It was Matthew's second birthday and she'd promised Frederick and Elizabeth that they could see him on his special day. Grace had wrapped up a toy train and a new outfit for Matthew and Lizzie, proudly gave him his present and then set about helping him open it. While the children played and Elizabeth made tea, Ruth told them about the presents Matthew had received and about the party they were having for him that evening.

When there was a lull in the conversation, Grace started, "Mother, Father, I have something to ask of you. Could you look after Michael and Lizzie for the weekend? Alex and I are going to Gosport to Doctor Gregson and his wife."

"Of course, we will look after them," Frederick said.

Lizzie had constantly pestered him all morning and he loved it. Lizzie was almost three years old and was the image of Grace at that age. Frederick marvelled at their likeness and she adored his attention.

"It's not just a visit, there is a purpose to the trip." She was losing her nerve, finally she explained, "They are just days old."

Ruth exclaimed, "How could anyone leave their children? She must have been desperate."

"No one knows," said Grace. "The police haven't been able to find her."

"Are you going with the intention of adopting them?" Elizabeth asked gravely. "You've two children Grace, they're both young, they demand a lot of your time and attention. Do you think you could manage more?"

"I'm not going blindly into this, Mother. The call has taken both of us by surprise. Alex and I talked extensively all evening and some of the night. We're going with an open mind just to see what the girls are like, see if we feel anything for them, see if there is any glimmer of attachment between us and them. It's important that we're good for them, as parents. One never knows if you have an affinity with a child. You have to feel it's right."

Elizabeth understood what Grace was saying. When they'd gone to see Lizzie that first time, both Alex and Grace had felt as if the little girl was their own and that they had been right to adopt her.

"I believe you're being sensible. Just keep in mind that another two babies would be hard work."

"I know."

"You and Alex are good parents. It would give the two babies a wonderful chance to have a good life. If it feels right, go ahead. I applaud you."

"We are being cautious, really we are. We know nothing of their backgrounds. We don't know what they look like. Irene said her friend at the hospital says they are healthy and pretty, but we'll find out soon enough."

Grace thought Ruth seemed to approve. She wasn't so sure that her parents did but at least, they were taking care of Michael and Lizzie so that they could go to Portsmouth and make an informed and competent decision. The more she thought about the girls, the more they appealed to her. No one knew about Lizzie's real heritage. No one had suspected. This time would be different. There would be no subterfuge but they could still be the girl's real parents.

During the next few days, Grace tried to gauge Michael's reaction to the suggestion of more children in the family.

He'd shrugged. "If they are like Lizzie, that wouldn't be so bad. She's been really fun, mummy."

They had bonded well, inseparable in many ways. Lizzie adored her big brother and he was her hero. He helped her to walk when she'd struggled. She played with his train set and he always told her what to do when playing with it and to be careful with his toys. When they went to the park, she would run after him to play. Lizzie got upset if Michael brought a school friend home or went to a friend's house, as she didn't have his attention. But woo be tide anyone who would hurt his sister or if she fell and hurt herself, he was immediately there to comfort her. It brought tears to Grace's eyes as it was so reminiscent of her relationship with her own brother. She still missed him terribly.

Finally, it was Saturday. Frederick and Elizabeth were going to stay at Grace's home. It will be less of an upheaval for the children, they'd said. The train journey passed quickly and as promised, John Gregson was waiting at Fareham station for them. He drove them to Queen Alexandra Hospital. Alex took hold of Grace's hand and held tightly as they entered the room where the girls were. For a moment, Grace wanted to flee, too scared and nervous to go in.

Alex sensed her fear and put his hand around her waist and pulled her to him, kissed the top of her head and softly said, "We're here darling. There's nothing to fear."

She gazed up and looked into those green eyes. He smiled at her and that gave her confidence to enter the room and meet the twins for the first time.

One was awake, the other was asleep. Both had dark hair and pale skin. Their colourings were a lot like Alex's, Grace thought. One slept silently, the other gurgled and wriggled. They were both tiny. Alex put his hand into the crib where the one lay awake. His hand in comparison looked enormous. He put his index finger towards the infant's tiny fist and she unconsciously gripped it. She was far too young to know what was going on, far too young to know what she had done by holding Alex's finger.

Grace caught her breath. This picture of Alex and this baby would be another memory she would hold dear and never forget. It was magical. She had slipped back a couple of years to when they'd first seen Lizzie. She had been desperate for another child then and Lizzie had won them over in an instant. Now, she wasn't so desperate. Now, she was clear headed and not impulsive. John and the doctor were talking. Grace moved closer to Alex. He hadn't taken his eyes from the girls. Grace touched his arm lightly and he looked at her His eyes were glowing with love. *The tiny bundles have captured his heart,* she thought.

115

"Is it all right if I pick her up?" he asked, not really addressing anyone.

"Of course," said the doctor and carried on his conversation with John.

Alex reached into the crib and picked up the little girl; she fit in both his hands. Grace looked at the baby and was stunned by her expression. She was as hypnotised by Alex as he was with her. The other baby began to stir. She blinked a couple of times then started to cry. Immediately, Grace picked her up.

"What's wrong, little one? There's nothing for you to cry about. Look, your sister is having a cuddle and now I'll cuddle you, there, there."

She didn't cry for long, soon soothed by Grace's affection. The doctor had left the room and John joined them at the cribs.

"You seem to be getting on well. The doctor will instruct the nurses to make up a feed and bring a change for them. They are probably hungry."

"Did he tell you anything more about their mother?"

"No, no one knows anymore, really. She didn't look poor. She was well-clothed and spoke well. She wasn't recognised as being local. She didn't appear upset or about to run away when she was first here, just wanted help with the labour. It's all a bit of a mystery."

"I'd be concerned that she may come back and try to claim them," Alex said.

"It's unlikely," John said, "for if she did, she would likely be imprisoned."

When the feed arrived, John left the couple with the excuse to get them all some refreshments. *They need time alone,* he thought. The girls were alike but not identical. One's hair was black, the other had flecks of brown. One had a smaller mouth than the other. One wanted to sleep more and the other was alert and looking around at her surroundings. Alex and Grace discussed the twins looks, their differences, the way they fed. One had moaned more about being changed than the other, but neither adult had stated the obvious. What were they going to do?

"This one gurgles like Michael did," Alex pointed out.

"This one just eats and sleeps. Remind you of anyone?" Grace asked.

"Lizzie," Alex agreed.

"They are adorable Alex, such characters and at such a young age. They've no idea of what a grave start to life they've had."

Each holding a baby, they looked at each other. Both babies were asleep now. They put them back into the cribs and covered them with their blankets.

"It feels right, just like it did with Lizzie, don't you agree?"

"It does feel right, very right, Alex." She looked straight at him.

"I think we have two more daughters, my dear." He kissed her passionately then picked her up and whirled her around. Finally, he put her down when she said she was giddy. She put her hand on the crib to steady herself.

"I do believe girls that your father has gone slightly mad."

"I know it's soon but names, Gracey, they need names."

"It is a bit soon. Do you have any in mind?"

"Well, I had put some thought to it just in case."

"And..."

"The one that clenched my finger," the one he'd held and fed, "this one she's alert, sharp. Victoria, I think. Strong and clever like the queen of the same name."

116

"Victoria Whitfield. That does sound grand. I like the name Amelia, so this little one," she indicated the quieter of the two, "so you my darling are Amelia Whitfield. Two beautiful names for two beautiful girls."

John returned with tea for everyone.

"John," said Alex, "meet Victoria and Amelia Whitfield."

Chapter 25

Alex and Grace were so excited. They talked incessantly throughout the journey back to John's home in Alverstoke. It was a pretty little village that Grace vaguely remembered when she stayed at the Anglesey Hotel nearer to the coast at Stokes Bay. The couple had a cottage in the village. Irene greeted them warmly and soon, they were all having tea and sitting comfortably.

"We lived in a bigger house out of the village a little," Irene explained. "But when the children grew up and married and moved on, it seemed a better idea to have a smaller house."

"It's lovely, Irene and thank you for letting us stay. It's been such a busy and thrilling day. It's nice to finally sit and calm down in a lovely home."

"The girls, you'll be adopting, I think," Irene quizzed.

"Absolutely," said Alex. "We fell in love with them immediately." Alex carried on explaining about their visit. "We've named them Victoria and Amelia."

"Very grand names for two tiny mites who haven't had much luck to start with but I expect that's all about to change."

"John's kindly started the process with all the legalities. Hopefully, we can take them home soon and start as we mean to go on," Alex said.

"How do you think your son and daughter will react?" Irene asked.

"Michael will probably say, 'not more girls' and then protect them until such time he can tease them. As for Lizzie, I'm not sure. She's her grandfather's little princess. I don't think she'll be too happy with the completion," Grace said.

"I expect there will be a few problems, but nothing you won't be able to sort out," Irene encouraged.

"Show Grace and Alex the guest room, John, as they may want to freshen up before dinner. I've done roast beef. I hope that's alright."

"Sounds wonderful, Irene," said Alex. "Hadn't thought about food much today, but now, I'm famished.

Once alone in their room, Grace said, "Are we completely stupid?"

"Totally, my darling, but those girls were too lovely to leave to someone else."

"You're right," Grace paused, "does it worry you at all that we know nothing of their backgrounds?"

"Not really, they are healthy and beautiful that's all that matters."

"Their hair and skin colour is much like yours, Alex. They'll definitely look like part of the family."

"They'll have known no other family but ours, Gracey." He put his arms around her and kissed her. "They'll fit in and be as smart and pretty as their mother and they will be our daughters as much as Lizzie is."

She kissed him passionately. She wished they were home and alone now.

Dinner was delicious. Irene was a great cook and the four of them enjoyed the evening immensely.

"I'd invite you to come again but with your extended brood, we may not fit you all in," said Irene. "But if you ever want to come for a break just the two of you, we'd be delighted to have you back."

"Thank you," said Alex. "You've made us very welcome and your cooking is excellent. Perhaps, if you and John want to come to London, you could stay with us. If not with us, then Grace's family live close and they usually put up my family when they are down from Yorkshire. My family!" he looked at Grace, "I wonder what they will think."

"They'll be all right like my mother and father. They'll just be glad of more grandchildren."

"Just like this one." Irene nodded towards her husband, "He adores his grandsons."

The rest of the evening was taken up with talk of families, children and showing of photographs. Grace and Alex were exhausted when they finally got to bed. After breakfast, John took them back to Queen Alexandra Hospital to see Victoria and Amelia again. John was to sort out the paperwork as Alex had given him the authority.

"I'll make sure my solicitor has all the details tomorrow, John."

Their birth hadn't been registered so they would do that and Grace and Alex would be named as their parents on their birth certificates.

John had been speaking to the doctor in charge and as long as the legalities were finalised, Victoria and Amelia would be with them in the next couple of weeks. Grace was tearful, she really didn't want to leave them.

"They will be fine, darling and they'll be home with us soon."

On leaving the hospital, John took them to Fareham railway station.

"Thank you for everything, John, "Alex said, shaking the other man's hand strongly.

"You're very welcome. I knew you'd want the girls and I didn't want you to miss out on the opportunity."

John hugged Grace and kissed her on both cheeks. "I promise you both, as soon as I hear that everything has gone as it should, we'll get them to you as soon as possible."

"Thank you. We're sorry to burden you so much, John."

"Grace, you are no burden. It's an honour. You've been through so much together, I just wanted you to have the family you've always dreamed of and I'm pleased to have been of assistance."

Grace stood on tip toe and kissed his cheek. "You are a good friend."

"Let's get you to your platform. You don't want to miss your train," John said, linking arms with Grace and they made their way into the station.

The next few days were a whirl of telephone calls and solicitor meetings. Alex's connection with the law helped and finally, everything was complete. Victoria and Amelia would arrive in London on 17th April. Irene and John were coming to town especially, to bring the twins. Telling Michael and Lizzie hadn't gone too badly either. Michael had said, "More girls, why not a brother?" Lizzie had gone quiet, asked if she had to share her toys and then when she was promised that she wouldn't have to, seemed to think the girls' arrival was all right. Frederick and Elizabeth were cautious, but as the week progressed, they too were growing used to the idea. Alex's family were not so enthusiastic, as they thought they were taking on too much. Alex persisted by telling them that the twins would probably have had to go to an orphanage and that was too awful to contemplate, having seen the two sweet innocent faces of the girls. It was going to be a squeeze at home at first. The twins would share a cot in their parents' room so not too much disruption, but Alex had already remarked that they would have to move in the not too distant future.

Friday the 17th soon arrived. Alex was nervous and excited as he set off for Waterloo Station to meet John, Irene and the twins. When they arrived home in a taxi cab, Grace, her parents, Michael and Lizzie were waiting on the front doorstep. Seeing the taxi, Grace ran out to greet everyone. John got out first, helping Irene out as she held Amelia and then Alex got out holding Victoria. With tears in her eyes, Grace took Amelia, kissed Alex and touched Victoria's cheek.

"Sorry, John, Irene, welcome and thank you."

"It's lovely to see you, Grace. Let's get these girls inside," said Irene. She took hold of Victoria so Alex could pay for the taxi. Grace led the way. Inside, Frederick and Elizabeth started to greet everyone.

"Welcome to your new home and to your grandparents, your brother and sister," Grace said as she entered the sitting room.

"Lovely to meet you, Irene. Did you have a good journey?" Frederick asked, as he walked over to see one of his new grandchildren.

"Very good actually and this little one was as good as gold. Would you like to hold Victoria, Frederick?"

"Yes," he said smiling at Irene as he took the small bundle in his arms. She stirred as he took her. "She looks a lot like Michael did when he was born."

"I didn't look like a girl, did I?" Michael said crossly.

"No, not like a girl, but you were tiny like this and your hair was much like this too."

"Oh."

As Frederick sat, Lizzie approached her grandfather. "So, Lizzie, your new baby sister. You and Michael will have to help look after these two as they are so small."

"Was I that small, Grandpa?"

"Yes, you were and I used to hold you like this and sing to you." Lizzie sat beside her grandfather and watched as Victoria started to wake.

"Welcome, Irene. Please sit and I'll get some tea. I'm Elizabeth."

"Nice to meet you, Elizabeth."

"No Mother, here, take Amelia and I'll get the tea," Grace said. Elizabeth took hold of her new granddaughter and sat next to Lizzie and Frederick. Michael walked over to see the babies.

"They are tiny, aren't they?"

"Yes, darling, they are," said Elizabeth, "and they are going to need all our help and love to be able to grow up like you and Lizzie."

"I'll help you make the tea, Grace," said Irene and the women left the room.

"I think it's a good idea that they all bond in their own time and way."

"I think so, too," said Grace and indicated to the two men entering the house to come into the kitchen.

"Thank you, John, for everything."

"No thanks required, Grace. You have given these girls a future and that's what counts."

"We'll make sure they never go without."

Once the tea was made and the cake was cut the quartet, went back to the sitting room to find Lizzie still between her grandparents and telling the twins what they could all play when they got bigger and Michael telling them he'd teach them to swim and he and Lizzie as the older children, would look after them.

Alex introduced his in-laws to John and Elizabeth, and confirmed the arrangements that John and Irene were to stay with them. It wasn't too long after that, Victoria started to cry and that woke Amelia.

"They're hungry. It's been a while since they were fed," said Irene.

Grace prepared bottles and then took Victoria from Frederick to feed her and Elizabeth fed Amelia. Once the twins had eagerly drunk their milk, Elizabeth and Grace took the babies upstairs to change them. Two baskets had been made up so once both girls were changed and content, they were placed in the baskets and brought back down to the rest of the group.

After a couple of hours, Frederick said, "We'd better make a move. I'm sure John and Irene are tired. They've had a long day what with all the travelling. We don't live too far, just a short walk."

Everyone said their goodbyes and made plans for the next few days and then Alex and Grace were left alone with their family. Michael wanted to play in his room so he went upstairs, but Lizzie wanted to stay and help her mother and father bathe the babies. Alex took Amelia as she was the quieter and easier to control. Victoria was far more animated and they weren't sure if she liked the water or not, as she squirmed and wriggled a lot. Lizzie thought she was funny. When both were settled into their cot, Lizzie brought in her Beatrice Potter Book.

"Do you think we should read them a story?"

"That would be a lovely idea," said Alex. "But they're both asleep already, but what about if you get ready for bed and I read you Peter Rabbit?"

"I'll go now, Daddy," and off she ran. Grace and Alex stood, looking down at the twins. Alex's arm was around Grace's waist.

"Happy?"

"Very, you too?"

Alex nodded. "It's perfect now, Gracey. The big family we've always wanted."

"You're right, it certainly doesn't hurt as it once did. I was so devastated when I thought I couldn't have any more children after Michael, but look at us now." She looked at Alex. "They are all our children and I love them all."

"I know, we are blessed."

She kissed him passionately. "You had better go and read to your eldest daughter or you'll upset her."

"I'm going and once I know Michael is settled too, I think we should get to bed too. I feel we may have an interrupted night if Victoria has anything to get unsettled for."

"I think you are right. She's much more active than Amelia."

The weekend was fun. John and Irene went shopping in Bond Street and then went with all the family to the park. Elizabeth and Frederick hosted the Easter Sunday dinner and invited Ruth, Robert, Rachael and Matthew. Ruth loved the girls instantly and kept holding them in turn and Rachael joined in too. The weekend was over far too soon. Frederick and Elizabeth gave an open invitation to John and Irene to visit whenever they wanted and then Alex saw them off to the station.

The next couple of months held a few sleepless nights until Victoria and Amelia settled into their new life. Lizzie invariably woke up if either of the twins cried out in the night and Alex usually had to settle her again. Even if tired, Alex and Grace were still happy. Elizabeth and Frederick helped most days and even had the twins for a couple of nights so Alex and Grace could rest. All of their friends and family took to the twins and were all there for their christening on 31st May. The next change for the family came in July.

Chapter 26

Days were hectic. Alex helped whenever possible but getting four children up, breakfast eaten and dressed in the mornings were no easy feat, Grace discovered. Michael and Lizzie would have breakfast and Michael would get ready for school, then Grace would help Lizzie dress. James and his mother would call for Michael to go to school. James and Michael started school together and become firm friends. James's parents lived only a couple of roads away. They were very wealthy and James was their only child. Constance had insisted that she didn't need any help to look after her son, although her family had always had nannies. She was going to be with him as much as possible as she wasn't going to have any more children. Constance's help was invaluable to Grace. Michael would happily go off of a morning with his friend and Constance would always pick up some essential Grace had forgotten on her return. Lizzie would play contentedly while Grace fed Victoria and Amelia, washed and dressed them and settled them for a nap. Amelia always slept but Victoria was more restless, always cooing and wriggling as if she had something to do. Elizabeth and Frederick visited several times a week. Lizzie liked these days best of all. Grandad Frederick would take her to the park to feed the ducks or would play in the garden. Sometimes, he fell asleep and snored loudly which made her laugh. He was 69 years of age now, but was still sprightly most of the time.

As a family, they were feeling that the house was splitting at the seams. So, when the unexpected news arrived, it came with a possible solution. With the twin's arrival and chaos of everyday life, they hadn't considered the summer holiday plans. Millie had contacted Elizabeth and Frederick at the beginning of July. The naval officer who owned the house in Bideford had put the house up for sale and Millie wanted them to know for two reasons. One, if they were planning a holiday again, it wasn't likely to be possible and two, were they interested in buying the house as they seemed to enjoy their time there. Frederick did indeed love the house. It was much like his home here in London, but it was in the beautiful setting of Devon that he had grown to adore. He loved walking, enjoyed the scenery and liked the locals. His immediate reaction was to buy the house, but Elizabeth was a little reticent. Would they live there all year round or just for the summers? If it was all year around, they wouldn't see Grace and the family as much. Grace was her only living child and she didn't want to see her less, especially now when Grace needed her help with the twins.

"Lizzie would miss you so Fred, if we moved to Devon."

"She's not at school yet, she could come and stay often. Michael loves the freedom there too. They could all come during the holidays and we can always travel back any time," he paused. "We're not getting any younger, Elizabeth. We deserve a peaceful retirement too."

"How peaceful will it be if the children are always visiting?"

"It won't be all of the time and even if it was, then we can get help."

"I don't think Grace would be happy if we got a nanny."

"Grace and Alex have been talking about getting a bigger house. What is more appropriate than this house? Grace grew up here. Michael and Lizzie see it as a second home anyway. What if they move here, sell their own house and they buy the Bideford house? That way, we can all live in either house whenever we want. We could spend a good percentage of the year in Devon with the family visiting us and we can come back to London for birthdays and Christmas and all be together."

Elizabeth considered this idea. It did seem workable and she had to admit she liked the Devon house and always enjoyed her visits and Millie's company.

"We'll have to talk to Grace and Alex. They may not like the idea. They've always been very independent and liking their own space, but I can see it working well."

Two evenings later, when the children were all settled and asleep, Frederick spoke of his plan. Elizabeth was watching the couple for their reaction.

"We'd miss you terribly, Mother, Father and so would the children, but they would also gain the benefits of going to the country on a regular basis."

"Arthur and Maggie have been looking for a new home in this area," Alex said. "Somewhere closer for him and work and Maggie wants to be nearer us, but they've found the prices around here too expensive. If we were to buy the house in Devon, which is cheaper than the value of this house and then they could have this one at a reduction and Maggie would be more on hand to help you, Grace."

"So, we would own the Devon house, Alex."

He nodded.

"And live in Mother and Father's house."

He nodded again.

"There's enough room in each house then when we visit each other, Grace," Frederick explained.

"After all, my dear, both houses will be yours one day."

"Oh, Father, don't talk like that."

"It's true, darling. You are all we have now. You, Alex and the children. I think this idea would be good for all of us."

"Let's not talk of it anymore this evening," said Elizabeth. "Let them discuss it alone and they can let us know."

And that was exactly what Grace and Alex did later that night as they lay in bed. It really would be advantageous to live in the bigger house she'd grown up in. They all liked the Bideford house too.

Grace's only disappointment would be that her parents would be far away for a portion of the year and that would be odd for them to not be to hand. She would miss them but she had to think about what they wanted too. Her parents seemed to have given the idea a lot of thought and seemed excited by the prospects. They slept that night, agreeing to speak to Arthur and Maggie. If their friends did want their house, that would help the plan along.

The next evening, they approached Maggie and Arthur who instantly loved the idea.

"I've always liked your house," Maggie said. "And Grace, I'd only be around the corner from you. With your parents in Devon, I could be there to help you."

124

Alex and Arthur talked figures and agreed upon a reduced price that suited everyone.

"Now, all we have to do is confirm the deal with Mother and Father," Grace said. "It's such a big step for everyone, but I believe it's the right one."

Frederick and Elizabeth were delighted. Frederick contacted Millie to find out which solicitors were dealing with the Devon property so he could make an offer. Millie was happy too as Frederick wanted to retain her in her position. It was only a matter of weeks and all the deals were sealed. Removal companies were hired to move the families into their new homes. Alex and Grace sorted out The Royal Crescent House to a workable degree and then went to Devon for August. Frederick and Elizabeth had already started having tradesmen in and getting quotes for new decoration and Grace helped Elizabeth pick out new curtains and soft furnishings. The house was crowded, but everyone was happy. Lizzie would go out daily with her grandfather and Michael and Alex would go swimming or play football in the park. Millie made a fuss of the twins and spent more time than ever with Elizabeth and Grace, and helped with the twins like a surrogate grandmother.

After the summer, Elizabeth and Frederick stayed in Bideford, wanting to get on with the redecorations. Grace and Alex settled into Royal Crescent. There was more room and the family seemed happier here. Arthur was pleased as he was nearer to the hospital and Maggie was happy to be so close to her friend. Elizabeth and Frederick returned to London at the end of November and spent Christmas and the New Year with their family. Grace had organised a Christmas party, much like those her mother had hosted over the years.

What a year, she thought as 1926 dawned. *All of us living in different homes and so many children. How did it all happen?*

Chapter 27

Michael

By 1926, Michael was seven he would be eight that November. He enjoyed school and excelled at all subjects. He had lots of friends but James was his best friend. He was in the football and ruby teams and was constantly invited to parties. He was tall for his age. Mother always said he took after his father. He was dark haired and his eyes had turned almost the same green as his fathers. He was handsome. He was slender and the amount of sport he played was starting to produce muscle. He missed his grandparents when they weren't around, but they always spoilt him when he visited them or when they returned to London. Holidays from school meant Devon, the sea and swimming. School and London was the normal everyday life. Having so many sisters in the house wasn't that good sometimes, especially Victoria and Amelia. They cried, they needed a lot of attention and they wouldn't play anything properly. Him and Lizzie stuck together in those early years when the twins were young. When he wasn't with his school friends, he was with Lizzie. She could play games with him; she was clever for someone her age and she looked up to him and he liked that. Grammar school was easy. James had gone to the same school too.

They were both good at sport, but James struggled with some of his academic subjects. If they were to go to college together, Michael would have to help James get his grades. It was an all-boys' school, so they didn't meet many girls but as the years went on, having sisters, especially of Lizzie's age around, he and James met a lot of girls. His family were always having parties and family and friends were always calling round. His second cousin, Jack, being two years older, would give them 'girl advice'. But to Michael, the next special girl in his life after Lizzie was Mary, Maggie and Arthur's eldest daughter. As Michael was getting ready to go to university in the autumn of 1937, Mary was still only sixteen years of age, but Michael thought she was the most beautiful girl he knew. She was doing well at school and was talking of going to a ladies college for two years, before starting her nursing training.

"It was good enough for mum," she explained, "and who knows in the future? I may be able to become a doctor like Dad."

Michael wasn't sure if it was Maggie or whether Arthur's company over the years that had steered him the direction of medicine. Alex had been a little upset that he hadn't chosen law to study at university, but he'd explained to his father that it was the sciences that he excelled at and that he hoped eventually to be a surgeon. He had also discussed his career path with John Gregson over the years and had even taken a trip to Gosport to see the naval hospital. So, Alex had wished him well and praised his son for coming to a decision about his future.

He was going to miss his family. Amelia and Victoria were now quite interesting company and of course, Lizzie, dear Lizzie, they would miss each other. Then there was Mary. She had kissed him goodbye two days before he left for university. Mary's dark brown eyes and long dark brown hair had been more vivid that evening than ever before. She was fun like her mother, always cheerful and optimistic and was studious like her father. That innocent first kiss changed things for both of them. They had grown up together, been indifferent at times, friends and had taken each other for granted, but now that had all changed. She kissed him on his cheek and then looked at each other so intently, realising what was happening. He kissed her on the lips as if he'd always known she was the one. He would miss her, but she promised to write and he would reply. They kissed again before he left and he knew that his life would never be the same again.

Chapter 28

Lizzie

The news that her grandparents would not be living so close upset Lizzie. Grandpa Fred would always play with her, take her to the park or read her stories. It wouldn't happen now. She made the most of the summer of 1926 being in Devon and spent as much time with him as she could. Michael read to her sometimes when he returned from school in the early days of grandpas move to Devon. Her brother was her best friend. He teased her a little but he was mostly kind to her and since the twins arrived, he looked after her more as Mummy and Daddy were busy with the babies. Living in Grandpa's old house was good though. She liked her new room and she felt her grandparents close to her.

Christmas was fun with Grandpa and Grandma coming to stay and the Christmas party. Mummy let her stay up for a while and see as everyone arrives. She'd had a pretty silk dress to wear and in her long hair, she had ribbons to match her dress. Her long hair was a lot like Mummy's—dark blonde with red bits. She really did look like Mummy.

In 1927, Lizzie started school, the same one Michael had been to. She was bright and enjoyed joining in with her peers, immediately making friends and one especially, Amy. As the twins grew up, they became more interesting. Victoria was always looking in her wardrobes, wanting to try on her shoes and dresses. Amelia would sit with her and ask her big sister to read her stories. Victoria demanded attention from their father constantly and Amelia quietly got on with things alone, occasionally going to mother for help or assistance. They were similar to look at but their personalities were quite different. Michael said Victoria was a little madam and Amelia was like a quite princess. But she loved them. When Michael boarded at school, she missed him terribly but the twins were now nine years old and good company.

School continued to be easy and she was a good student. Whenever there was a chance during the holidays, she went to Devon. Sometimes, she stayed there when her parents returned home and then Grandpa would travel back to London with her at the end of the holiday. He was getting older and couldn't do as much as he once had, but he still made a fuss of her and made her feel special. He was always interested in what she was doing at school and she could tell him anything.

When she'd told him she'd like to be a teacher, he said it would be a good profession for her and she would be following in her uncle's footsteps; an uncle she had never known, but Grandpa and Grandma had pictures of him all over the drawing room and of course, she knew he had once been married to Auntie Ruth and cousin Rachael was his daughter.

She liked Rachael but she was quite a bit older than her. Cousin Matthew was all right but it was Mary and Jessica she enjoyed being with. While she was growing up, Maggie was always calling in to their house or Grace would take her and the twins to their old home and visit Maggie. They played together shared secrets and promised to be friends forever. She hadn't realised that Mary liked Michael but when he'd left for university, Mary had confided in her that she really liked him and would miss him. Michael hadn't said anything, which surprised her, because he told her everything. What a surprise Mary and Michael liking each other like that. At first, she'd been hurt that Michael hadn't told her but after some thought, she was happy. Her beloved brother and her dear friend, they are a good-looking couple. Maybe they might get married and she could be a bridesmaid.

Chapter 29

Victoria and Amelia

The twins only remember the Royal Crescent House. They shared a room till they were seven years old and then they wanted their own rooms.

Victoria opening her eyes that first day and squeezing her father's finger started the beginning of a lifelong connection with Alex. If she wanted her own way, she would always go to her father and plead and wangle what she wanted from him. He knew what she was like but most of the time, he gave in. Amelia loved it when her father read her stories and played tickling games with her, but she spent most of her time with her mother. Amelia was quieter and was more studious. She learnt to read faster than Victoria and spent hours learning how to cook and sew with her mother and grandmother. Victoria liked Lizzie's clothes and how grown up her sister was. Amelia liked Lizzie for the help she gave her with her reading and sewing. Both girls looked up to Lizzie and tried to be like her. Victoria mimicked Lizzie's manners and gentle ways. Amelia wanted to be as clever as her older sibling.

Michael would be a tease and a pain, but was always there to help if they were hurt or sad. He did spend more time with Lizzie though and Victoria was always jealous if Michael and Alex were doing boy stuff. She couldn't get her father's attention then.

As they grew, both were slim and pretty but not as willowy as Lizzie. Both had long dark hair that made them look like Alex and Michael. Victoria's eyes had changed to grey-brown, somewhat like her Mothers and Amelia's had remained blue, green. Amelia was slightly the shorter of the two but both were attractive and no one would ever believe they weren't born to this family. Both did reasonably well at school. Victoria was criticised for her lack of concentration. Amelia always joined in with sports and group activities while Victoria had a smaller group of friends and preferred not to join in with social groups.

Despite their differences, the sisters were close, standing up for each other if there was trouble, helping with homework or sharing dresses. There was never any talk between the family or friends that they were adopted, so the conversation with the girls never took place. As Michael and Lizzie had been young when the twins arrived and although Michael had known things were different at the time, all the children accepted each other as their natural siblings and had bonded as one big family.

The twins were nine years of age when Michael asked if he could board at school. His friends were all staying and he didn't want to be left out. It was also at that time that Grandpa Frederick had been poorly and mother had wanted to be in Devon more. Their parents had spent some time wondering what was the best course of action. When they'd decided, they called all the children together and announced that they would all be moving to Devon to live with their grandparents.

Lizzie was upset when Michael starting boarding at school and was at first unhappy to be leaving her friends, but she was concerned about her beloved grandpa and was soon excited to be leaving London. Victoria was upset. Devon was alright, but London was better. It was busy and there were a lot of shops to look in and parks to play in. Amelia had always loved Devon. She liked the beaches, the open space and wanted to learn about all the wildlife. When Lizzie and Grandpa went for walks, Amelia always wanted to go too. Amelia had made friends with a lot of the local children on her holidays to Bideford, including Millie's grandson, Paul and granddaughter, Amy. As a group, they'd played at Chudleigh Fort in East the Water the opposite site of the River Torridge to their house. The fort was from the English Civil War days and was a great place to play. Victoria would only join in if the game involved a princess which was obviously her.

Alex convinced Victoria that it was best for the family and assured her that she would enjoy it once she was there. Her father couldn't be wrong, she thought and eventually came around to the idea. It turned out not to be as bad as she thought. School was alright and she made friends too. Some of the holidays, she went back to London; sometimes, with the family or to stay with Maggie and her family. Her parents had kept the London house going in case they ever wanted to go back and also for Michael once he was finished with schooling. Amelia fell straight into life in Devon and was glad to be around all the friends she had made over the years. Lizzie concentrated on her school work and spent long hours with Grandpa, but Grandma liked to take the twins out to Barnstaple and the local shops of Bideford and treat them to tea and cakes or ice cream. Soon, Devon life wasn't too different to London life and as Victoria realised, Daddy was home more now. She liked that very much.

Chapter 30

1926 dawned and life was hectic. The twins always seemed to be doing the opposite of each other. One had a nap while the other was awake. One would want to eat while the other rested. They were keeping Grace on the go from morning to night. Lizzie was an angel, still only three years old but helping whenever possible—Mummy's little helper. Michael just came and went; school and friends important above all else. He would look in on Lizzie when he came home but would escape to his room if either of the twins started crying. Lizzie and Michael were close, Grace had had that with her own brother and the twins had each other.

Grace did miss her parents terribly. Lizzie especially missed her grandfather. Maggie, now only around the corner, was more of a constant companion, thankfully. Maggie would take Mary to school and bring Jessica around to Grace's. Jessica and Lizzie would play contentedly while Maggie helped Grace with the twins and the house. Grace knew she wouldn't have coped without the help of her friend.

They would visit Ruth and Eloise quite a bit. All the women liked the children to be together as much as possible. Alex continued to work but was as helpful as he could be when he returned in the evenings. From the earliest days, Victoria gravitated towards him and he liked it. Helping to bathe the twins and putting them down became routine. Michael now wanted to talk to his father about football and rugby. He was quite the young man at times and then there was Lizzie, the little princess—the pretty, sweet, good-natured daughter who never seemed to be upset. She was so like Grace, he marvelled at their likeness. He was a proud father. He knew that days were endless for Grace, so whenever possible, he would take her out to the cinema for a meal, or to the theatre.

At 30, she was a beautiful woman. She had never had her hair cut to the short style that most of the woman had in the early twenties. She had kept hers long and now longer than ever. Her skin was creamy and glowing and she always looked gorgeous even when she had a day of it with the children. She was still slim, petit and he loved her more than ever. She flourished as a mother and he knew she was now content. Still a little upset that she'd only been able to give birth once, but she had quite a brood and she loved them so.

The country as a whole wasn't the one men had fought and died for only a few years before. There had been high unemployment and by May 1926, there was a general strike. The country was struggling financially, with armed troops in the streets keeping order along with armoured cars. The miners around the country had been on strike for six months. Alex and some of his colleagues and the like of Robert, Ruth's husband and Eloise's husband, Stephan were among many volunteers that kept essential services going, as well as keeping up with their own jobs.

Alex got the family out of London whenever possible. Mostly when Michael had holidays from school, he would pack them up and get them to Elizabeth and Frederick. Michael liked Devon and would soon be at a beach in good weather, usually Instow beach. Lizzie was just glad to be back with her grandfather and the twins grew up thinking Bideford was as much home as London. Millie's grandchildren were always around. Paul, the same age as Lizzie and Amy, the same age as the twins, all got on well together.

On occasions, Maggie would arrive in Devon with Mary and Jessica. During the summers, they would crowd down to Westward Ho! and spend long days building sand castles, swimming and having picnics. Life was treating Grace, Alex, their family and friends well and Grace was always keen to remind Alex that their luck had changed and they were looking forward to a more settled future. As the years ticked by, Alex and Grace watched their children grown up, mix with other children and develop their personalities. Michael, a typical boy at times. Football, cricket and swimming took up his time. He was naturally clever and never had to try too hard academically. Both Michael and his best friend James made it to Grammar School and as the term finished in the summer of 1934, James and Michael decided that they wanted to board from the next term. Grace was sceptical, he seemed so young still but Alex said it would be good for him and after all, he had made up his own mind. Lizzie would miss her brother. They had been each other's allies throughout their childhood. Michael took care of all his sisters but Lizzie was his friend as well.

Lizzie grew into a pretty young girl—slender, long hair, graceful and looked a lot like Grace. The mother and daughter were close. Lizzie was intelligent and her parents encouraged her talents, and Lizzie aspired to go to college and perhaps become a teacher or a lawyer.

Victoria was a proper little madam at times. She looked up to Lizzie and wanted to be as elegant. When Lizzie joined a dance class, Victoria wanted too as well. She would forever go through Lizzie's wardrobe to play dress up. Amelia was the quietest of them all, studious and analytical. As she grew, she would try anything. At first, not being very good, but she would try and try again and she would always achieve what she set out to do.

The twins kept their dark hair, which copying their mother and sister, they grew long. Victoria was slightly taller and had her mother's grey-brown eyes. Amelia's eyes were blue-green in colour, more like Alex's. Again, their likeness to their adoptive parents was uncanny. As the years went by, no one ever made reference to any of the girls having been adopted, so Grace and Alex decided never to tell them. Neither of the twins found school easy at first. Victoria would get bored easily and Amelia would plod through lessons till she gained confidence in a subject. After the first couple of terms, they settled and Victoria's competitiveness kicked in and Amelia's confidence grew and their grades improved. Victoria always wanted to look like a perfect young lady. Amelia would have been happier baking in the kitchen or climbing trees in the park. All three girls enjoyed afternoons with their mother. Grace taught them all how to sew and make lace, knit and make alterations to their dresses. Victoria would have a grumble at first, but enjoyed it all the same.

Their differences disappeared when they were in Devon and played on the beach. This seemed to be when Amelia took charge as they grew up. She always had some adventure planned and she would recruit the others and Millie's grandchildren to join in.

No one took much notice in 1930, when the Nazi Party in Germany won 100 seats in their election and then in 1933, Adolf Hitler, their leader, became their chancellor. The world was yet to know what that would mean.

In early 1934, Alex's parents sold the mill. James had retired 11 years before but had kept the business on, but his health was failing and knowing that Alex didn't want to take the company on, he sold it. He gave his son and daughter-in-law a considerable amount of money, enough that Alex didn't really have to work. While the children went to Devon in the Easter of 1934, Grace and Alex visited James and Helen. Grace wanted to make sure her father-in-law was not too ill. James wasn't too bad and Alex made his parents promise that they would come to Devon to spend the summer. This change in their lives and Michael's decision to board from the following term made Alex's mind up. The family would move to Devon permanently. Grace was all for the move, so was Lizzie as it would be more time with her grandpa. Amelia loved the country but Victoria took more convincing. The bribe of a pony of her own finally won her over, as well as promised trips back to London to stay with friends.

The Royal Crescent House would be there for the family whenever they came to London. Maggie would look in from time to time, but Sally and George would still manage the household along with Cassie, who now did all the cooking and Mary had left when she married and had been replaced by Louise, her cousin, last year. Sally and George should retire really, but the house was also their home and as the property would be vacant most of the time, Grace thought they may well take it a bit easier.

Maggie was sad her friend was leaving. They were closer than ever since they only lived streets apart, but there were holidays to be had and Maggie said she would convince Arthur one day to leave the hospital and move to the country too. John Gregson and his wife, Irene, had kept in touch over the years and the family had gone to Alverstoke on a number of occasions. John was keen to see how the twins had grown and was pleased to see them becoming quite the grand ladies. He'd hoped they'd be when he'd told Alex and Grace about their bad start to life. The beaches of Stokes Bay and Lee on The Solent were great days out, as well as the Lee Tower.

Frederick and Elizabeth were delighted that the family were going to be reunited. The London house would be there for Michael in case he wanted to reside there when he finished school and also for family visits to the capital.

Alex was pleased to be leaving the law firm. He wanted more free time, but when they settled into their new routine in Bideford, he soon found that his knowledge of the law could be put to use. First, he took a few clients on from home but then took a small premise at the top of the hill in town and soon had two people working for him. The work was different; mostly about land sales and farm business but he enjoyed it and he chose the hours he worked. Lizzie took to school as easy as ever, getting into Grammar School easily with such good grades. Victoria did get her pony and this was stabled at Millie's son-in-law's farm. All the girls and Michael learnt to ride. While Victoria tended to her pony, Amelia wanted to learn about the farm and the other animals. Paul, Millie's grandson, taught Amelia how to milk the cows and how to sow the seeds for the crops. Amelia was in her element. Grace joined in the local community as her mother was already heavily involved. They regularly helped with church functions and joined in with fetes and dances.

The country mourned in 1936 when the King, George V, died. His son, David, became King Edward VIII, but after 11 months, he abdicated over his love for an American divorcee. The new King was George VI and his Queen, Elizabeth.

The Nazi party were growing stronger in Germany. Germany and Italy's leaders had been having meetings. Back at home, hunger marches from Jarrow had hit the news. On average, seven out of ten people were unemployed.

By 1938, the country was worried that war might be at the door again. In September of that year, Prime Minister Neville Chamberlain, after effectively granting Adolf Hitler the right to dismember Czechoslovakia, returned to Britain promising 'Peace with Honour'.

On 9th and 10th November, Nazi youth groups destroyed 101 synagogues and more than 7,000 Jewish businesses. Some 26,000 Jews were sent to Concentration Camps. The world was watching and waiting. Some 38,000,000 gas masks were issued to the British people.

Grace was worried. Not again. She'd seen the war to end all wars. She'd lost her brother to it. Her husband had been wounded and had spent many years trying to forget the horrors. Her son, her only son would have to fight, so would her cousin Eloise's son, Jack. Fortunately, her nephew, Matthew, was too young, but how long would another war last? The Great War as it was now known lasted four years. She kept up to date with the news, always hoping that war could be averted, but Hitler seemed to be preoccupied in ruling the whole of Europe. Michael was finishing Medical School and was taking up a position at Charing Cross Hospital. Arthur had put in a word for him and Michael was keen to get started.

Lizzie was still at college. She was studying English and History and wanted to be a teacher. Alex was extremely pleased as a profession, teaching was good for a woman and had prospects to go far. The war would disrupt all their lives. On 1st September 1939, Germany invaded Poland. The clock started ticking, Germany were given time to withdraw. On 3rd September, the Prime Minister addressed the people of Great Britain; the deadline had passed with no withdrawal and the country was at war with Germany. Grace cried, "Not again."

Chapter 31

There wasn't time to cry, everything was changing as the country prepared for war. Everyone was issued with gas masks in case of a gas attack and were to keep them with them at all times. As Germany invaded Poland, Britain started its evacuation of its children from the cities to safer parts of the country.

Victoria wouldn't be happy, but if she and Amelia shared, Grace could take two evacuees. Grace and a couple of women from the church had organised the receiving of children and were rounding up families who could take the children in. Some were only too pleased to help, feeling they were doing their bit. The cities were likely to be bombed and the children needed to be out of that terror. Others were reluctant, where were these children coming from? Some reports that children from London were dirty and carried diseases. Grace was appalled and told these unpatriotic people. She was from London. Was she dirty or diseased?

Most of the locals had taken to Frederick and Elizabeth and later Grace, Alex and their brood, thinking of them as their own. A lot of thanks for their acceptance was due to Millie and her family, who had lived there all their lives.

Victoria had moaned but finally gave in. There was a war on after all, she exclaimed. Most of her belongings fit easily into Amelia's room that was sparser.

"I suppose I could have used Michael's room," Grace thought but was reluctant to give over her son's room.

He hadn't been home much this year. He had visited Devon in August for a couple of weeks. He had grown so much while he was at university. He was not far short of his father's height. The same hair colour and complexion as Alex but those piercing blue eyes still reminded her of her brother's. The same mischievous look. He'd hugged her then picked her up when he got home. He was strong and muscular. He'd played rugby and cricket at university and it showed in his athletic physique. He was handsome and she was very proud of him. She hadn't realised how much Michael liked Mary and neither had Maggie till the letters from Michael at college started to arrive. Grace loved Mary as one of her own children, but wasn't sure about the pairing. She wasn't being a snob about class at all. Many thoughts of class boundaries and such like had diminished in the last war, but they were both young and had grown up together, would they both not want to see other people, see the world. She was pleased to hear from Maggie that their relationship was going slow at first.

"I think it's a surprise for both of them, Gracey. They've known each other for so long, I don't think it's entered their heads there might be more to their feelings. Besides, Mary will be starting her nurse's training before long and I'm sure she won't have any time on her hands then."

By the summer of 1939, there was no doubt that Michael and Mary were in love. Michael's studying and Mary's training left them little time, but they spent holidays together in London under Maggie and Arthur's watchful eye. Michael's two weeks with Grace were precious. More so with the hint of war and he'd also announced Arthur had pulled strings and that his medical training would be at Charing Cross. He was grown up and really had flown the nest. She was elated and upset. Her little boy was now a man, would soon be a doctor and very likely a husband, all good, but what would happen to all these young men and women? She recalled her anxiety of the years waiting till her brother and Alex had had to go and fight, the nights she would pray they would both return home safe, then the agonising times waiting to see if Michael would survive and then watching Alex recovering from his injuries. She worried for her children, but she tried not to let them see. *It was never meant to happen again,* she thought. *Didn't we go through the war to end all wars? Why were we here again with the same enemy?*

Preparing for the war to begin and getting ready for the evacuees filled up her time. Their garden wasn't big enough for a shelter but Millie said the one in her garden would accommodate them if need be. She wasn't far away for them to get to in case of a raid. Grace and Alex had an indoor shelter put in the basement. It looked much like a table and was used as one too.

The evacuees didn't come to Bideford. They were mostly taken to South Devon to Totnes and villages such as Ugborough and to South Hams and Dawlish. Victoria moved back to her own room. By Christmas, not much had changed for the family and the war was mostly being fought at sea. HMS Royal Oak had been sunk at Scapa Flow in October and many merchant ships bringing supplies had been sunk off the east coast of Britain in November by magnetic mines. Some were calling it 'The Phoney War', but still, there were people being killed.

It was Christmas and at last, her family got together. Michael was spending Christmas with them but had promised to go to Mary for New Year. Alex had brought her a new dress. It was navy in colour and fitted closely over her bust, waist and hips and pulled tight with a belt around her tiny waist. The material was chiffon crepe and had a leaf motif starting at the right shoulder that went diagonally to the left, finishing on the left thigh all in a silver thread. The dress came with a little matching jacket. Having put her long hair up and applied a little make up, Grace got up from the chair in front of the dressing table and turned to face her husband.

"What do you think, will I do?"

Grace had not that long ago celebrated her 45th birthday, but as Alex gazed at her, he thought back to the Christmas he'd first met her and how beautiful she'd looked. Looking at her now, she had hardly changed. Yes, she had a few grey hairs peeking through her gold and auburn locks and a few lines had taken their place around her eyes over the last couple of years, but she was still as beautiful as that Christmas ball so many years ago. She was still slender and the dress he had admired in the shop hugged her figure to show her at her womanly best.

"My darling, you look wonderful, so good, I don't think we'll join the others, I'm going to take you to bed."

He kissed her and held her close to him. They had been through so much together and he knew that this war was weighing heavy on her mind so he had made every effort to make this Christmas special. "I've something else for you, "he released from his embrace. He reached into the pocket of his jacket and produced a ring box and handed it to her.

"You've bought me so much, Alex. I don't want anything else," and stopped as she opened the box and looked at the sparkling diamond eternity ring. "Alex, it's gorgeous."

He took the ring from the box. Grace removed her engagement ring and Alex slipped the eternity ring on and Grace replaced her engagement ring. She held up her hand to admire all three rings that looked perfect together.

"Oh, Alex," a tear came to her eye. "Thank you, it's lovely." She wrapped her arms around his neck and kissed him. Did they really have to host Christmas dinner? She too wanted to get him into bed. As they released, Grace said, "I love you Alex."

"I love you so much, Grace and as the ring says, it's forever."

"And maybe one of these days, you will take me to Paris like you promised," Grace smiled.

"Not if Mr Hitler has anything to do with it, my dear. I think we'll stay in good old Devon." Then they heard Elizabeth and Lizzie calling them to dinner.

On Boxing Day, Millie and all her family came for dinner and stayed playing games and singing late into the evening. Too much fun had made Frederick take to his bed on New Year's Eve, but he felt better in a couple of days.

Meat rationing started in December 1939 and was followed by rationing of butter, bacon, sugar and ham in 1940. Eloise had telephoned to say that Jack had been called up and was soon off for training.

"He'd be sent to France for sure," Eloise had said. Jack had been engaged to his fiancée, Cara, for a year, but with his call up, they bought arrangements forward and married at Kensington Registry Office before he went training. Eloise apologised there was no time to invite family, but Jack and Cara wanted to be married before he left.

Frederick's health deteriorated throughout January. The doctor had said he had pneumonia and had to stay in bed and rest. Elizabeth, Grace and Lizzie took it in turns to sit with him during the day and Alex would sit and update him of world events and local gossip of an evening. On the morning of 2nd February 1940, Frederick didn't wake up.

The darkness of the blackout and the silencing of any church bells paid a silent and dark homage to Frederick Richardson; beloved husband, father and grandfather. Everyone was devastated, none more so than Lizzie. His funeral was held at St Mary's Church in Bideford with as many of the family who could attend and then Millie laid on lunch for everyone after. Millie herself was upset and kept weeping while she prepared the food. She had taken this family to her heart and she hated to see their pain. *They would now have to look after each other more than ever*, she thought, *and what with this blinking war to content with, whatever next.*

Chapter 32

The rest of the winter was bleak, everyone was mourning the loss of Frederick. Locally, not much had changed but the war was gathering internationally. On 10th May, Winston Churchill became Prime Minister. The Germans were advancing and the British Expeditionary Force was in retreat. Between 27th May and 4th June 1940, 338,226 troops were evacuated from Dunkirk. All manner of ship and boat, whatever its size, crossed the English Channel to rescue the British servicemen and The French allies. Eloise was anxious, Jack had written many times in his early stationing that he hadn't had to fight and things had been relatively calm, but on hearing about the evacuation, she hoped he would get home safe. Some British servicemen were captured and remained prisoners of the Germans for the remainder of the war, but the majority of our army was back home, ready to plan the second front. A failure was made into a victory as so many men were now safe, but all thoughts turned to a German invasion. At the end of June, Jack was home. He'd been injured during the evacuation and had been treated at a hospital in Kent.

On 14th June, German troops entered Paris, France had fallen. The Phoney War was coming to an end and the country was on red alert.

It was June when the first evacuees arrived in Bideford. Elizabeth threw herself into volunteering, wanting something to take her mind off her loneliness and despair from losing Frederick. Two boys, Dennis and Alan, were boarded with Millie's daughter at the farm. Neither of the lads had ever been to the country before and had never seen live cows or sheep and were a little frightened. Elizabeth chose sisters Maureen and Iris from Stepney, East London. Like Dennis and Alan, they were aged nine and seven, respectively, all with just a few belonging and their obligatory gas masks. Victoria's reticence at giving up her room the previous year wasn't there this time. It was amazing. The change in her personality amazed her parents. The 'Little Miss, I'm centre of everything' had completely disappeared. The prospect of invasion had scared her more than anyone and she had been really sad at her grandfather's death. She would sit some evenings after dinner with Alex in his study. She would ask about the German advancement in Europe and the impact on the war. She asked him about his experiences in the Great War. She would sit and listen with tears in her eyes. She hadn't realised how much her father had gone through and she would hug and kiss him goodnight, loving him more than ever.

While Dennis and Alan got used to life on a farm, Maureen and Iris tried to fit in with the Whitfield household. Home was a two-up two-down house with an outside toilet. The house in Bideford seemed so grand, they were afraid to move at first in case they broke something expensive. Both girls had blond short hair and blue eyes and were very thin. Millie took one look at that and made it her mission to feed them up rations or not. Amelia helped them settle in their room and sensing their nervousness, tried to get them to talk; asking about school, friends, or whether they went to the cinema. She got the girls chatting and by the time they came down to dinner, she had helped with their shyness and neither girl looked like she'd now burst into tears.

"When you've finished eating my dears," Elizabeth said, "you have to write to your parents with our address so they know where you are."

"I'll help you," said Amelia.

"Thank you," said Maureen.

The conversation carried on, encouraging the evacuees to join in but they were soon tired.

"I think it would be better if you two young ladies took a cup of Ovaltine up to bed and get settled for the night," Alex suggested.

Maureen agreed, Iris was almost asleep all ready. Amelia helped them with their drinks and once settled, they were soon asleep.

"I'll check out some of the twins' old clothes, see if there's anything we can make up for them," Grace said when the girls had gone upstairs. "I don't think they've got much and we won't be able to keep washing the same things over and over again for them."

"Well, I can always knit them a cardigan each," said Elizabeth.

As a member of the Bideford Women's Emergency Committee, she had swung into action on the evacuee's arrival. Collecting blankets and mattresses and knitting had started in earnest. *Life was quite different,* thought Elizabeth. She had been brought up as a young lady of the upper-class. Taught to read, embroider and dance, with the ambition of achieving a good marriage and give her equally upper-class husband a well-run and staffed home and a family. This was the second world war she had had to cope with and although her daughter had mixed with all types of people due to the Great War, she was now having to look after working class evacuees and knit for England. It did bring a smile to her face though.

"What you smiling at, Mother?" Grace asked.

"Oh, just thinking that I'm doing my bit for the country by knitting, doesn't sound very grand does it."

Grace got up from her chair and lent over and kissed her mother's cheek. "You're doing great, mother and I'm sure Maureen and Iris would be happy for any new clothes."

Lizzie had been out with some friends and had only just got home. She'd had her exams the month before and in a few days, she would be 18.

"Hello everyone, how are Maureen and Iris settling in? Any food left?"

"Some," said Alex, "but I thought you were eating out."

"I have, Papa, but still hungry." She kissed the top of Alex's head as she passed him to sit down.

Lizzie was a beautiful young lady but still his little girl, he thought. She was slim and now taller than Grace. She usually wore her long hair flowing down her back. She was exceptionally clever and upon her results, she could be going to Oxford University if the war didn't put a stop to that. She had been inconsolable when Frederick died and Alex was worried that she wouldn't get through her exams. She had spoken at length with him over her career choices and wanted to succeed to make her father and late grandfather proud of her. Alex was proud of her and knew that Frederick had idolised this bright garland whatever her choices, they were overjoyed at her achievements and loved her dearly. She was also helping her grandmother with knitting and collecting. He knew that she would enjoy a party for her birthday.

"They are tired, poor little mites," said Alex. "Amelia's settled them in. I expect it's been a hard and emotional day for them and they're probably missing their parents."

"They'll be fine here with us, Papa. We'll look after them. Any news from Michael, yet?"

"No, no more than we'd heard two days ago. He was going to get stuck into hospital duties. It's shame, really," Alex said. "He should really be going to medical school first, but what with Dunkirk and the injured from that and the ships, he's learning on his feet."

"He'll probably learn more," said Grace, recalling her volunteer work many years ago. "He'll get more experience this way and learn out of necessity. He can do exams later. Maggie and Arthur will keep an eye on him, thankfully, but if the Germans do start bombing, I'll be worried about him being in London."

"He'll be fine, darling. The hospital will have made provision and Maggie's made Arthur put a shelter in the garden. He'll probably spend most of his spare time at theirs with Mary anyway."

The fine weather continued throughout the summer. The family got into a routine with the newcomers. Amelia would make sure they got to school and either her or Victoria would help them write home.

The girls would meet up with other evacuees sometimes after school, but the whole family tried to make the most of the good weather and tried to forget that an invasion could be imminent.

Alex had become a member of the local defence volunteers of Bideford recently. He would be on guard duty, ensuring that everyone abided to blackout conditions and be there if they too were bombed.

On 10th July, the Luftwaffe bombed military targets in Southern England to test the RAF's response.

This was the start of what came to be known as The Battle of Britain. These daylight raids were a prelude to invasion. 13th August was the first major action and daylight raids became part of the normal day, even in North Devon. A bomb dropped in Instow. No one was killed or injured, but The Jubilee Hall and The New Inn were damaged. The raids on Britain continued till 15th September 1940 when there were 56 German aircraft losses to 26 British. This signalled the Luftwaffe's failure to gain air supremacy. This day was celebrated as Battle of Britain day.

Devon had taken a beating. Each week in July, Plymouth had been attacked and other places such as Brixham and Exeter had also been hit. September saw the London blitz, but with the season changing and Britain not having given in as easily as he'd hoped, Hitler postponed invasion 'Operation Sea Lion', until the following spring, but it didn't stop the air raids. On 14th November, the City of Coventry was devastated. 500 people died and there were some 800 casualties.

So far Alex, Grace, family and friends were still alive and safe. Michael had taken shelter either at the Smith's or at the hospital, occasionally getting caught out during daylight raids and ran to the nearest underground railway station. Eloise's son, Jack, had recovered, but was soon to be posted to the deserts of Africa. The only good news was that Cara was pregnant. Grace worried now for Michael. He would soon have to go probably with the Medical Corp, but he'd still have to go. She hated reading the newspaper but felt compelled to. *We've got through one war against Germany, we'll get through this one. We've stopped Hitler so far. We'll just have to keep going whatever is thrown at us and we'll win.*

Chapter 33

January 1941 was cold and the snow fell. Alex worked at his small legal practice by day and then did his home guard duties by night. The blackouts and the cold were hard to bear and there were times he drifted back to the trenches of the Great War. He had to shrug it off, there was too much to do and moral had to be boosted. He had the role of sergeant due to his war record. Bryan, Millie's son-in-law, also was in his battalion. Duties included patrols, road blocks and checking identities. There were manoeuvres done at night too, to practise in case of invasion.

Bideford was looking a little different now. The Royal Hotel was headquarters for the Department of Miscellaneous Weapons. Concrete bollards, tank traps and pill boxes were set up. A pill box was essentially a mini fortress and minefields were buried in the sand and shingle of the beaches. Anti-aircraft guns were mounted on the top of the Strand cinema in sight of their home. Alex had joked 'there won't be any Germans getting to our house, I'll be up there in a shot.' Emergency gun batteries were established and manned by the Royal Artillery Special Battery with its headquarters at the Marine Hotel in Instow. Everything seemed terribly close when the Hartland Lighthouse, just a little up the coast, was bombed on 12th January. Grace was relieved they weren't in London, but she was still worried about Michael and Maggie and her family. She knew they wouldn't take any risks but it was a constant worry.

She was also keeping a watchful eye on Alex. With too much war talk and news, she could see that it got to him sometimes. His face would glaze over, become silent and gradually, a look of haunted reflection radiated from him. Even after all these years, it still frightened her. What if he became ill because of all his duties and the memories? She would keep him going, she'd make sure time spent at home was as pleasant as possible to stop him mulling over old times. Grace wasn't idle either. She had started to help out at Bideford Hospital. It wasn't long before she was cleaning and changing the beds and assisting the nurses much like she had done in the last war. Elizabeth had encouraged her to do her bit.

"I'll look after the twins and the evacuees. I've got Millie's help in the kitchen and after all, I need to keep myself busy."

Grace had agreed with her mother. Elizabeth still missed Frederick immensely and often wept. If her mother thought she was up to running the household again, she could do her bit. Not that either of the women and Millie and her daughter weren't always doing something for the war effort arranged by the church, but it made her feel useful. Now, she did as many shifts at the hospital whenever they needed her.

Maggie had done the same. With so many injured soldiers back from Dunkirk the year before, she couldn't sit back and watch. She'd been a good nurse and would easily fit right back into the routine. Arthur didn't want her to, but needs must and she would be more than useful. After all, she had seen many injured soldiers before.

Mary's training had gone well and when the war victims started to arrive, she was doing full days and nights. She didn't mind though as Michael was always nearby. They spent most of their spare time together. There were still rules about nurses and doctors dating, but it was war time. No one knew if you'd be alive tomorrow. So long as you did your work and behaved impeccably during these hours, most people were living for the day. Mary was getting scared at the thought of Michael's inevitable call up. This made her more intent of them spending as much time as possible together. Jessica, the youngest of the Smith Clan, had also decided to give the medical profession ago.

Arthur had laughed when she had first mentioned it, he said to Maggie, "I don't think our apples have fallen far from the tree, have they?" Maggie had agreed. "But it's good that she has chosen a career, I'm proud of both our girls. "

When Grace had heard about the severe bombings of Portsmouth and Gosport, she'd written to John and Irene Gregson. The High Street in Gosport had been bombed in March and Alverstoke, where they lived, had been bombed too. John, who should have retired, was doing more work at Haslar Hospital. Irene was tired of the bombings, so Grace had invited her to stay with them for a few weeks. Travelling was difficult but she made it down and the break did her good and when she was due to go home, she was reluctant to leave, but there had been some respite in the bombing and she felt much better. Eloise's son, Jack, was back fighting in Egypt and the cousins kept in touch to give each other support. Grace was always checking on Cara's health and making sure her pregnancy was going well.

"Poor thing. Jack probably won't be able to get back for the birth." *But at least Cara had Eloise close by*, thought Grace.

Also, in constant contact was Rachael, who was now in her late 20's and had never married. She'd become a school teacher, following in her father footsteps. She loved her work and loved the children she taught. She had men friends but no one special and she was happy with her life. When war was declared, her school was evacuated. Rachael volunteered to go with the children. She wanted to ensure they were all right. They were placed at Dawlish, Devon. Some of the families her students were placed with weren't that good. So, whenever possible, she interfered and had them re-allocated. She didn't have much time off and certainly not that much time to go back to Richmond and see her mother and step father, but for Easter this year, she would be going to stay with Auntie Grace. She was so looking forward to the stay. She missed her cousins and hoped that Lizzie would be home from college. Their family get togethers of years gone by seemed to be distant memories and she missed those times. Since the war began, she'd thought even more of the father she'd hardly known. *How many more children would lose their fathers?* she thought. She also wanted to talk to her Aunt about Edward. She met Edward since arriving in Dawlish. Edward had been hurt when the troops had been evacuated from Dunkirk.

His leg injury meant he couldn't go back into the services but had to go back to his family's farm. Rachael met him at a dance one Saturday before Christmas. He had fair hair and the bluest eyes. He was tall about six feet and although he had a limp from his injury, he'd still managed to dance for most of that first evening. She was falling in love with him and just wanted to have that mother-daughter conversation. *Mum was too far away and Auntie Grace would be just as good for advice.* Rachael finally got into Bideford station at just after 6:30 pm on 9th April.

Alex and Lizzie had gone to the station to meet her. Lizzie had got home only two days before.

It had been a long and tiring journey, crowded all the way mostly with soldiers. She was so pleased to see her uncle and cousin. She dropped her case on the platform and hugged them both. Tears were in her eyes and for the first time in a long time, she felt home sick.

"Oh, Rachael darling, don't be upset," said Alex, giving her another hug.

"Sorry, Uncle Alex, just relieved to be here and happy to see you both so much. My, Lizzie you've grown so much and you look even more like Aunt Grace."

"Grandma always says that."

"Sorry, I missed Grandpa Frederick's funeral. Is Grandma doing all right?"

"She's concentrating on the war effort, keeping home and organising the evacuees. She's not too bad but she does cry a lot. You'll do her the world of good. I think she's looking forward to having a full house."

Alex took her case and the girls linked arms. They walked over the bridge along the river side and finally reached home. As Alex opened the door, Elizabeth came into the hall.

"Rachael, it's so good to see you. Come on in and get comfortable, I bet you are tired after that journey!"

"Grandma, I'm exhausted." She embraced Elizabeth and then the pair of them went into the living room.

"We kept dinner to later, hoping you'd get here to join us."

"That's good, I'm famished."

Grace had heard their arrival and finished making a pot of tea. Alex had joined her in the kitchen, ready to bring in the tea things on the tray. As they entered the living room, Victoria and Amelia were greeting Rachael. Rachael again exclaimed how the two girls had grown and were proper young ladies now. Upon seeing Grace, Rachael went over to her Aunt and kissed her.

"I'm so glad to be here, Aunt Grace. I've so missed our family get togethers. I'm going to make the most of this Easter."

Grace hugged her niece again. She was so like Michael and having not seen Rachael since the war had started made this time even more poignant. She missed her brother but his daughter was here and that pleased her greatly.

"Millie's prepared a roast dinner for us all," Grace said, "and once we've had tea, we'll go and eat."

Then into the room, came Maureen and Iris. Amelia introduced them to Rachael and Rachael explained that she was with a lot of evacuees in Dawlish from her school back in London. So, the girls chatted to her, finding her easy to be around. They were as much a part of the family now and joined in with whatever was going on. Dinner was a noisy occasion; everyone catching up on news of other family members and what was happening to them all. Maureen and Iris went to bed first. Lizzie had Michael's room and the twins were the last to be up along with Elizabeth. Everyone had had a lovely evening and laughed a lot, which didn't happen much these days. Alex also wanted an early night. He had a night off from Home Guard duty and wanted to take advantage of it. He said 'Goodnight' to Grace and Rachael and left the two women alone.

"You must be shattered," Grace said.

"I am, I'll go up soon. It's just nice to be around everyone again. I miss Mum and Dad and Matthew, and I know that I can't get back to London. Coming here was hard enough but I just want a chance while I'm here to relax, talk and enjoy everyone's company, just like we did before the war. I want to talk about Dad and I want to tell you about Edward."

Grace noticed the soft dreamy look that had come over her niece's face at the mention of this man.

"Is he your sweetheart? Edward, I mean."

"Yes, I've never met anyone like him, Aunt Grace. He's a farmer. He was hurt during the evacuation of Dunkirk and couldn't re-join his regiment. I met him at a dance and we've seen each other ever since."

"He sounds nice and you obviously like him."

"I love him."

"Quite a declaration."

"I know. It's never hit me like this before, I've never been interested in marriage. I'm married to my job, I suppose, but he's different. Do you know what I mean?"

Grace laughed. "I know exactly what you mean. I was younger than you when I first met Alex, but before him, I was determined not to get married and have children. I, like you, was going to have a career." She smiled recalling that first meeting. "Alex just stunned me. That Christmas party, I've probably told you before, your mother and father had asked Alex along and as soon as I set eyes on him, I changed. I was hooked. I just wanted to talk to him. I danced all evening with him and when he left, he kissed me goodnight. I prayed he'd call on me again. So, my dear, I know exactly what you mean."

"I knew you would."

"Then, we'll talk more over the next few days, but we're both tired and I definitely need some sleep."

The women rose from their seats, Grace turned out the light and they both ascended the stairs. Rachael was going to share with Lizzie. Outside their room, Rachael kissed Grace's cheek.

"Good night, Auntie."

"Good night, Rachael darling, sweet dreams."

Grace had to go into the hospital for a shift the next day and Alex had two clients to see. The plan at breakfast was that all the girls were going to Barnstaple to do some shopping and then later go to the farm to see if they could ride the horses.

Once at the farm, Amelia went to find Paul. Amy found the girls at the stable and they all took turns riding.

"I think our Amelia is sweet on Paul," Victoria explained to Lizzie and Rachael. "They're always together when we come here."

"Does mother know?" asked Lizzie.

Victoria shrugged.

Lizzie still thought of her sisters as little things, she had to remind herself they were about to leave school and go to work. So, if Amelia was sweet on Paul, what was there to do?

The meal was a noisy affair again that evening. Alex was reluctant to leave the jovial scene and go out on patrol. On Saturday evening, there was a dance organised in town and everyone went. A great time was had by all and a brief respite from the worry of war. The day before, Paignton in the south of the county had been bombed.

Grace was relieved Rachael was with them. The south was more at risk of raids due to the naval base at Plymouth, which had already been bombed last month.

On Sunday, the family went to church and came home to an Easter feast; well as much as they could with rationing. Although Grace knew they did fair better here than those in the cities, so she never complained. Rachael and Grace had many occasions to chat. Rachael spoke of Edward and hoped he'd ask her to marry him. They also reminisced about Michael. The week passed all too quickly and soon; it was time for Rachael to return to Dawlish. She kissed everyone goodbye at breakfast and this time, it was Grace and Amelia who took her to the train.

"I'll miss you all," Rachael said, giving her aunt and cousin hugs.

"We'll miss you too," Amelia said.

"At least you'll be able to see Edward. I expect he's missed you," said Grace.

"I hope he has. He may ask me to marry him."

The train arrived and Rachael boarded; at least, it wasn't crowded this time. Rachael had tears in her eyes as did Grace. Rachael continued to wave from the window till she could no longer see her aunt and cousin. It had been a real treat this week. She would make time to go back, maybe with Edward next time. She really hoped he'd missed her so much that he might pop the question. Talking with Aunt Grace about her family, her real father and her love for Edward had made up her mind. She was ready for marriage and children and Edward was the one.

It wasn't long after Rachael's departure, that Plymouth was hit again. 120 bombers attacked the city in six hours of raids. On 21st April, an underground shelter in Portland Square in the city sustained a direct hit from a high explosive bomb and killed 62 people sheltering, only 2 survived. People began to leave the city at night, sleeping out in the open, believing it to be safer. April had also seen the registration of women aged twenty and twenty-one and June brought rationing on clothes to 66 coupons a year.

Victoria was appalled, "It's sixteen coupons for a coat, I'll never manage." Victoria had left school and started work at Lloyds Bank in the town. She was doing mostly filing or typing, but she enjoyed it.

Amelia was working at the drapers Villacot, Teapnell and Merefield. She didn't really like it much and spent most of her free time helping at the farm and of course, seeing Paul. What she really wanted to do was nursing. So, Grace was going to see if she could volunteer at first and go from there. Lizzie had her first-year exams and then came home in July. Her 19th birthday had been on 25th June, so on her return, Grace threw her a party. Lizzie joined in with the family as usual, but Grace thought she was pre-occupied. Maybe she had met someone special like Rachael had. The most recent letter from Rachael had said she was safe and the bombings in Plymouth had devastated the city, but the best news was that on her return, Edward had missed her so much that a month later, he proposed and had bought her a sapphire and diamond ring. Grace had written back, congratulating her and hoped they could all come to the wedding whenever it would be arranged for.

Maybe Lizzie's the same, wondering about love. *She'll talk to me when she's ready,* thought Grace. It was little over a week since her return when a letter arrived for Lizzie. She took the letter straight to her room. Grace was more puzzled than ever.

Elizabeth, Grace and Lizzie wanted to go to the beach as it was warm, but the beaches weren't the same now, so the park was the destination for their picnic. Grace was pleased to be having a day off, a time to catch up with her daughter. They packed a hamper and went and sat in the park. After her lunch, Elizabeth dozed in her deck chair.

"Is everything all right, darling?" Grace inquired.

"Yes, mother, I'm fine. The exams were a little harder than I imagined but I think I did enough for next year."

"If there is anything wrong or you are worried about anything, you can talk to me."

"I know," Lizzie said, "I know."

That evening when everyone had retired for the night, Lizzie took the letter and found her mother and father together in the living room.

"Lizzie, my little princess," Alex said.

"Oh, Dad, I'm hardly a little princess."

"You've always been my little princess and you always will be."

Lizzie took a seat opposite her parents who were sharing the sofa.

"Mother, Dad," she opened the letter and handed it to them. "A few weeks ago, a few of us at the top of our class were asked to do a test."

Alex had taken the letter and had started to read it, also listening to his daughter.

"We weren't told too much at the time, but we all guessed it must be something to do with war work."

Alex had read the letter by now.

Lizzie focused on her father. "As you see, I passed with flying colours," she paused. "They want me to start in September."

"What is it about?" Grace asked Alex and Lizzie.

"I'm to go to Bletchley Park in Buckinghamshire. They haven't said too much, secrecy act and all that, but it definitely is important war work."

"Why haven't you said anything?" Alex asked.

"I didn't see much point till I knew if I'd passed or not."

"Do you have to go or is it voluntary?" Grace asked, taking the letter from Alex.

"They say I have a choice, but really, I think they picked those they thought could pass the test so I think they're expecting us to accept. I'd get called to do something soon anyway."

"Well done, sweetheart. It must have been quite a test," said Alex.

"It was hard, but I found my end of year exams harder. I don't know how you studied law, Dad."

"It took a lot of hard graft and help from your Uncle Michael, but I'm sure you'll do just fine. What happens to your education if you go to Bletchley?"

"They said they will take us back as soon as we're done or the war ends, whatever's first."

"Is it safe? I'd really rather you were at college if your safety is an issue," Grace asked.

"The location is pretty much secret and what they do there is too. There are forces there too, not just civilians. I think it is as safe as anywhere these days. At first, I wasn't sure I wanted to go, but as I said, if the war goes on much longer, I'll have to sign up to something. At least, this way I'm already doing my bit and after, I can finish my degree."

Grace watched her daughter. She was so grown up. She too had been faced with war at her age. Married and worried when her husband would be called to fight and now here was her daughter, having to consider her part in this war. Where had all the time gone and why were they in this position again? Families all over the country were being pulled in all directions. Men fighting, women taking on men's work. Lizzie looked more relaxed now, though. *I think she'd already worked out what she was to do,* thought Grace.

"Well Lizzie, I'm sure, I'm speaking for your father too. We are incredibly proud of you on passing this test. Actually, we are always proud of you. You always work out what you want to do and set your mind on achieving whatever it is."

Alex nodded in agreement.

Lizzie smiled, "Then, I'll go to Bletchley and pick up my studies when I can, if that is all right with you both?"

Alex got up and walked over to his daughter arms out stretched, Lizzie rose and embraced her father. He kissed the top of her head.

"Of course, it is fine with us. Just promise you'll look after yourself and write as often as you can."

Grace got up and embraced them both. She had a mixture of feelings. She was so elated by Lizzie's achievements but worried that her eldest daughter could be at risk. There wasn't time to worry because two days later, Michael arrived for a brief visit. Great excitement and happiness filled the house. Everyone was pleased to see him. Lizzie, as they had in childhood took Michael off one day to chat and tell him all about Bletchley. Victoria and Amelia wanted him to see where they worked and took him to a dance one evening. He said Mary would have liked to visit, but she was doing extra training and shifts at the moment.

One evening, when he knew his mother and father were alone, he joined them in the sitting room. Alex got them all a drink.

"Not a lot to go around now."

"No, shortages in everything, especially back in London," Michael added. There was a pause while he took a sip of his drink. "I've got to go training for the army next month. I'm to be posted with the Medical Corp. Not sure when I'll be off and in the thick of it but I've got to go to Aldershot in two weeks. That is why I have some time off to be able to visit and tell you."

Grace's eyes welled with tears. Alex took hold of her hand and squeezed it tight.

"Son, I thought we'd get to this point sooner or later." He leaned over and shook hands with Michael.

"You will make a good soldier and they need good doctors out in the field. Take my word for it, I owe my life to men like you Michael and I'm sure you will do a good job."

"Thank you, Dad. Mother, are you all right?"

She sniffed, wiped her eyes with her handkerchief. "Yes Michael, your father's right. We had to expect it sometime and you will be helping soldiers with their injuries. I don't expect you will be fighting too much." She really prayed he wouldn't be fighting.

"Maybe I won't, but that's what they'll be training me to do. Don't worry about me, Mother, Dad made it through. I will, too." He stretched out his hand and Grace held it tightly.

"I'll pray all the time that God keeps you safe, darling."

"It worked for Father, say a lot for me too."

"I will, every day, without fail."

The next day, Michael told the rest of the family. It was a mixed reaction and made his last few days more sombre than Grace would have wished. There were a lot of tears when he left. He promised to write and let them know about his training and he would try and see them again before he went overseas.

The summer ended. Lizzie started at Bletchley; Michael was already at Aldershot. Another winter approached and still the war continued. Local RAF Chivenor reopened as an airfield in October. More troops about and even Bideford was hit by a bomb on 25th October. Paul got his call up in December and Amelia was distraught. Grace had realised Amelia didn't only go to the farm just to help out but also to see Paul and realised that her daughter was sweet on Millie's grandson. She had found Amelia crying in her room the day when Paul had heard his news. She consoled her daughter. So grown up to fall in love, but too young to cope with the possible loss.

"Paul has to do his duty just as Michael has to and just like your second cousin Jack. We'll pray he keeps safe and when this war is finally done with, if you still feel the same, then who knows you may want to marry." Grace was trying to be positive.

"I wish I was old enough to marry now," said Amelia between sobs and more tears. "I'll die too if he gets killed. How did you cope, Mother? Worrying about Father all the time?"

"You just do, my darling. You have to be brave for the man you love. They need all your strength to go off and do their bit. You will be brave Amelia. Your belief in his return and the strength you have for both of you and we will all include him in our prayers."

Amelia cried some more and Grace continued to hold her daughter, knowing only too well how she felt.

She had to be strong for her family once again. She knew there would be more fraught times ahead, more worry. This Christmas maybe the last time everyone could be together for a while. She really hoped Michael could get back. She needed all her family together. When would this war be over? Michael's training had completed and he was temporarily back on the wards at Charing Cross. It wasn't likely he'd get time off to go to the family in Devon as he was being sent away before Christmas.

On 3rd December, he telephoned his mother to wish her a happy 47th birthday. He couldn't bring himself to tell her he was going off soon. They chatted for a few minutes, told her to tell everyone he missed them and rung off. Then he went to dress. Dressed in his best suit, he met Mary and two colleagues from work at All Saints Church, the church where his parents had married, where he and his sisters were baptised and married Mary on her 21st birthday.

They both felt guilty at not letting either set of parents know, but they didn't have much time before Michael had to leave and they both wanted to be married and spend some time together. They went for a quick drink to celebrate after the ceremony and went back to Crescent Road for their wedding night. Mary had worn a cream suit and held a small posy of cream roses. Michael thought she had never looked more beautiful.

Finally, alone in his childhood home, they were soon in each other's arms. They headed straight for the bedroom, tugging at each other's clothes, desperate to touch each other, taste each other and make love. Whatever guilt they felt at their deception slipped away. They had waited a long time for this moment and they weren't going to waste a single minute.

On 7th December, Japan bombed Pearl Harbour in Hawaii. As a result, the United States declared war. The USA would become allies to Britain. Could this change the course of the war?

Chapter 34

Grace had really hoped that all her family would be home for Christmas. The weather was awful and she needed the festivities to look forward to. Pearl Harbour had brought the Americans into the war. On 11th December, Hitler declared war on the United States. Lizzie came home on 19th December. In January, she would be going back to Bletchley. She was a little stressed and just wanted to spend time with her family and relax. Maureen and Iris liked it when Lizzie was there. She played games with them more than Amelia and Victoria did.

It was on Monday, 21st December, when a letter arrived addressed to Mr Whitfield. Alex had already decided that he would not go to the office again till after the New Year. He too wanted to relax and enjoy his family's company. He knew Grace was growing weary with everything and his night watch duties were exhausting him.

Maureen and Iris had said they would go to the farm and help out and Amelia and Victoria had left for work. Grace and Lizzie were just finishing breakfast sitting in the kitchen, when the post arrived. Alex had been descending the stairs at the time, having washed and dressed and ready for breakfast. He opened the envelope and inside was a Christmas card and a letter. The greeting in the card was to all the family and signed with love from Michael and Mary— 'Signing as a couple now'. Alex thought and unfolded the letter. He was unconsciously walking into the sitting room and stopped in front of the roaring fire. The letter said:

Dear Father,

I hope this will not come as too much of a shock for you both and I beg you to help Mother through what I'm about to tell you.

I won't be home for Christmas. I've been attached to a unit and by the time you get this letter, I'll have shipped out to Egypt. Don't worry about me, I'll keep safe. I'm there primarily to look after the injured soldiers and that's what I'll do. You got through the last war Dad, I'm sure I'll make it through this one. My other surprise is that I left a wife at home. Yes, I married Mary. It was just a small affair on 3rd December, Mary and I and two witnesses. I couldn't leave to fight for the king and country without marrying Mary. I know you'll understand Dad. You were already married to Mother when you went off to fight. Gives you more to fight for, doesn't it? Knowing your wife is waiting for you. I'm sorry we kept it a secret and I know you will be angry at my deception, especially mother, but I love Mary and I wanted to spend as much time as possible with her when I found out about my posting. We hadn't told Maggie and Arthur either. Unfortunately, I've left Mary to deal with her family. That seems cowardly, but it's the way Mary wanted it. We've been staying at Royal Crescent; we want to make it our home in the future if that's alright with you.

I'm sorry if I have disappointed you both but I had to go with my heart. I've learnt that from you and Mother. You have always made my life feel safe and loving.

You have allowed me to make up my own mind and helped me through any of my mistakes and rejoiced in my successes. Mother always told me she prayed for you to return safe from the Great War. I hope she will pray for me to return safe from this one. Please don't be too angry with Mary, she's all I've ever wanted and I know that she too is worried sick about me.

Thank you for all you've done for me. Give my love to all the family and to Maureen and Iris too. When this war is over, Mary and I will have a blessing at St Mary's in Bideford with all the family together and we'll have a big celebration. Till I'm back then. Have a great Christmas. I love you all. I'll write when I'm settled.

Love Michael x

Tears had come to Alex's eyes. He was fixed by mixed emotions. He was angry at his son's deceit. Grace would be livid, but most of all, he feared for his son's life. He loved all his children dearly, but Michael's arrival had led to Grace never being able to carry another child. It had been a frightening time in which Grace could have lost her life. Michael was their only son and the only one they had conceived. He knew the horrors of war only too well and still, those horrors plagued him sometimes in his nightmares. He offered a silent prayer to keep his son safe. He'd have to write to him. Mary must know the regiment he's with so she can ensure him that they don't blame him. God, how would they all feel if he did get killed not knowing his family forgave him, cared and loved him the same as always? Alex heard Grace coming up the hall.

"Alex, where are you? Do you want any breakfast?"

Alex quickly wiped his eyes as Grace peeped into the sitting room.

"There you are, I thought I'd heard you up and about but you hadn't appeared in the kitchen. Are you all right, darling?" She noticed the letter. "The letter, business, is it?"

Alex had slumped into the chair nearest the fire while reading the letter. Grace came and sat opposite him on the settee.

"Alex darling, why aren't you saying anything?" Suddenly, she was frightened, his eyes glistened as if he had been crying. "It's not your parents, is it? Maggie, Arthur, who's the letter from?"

"From Michael, He won't be home for Christmas, Grace. He's… he's been posted to Egypt."

"Oh God, Alex, I knew this was coming but I hoped it would be after the New Year. I just wanted everyone together again."

"That's not all. Try to understand how we felt when I went off to France."

"I was terrified, I'd wished as soon as you were gone that we'd had our family. I was so scared you wouldn't come back," she stopped. "I don't see what you mean."

"Michael married Mary on your birthday. Arthur and Maggie didn't know about it either. Just the two of them and two witnesses." Alex handed Grace the letter.

Through tears, she read the letter. She was so angry but her heart went out to her son. She did know what it was like when the man you loved went off to fight for his country. Alex was now seated beside her and as she let the tears fell, he held her close. They'd had so many troubles in their lives. He had hoped that as they reached middle age, they could lead a quiet life, but this war was not allowing that. But they weren't the only family dealing with separation, death and fear. Grace was still crying, Alex still holding her tightly when Lizzie came in. Alex gave her the letter. She kneeled on the floor in front of her parents and read the contents.

She looked up at her father, "He told me at the end of the summer that he wanted to get married, but he asked me not to say anything as he wanted everyone to get together to celebrate. Oh, I hope Mary is all right." She put her hand on her mother's that held a sodden handkerchief. "Don't be sad, Mother. Michael won't be hurt. He'll be back in no time and then as he says, we'll have the wedding party of a lifetime."

Grace patted her daughter's hand. "I know dear, I know. I'm so angry at him for not telling us. For not being able to see him off and so scared for his safety, I just want him to know we love him."

"He knows, the letter says so and we'll pray for him, won't we?"

Grace nodded and sniffed.

"I'll get on to Mary, see if she knows where he'll be stationed and we'll get a message to him soon," Alex said. "Dry your eyes my brave, beautiful wife." Alex wiped tears off her cheeks and held her face in his hands. "You've done this before; my girl and you can do it again. As Lizzie said, we'll pray for him. We'll let him know we're all right with his marriage and that we love him very much and all he has to concentrate on is doing his duty and getting home, right?"

Grace nodded.

"I love you, Grace, so very much." He kissed her. Lizzie smiled, she had always seen her parents cuddling, kissing, always loving towards each other but this moment was so touching. It brought tears to her eyes. *I hope I love someone that much one day,* she thought.

"Right, you two beautiful ladies, I'm going to get some breakfast and then the three of us are going out, to brave the cold and walk up to the fort and talk of Michael and all the holidays we had before we moved here. Then when we get back, we'll speak to Maggie and Arthur and see if Mary's told them yet. Is that a good plan?"

"I think that sounds smashing, Father. I'll go and get some bacon on for you," Lizzie got up, kissed her mother's cheek and left the room.

"All right?"

Grace nodded, "Why wouldn't he tell us?"

"I don't know, darling. Perhaps, it was just the time element. He found out he was going and they just got married. He wouldn't have wanted us not to be there. He'd know it would mean so much to you."

"I knew he loved Mary, thought it was inevitable she would be our daughter-in-law, but this bloody war has taken all control away from us and what we want. He will be all right, Alex, won't he?"

"I do hope so, we'll pray for him and keep up our spirits. We've got to tell Amelia and Victoria and Maureen and Iris yet."

"And Mother."

"She'll be the bravest of all. She's been through so much, she'll handle it. Now go and wash you face and get prepared for a walk in the cold."

"I love you, husband. What would I do without you?"

As they rose from the settee, she hugged him close. Trying to hide his own fears from her, he said, "What would I do without you, Gracey?"

They went for a walk trying to be cheerful, remembering all the good times, the holidays, like long days spent on the beach at Westward Ho! Lizzie got upset. Grace knew that Michael's call up would eventually hit her daughter. Michael and Lizzie had always been close. If anything happened to Michael, Lizzie wouldn't only be losing her brother but her best friend. With Lizzie in the middle, Alex holding one hand and mother and daughter with their arms around each other waists, they stood on top of the hill by the fort and looked out over Bideford and the river, each sending their own personal message of hope and love across the continents to Africa and to Michael. When they returned, they told Elizabeth, who after a few tears did much as Alex had predicted.

"He'll be fine. He's strong and brave and apart from all of us, he's now got a wife to come back for now." There were more tears from Amelia and Victoria, especially Victoria.

By 7 o'clock, Alex was about to telephone Arthur when the ringing startled them. It was Arthur. The men talked for a while then Alex passed the telephone to Grace.

"Arthur's getting Maggie."

After a few moments, "Grace…"

"Maggie."

"Oh Grace, I'm so sorry. We only found out this weekend just gone. Mary said Michael had written the letter and told her to post it last Friday. So, we guessed you would get it today. I was so angry at first, but Mary's so upset at his leaving. I couldn't help but just cuddle her up and tell her that everything will be fine."

"I know the feeling, Maggie. I'm so scared for him, for them. I know what it's like. We've had tears all round today. I don't think we will be celebrating much this Christmas now."

"We've got to, for Michael's sake. He wouldn't want us not to enjoy ourselves. I wish we could come down to you but we're all working so much at the hospital."

"I understand, Maggie. I wish you could too."

"We're family now, Grace."

"You've been a part of my family for so long Maggie. Michael and Mary have just made it official."

"Oh, Grace, thank you."

The women carried on talking for a few more minutes then wished each other Merry Christmas and ended the call. Grace joined the family and related her conversation. What a day it had been. They would try and enjoy the festive season, just for Michael.

Chapter 35

1942

Lizzie was back at Bletchley. She stayed at a local house and shared a room with another Bletchley colleague named Florence or Florey. Saying goodbye to her family had been hard this time. Everyone was worried about Michael and she was still nervous about her job. Alex had seen her to the station with her case, wished her well, kissed her and then she was on her own.

Once settled in, she was hardly alone. The place was full of civilians and service personnel and top boffins. Work was top secret and she sworn to secrecy, including her family. Work was repetitive and she worked long hours. Florence had been a quiet sort at first, but they were getting on better now. Lizzie made friends and soon had a group of girls to go around with. She, along with Florence, joined in sports and they often went to the cinema or for drinks. She wrote home telling everyone she was enjoying what she was doing and not to worry. At least, being busy kept her mind off Michael, so far away, fighting.

Michael had reached Egypt. He sent word back to Mary and to his family. He really hoped they were alright about his marriage. The desert was hot and dusty during the day but got very cold at night. There was no time to settle into army life. He was set to work as soon as he stepped off the truck. It was real life horror. Men are wounded everywhere, the smell and noise and people bustling all around took him by surprise, but within days, he was used to his surroundings and had become part of the machine. There wasn't much time to rest, so Michael felt tired all the time.

Mary's first letter arrived, confirming that both families were happy for them both and they all wanted the same thing: for him to get back safely. Then his mother's letter arrived. He kept both letters in his medical book by his bed. Mary had signed 'all my love, Mary' and his mother had signed 'We miss you and we love you dearly, keep safe. Mother, Father and the rest of the family'. He still felt guilty over the secret wedding but he'd had to marry Mary. Their nights together were fantastic and memorable. They made love two or three times a night, wanting to know each other as much as possible before their inevitable separation. He had to get through this and get back to his wife. He missed her. He wanted her.

Jack had managed to get his first leave since his daughter's birth the previous July. Cara was so relieved to see him. She was so busy with Laura but so worried about Jack that she felt anxious all the time. At least, he was home now even if it wasn't for long.

South Devon was still being hit. Torquay was hit on 12th February. Only two days later, Rachael married Edward at the church, where Edward had been christened at and where his parents had married. It was a small affair as far as family members. Ruth and Robert had made it down for a few days. Robert proudly gave his step daughter away. Rachael had made her own wedding dress from material that had been hard to come by, but she didn't care that it was war time and the wedding wasn't as grand as it might have been. She was happy, really very happy. She was marrying the man of her dreams. Yes, she'd managed to find him and this was for keeps. She was emotional as she walked up the aisle. She wished her brother and Grace, Alex and the brood were here and as much as she loved Robert, he had been a great father, but she still wished her real father could have seen her on her special day. Then she spotted Edward and her heart soared. *Soon, I'll be Mrs Edward Thompson.*

After the ceremony, there was a wedding breakfast at Edward's parent's home. Ruth and Robert were staying with Edward's parents for another day then they'd travel home. Matthew was due home for a few days before he would be off fighting abroad. Rachael feared for her brother. He seemed so young but so were many others. She knew her mother and father were worried too and could understand that they wanted to get home. She was glad they'd made it to her wedding. There wasn't time for a honeymoon, but as she looked at the card and gift from Aunt Grace, she thought, *when the summer comes, I'll take Edward to meet them all and we'll have a great time. Honeymoons will have to wait till the war's over.*

Days after Rachael's wedding, Grace picked up the telephone to a tearful Helen. James, Alex's father, had died in his sleep at the age of 84. His failing health some years before had improved once he had retired, but lately he had become frail and passed away peacefully. Grace tried to comfort her mother-in-law and promised that she and Alex would be up to see her soon. Alex was rather upset. He hadn't been able to see his parents much these last few years. They quickly made plans to make their way up to Yorkshire. Elizabeth said she would be fine left in charge with Millie's help.

On the morning they left, a letter arrived from Mary. She was pregnant, Michael knew and they were extremely happy. Grace wept tears of happiness. Good news and bad news, there was more of one than the other but she was going to be a grandmother and that cheered her. *Life's rich circle*, she thought.

Paul was sent to Malta. Amelia was beside herself. She'd always liked Paul but over the last couple of years, their feelings had changed towards each other. She loved him, but she knew she wouldn't be allowed to marry him before he left to fight. She was only seventeen, her parents would forbid her. He'd managed to save a little money and bought her a gold ring with a heart on.

"It's not an engagement ring, coz I haven't asked your father's permission to marry you, Amelia, but to us, it's for real. I love you, Amelia and when this war is over, we will marry."

There was a great many tears when he left in March. Millie, her daughter and son-in-law, granddaughter and Amelia saw Paul off.

Amelia kissed Paul goodbye. "Be safe and come back soon, my love," she whispered in his ear. "I love you."

"I love you too, Amelia and remember what I said, we'll marry soon."

Later at home, Amelia cried alone in her room. Victoria arrived home from work to find her twin in a terrible state.

"Come on, Amelia," she said cuddling her sister, "Paul will be fine, he can look after himself and he'll get back, you'll see."

But Amelia still cried.

I'll have to look after her, keep her busy, thought Victoria. Amelia continued to cry. Back from Yorkshire, Alex was busy finding his mother a new home. Helen agreed a couple of days after the funeral that it would be for the best if she moved nearer her son and his family. She was now 81 and it would be good to really get to know her grandchildren before it was too late. Along from Millie, there was small cottage for sale. Alex got on with the negotiations and then Alex's cousin brought Helen down at the beginning of April.

Whatever training Paul had received, he soon realised he was a novice and totally out of his depth. Malta was an important British base in the Mediterranean, midway between Italy and North Africa. The British Navy used the Maltese Capital Valetta's harbour for repairs and refuelling and there was also an airfield. The Germans and the Italians were trying to starve Malta into submission by attaching convoys, bringing in fuel, food and other supplies. Within days of his arrival, a needed convoy fought its way through, but two large cargo ships were sunk in sight of the shore and two were sunk in the harbour while unloading. Prospects for the island were grim, but Paul had been drafted with a friendly group of men and they were going to make the most of a bad situation.

Lizzie was already in a fall swing with her work and her social life at Bletchley. She was enjoying the feeling of doing something for the war effort. It kept her mind off of missing her brother and worrying about him. Amelia had written to her, telling of Paul's drafting and how much she was missing the man she loved. Then there was Jack now back in the desert. Maybe he'll meet Michael and they can look out for each other. She was also going to be an auntie and she thought that was exciting.

One Saturday in April just after Easter, Lizzie hoped she would be able to have a lazy day. Maybe go to the shops and see what little was about and just relax. Florence had heard about a dance being held locally and convinced Lizzie to go. *I'll give up the shopping idea, relax, take a bath in an inch of water, as instructed due to conserving, then go to the dance.*

Other girls from work were joining them and when they all arrived at the hall, it was already crowded. Florence managed to get them a drink but it wasn't long before they were asked to dance and their drinks forgotten. After five dances, Lizzie was hot and thirsty, excused herself from her partner and went in search of another lemonade.

She was drinking, relishing the cool liquid when someone said, "It looks like you needed that."

Lizzie looked up to see a handsome air force officer smiling at her. She blushed, "Yes, it's quite hot out there on the dance floor."

"I hope you're not too tired to dance with me, "he enquired.

"No, just a quick drink to recuperate and I'll be right with you."

"Good. I'm William Havers and you are?"

"Elizabeth Whitfield, most people call me Lizzie."

William took her free hand, held it to his lips and gently his lips brushed her hand. "It's a pleasure to meet you, Lizzie."

He led her to the dance floor as a Foxtrot began. He held her closer than needed but she found that she liked it. He was tall, must be over six feet like her father. His hair was fair, light brown and he had very deep blue eyes that sparked. He looked dashing in his uniform and he danced expertly.

As they glided across the floor, his strong hold guiding them amongst the other couples, Lizzie was struck by her feelings towards this stranger. He was strong, well-built. She wondered what he was doing here in Bletchley and not abroad fighting. Perhaps, he was on leave. After several dances, he led them off the floor, both were hot so they went out of the hall.

"You dance well, Lizzie."

"Thank you, so do you."

William smiled and his eyes sparked.

"So, what do you do? I would guess you have something to do with Bletchley Park."

Lizzie nodded, suddenly aware that she really didn't know this man, could he be a spy. 'Walls have ears' and all that. William realised what she was thinking and laughed.

"It's all right, don't be worried. I'm at Bletchley too. Only arrived a week ago." He went on to explain that he had been shot down in a dog fight at the end of 1941. Fortunately, he was nursed back to full health. He was stationed at Bletchley to give information from the raids he'd taken part in, then he would be back on active service and training other pilots.

"You look so well. I'd never have dreamt you had been hurt."

"Good nursing, I suppose and I wasn't going to let Hitler and his army stop me. So, Lizzie where do you hail from?"

"London, originally, but most of my life has been in Devon, Bideford. Do you know it?"

"Near Westward Ho!"

"Yes."

"You don't have a Devon accent."

"No, perhaps I had a little when I was younger, but I was studying at Oxford, mixing with all sorts of people. I don't think I have an accent at all. What about you? Where did you come from before this war took you all over?"

"London, Kent, Hampshire, Father's career in the navy made us move around a bit. He's quite high up and he was disappointed when I decided to join the air force. I went to Cambridge, studied law, but the war started and I thought I'd better do my bit."

They were silent for a while.

"Shall we dance again, William?"

"Yes, I think we shall."

He spoke politely and he was probably from a well-to-do family, Lizzie thought and he studied law just like father. Just before they entered the hall again, William turned to face her.

"Lizzie, is there anyone special in your life?"

"No, there isn't."

"I know we've only just met but I would like to see you again, if that's all right with you."

"I'd like that, William," she smiled and looked straight into those sparkling blue eyes. Her mother had once told her that on her first meeting with her father, she'd known he was the one for her. Was it happening for her the same way tonight, history repeating itself? She hoped so.

Taking her arm, William led her back to the dance floor and began to waltz. Was that what it was like to fall in love? She thought. They didn't leave each other for the rest of the evening. Florence had introduced herself sometime in the evening and was ready at the end of the evening to leave with Lizzie.

William kissed Lizzie lightly on the lips, "I'll get to see you sometime this week, won't I?"

"Yes, you will, you have my address, call for me on Wednesday, we'll go to the cinema."

"Wednesday at seven then," he kissed her again, said goodbye to them both and was gone.

"Well, I think you like him, Lizzie. You didn't give any of the other chaps a look in tonight and to think you didn't really want to come out."

Lizzie linked arms with her friend as they started to walk home in the blackout. "I'm so glad you convinced me to come out, Florey, really glad."

Florey looked at her friend and saw her happiness. "Gosh, girl you've got it bad."

Lizzie laughed. "I think you're right."

Malta was still having heavy bombing. In the desert, Michael was being kept busy at the field hospital. He felt constantly tired but had to keep going. Now more than ever, he had to get through this as he was now going to be a father. Mary's letters were getting through regularly and that kept him positive. He heard from his friend James from school and college. James, who obviously couldn't give too much detail, had joined the air force and would soon be on a special mission. He was also keeping a lookout for his second cousin, Jack, as Alex had written to him telling him Jack was in the area. Lizzie had written, telling of her boyfriend who was in the air force too.

With the news of Air Marshall Harris bombing Cologne, Michael wondered if that was the raid his friend had spoken of and possibly his sister's boyfriend had been a part of it.

On 21st June 1942, Tobruk fell to German Field Marshall Rommel and 20,000 allied prisoners were taken. By July, British General Auchinleck stopped Rommel at the first battle of Al Alamein. A good turning point, but despite his victory, the General was sacked and Prime Minister Churchill appointed a new commander, General Montgomery. Jack had avoided capture when Tobruk fell, but Michael had only found this out when Jack arrived at the field hospital. Broken ribs and a badly injured leg had put pay to Jack's battle. The cousins were relieved to see each other and Michael visited Jack every day. By August, Jack was well enough to be shipped back to England. The men shook hands.

"If you get the chance to see Mary, tell her I love her and I miss her."

"Cara and I will look out for her, Michael, don't worry and when the baby comes, we'll help out."

"Thanks, I know you will."

They slapped each other on the back. Michael said goodbye and went to work. Soon, Jack was on his way back home and Michael wished it was himself instead.

A letter came from Rachael at the beginning of August. Grace read it, as always mixed news. The good news, Racheal was pregnant. She and Edward were delighted. She also hoped to get to see her aunt and uncle sometime, but although the school was on holidays, she was now busy on the farm too. Rachael was now worried about her little brother Matthew. Now, 19 years of age, he was in the air force and was training at Northolt in Middlesex. She wasn't sure what his next posting would be and as worried as she was for him, she was as concerned for her mother. She went on to say she'd tried to get Ruth and Robert down for the summer, but both said they wouldn't leave London in case Matthew got leave. She rounded off, wishing everyone well and said she was looking forward to becoming a mother.

The rationing of sweets had upset Maureen, Iris, Dennis and Alan when announced on 27th July, but Millie explained that they all had to give up something for the war. They couldn't get to the beaches now, so they either helped at the farm or would go and play in the park. Amelia would go to the farm sometimes, but it reminded her so much of Paul and it hurt too much. In any case, she now had to concentrate on starting her nursing career. So, she had to keep a stiff upper lip and keep going.

More and more Allied and British servicemen were stationed throughout Devon. There was a troop stationed at Instow. Victoria had a couple of Americans in the bank during the last couple of weeks. It made a nice change to see young men around, she thought. Everyone seemed to have a sweetheart, even her twin. Alright, it was only Paul they'd all grown up together, but she knew her sister desperately missed him and she felt for her. *I wonder if I'll ever meet anyone special. I'll probably have to wait till the war has ended. And no one knew when that would be.*

Lizzie had a few days off in August and made it home briefly to see her parents and then stopped in on Mary to see how her sister-in-law was, now that she was into her final month of pregnancy.

"I think I'm carrying an elephant," Mary exclaimed. "I'm so tired, Lizzie. I can't wait for the birth."

"Are you nervous?" Lizzie asked.

"A bit but with all the medical knowledge in my family, I'm in the best hands." The women laughed.

"I do hope Michael gets home soon," Lizzie said. "He's not had any leave long enough to get home, has he?"

"No, he hasn't. I would like him here for the birth but as soon after would be just as good. He tries to sound optimistic but he is tired, Lizzie and when he knew Jack was home and recovered, he was really envious."

"It must be hard for both of you. I miss him so much, so you must."

"What about William?" Mary asked as she got up to make tea.

"Don't get up Mary, let me make the drink. Oh, William, he took part in the raids on Cologne. He hasn't been able to say much in his letters but he's constantly on call. I can't wait to see him again. Mary, I've found the one," she blushed. "I know we haven't known each other long but I love him and I just hope he gets through his missions and that we can have a future together." Lizzie made a pot of tea and sat at the table with Mary.

"I couldn't get any sugar this last week," said Mary, "you alright without it?"

"Of course."

"I wouldn't worry about not knowing him long, not these days. I think you have to grab hold of each day and live it to the full because you never know when it will be your last. Not the best outlook for my baby," Mary patted her bump. The baby responded with a kick. "Quick, Lizzie! Your niece or nephew is making its presence felt."

"Does it hurt?"

"Depends, it makes you jump sometimes. I've been very lucky that although it's a big baby, it hasn't sat on a nerve, just made my back ache a bit, so the odd kick is quite easy and reassuring."

Her visit was short but it had been great to catch up with Mary. It made her feel closer to her brother. Back to work at Bletchley, she and Florey had more duties that kept them busy. In their spare time, they played tennis or went to the cinema. On one particular Thursday at the end of August, Florey had a date with an officer from work so Lizzie thought she would take a bath and rest for the evening. Having bathed, she dressed in her nightdress and dressing gown and was reading, when there was a knock at the door. Her landlady was away visiting relatives in Blackpool, so she went to answer the door, tying the belt of her dressing gown as she made her way up the hall. She could hardly believe her eyes when she saw William standing there.

"Lizzie."

"William."

She couldn't help herself. She flung her arms around his neck and kissed him full on the mouth. He responded hungrily.

"Now, that was worth waiting for," William said when they parted, "but I think we'd better go inside if that's alright with your landlady and in your state of undress."

Lizzie took his hand and almost dragged him into the house.

"Mrs Barton's away and Florey's out so we're quite alone and I'm so pleased that they are so I can kiss you for the whole evening." She led him into the front room and they sat together on the sofa. He touched her face lightly and kissed her again.

"You look better than I remember. Oh, Lizzie, it seems so long since I've seen you. It's for this moment that has got me through all those raids."

"Was it awful? Silly question, it must have been terrible!"

He explained briefly his part in the missions and how tired he's felt at times.

"But I don't want to talk any more, darling."

"Me neither."

Again, they were in each other's arms, kissing eagerly. Mary's words of making every day count popped into her head. She certainly was going to make the most of their time together. She had laid back her head on a cushion and William was almost on top of her. His hands moved over her body and with only her nightdress and dressing gown on, his hands felt close to her skin. She kissed him with such hunger and her body was responding to him in ways she had only imagined. He undid her dressing gown and the buttons at the top of her nightdress. He kissed her neck and then her exposed chest. Her body was on fire. She'd undone the buttons of his shirt and he'd wriggled out of it and his vest. Their bare chests touched and she knew that she could not resist it. He could take her here and now. William looked down at her and she smiled, he was fully on top of her now and she wanted him. It was at that time they heard Florey coming into the house. Quickly, they dressed.

"You still up Lizzie?" Florey called on her way to the kitchen.

"Yes, I've got company, I'll be out in a minute." When more fit to see anyone, they faced each other and laughed.

"Nearly caught in the act," William said. "I'm sorry, Lizzie, I shouldn't have gone that far."

Lizzie put a finger to his lips to silence him and he kissed it. "No apologises. I wanted it as much as you and if Florey hadn't come home, we would have finished what we started."

He smiled at her. "You are something special, Elizabeth Whitfield. One day I'm going to marry you."

"Is that a proposal, Mr Havers?"

"It sure is, Elizabeth. When there's a suitable time. Will you be my wife?"

"Yes. "They were back in each other's arms, kissing again.

"I'll probably have to wait till I'm 21, William. I think my parents will insist."

"When you are 21 or at any other time, I'll wait for you my love. What I came to ask you was if you are off this weekend. I know it's not the proper thing to do but after what's just happened between us, I feel we need some time alone now more than ever."

"What do you have in mind?"

"Will you spend the weekend away with me in a hotel?"

"It's not the done thing." Lizzie tried to seem offended but couldn't, while smiling, she said, "Try and stop me, William. I can't wait to be with you properly."

"That's settled then. Had we better go and see Florey and tell her our news?"

"I'm not telling her about our weekend away."

"No, Lizzie, about us getting married."

"Oh, yes."

William had borrowed a car and they went to Brighton. They booked in as Mr and Mrs Havers and as soon as they were alone, she became, in her eyes anyway, the real Mrs Havers. They were both a little nervous but had undressed hurriedly and it didn't take long for them to be back to where they were two days ago. As he took her, she cried out. She had wanted this so much since she'd met him and as they climaxed, she knew that she would love this man forever.

They dressed and went for a walk, had dinner and went straight to bed again. Making love several times that first night and again the next. On Sunday morning, they made love for the last time for what would be a while.

"I really don't want to go back," said Lizzie, as she lay half draped over William. Each coupling had been better than the last and she wondered when they would be close again.

"Me neither, but there is a war to win, my darling and once it's over, we've got the rest of our lives to make love, have babies and live where ever you want."

"We could live in Devon. My father has a small law practice, you could work with him."

"You've got it all worked out, haven't you?" his hand was stroking her body and she felt the heat of excitement flowing through her again.

"No, all I've worked out is I love you and I'm not about to let you out of my sight once this war's over. So, you are not allowed to go and get yourself killed."

"I'll try my best and Lizzie, I love you too." He kissed her deeply. "Come on my dear, time to go back to reality."

"I know," she said sadly.

Mary woke early on 10th September. Her back had been aching the whole of the day before so she'd taken to bed early. With some difficulty, she got up to go to the bathroom when a pain so severe doubled her up. She sat back on the bed for a few moments till the pain subsided. Relieved that it seemed to pass, she left her room for the bathroom. She just made it in time as her waters broke and another pain gripped her body. *Keep calm, keep calm,* she told herself. She threw some cold water on her face and went back to her room to dress. It was just after 6 o'clock. Her father was on nights and she hadn't heard her mother get up. Another pain had racked through her body. *I think this baby wants to come quickly.* She called out for her mother but it was Jess who came to the door.

"Are you alright, Mary?"

"The baby's coming, Jess. Is Mum about?"

"Yes, she got up early said she couldn't sleep."

"That makes two of us. Can you go and get her?"

"Shouldn't we be getting you to the hospital?"

"No, I think it's too late for that this baby wants out and soon."

Jess ran off down the stairs as Mary got another pain. She'd better count how long between them. Then Maggie came in.

"How you feeling, love?" she asked. Going through this yourself was one thing but she was about to see her daughter cope with childbirth and that made her nervous. She wished Arthur was home. "Jess has gone to get the midwife, how quickly are you getting the pains?"

"I haven't counted properly yet but they are pretty regular." When the next one started Mary looked at her watch. "Every six minutes."

"You're right, it's too late for the hospital. Come on, let's get you back into your nightdress and get the bed covered."

The women worked together.

"I wish Michael was here, Mum."

"I know, love," she hugged her daughter. "I know, but we'll cope and when he gets home, he'll be able to see both of you."

By the time Jess returned with the midwife, Maggie had examined Mary and could already see the baby's head. Jess had contacted the hospital and said she would be late and her mother wouldn't be in. Arthur arrived home to what seemed a quiet house until he heard someone scream out.

He rushed up stairs, "Maggie, Maggie are you all right?"

Maggie had been helping Mary, keeping her calm and mopping her brow, left her daughter's side and went out to her husband.

"It's the baby, Mary's doing well. She must have had most of her labour during the night without knowing because this baby's almost here."

Arthur hugged his wife. "Well, Grandma, you'd better get back in there. I take it the midwife's in."

"Yes."

Another scream.

"Go back in, Maggie, I'll get the kettle on."

Just before 10 o'clock, Mary gave birth to a boy. The mother and baby are doing well, the midwife told Grandfather. Arthur had made tea that had gone cold a couple of times but he ran excitedly up the stairs at the sound of the baby crying.

After knocking on the bedroom door and peering around, Maggie said, "It's a boy, Grandad."

Maggie was tearful and Arthur started to fill up with emotion. "I'll get the kettle on again, are they both all right?"

"Yes, darling, mother and baby are great."

With Mary changed and the bed cleaned up, she held the baby when Grandpa returned with tea.

"Congratulations, my dear girl. Can your old dad get a hold then?"

Mary handed her son to her father.

"He's a strong-looking lad and look at all that dark hair, takes after his dad then!"

"Yes, it looks like he does," said Maggie, looking over her husband's shoulder and putting her finger to the baby's tiny hand.

"Meet James Alexander Arthur Whitfield."

"James, meet Grandad and Grandma."

The news reached Michael two weeks later. He had been trying to get leave but now he wasn't going to take no for an answer. Finally, he was granted leave. H would leave for England in one week.

Grace and Alex celebrated, throwing an impromptu party with as much of their rations as they could manage. Helen and Elizabeth couldn't believe they were great grandmothers. Millie went into overdrive, preparing food for the party while listening to the great grandmother's happiness about the new arrival. If her grandson and Amelia married, they would all be family and if they had children, she would also be a great grandmother. She hoped that it would happen. Grace had spoken to Lizzie and she said she would try and get to see Mary and James soon. The party was fun, the evacuees, Millie's family and neighbours joined Alex and Grace. Amelia and Victoria and made a toast to wet the baby's head. Grace would time a visit to London near the time Michael would be home on leave and see her grandson.

Grace and Alex arrived in London three days before Michael's arrival. They stayed at the Royal Crescent house and were pleased to see George and Sally still in good health and the house still in one piece despite the bombings. Seeing Maggie and Arthur was great, but seeing her first grandchild topped everything for Grace. As she held little James for the first time with tears in her eyes, she couldn't believe how she was transported back in time. It was as if she was young again and holding the new born Michael. This baby was so like his father. The reunion of friends and family was exciting and joyous, but everyone was waiting for Michael's return.

A tired and older looking Michael got home on 5th October. He went straight to his wife and child and wept tears of joy and relief while holding them both. It had been a long nine months away. Once he had seen his wife and child, Michael, embraced his mother and mother-in-law, shook hands with the proud grandfathers.

"I'm sorry we kept everything secret…"

"No apologies, son," Alex said. "No need, we're all here, safe, you've got a son now. What is there to apologise for?"

Michael hugged his father. Sometime he wanted to sit down and talk to his dad, ask him how he coped with the battle, the tiredness and the loneliness of being away from those you loved.

The days were precious, but Grace knew Michael needed time to be alone with Mary and James. There were tearful goodbyes but she knew it wouldn't be long before they'd all be together again. At least, she would pray for it. Before going back to Devon, they diverted to Gosport and stayed a couple of days with Doctor Gregson and Irene. Catching up with old friends was good, but looking around, Gosport now looked so battle-worn due to the bombings. Grace couldn't believe the state of what she'd seen here and in London, but everyone just carried on.

While Michael was at home, the second battle of El-Alamein began on 24th October. On 25th October, a milk ration of two and a half pints per person per week was introduced. Millie said she would see what she could do to get more from the farm, but things were getting tight with regulations. Grace had to admit they'd had it easier here than her friends in London and apart from the main rationing items, they hadn't gone without much.

On 3rd November, General Montgomery successfully broke through the Afrika Korp front line at El-Alamein. The victory caused great rejoicing throughout Britain and for the first time in a long time, church bells rang out throughout Devon, celebrating the breakthrough. General Montgomery was an overnight hero. Rommel began to withdraw westward as there were now more allied troops in Morocco and Algeria. German and Italian armies were trapped.

Grace and Alex made every attempt to make a good Christmas this year. The war was far from over but the news from Africa was uplifting. Michael had to go back to his unit two weeks before Christmas, but Grace was hopeful all would turn out well and he would be back home again soon. 1943 would begin with hope. Lizzie came home full of talk about her boyfriend. She asked permission to get engaged and although Alex had really wanted to meet this William before he made his decision, he said she could. Lizzie told him so much about the airman he felt he did know him and as usual, Lizzie could wrap him around her finger. He realised that in days like these, his children had grown up quicker than he'd have liked, but grown up they were.

"But Lizzie, no secret weddings, please and wait till you are 21."

Lizzie kissed her father, "Thanks, Dad. You're the best and you will really like William, I promise."

Everyone had a great Christmas dinner, a little more sparse than in years gone by and later, sang songs like the new one from Bing Crosby 'White Christmas' and 'The White Cliffs of Dover' and 'Don't Sit Under the Apple Tree." Amelia pined for Paul and Victoria was talking about an American soldier who had asked her to a New Year's Eve dance. The family wasn't fully together but life carried on; everyone making the most of each day.

Chapter 36

1943

Victoria wasn't going to get serious about any man, it was war time. No one knew if today, tomorrow was their last and certainly, American GI's were out of the question. Much of Devon was filling up with Allied soldiers. Liam O'Connor had been into her bank several times and she tried to treat him like any other customer; smile, be polite and then on to the next person. Although she'd given him the cold shoulder, Liam wasn't going to give in easily. One lunch time, she was going to go up to the hospital to meet her mother and Amelia when she found him outside the bank waiting for her.

After greeting her he said, "Can I take you for something to eat?"

"No, I'm sorry. I'm meeting my family."

"Oh."

Victoria couldn't help herself. He was handsome and he had really tried to get to know her. "When will you be free again, Sergeant?"

"Tomorrow."

"Tomorrow it is then, about 1 o'clock, meet me here."

"Yes, ma'am," he saluted.

Victoria smiled, "You'd better tell me your name."

"I'm Liam O'Connor from New York, United States of America."

"I'm Victoria Whitfield from Devon, England."

He took her hand and held it to his lips. "It's nice to meet you, Miss Whitfield."

"So, tomorrow it is."

"Yes, goodbye for now." He turned and walked on, turned and waved and then was gone.

Liam told Victoria about home, that he worked in finance for a bank in New York. He was stationed at Instow and was training new recruits. He liked Devon, thought the countryside was so green and beautiful. He wished he could see it at peace time. Victoria told him about her family, their move from London. Michael was fighting, Lizzie doing war work that was top secret and her twin Amelia was studying to be a nurse.

"And you, Victoria?"

"Apart from my job at the bank, I help my father with his small law company and I do some volunteer work with the church and Amelia always gets me involved with hospital work whenever she can."

"Do you think you'll volunteer for one of the services?"

"I'm not sure," Victoria became sad.

"Sorry, Victoria. I didn't want to upset you," he reached across the table and put his hand on hers.

"I'm all right, really. It's just with Michael and Lizzie away and Amelia caught up with the nursing, I'm the only one at home regularly. I don't want my grandmothers and my parents worried about me too."

"You may have to go."

"I know, I'll face it when it comes to it." She gazed into his eyes. She realised he was thinking about those left behind in his own country. "Sorry Liam, I'm sounding so selfish and you're thousands of miles from home."

He smiled. "So many of us are but I'm lucky cos I've met you." He held her hand. "Being able to talk about home and family and listen to you about your life is refreshing and so much better than talk of the war. We could be good for each other, Victoria."

His blue eyes sparkled. His black hair was cut regulation short by the army. His smile was cheeky and infectious. He was smart in his uniform and he was tall like her father. *Would it hurt to get to know him?* she wondered. He met her as much as he could at lunch times and after a couple of meetings, he invited her to the New Year's Eve dance at the barracks.

"I'd like to, Liam, but my sister is off duty and with her man so far away, I said I'd keep her company."

"My friend John is missing his wife and family, he could do with a friend for the dance, cheer him up. Amelia could go with him."

"I'll ask her but I don't think she will want to."

Amelia wasn't sure. Paul's last letter had been some weeks ago and she could tell things weren't too good all be it that he couldn't possibly be specific, but she knew.

"Amelia, John's missing his wife, you're missing Paul. It's just for the dance, it might cheer you both. Come on sis, you don't get many nights off. Come and enjoy yourself."

"Oh, all right, but he's got to know no funny business."

"Of course."

Grace was pleased to see the girls going out. Maureen and Iris would have liked to have gone, but Grace promised them they'd have a bit of a party at home. Amelia was working so hard to pass her nursing exams that she was wearing herself out. Then there was Paul, Grace knew Amelia was worried and pinning. *What can I say to her?* Grace thought. *I've been through this and yet I can't help her, tell her everything is going to be fine when I truly don't know.*

Grace did have a small party with family and Millie's family together and some neighbours, all pitching in with food and drink and music from the gramophone. When in bed in the early hours of 1st January 1943, Grace laid in Alex's arms. It had been a fun evening and when they'd retired to the bedroom, they made love for the first time in a while.

"1943 Gracey, do you think it's going to be better than the last?"

"I do hope so my love, I'm just happy for now." Their coupling had made her feel whole again. "I take each day as it comes and pray that all those dear to us are alive and safe."

He squeezed her tighter. "I know what you mean, darling," then started kissing her neck and stroking her hips and legs.

John was a kind man, desperately missing his family and Amelia had told him about Paul. They got on well and relaxed in each other's company. John had shown her pictures of his wife, Margaret and his little girl, Anne. They had a drink and danced. *It did feel good to have fun*, thought Amelia.

When Victoria looked back, she would recall that it was at this dance that she fell in love with Liam. She kept an eye on her sister making sure she was all right but most of the time, she was dancing with Liam. The music and the dances were a little different but Liam was a great teacher. They jived and then did the Foxtrot and then Waltzed. In the Waltz, he held her close and tight. She rested her head on his chest, wishing this night would never end. Caught up in the romance of the dance as the music ended, Liam kissed her. Liam saw them both home once they'd celebrated the New Year in. Amelia said goodnight and asked Liam to thank John for a lovely evening and went inside the house. On the steps, now alone, Liam lightly touched her face and moments later, they were in each other's arms and kissing more passionately than before. Her body felt weak and she felt light-headed. He stopped and she opened her eyes, he was smiling at her.

"I've had the best night of my life, Vicky."

"No one calls me Vicky."

"I do, my gorgeous sweet Vicky." They kissed again.

"When do I get to see you again, my Vicky?"

"Whenever you are free."

"I'll always make time for you." He kissed her again. "I'd better let you go and get some sleep, you must be tired from all that dancing, we hardly missed one."

"I could dance forever…with you."

"I think we might just do that." This kiss lasted the longest and was the most delicious. "Goodnight my Vicky, Happy New Year."

"Happy New Year, Liam."

He turned and descended the steps. At the bottom, he turned and blew her a kiss. "I'll see you on Sunday."

"I'll look forward to it, Liam," she returned his kiss and then he runs off back to the barracks.

Inside the house, Victoria recalled the kisses, his strong arms around her. She did like him a lot. She was breaking all her own rules but what a rule to break when Liam kissed her like that. Now, she knew how Amelia was feeling. *If I couldn't see Liam and kiss him and be in his arms, I'd be miserable.*

She locked the front door and went up to the bedroom she shared with her sister. *I'll be extra kind to her from now on, she must be really hurting,* Victoria thought. Amelia was already in bed; she'd kept a lamp on so Victoria could see to undress. Once ready for bed, instead of climbing into her own bed, she squeezed in with her sister.

"Victoria, what are you doing? You haven't done that in years."

"I know, I just wanted to be close to my twin and thank her for coming out tonight. Did you enjoy yourself at all, Amelia? I know it wasn't the best it could be because Paul wasn't there, but it wasn't that bad either, was it?"

"Victoria, I had a good time. John's a nice man and I got to dance. You didn't leave Liam alone though, no one else got a look in."

"Oh Amelia, he's lovely. I think I understand how you feel about Paul now. I know you've known Paul along time and I've only known Liam a short time, but I would be very sad if he was to leave now."

"My sister's found love, at last."

"I think I have."

"Come on then, tell me all about it."

17th January 1943, London was subjected to a night time raid by German bombers the first time since May 1941. Mary with baby and Maggie went into the shelter. Jessica and Arthur were on night shifts. Maggie worried about them when the raids started as it took so much time to move the able-bodied patients, but not all could be moved. Arthur had during past raids gone back to check patients, risking his own life if the hospital was hit. But here at home, it was important now to get James in the shelter and safe. *Poor little mite,* she thought. *What a way to start your life sheltering from bombs and your daddy miles away.*

Between 14th to 23rd January at Casablanca, Churchill and President Roosevelt of America agreed on the unconditional surrender of Germany and Japan. They discussed their aims to drive the Germans and Italians from North Africa then land in Sicily.

Michael was as busy as ever. Now there were US troops in Morocco and Algeria getting their first taste of serious fighting. There were American medics about too and a lot of casualties. He just set his mind on getting the job done and getting home to Mary and James. Now more than ever, he wished the war would end. He wanted to get back to work at the hospital and live in Royal Crescent with his family.

Grace was becoming an avid letter writer, trying to keep in touch with every branch of her family, but she was getting less responses as everyone was so tied up with their busy lives. When there was any news of bombings in London, she would contact Maggie and family. If South Devon was hit, she would write to Rachael and to John and Irene when raids on Portsmouth were reported. On 13th February, two bombs dropped near Dartmouth Old Mill Creek and over 50 people were killed. Grace knew Rachael wasn't that close, but still wanted news that Rachael and Edward were fine. She also wanted to know that Rachael's pregnancy was going well.

Everyone was tired of the war but all had to make the effort to stay positive. There always being a house full, always helped. Maureen and Iris kept everyone on their toes. Helen always popped in for tea and a chat. Amelia emersed herself in nursing but it was Victoria's change in personality that had surprised Grace the most. Her most self-obsessed daughter had become the most selfless of them all, always keeping upbeat and positive. She'd been a great help to her twin over Paul, giving her a shoulder to cry on when Amelia worried over him. Victoria helped her father with paperwork at his law practice, did her own job at the bank and was now considering which of the forces she may have to join next year when she turned 19. She had said she'd rather stay close to home to stay near her family but if she had to go, she would do her duty. Even meeting her American friend, Liam, had been kept low key to not upset Amelia, but Grace knew that this was a budding romance, that wasn't just a puppy love.

When Liam was free and his friend, John, they joined the Whitfields for dinner, bringing food with them as they knew rations made things difficult for British families. Liam and Victoria were so at ease with each other and talked for hours. Grace had never seen Victoria so smitten. This cheered her along with Victoria's change of personality. Alex had always been close to Victoria, but she had always felt unimportant in this daughter's life. Now, they would sit in the evenings chatting about all sorts, including Liam and Grace felt a closeness she hadn't before. Grace realised that Victoria was actually the least confident of her children and needed all of them around and their love to boost her.

Liam was a nice young man and intelligent. He seemed to be in love with Victoria very much. Her children were all grown up and with any luck, they would all marry their chosen partners and have children and her family would grow some more. She prayed this would happen, she had to believe they would all live happily.

There was further good news. Lizzie had got engaged to William on Valentine's Day. Lizzie had told her parents so much about William, they felt they knew him. William had got two days off and had taken Lizzie to a hotel in Oxford. They'd made love as soon as they were alone and then William proposed and placed the diamond solitaire onto the fourth finger of Lizzie's left hand.

"No one can plan these days, Lizzie, but we'll try to get time in August to get to Devon and marry with as many of your family there as possible."

"Oh, Will, that would be lovely. What about your family?"

"I'll invite them but they'll probably be too busy. Your family have taken to me without even meeting me, so your family are now my family and when this war's over, I'd like to live in Devon with you and maybe your father will let me come in with him and build on his law firm."

"Are you sure you'd like that?"

"Where ever you are my love, will be home."

She snuggled up to him looking at the ring on her finger "Mother said she prayed every day when Dad was over in France. She carried on praying once he was home and hoped he would survive his injuries. It worked for her so I'll do the same. I'll pray every day when you are on raids that you come back safe to me. We will marry in August and when this war is over, we'll have many children and settle in Devon."

"I'll have to fight harder now than ever, as I've so much to come home to."

Lizzie kissed him. "Now let's not waste any more time, husband to be, make love to me again."

It wasn't long after that Valentine's Day that American and British Bombers began around the clock bombing attacks of German cities. William was involved as was Matthew. Ruth continually wrote of her fear for her son's life when she wrote to Rachael. Rachael tried to lighten these worries with the impending birth of their first grandchild, but she herself was worried. It was generally known that the pilot's luck ran out sooner or later and of all those that went out, not all came back. Lizzie did pray every day. She filled her days with her job and just hoped, like her aunt did that their loved ones came back after each raid.

After victory at Al Alamein, the British Forces pushed further west to link up with the US Troops in Tunisia in April 1943. The Germans were now sandwiched between two allied armies. On 13th May, German and Italian armies surrendered in Tunisia. German General Rommel was sick and had left North Africa. Now, the way was clear for Britain and the Allied Forces to invade Italy. Paul in Malta was given the news and orders that he would be heading to Italy, as was Michael in the desert.

The raids had continued between March and May. Dams were being targeted to flood factories and power stations. So far, William had come back each time, but in late April, as his sister, Rachael gave birth to his nephew, Adam Thompson, Matthew was hit on his return from a raid. His plane took a direct hit. Ruth fainted at the news of the loss of her son. She had lost her first husband in The Great War and now this one had taken her son. How could she carry on now? Rachael had had a hard and long delivery and was extremely tired. Edward had contacted his own family when Adam was born and immediately, his mother came around to help out. He then telephoned Grace to let her know of the new arrival. Grace wished mother and baby well and said she hoped to be able to travel down to see them soon.

It was only the next day when Edward made another call with the sad news of Matthew's death.

He told Grace, "Ruth is inconsolable, Robert is really worried about her health. I've suggested we talk her into coming to us for a while. It's no consolation, but maybe seeing Adam and helping Rachael get back to health might distract her."

"How's Rachael?" Grace asked.

"She's taken the news badly, Grace, She was weak after the birth but now, with this news, she's worried about Ruth and has cried a lot of the time over Matthew since she found out."

"Oh, the poor dear. It must be very hard for you both. Somehow, you have to find the strength to carry on for Adam's sake. You really don't want to miss these early days of his life. Take my word for it, Edward, the time rushes by and in no time, he'll be leaving home himself."

"I know and what with the war, we all feel time is more precious than ever."

"Do you think you'll be able to convince Ruth and Robert to come to you?"

"I hope so. I'm not sure what's happening about a funeral, maybe after that. I don't think Rachael will be well enough to travel to London and that's upsetting her too."

"Just let me know what's happening. I'd like to call Ruth but I don't want to upset her more. Alex and I wouldn't be able to get to London either, but I will try to get down to you as soon as I can to see if I can help with Rachael."

"That would be helpful, I'm sure you would cheer her. She loves you very much."

"She's like a daughter to me, too. Give her my love, Edward and look after yourself and your family and I'll see you soon."

"Goodbye, Grace. We'll look forward to your arrival."

That evening, Grace discussed her going to Dawlish with Alex.

"If you can change your shifts at the hospital, go for as long as you like. I'd like to come with you but I don't think I can. Rachael will need you especially if Ruth doesn't get down. It's a shame we can't get up to London either. Perhaps, Maggie can call in on Ruth and Robert in a few days just to check up on things, they know each other well enough."

"That's a good idea about Maggie. It's just so hard to travel around now, I'm not sure how easy it's going to be to get to Dawlish."

Victoria came up with an idea when she came in that evening. The next day, it was sorted. Liam was to go to Plymouth to pick up something, she couldn't ask what obviously, but he said he'd detour and take her mother to her cousin Rachael.

Three days later, Liam and a private named Peter, picked Grace up from home just after 8 o'clock in the morning and took her to the farm in Dawlish. Seeing Rachael so tired and weak upset Grace and once they greeted each other, they were in tears, remembering Matthew and worried for Ruth and Robert. Grace had enjoyed the ride down with Liam and Peter, learning more about his life in the United States. Victoria had met a lovely young man and Grace only hoped they could have a long and happy life together. Liam had certainly hinted at that. She was a little tired on arrival, but having seen Rachael and then little Adam, she regained some of her strength. She had to help her niece get better and Adam was adorable. Edward was doing his best but he had to run the farm.

There was going to be a memorial service for Matthew and then Robert had made Ruth agree to go to Devon. By the time Ruth and Robert arrived, Rachael was up and about feeling a great deal better. Grace couldn't believe Ruth's appearance. It had been a few years since she'd last seen her sister-in-law, but she had aged a lot. Robert explained later when Ruth had retired for the evening, that she had been working so hard volunteering, to keep her mind off of Matthew. On hearing of his death, she hadn't eaten for three days. Grace agreed that Ruth was thinner than she'd ever been and so pale. Robert wasn't going to be able to stay long, but was hoping Ruth would remain in the country.

"It would be good for her to spend time with her grandson and daughter."

"What about you, Robert? You've lost a son too."

"I know, Grace, but I think I've been preparing myself for this since Matthew joined up. I tried to convince him to join the army but he insisted on the air force. I loved my son and I'll miss him forever, but Ruth lost Michael in the last war, now Matthew. It's a double blow and I don't think she can comprehend the loss. Her grief is too consuming."

Grace had realised just how devastated Ruth was from the off. Rachael had greeted her mother and had cried. She held her grandson and she cried. She was drowning in her grief. Grace had worried that Rachael would deteriorate again, but she had summoned up more strength and consoled her mother. Grace left them together. She helped Edward with some of the farm duties, cooked and cleaned the house and kept Robert company. Grace and Ruth talked over old times about Michael, about their children. Ruth was improving. She was eating and not crying so much. When Robert was due to go back to London, he was relieved to see his wife coping a little better and now eating. She had put a little weight on. He didn't want to leave her and he said he would be back as soon as he could. Grace and Edward took Robert to the station. The men shook hands and Grace hugged Robert and kissed his cheek.

"Whenever you want to talk just call."

"I will do, thank you, Grace. Ruth is getting better, thanks to all of you."

"She is and I'm sure Rachael will continue to help her, but you must take care of yourself too, promise me you will."

"I will, Grace," he kissed her again and then boarded the train.

These days, she thought, *it's all goodbyes.*

It was goodbye again two days later. Grace thought it best to leave the mother and daughter together. Edward took her to the station and Alex met her at Bideford Station at the end of her journey.

"I'm glad I went."

"How are they all?" Alex enquired.

"Not too bad now. Ruth really did need the change of scenery and they are helping each other through their grief."

"And what's Adam like?"

"A lovely little boy."

Bideford and surrounding areas had more troops. The Americans had taken over The Shandfield Hotel in Instow and were practising exercises, using landing crafts on the beach. The MV President Warfield arrived. She was a passenger ferry from Baltimore that had been towed across the Atlantic and moored at Zeta berth and was now being used as the US Navy officers' quarters. The Quay Café became a Sergeants' Mess, the Jubilee Hall became the Naafi and the Marine Hotel was also partly taken over for catering. Hotels in Ilfracombe where Grace and Alex had spent holidays many years before, were taken over by American Servicemen. Many troops moved onto Braunton and Saunton to build camps. US Troops practised amphibious exercises on Woolacombe beach, all of which were sectioned off from the public with barbed wire. Quite different from their holidays spent relaxing on the beach, Grace thought. But all this activity brought hope that this war was turning in the Allies' favour.

As Allied troops began landing in Sicily, Paul and Michael both had leave. With Michael back in England, Lizzie thought it best to arrange the wedding quickly. William was in total agreement. He applied for forty-eight hours leave and was granted a week due to the circumstances. Lizzie did the same. They contacted All Saints Church in Notting Hill to carry on the family tradition. Grace and Alex weren't going to miss this wedding. Travelling was becoming increasingly difficult and it was going to become impossible if the authorities persisted in stopping the freedom of movement. In the south of Devon, whole towns had been evacuated to accommodate troops; lives were still changing for some.

On Saturday, 7th August, Lizzie walked up the aisle in a dress made by herself and Florey. She'd managed to get some silk and made up a simple dress. She held a small posy of yellow roses and tiny bud roses held her veil in place. Alex proudly walked his daughter down the aisle to a man he'd only met two days ago. He had taken to William though and had no fear that Lizzie was marrying a decent man, who was proving each day of his bravery during the bombing raids of German cities. They appeared to be very much in love and happy, considering the circumstances of the time. All from home had sent their love.

Amelia had taken some time off because Paul was home and Victoria was seeing Liam as much as possible. Elizabeth and Helen were looking after Maureen and Iris and Millie were spending more time at the farm to be able to see her grandson.

Looking around the church, there wasn't many of William's family, just an aunt and uncle and a few cousins who lived in London. Michael, Mary and James were there, as were Maggie and Arthur. Eloise, Stephan, Jack, Cara and Laura had come too. Ruth hadn't long come back from Devon and Grace wasn't sure if she would come, but she had with Robert and was now standing next to Grace in the front pew. Ruth looked a great deal better, had colour to her cheeks and had put on a little weight. As tears came to Grace's eyes at seeing her daughter walking down the aisle looking so happy and beautiful, Ruth squeezed her arm. Grace turned to her and smiled. It was good to have her sister-in-law there.

The ceremony began. They sang a hymn and then the couple made their vows. Alex had given his daughter away and slipped into the pew next to Grace. As the young couple vowed to love in sickness and in health, Alex put his arm around his tearful wife. He too was filled with emotion at seeing his eldest daughter marry. She still seemed too young to be a wife. Another hymn, the Register signed, the proud husband in his air force uniform took the arm of his bride and led her out of the church into the summer sunshine. A couple of photographs were taken and a reception was to be at the Royal Crescent house. Mary and Maggie had made most of the arrangements along with Sally and the other help, the reception had been catered for.

Jessica and Florey had been Lizzie's bridesmaids and a friend of William from his squadron, Luke, had been his best man. Not long into the reception, Florey and Luke had to leave to go back to their work. Michael was pleased to be home with Mary and his son James, who was nearly a year old. They were spending their time at Royal Crescent, but for the next two nights, they were letting Lizzie and William have the house to be alone as a honeymoon wasn't on the cards. He and Mary had wasted no time. They had spent a lot of their time in bed. So many times, he had yearned to hold her, to love her and she had been the same. It was going to be tougher than ever to go back this time.

Maggie had done Lizzie proud with the wedding breakfast. She had felt awkward as it was Grace's place as mother of the bride to take centre stage, but Grace had assured her that as Maggie had been the one close to hand, it was for the best.

"Anyway, Mags, you've been around all of Lizzie's life. You're like her auntie anyway."

Ruth and Robert had enjoyed themselves. Robert had told Grace that although far from over the loss of their son, Ruth was doing better and positive when talking about their grandson. Grace said she was pleased, but still asked after Robert's own well-being.

"I'm not too bad, Grace. It gives me strength that Ruth is better. I now feel I have someone I can lean on too."

As the afternoon went into the evening, everyone said their goodbyes. Maggie had made up beds as not only Mary, Michael and James were staying with her, so was Grace and Alex. It was going to be crowded.

"Let's hope there are no raids or we'll have to run off to the underground station," said Arthur.

"I don't care how squeezed we are," said Maggie. "It's just good to be all together again."

Once alone, Lizzie and William went to the bedroom that had once been her grandparent's bedroom. He kissed her tenderly.

"You are the most beautiful woman in the world, Lizzie. I was so happy and proud when I saw you walk into the church."

"I was nervous Will, I'm glad my father was there for me to hold on to."

They kissed again. Obviously, it wasn't their first time but strangely, Lizzie did feel a little nervous. They were married now. She took off her dress with care and William took off his uniform. Soon, their bodies were joined as one, enjoying the pleasure they were giving to each other. Each time had been good between them but this time was special. She was now Mrs William Havers. They climaxed together and Lizzie cried out in ecstasy.

"I love you, Will."

"Oh, Lizzie, I love you too."

On the Sunday after Lizzie's wedding, Amelia finished her shift at the hospital at lunch time. She had the next day off and was going to spend as much time with Paul as possible. She thought he had changed a bit. He certainly looked older. He'd had a beard when he'd first returned but had since shaved it off. He was tired and just wanted the peace of the farm at first. Malta had been a nightmare; he'd explained to

Amelia. There was continual bombing and at times, there were hardly any provisions. Amelia had held him close and let him tell her all he wanted to. She couldn't wait to see him today. He was in the barn cleaning out while the horses were in the field. She crept up behind him, but he sensed someone was there and turned around looking nervous and anxious. Realising it was Amelia, his face changed to smile and he opened out his arms to her. She rushed into his arms and kissed him.

"You'll have to get out of your uniform, you'll get it dirty."

"And I thought you were a gentleman. You want me to take my clothes off. I don't know a short time in the army and you take the first girl you find," she was smiling.

"I would like to get you out of your clothes, Amelia. I want you so much. I want to marry you. "Their kissing was more urgent and passionate.

"We'd better stop," Paul said. "Go into the house and change and when I've finished here, we'll go for a horse ride like old times."

She kissed him once more and ran into the house. Millie was out with Jane. Bryan was out getting ready for the forthcoming harvest with the land girls. Dennis and Alan, their evacuees, were off playing somewhere. There was some bread on the kitchen table. Instantly hungry, she cut herself a couple of slices. Millie made her own cheese so Amelia quickly made herself a sandwich. There was a strong smell of beef cooking and that made her feel even more hungry. She gobbled down her sandwich and went up to Paul's room, where she had left some clothes a few days ago. She took off her uniform and put on trousers and an old blouse. She sat on Paul's bed and his words came in her mind. 'I want you Amelia, I want to marry you.' She wanted him too.

They went out for a ride. Then upon return, all the family, the land girls and Dennis and Alan sat together for a Sunday roast. It was a jovial time and for the first time in a long time, Amelia relaxed. The hospital had taken up all her time. She'd done that on purpose to keep her mind occupied to stop thinking about Paul away fighting. She was sorry she'd missed Lizzie's wedding but she didn't want to miss any of Paul's time at home.

She helped with the milking when the cows came in for the night and finally, it was just her and Paul alone in the barn. The sun was going down. In a corner of the barn where they kept fresh hay, Amelia and Paul sunk down to rest. It had been a good day just like a Sunday had been before the war had started, but it was different now. They were older, a man and a woman, wanting to get to know each other physically. Paul turned on his side, his head resting on his hand. Amelia's heart started to race with excitement.

She touched his face. "I want you Paul."

"Are you sure?"

"I've never been more sure of anything. Love me Paul, make me your wife."

He sat up and unbuttoned her blouse. He took off his shirt and then his trousers. Amelia took off the rest of her things. Laying back on the hay in the dusk of the evening, they kissed. He gently caressed one of her breasts. Desire soured through her body. Paul's hands were exploring her whole body. She stroked his back, his chest, feeling his toned muscles. He got on top of her.

"I love you, Amelia."

"I love you, Paul."

She was his now. The pleasure took her and she cried out. They laid in each other's arms for some time afterwards.

"I suppose we'd better go in to the house," Paul said.

"No, my darling, let's stay here. We won't have too much time before you have to go back and I want to spend as much time as possible with you. And I want to do that all over again."

Paul smiled. "Then we'll stay here and in the morning, we'll tell them we got an early start."

Amelia rolled on top of him. "Then let's not waste our time." She kissed him and soon, they were making love again.

Jessica had left the wedding to go back to the hospital. She was tending an injured Canadian soldier named Patrick. All her training had told her she shouldn't get involved with patients, but Patrick had been special. He had been brought back from the desert. His injuries weren't so bad but infection had set in. It had been touch and go for a while for Patrick, but Jessica had persisted. On waking from his fever, he had smiled at Jess and said he thought she was an angel. During his recovery, she took whatever time she could to talk to Patrick. Today, he was being discharged and would have to go back to his regiment. He had packed up his belongings and was saying goodbye to the other nurses and patients. Her shift wasn't due to start yet. She'd made sure she had enough time to say goodbye properly. She was at the door to the ward. Patrick spotted her, said his final goodbyes and left the ward. The couple greeted each other and went outside the hospital.

Outside, Patrick turned to her, "Have you enough time to have some tea?"

"Yes."

He took her arm and they walked to the nearest café. Patrick ordered two teas and they sat at a table for two. He put his hand in his top pocket and pulled out a slip of paper and handed it to Jess.

"This is the address of my barracks. Will you write to me, Jessica?"

"Yes, I'd love to, Patrick."

"Thankyou. If it wasn't for your care, I might not be here now."

"Oh, you were strong, you'd have made it."

Patrick smiled. "I don't know if you feel the same, but I'm going to miss you and I was hoping that when I'm next on leave, I could come back and see you," he paused, "I'd like you to be my girl, Jessica."

Jess blushed, she did feel the same. "Come back and see me as soon as you can. I'll write to you often and I would be proud to be your girl."

He held her hand to his lips and kissed it. "Good, I'd hoped you would say that. We've had so little time to get to know each other, but I feel I know enough about you to say I'd like to spend my life with you. You are my angel."

Time was slipping away and they had to leave the café.

"I'd better get back to the hospital," Jess said.

Patrick cupped her face in his hands and kissed her gently on the mouth. "I've been wanting to do that for weeks, Nurse Smith."

"I've wanted you to, Sergeant Baker and I want you to do it again. "This time they held each other and kissed with much more passion.

"Wait for me, Jessica."

"Of course, I will. Keep safe and come back soon."

"I will, for you."

177

They kissed again and then Jess had to run back to the hospital. Just before they were out of each other's sight, Jess turned and Patrick was where she'd left him. He blew her a kiss and waved. She waved back and hurried on.

"I love you, Patrick Baker. Come back to me soon, "she said to herself and ran into the hospital to do her duty.

On 15th August, the Allied Forces invaded the southern Italian mainland. Paul and Michael joined their regiments in Italy. Celebrations and the ongoing breakthrough had happened and on 8th September, Italy surrendered unconditionally and signed an armistice with the Allies. This was a good turning point and a chance for people at home to celebrate. The Allies now had to push North and they took Naples on 1st October.

Grace and Alex had returned a few days after the wedding. They had said their goodbyes to their new son-in-law and Lizzie and to Michael and his family. It had been good to see so many people she loved all in one place, together and happy and Alex had said when they got on the train to return home, "Let's hope we can all be together again soon. I've enjoyed the normality of the whole time."

Grace had agreed she wanted her family all together again. She knew what with marriages and children, it wasn't going to be as it was before the war, but they would all be able to see each other more. Paul's leaving had made Amelia upset again, but she'd thrown herself into her work. She was going to talk to her parents and ask that when Paul got leave the next time, she wanted to get married. She'd pick the right time though, she thought.

Victoria was seeing Liam a lot. They wanted time alone but there never seemed the chance. Liam had suggested that when he was free from duty, he would take her away for a few days, but she said her parents wouldn't agree to that. Victoria was serious about Liam and he was about her. He spoke of taking her to the United States after the war to meet his family and show her where he'd grown up. She couldn't believe that she may someday leave England, but it was exciting to think about it. Would her family let her? She wondered and would she be able to leave them?

Christmas was soon upon them again. Some 900 children were treated by the American soldiers to films and sweets at the Strand Cinema. It was a festive time and Maureen, Iris, Dennis and Alan enjoyed themselves. The boy's parents had managed to get to see them in November, but Maureen and Iris's parents hadn't been down since they'd been evacuated. Grace felt for them both and had made them even more part of the family.

Liam and John joined in the Whitfield Christmas festivities, bringing chocolates and other food with them. Boxing Day was at the farm with Millie's brood and again, the Americans were invited. Bryan, Liam, John and Alex had gone out to the barn after dinner. John helped Bryan with horses and their feed. That left Liam and Alex.

"I can't say too much, sir," said Liam, "but there are plans afoot. There are more troops arriving next year and I'll be gone once they're all trained."

"Do you think it's an invasion?" asked Alex.

"I'm not sure, but I would guess that's what's going to happen."

"It's about time, now with all of you involved, we stand a good chance at finally giving Hitler a beating."

"It's because I may well be leaving that I would like to ask you something, sir."

"What's that, Liam?"

"I know that Victoria isn't 21, but I would like to ask her to marry me before I go. I would like her to be my wife before I go, but with your permission, I would at least like to be engaged to Victoria," he stopped. He couldn't read Alex's expression. More nervous now, he said, "I love your daughter, Mr Whitfield and I will make her a good husband."

"I'm sure you will, Liam. Victoria is young though. Does she feel the same?"

"I know she loves me, but I've not made any promises to her, that without your permission I could not keep."

"I'll have to speak to Grace, but you have my blessing, Liam."

"Thank you, sir," Liam shook hands with his future father-in-law. "I'll wait till you say you've spoken to Mrs Whitfield, then I'll propose."

Grace was concerned that Victoria was too young but she and Liam did make a lovely couple and in this day and age, you had to live your life. With both Victoria's parents' permission, Liam proposed on New Year's Eve and Victoria accepted. Grace congratulated the couple. Victoria embraced her mother and father.

"Thank you, both of you. You've made me so happy."

Grace kissed her daughter, she marvelled at how much she had changed. *My family is all grown up, she* thought.

Chapter 37

Hitler, after the raids on German cities ordered retaliatory raids against London and Southern England. On 21st January 1944, the RAF sent 700 bombers on raids on Berden, Kiel and Magdebury, and was successful. William was involved in these raids and wasn't able to get much time off these days to see his wife, Lizzie. There was even little time for sleep with the raids. Lizzie tried to get on with her work to put William's dangerous tasks to the back of her mind. She prayed every night that he came back each time and soon, they can be together again.

On 22nd January, British and American forces landed at Anzio, Italy. Paul and Michael's regiments were still pushing further north in Italy. The Germans were still trying to hold on. Michael did feel that there had been some breakthroughs and truly hoped that the tides were turning in the Allies' favour. He wrote whenever possible to Mary, asking after her and their son, James. There was talk of an expeditionary force going to France again. He really hoped there would be, Hitler had to be beaten. The Russians were holding fast in the East so Allied forces invading in the West might finally finish off the Germans. There were still many casualties and Michael was operating on colleagues daily. He had rarely had to fire a shot. It had only been on the advance that he had been involved in combat. He was even considering if he wanted to carry on being a doctor when the war was finally over. He had seen so much death and horror for one lifetime. It didn't seem such a vocation anymore. He would need to talk to Doctor Gregson when he got home. John Gregson had been a doctor in the services his whole life. How had he coped? Michael also remembered conversations with his father about the trench warfare from the Great War. Would any generation ever be free to not endure this type of existence?

Grace and Alex tried to keep Maureen and Iris occupied during the winter months. Helen hadn't been too well in February. She had caught a cold and it had developed into pneumonia. Grace was always fearful of this ailment, as she had been ill with it many years before. So, she, Elizabeth and Victoria took turns to nurse Helen. Finally, by the end of February, Helen started to feel better and the risk to her health seemed to have passed. Grace marvelled at her mother and mother-in-law's resolve.

At 76 and 83 respectively, they had such grit and determination. They really kept the household running, ensuring that whatever could be saved and not wasted was recycled. They kept to rations along with Millie's help and they'd made up creative recipes from hardly any ingredients. Clothes were so sparse so Helen put her clothes, making talents to good use. Jumpers were unpicked and knitted again as something to suit Maureen or Iris. Dresses were made into blouses. If the war could be won on determination alone, thought Grace, these women would win out right. They seemed to have endless energy and hopefulness. When Helen had fallen ill, they had all worried as it was so unlike her. These women, especially her mother, had never been brought up for this type of life. It had been all privilege. No austerity. Grace and Alex still had their duties towards the war effort. Grace still did shifts at the hospital; Alex did night duties with the ARP. The bed felt empty without Alex and she was always relieved when he climbed into bed for just a couple of hours to sleep. She would cuddle up to him and finally sleep soundly. They still needed each other for strength and Alex knew how Grace worried about all their children. He tried so hard to keep her positive. He had to; it was his duty. When Alex had a night-off, they would go to bed early, not always to make love but more often than not, they did. Grace still enjoyed their intimacy. She was still attracted to Alex as much as she always had been. He had grown even more handsome as the years had passed and she revelled in the way he made her feel loved and desired.

Victoria and Liam weren't getting so much time together. So many troops needed to be trained; therefore, Liam left the base less. At least, they were engaged. Amelia had been jealous of her sister when she got engaged. She should have made Paul ask her parent's permission so that they could have done the same before he'd left, but they had made love. She had kept their special time to herself and thought about it a lot. Paul had to come back. She wanted to be his wife, have his children. She recalled his strong body and how he had excited her. *Had Victoria done anything yet?* She wondered. If she felt jealous regarding the engagement, she wouldn't let it show. Victoria had been supportive all the time Paul was away and she had been grateful for that. At one point, Amelia thought she may have got pregnant and although she had never confided to her twin, Victoria had sensed her worries and had been there for her. They were both in the same boat, really.

The family were writing constantly to keep in touch. With the raids in January, Rachael wrote to say they were all fine. Adam was growing so quick and Edward was working hard on the farm. Another teacher had come from her school in London, so she wasn't teaching at all now. Ruth and Robert had made it to Devon for Christmas and everyone had enjoyed themselves. Rachael wrote that her mother was doing well, keeping busy with her charity work and she and Robert were as close as ever. Robert had said they were helping each other through their grief of losing Matthew.

In March, Eloise wrote to say that Clara was pregnant again and both Cara and Jack were pleased. Maggie wrote with news of their grandson James, who was now very capable of walking and getting into mischief. She told them of Jessica's romance with the Canadian serviceman, Patrick, who had recently been back to visit and he and Jess had been out several times. Maggie said she missed them all and couldn't wait for a time when they could all be together again.

Irene Gregson had written a few times to say Gosport had been hit a few more times, but they had all escaped unhurt. When Alex and Grace sat at dinner with the family still with them, they would all talk about their memories of their friends and family and keep up with all the news and updates and pray that they would all still be alive when this sorry war was over.

On 4th March, US bombers began daylight raids on Berlin. On 18th April, the heaviest Allied air raid of the war sent 2,000 bombers, dropping more than 4,000 tonnes of bombs on Germany. Grace thought of all the families that would die, but Helen pointed out, "It's retaliation, Grace dear, they did it to us. They only understand one way; unfortunately, it's the innocents that suffer." Helen was right, but Grace still felt sorry for all those that were dying.

Liam had sad news at the end of April. On the 28th, the US 4th division had been out training off the Dorset coast and their ships had been torpedoed and 749 servicemen had been killed. He had known some of these men. Victoria had never seen him so low and tried her best to lighten his mood. He was going to have a few days leave soon and she would get the time off too. They needed some time alone. There was the talk of the second front happening soon. Liam would be gone. She wanted them to have consummated their relationship before he went. She would have wanted to be married really, but there was no time. She asked Grace if she could go away with Liam for a few days. She was a little embarrassed at asking but was surprised when her mother agreed to her going.

"Go and have some time with your fiancé, Victoria. Just be careful, my darling."

Victoria kissed her mother. "Thank you, Mother. I just wanted some time with him before he goes off to fight. You understand, don't you?" she'd pleaded to Grace.

"I know exactly how you feel," Grace recalled how she felt the night before Alex had left to fight. She had felt like her heart might break, so how could she deny her daughter the chance of some happiness.

So, before the mass exodus of troops moving to the south of Devon in preparation of the second front, Victoria and Liam took three days off. They went towards Cornwall and found a small boarding house that had a vacant room. They booked in as Mr and Mrs O'Connor and once alone, made straight for the bed. They tore at each other's clothes and their bodies were soon entwined. Victoria had wanted this for some time now and she couldn't wait any longer. If she had been nervous on their drive down, that had soon evaporated when they were naked and he was kissing and caressing her. She didn't want this feeling to end and she didn't want Liam to leave her ever.

"As soon as I come back, Vicky, we'll be married."

"We're as good as now, my love. Who needs a certificate to prove we love each other and after what we've done? I feel married."

"It was good."

"Just good!" she tickled him.

"Oh, all right, It was fantastic."

"Too right, it was," she mimicked his American accent.

"All the same, we will be married, Vicky. I want you to be my legal wife."

"I want that too. Now, stop talking and do what you did to me all over again. I don't want you to stop and that's an order."

"Yes, ma'am." He started to kiss her again and the thrill and excitement started again.

The troops and vehicles lined up in South Devon and along the coasts of Hampshire, including Gosport, in preparation of embarking for France. On 11th May, a fourth attack on the strategic point of Monte Casino in Italy, the German line, is finally broken by Allied forces. On 4th June, Allied forces entered Rome. German forces retreated and the city was taken without fighting.

Lizzie had chance for a week's leave with William at the end of May. They spent time at Lizzie's lodgings. Florey kindly let them have the time alone and stayed with another friend. They talked of their plans for the future, of the children they would have. William still wanted to live in Devon and work at Alex's law office. They made love many times and Lizzie tried not to cry but couldn't hold back when William left. The invasion would keep him from her longer than ever.

Jessica's boyfriend had been sent to Gosport. They had managed a few hours together before he left. A few days later, the hospital asked for volunteers to go to the Royal Hospital Haslar in Gosport, as it was a military hospital and casualties from the invasion would be sent there. Jessica volunteered, as did Amelia. She felt this move made her closer to the man she loved and missed so much. The two women met on arrival and were sharing the same hall for sleeping. They both thought it was calming to have someone you knew in a different place.

In the early hours of 6th June, the streets of Gosport emptied. Stokes Bay and The Hardway were used to transport Canadian and British troops to France on what was being called D-Day. The weather was bad for the time of year and troops were being sick around him, but all Patrick Baker could think about was his family he had left on another continent and of Jessica who he was leaving in England. Liam was thinking of Victoria as he boarded in South Devon. He too, thought of his family in the US, but he longed to be with Victoria, his love.

Victoria had been upset to see Amelia go, but understood her need for going. Grace comforted Victoria, knowing full well how she was feeling. Grace worried for Amelia and the sights she would see at the military hospital. She had hastily written to John Gregson to ask him to look out for Amelia and Jessica. Lizzie's husband would be involved in the air raids. Michael and Paul were in Italy. *When would all the worry be over*? she thought.

Liam was feeling sick and some of his comrades were actually throwing up. The crossing was rough and what was it going to be like when they reached the French coast? He had trained hundreds of soldiers, but would it be good enough? If the Germans were waiting for them, it would be a massacre. He just hoped that this invasion was more of a surprise; it was supposed to be, as the enemy thought that the Allies would try nearer to Calais. There were ships all around. Some men were singing, some smoking, some just trying to hold on to their breakfast. Liam was quietly reflecting on his weekend with Victoria. He remembered holding her in his arms, he'd kissed her, made love to her. He had promised her that when the war was over, he'd be back to make her his wife and he was going to make it back. Soon, he would be fighting for his life and for his regiment and for freedom. *A small prayer for luck wouldn't hurt*, he thought.

Patrick was feeling much the same, as was William. William was flying parachutists in to France. It had to work. Today, this was the Allies' biggest chance to turn the tide of the war and each soldier, sailor and airman had their duty to do. The longest day had only just begun. Where would they all be as night fell?

Bideford felt empty. The Americans had become so much a part of everyday life that it seemed strange that they'd all gone. Grace and Alex began to worry more than ever. D-Day could be a success, but Amelia was now in Gosport and Michael was in Italy. Lizzie's husband would be constantly flying to and from the continent and Victoria's fiancé would be fighting in France. If locally, it was quieter, all their family and friends were involved in greater things. Alex had recalled his time in the trenches and feared for these men. As Amelia and a couple of nurses had transferred to military posts, Grace was still busy at the local hospital. Alex had less to do with the ARP, so at least he and Grace could spend more evenings together. Maureen and Iris, with the rest of the family, would listen to the news on the radio to check on the progress of the invasion.

Amelia and Jessica's shifts had coincided so far. Doctor Gregson had called in to see how they were doing and invited them both to dinner, as soon as they had an afternoon or evening free. They were thrown into the work instantly. As ships were being hit, soldiers and sailors injured were being brought back and the nurses and doctors started their work. It had been quite a site; seeing all the ships leaving Portsmouth and Gosport on their way to France. All the patients and staff had been excited and worried what the next few days would bring. Both Amelia and Jessica were scared that the next man in would be their boyfriend. Amelia knew Paul was further away in Italy, but the thought had crossed her mind. So many men injured, some already dead as they came back to English shores. Someone was losing a son, a husband, a nephew; someone they cared for. Both women knew their job.

As Allied troops pushed forward on French soil, Hitler was retaliating. A new type of bomb called a VI was launched on England. They caused so much devastation that by July, over a million more children were evacuated from London. It was like the Blitz all over again.

Paul and Michael's regiments in Italy were pushing north. On 4th August, the Allies took Florence and the Germans withdrew. Eleven days later, Allied forces landed on the French Mediterranean Coast. Advances were being made on all fronts.

The summer had been quiet in Devon. No one came for holidays. The soldiers were gone. The excitement of the invasion was wearing off; everyone just wanted the war to end. Victoria had heard from Liam and cried with relief. *He was all right so far*, she thought. A letter from Paul had arrived and Grace redirected it to Haslar Hospital. She hadn't heard from Amelia much in the last couple of months, but knew she would be so busy. The Americans had taken a beating trying to take their designated stretch of the Normandy coast and there were many injured that would probably end up at Haslar. Lizzie came home for two weeks. Grace and Alex were pleased to see her and made a fuss. They walked and picnicked in the park. It was a shame they still couldn't use the beaches, but Victoria Park served just as well. One time, Maureen and Iris had gone off to play and Alex had fallen asleep, it just left the mother and the daughter to talk.

"I wish now that I had got pregnant. We'd discussed that it was better to wait, but now that I haven't seen William for three months, I wish I was having his baby," Lizzie confided.

"I know just how you feel. Your father and I had wanted to wait have time to ourselves. Then the war started and I wasn't sure if it was the best time to start a family, but as soon as your father was gone, I wished I was pregnant. I thought it would have made me closer to him." She took her daughter's hand. "You'll just have to be brave and believe he will be back and one day, you will have many children."

"I'll try, Mother, but it's hard to believe. His raids have always been dangerous, but now I think the Germans are more desperate and William's flying on more raids than ever."

"He's made it so far; Lizzie darling and he's got you waiting for him. It gives a man incentive. I'm sure he'll be back home."

Michael returned to London late August as Charles De Gaulle entered Paris to the cheers of his countrymen. He was still at home when Chiswick, West London was hit by the first V2 rocket sent from Germany; killing three and injuring ten. London seemed more dangerous than Italy, but it was good to be home. He was there for his son, James' second birthday. James was walking and talking and Michael made sure he spent as much time with him and Mary. He telephoned Grace and Alex to catch up and let them know that he would now be heading for France with some other medics from his regiment. When he set off again, little did he know that Mary was with child and again, he didn't want to leave the love and happiness of his family for the war field.

Paul had got back to Devon in September. He knew Amelia wouldn't be there but took the time to write many letters to her to tell her how he was and how much he loved her. It was good to be home and see his family, and he visited Grace and Alex too. He took the opportunity to ask Alex if he could marry Amelia when the war was over and Alex happily agreed.

Alex couldn't believe where all the years had gone. Lizzie and Michael were married already, Michael had a son, Victoria is engaged and Amelia as good as. They had all grown up so quickly and the war has hastened that. He was fifty-three years old. Sometimes, he felt old, but most of the time, he still thought of Grace and himself as they had been in their twenties with the children small. *Maybe we'll have many grandchildren to look after when peace comes; more long days on the beach and times to laugh and relax.* Lizzie had said William wanted to move to Devon and work in the law practice and maybe expand the business. This made him more hopeful of the future. This war had brought back so many bad memories of the Great War and that dragged his mood down. He knew Grace worried constantly about their brood and he tried hard to keep her lifted. Grace, the love of his life; what would he have done without her? When this war was over, he would take her on the trip of a lifetime, spoil her. That was something to look forward to.

September saw a set back at Arnhem for the Allies. Eleven hundred troops were killed and thousands were taken as prisoners. The news came from all quarters that all family members were safe. Grace was relieved. Everyone had hoped that by now, the war would be over.

Liam had written to Victoria to say he was safe, but John had been injured and was on his way back to England. Amelia had been working all day when the next group of injured came to the hospital. As they were being admitted, she heard John's name called and she made her way to him. John's injury wasn't life-threatening and Amelia soon had him settled and then into surgery to remove the bullet from his leg. John was thrilled to see a face he knew and Amelia was anxious for news of her twin's fiancé.

"When I left, Nurse Amelia, Liam was doing fine."

"Nurse Whitfield to you Sergeant," she said smiling and then making sure she wasn't seen, she kissed John's cheek. "Thank you, John. I can write to Victoria and let her know. Now, let's get you fit and up and about again."

Good news reached Grace in October. Cara and Jack had a boy named Christopher. Mother and baby were doing fine and Eloise and Stephen were overjoyed. Jack had been depressed for a while as he felt he wasn't doing his bit of war duty, but Cara's pregnancy had helped, and now, he had a son. He was now going to ensure that his son never had to go through what he had gone through.

Amelia had written to her parents, saying John was being discharged from the forces due to his injury and before he returned to the US, he had asked if he could stay with Grace and Alex. They were only too pleased to have him with them for Christmas.

William was on leave so he and Lizzie were staying at Lizzie's digs in Bletchley. Amelia couldn't get time off, so it was just her and Alex, the grandmothers, Victoria, and Maureen and Iris. John's presence would help Victoria feel closer to Liam, Grace hoped. Unfortunately, the Germans launched an attack on the US army at Ardennes on 16th December and by Christmas, Victoria hadn't heard from Liam. She was over wrought with worry. John tried to comfort her but she wanted a word from Liam. Grace tried to make the festive season as jolly as possible. The news in November that Mary was pregnant again and a letter from Michael saying he was chuffed over the prospect of becoming a father again, was helping. She would try harder than ever to cheer Victoria, as she knew only too well what her daughter was feeling. Roll in 1945, will it be the last of the war.

Chapter 38

The winter was cold and the snow fell. Everyone was demoralised. Maureen and Iris were bored of building snowmen. There was little to do at the farm at this time of year and everywhere seemed empty since the Americans had left. They were still luckier than most who lived in the towns and cities as far as food was concerned, but there was a coal shortage and the prolonged bad weather was making everyone feel worse.

Grace laid in bed with Alex the morning of 13th February. They had made love and their bodies were still entwined. It wasn't as athletic as it had been in their early years together, but just as fulfilling. Grace wanted his closeness more now of late. She was pleased his ARP duties were less and they could spend more evenings together. She didn't want to move. It was lovely and warm in bed with Alex and she didn't want to leave the feeling of his naked body close to hers. She traced his scar from the stabbing of many years ago.

"That tickled, Gracey," he laughed.

"Would you like me to do it again?" She moved on top of him and her long hair cascaded over him. God, he loved her and Alex felt the need for her again.

"I've got you now," she smiled at him.

"You can have me anytime." Slowly then faster, they moved together. "Not too fast, my love. I want this to last," he said.

She leant down and kissed him. "I'll go as slow as you like."

It was on that day that the Allies bombed the German City of Dresden. By the end of the raid, the city was completely destroyed. William was exhausted after the raids and he needed a rest. If he didn't get a goodnight's sleep soon he wouldn't be able to fly anywhere. He would make a mistake or fall asleep in the cockpit. He had seen so many of his colleagues die when they'd been too tired to react in the battle. They'd made an error of judgement and didn't make it back. It was months since he'd seen Lizzie. He wrote as often as possible, telling her he was keeping safe. He didn't dare let on about the extra raids he was doing. She would worry herself into a state.

Elizabeth and Helen missed John when he returned to America. He had been their patient and they had spoilt him. When he left, he promised to keep in touch and both grandmothers felt they were losing a grandson. John's absence and the cold had made Helen take a turn for the worse. Now 89, Helen had been a robust and healthy woman for the majority of her life; but now, she felt tired, worn out. She had wanted to be near her son when James died and she lived happily in Devon since her arrival. She and Elizabeth had taken to each other and with Millie's presence in the Whitfield household, they had spent the worrying days of the war laughing, trying to keep up morale as Mr Churchill had commanded, but she was weary now. She had hoped that all her grandchildren were home by now, but they were risking their lives or patching up servicemen or doing other important war work. Last night, she laid in bed in her son's home; the room that had once been young Michael's. Not so young now, a husband, father and another little one on the way. He was handsome, so like his father. Alex had come to sit with her and chatted as they always done with ease. She was proud of his achievements. He had left the life of the mills behind, gone to college and become a lawyer. He read her a letter that Michael had sent and relayed the news he'd heard on the radio. He kissed her cheek and said, "Goodnight ma, love you."

She held his hand. "And my dear Alexander, I love you too."

He kissed her hand and said, "Goodnight," and left her to rest.

She was comfortable and warm. 'Yes', she was warm for the first time in months, she thought. She settled under the blankets and thought how lucky she had been throughout her life. Her last thoughts were of James. He was smiling at her and telling her to come with him.

It was 1st March; Elizabeth had been up earlier than normal. She thought she had to rise, needed to make tea. She wasn't sure why but she needed to. She would make a warm drink for Helen. They both felt the cold more these days. As she entered the bedroom, Elizabeth knew Helen had passed away. She put the tea down and felt Helen's cheek. She was cold, but she was smiling and looked peaceful and happy.

"God bless, Helen, my dear." She kissed her forehead and left the room. Victoria came into the kitchen first. She was getting ready for work. She had been happier these last few days as a letter had come from Liam.

"Has your mother and father stirred, Vicky?"

"Yes, Grandma. Dad's on his way down. Are you all right?"

Alex walked into the kitchen, his face pale his eyes watering. Elizabeth rose and went to him. The tears had started to fall for both of them.

She hugged him and said "I'm so sorry, Alex." She hugged a little longer until he realised from her hold. "She looked happy; don't you think?"

"Yes, she does."

"Grandma, Dad, what's wrong?" Victoria was getting scared.

Alex took his daughter's hands in his. "It's Grandma Helen. She passed away in her sleep."

Tears welled in her eyes immediately and she began to cry. Alex hugged his daughter close to him.

Elizabeth asked, "Grace doesn't know yet?" Alex shook his head.

"I'll go," said Elizabeth. "I'll tell her."

Grace cried and clung to her mother on the news. She went into the bedroom to see her mother-in-law and knelt by the bed and kissed her hand.

"Sleep well, Mother, and I promise to look after Alex for you. I'll miss you terribly." She prayed and then went down to her husband and daughter. She fell into Alex's arms and felt his loss. Victoria sat close to Elizabeth and the four of them sat for what seemed an eternity, hardly speaking, just reflecting, thinking of Helen.

The funeral a week later was a small affair. Only Elizabeth, Grace, Alex and Victoria could mourn her passing. Millie and her family came to St Mary's church for the service along with neighbours and friends. Alex was upset that his mother couldn't be buried with his father, but Grace tried to console him and had said many times, "She's close to us, we can go and talk to her any time and she's with James now, anyway. "

188

"She loved being here. It surprised me. I thought she'd never leave the north."

"She was with family, Alex. She loved having all the company."

"I don't want to sell the house yet. If Lizzie and William are going to settle here, then maybe they will want it."

"It would be a good start for them, I think you are right." Grace realised that his mother's loss would affect Alex for a long time but she would help him.

When Lizzie heard about Grandma Helen's death, she felt more alone than ever. She couldn't get to Devon but decided she would visit Mary. Mary was having a more difficult pregnancy this time and Lizzie wanted to see her to put her mind at rest, but also to have family close to her. Mary was almost seven months gone, but looked like the baby would come any day.

"My poor Mary, you really have grown since I last saw you."

"I know, I think I know how an elephant feels now." The women laughed. James had been playing but now wanted to sit on Auntie Lizzie's lap and have biscuits. Lizzie cuddled her nephew and felt happier being close to her family. She ruffled his hair and he fidgeted and laughed.

"I'm sorry to hear about your grandma, Lizzie."

"Thank you. I suppose Michael should know by now. He'll be upset."

"I know."

"I wanted to get home but it's just not possible. I just wanted to hug Mother and Dad and Grandma Elizabeth. We may have grown up Mary, but we are still children when it comes to grandparents and parents, aren't we?"

"Yes, we are. I don't know what I'd do without my Mum and Dad with Michael away. You must be lonely without William."

"I do and I'm so envious of you and your little one and your bump."

"This bump," Mary said, laying her hands over her swollen tummy, "you really wouldn't want this one. I'm sure it's another Mr Churchill in here trying to win the war."

"I just want all our men home, Mary. I want to believe we all have a future. I want children at least two, if not four."

"Be prepared, Lizzie. You too could be the size of an elephant."

"I really hope I get the chance," Lizzie said sadly.

Between the 21st and 23rd March, US General Paton and General Montgomery sent troops across the River Rhine, Germany. By 1st April, the US troops encircled the Germans on the Ruhr and seventeen days later, the Germans surrendered in the area.

Liam's unit was in the area and the end of the war seemed in sight. Michael wasn't too far away and he too, felt home was on the horizon. Paul was in Italy still when on 28th April, Mussolini was captured and hanged by Italian partisans.

William had spent the last two weeks back with Lizzie. He had collapsed with exhaustion and been given special leave. Lizzie still had to work, but spent all her spare time getting her husband back on his feet. She snuggled up close to him each night. He was restless, still fighting in his dreams. She really wished she could reach him. Lizzie had written to her mother with her concerns and Grace had responded, telling her just to be there for him. "Just be close and look after him, be patient" and that was exactly what she would do.

News broke on 30th April that Hitler had committed suicide with his mistress, Eva Braun, in a bunker in Berlin. On 2nd May, Berlin surrendered to the Russians and the German troops in Italy surrendered to the Allies. Everyone waited with baited breath. Hitler was gone; the war was over wasn't it? On 7th May came the unconditional surrender of all the German forces.

Grace and Alex hugged and Grace and Elizabeth cried when they heard the news. It was such a relief but at what cost to so many. They were happy but also sad.

The news of the atrocities of the labour camps had horrified the world. So many civilians had died in so many countries. Most families had lost sons, husbands, daughters and mothers. The relief was truly wonderful. The war was over and now to the future.

8th May was to be a holiday—the Victory in Europe Day. Street parties took place all over the country. In Bideford, there were free trips on the amphibian crafts around the bay or taken up the River Torridge on landing crafts. Alex and Bryan took Maureen, Iris, Dennis and Alan on one of the trips to their delight. Elizabeth and Grace had been cooking and preparing food for the party.

"I wish Helen had made it to today," Elizabeth said.

"So do I, Mother, but she'll know all about it, won't she?"

Everyone enjoyed the party and spent a long time celebrating into the night. There was no longer the need for the blackout and lights shone all over Bideford.

Alex cuddled Grace close to him. "I can't wait till all our family is home, darling, then we'll have another great party."

Mary hadn't managed to enjoy VE Day in quite the same way, because at about 11 o'clock on the night of 7th May, her waters broke and she spent the next nine hours in labour. Just after 8 o'clock in the morning of the holiday, Mary gave birth to a girl. She and Michael had agreed her name and Helen Margaret Whitfield said hello to the free world. When everyone was settled and Helen had had her first feed, Maggie suddenly laughed.

"What's funny, Mum?"

"Michael was born on the eve of Armistice Day and now his daughter has been born on VE Day. That is quite poetic, don't you think?"

"Strange, weird. I just hope this little one doesn't go through war when she's married and about to give birth."

"They said the Great War was the war to end all wars, so who knows?"

"I hope that no one ever has to go through what we've had to cope with. Two generations scarred by war. I pray James and Helen never know about such things."

"I hope so too," Maggie agreed.

It was the day after the holiday when Maggie telephoned Grace to tell her of Helen's arrival. Grace asked if mother and baby were well, and said she would get to see them as soon as she could. It was only a couple of days when there were more 'goodbyes'. Before they left, Maureen and Iris went to Grandma Helen's grave to put some flowers. They had reluctantly tidied their room and packed up, ready to leave. Millie and Jane had thrown a party for them all at the farm. Maureen and Iris, Dennis and Alan hadn't seen their parents for some time and were excited to be going home, but sad to be leaving Devon and all the people who had been their family and friends for the war years.

Elizabeth said goodbye at the house and hugged them both. They weren't the little girls that had arrived five years ago. Maureen was fourteen and becoming quite the young lady. Iris was twelve and had become the country lass of the two. Elizabeth worried they would find it hard back in London. The country had been less restrictive and who knew what they were going back to with all the bomb damage. She would miss them. She and Helen spent hours teaching them to sew and mend clothes, knit and play games.

"We'll write to you Grandma Elizabeth and we'll come back for a holiday."

"You do that, I'll look forward to that."

At the station, there were crowds of people, lots of tears and goodbyes. Jane and Bryan had brought Dennis and Alan who now were fourteen and twelve, respectively.

Alex shook hands with both the boys. "Good luck back home."

"Thank you, Mr Alex," said Dennis.

Jane had been reluctant to cuddle the boys. They weren't young now, they were growing into men, but both the lads cuddled her before they boarded the train. Alex hugged Iris and Maureen. "Come back whenever you want. We'd love to see you again."

"I'll miss you, Daddy Alex," said Iris, her face sad.

"I'll miss you too, Iris."

Grace cuddled the girls. "Write and tell us about home and how you get on back at your school."

"Goodbye, Grace," Maureen paused and then said, "Thank you for everything. We'll write and come back sometime if that's all right. You've been a good mother to us and Iris and I will miss you very much."

"I'm going to miss you both very much. You've been like my own daughters and I'm sad to see you go."

They said their final farewells and the train set off. Grace wept, Alex took her arm and walked home. Jane and Bryan followed behind; all were sombre. *There had been so many goodbyes,* thought Alex. *I really could do with hellos and cheer.*

Chapter 39

Lizzie considered herself lucky to have William at home to celebrate VE Day. With Florey and the rest of the street, they had partied for hours; but end of war or not, there was still work to do and after the fun, William had to go back to his squadron. Lizzie wasn't so scared about him going this time. She'd nursed him back to health, he'd had time to rest, time to eat properly and hours that they had spent together. It wasn't long into June that she realised she was pregnant. Her time at Bletchley had come to an end and before she travelled back to Devon, she wanted to see Mary and her new niece.

Mary was excited with Lizzie's news. "Our children will be of a similar age. They'll all grow up together like we did."

Lizzie had always loved being in the company of Maggie and her family. They were all so down to earth and their home had always been full of love. She understood how her brother had fallen for Mary. She was a caring and compassionate woman and was a great wife and mother. *I'd like to be a good mother*, she thought.

Mary was concerned and distracted. "I haven't heard a word from Michael in over a month. I know that everything is in chaos in Europe, but I had hoped that there would have been some news. I just want him home, Lizzie. The war's over and I want to start living a life as husband and wife and bring up my family."

"I know what you mean, it feels like a lifetime since we were at peace. It's going to take some getting used to, I think."

"Not for me, Lizzie. I just want to get my family all together and start as I mean to go on. Are you and William definitely going to live in Bideford?"

"Yes, we're going to live in Grandma Helen's house. Mother and Dad have been keeping it going and after a few days back with them, I'll move in and wait till William's out of the air force."

"You won't be finishing your college course?"

"No, not with this one on the way," she patted her flat tummy. "William's keen to work with Dad and once the baby's born, I'll be happy to be a mother first and foremost for a while anyway. Who knows what the future will bring? There's been so many women doing jobs they've never dreamed of doing and I don't think that some will want to give up so easily."

"Do you think things will change much?"

"Yes, I do. I think we women, have shown what we can do."

"Things will have changed, for some already, lost husbands, sons, daughters," Mary said.

"Look at Auntie Ruth."

"I think she relies a lot on Robert. When I last heard from Mother, she said that Rachael was hoping to convince them both to move near the farm, so that they're near Adam to see him grow up."

"It's awful that she lost both her first husband and her son in two wars."

"It is so cruel. I do hope she and Robert move to Devon. I think it will be good for them. What's Jessica going to do now?" Lizzie asked.

"Amelia's coming home soon. She's hoping Paul will be back soon and she wants to be back in Bideford when he does."

"Oh, Jess is going to stay on a bit. Patrick's likely to come back to Gosport / Portsmouth before he heads home to Canada."

"Is marriage on the cards?"

"Yes, I believe so, I think Mum's worried she'll be heading off to Canada. I expect your mum is worried about Victoria going to the United States with Liam?"

"I think Victoria will convince Liam to stay here. She's become such a home body and Mother says Victoria's been very sad since Grandma Helen died, so much so that apart from going to work, she hardly leaves the house and the rest of the family."

"Who'd have thought Miss-Snooty-I'm-the-centre-of-everything would have become such a softy. I think you're right, Lizzie, the war's changed everything and everyone."

The women made visits to Ruth and Robert and to Jack and Cara. Little Laura was very nearly five and going to school, and baby Christopher born last October was the image of Jack. Jack had started working for the Civil Service and now that the war was over, he had relaxed, felt less guilty about his injuries and had started to enjoy family life. On her last night in London, Mary, the children and Lizzie dined with Maggie and Arthur.

"We'll try and get to Devon for Christmas this year, Lizzie. It's been a long time since we all managed to be together for any celebration."

"There'll be plenty of room. William and I are taking Grandma Helen's home so there'll be room there too."

As the evening wore on much reminiscing was done, Lizzie fell into bed exhausted but happy. She was glad to be getting back to Bideford and leaving war-torn London. She was sorry to be saying goodbye to the family, but she needed a bit of peace and quiet, and time with Mother and Dad and to get used to the idea of becoming a mum.

Lizzie loved Grandma Helen's house and moved in straight away. Grace was pleased to have her daughter home and was overjoyed at the news of Lizzie's pregnancy. Lizzie didn't want to change much about the house and each day, she and Grace busied themselves, moving Lizzie's personal things and clothes into her new home. Grandma Elizabeth lent a hand too.

Victoria was excited at her sister's home coming. She'd always looked up to Lizzie and had tried to emulate her ladylike demeanour over the years. Lizzie immediately noticed the changes in Victoria. She was softer, kinder and racked with worry over Liam. He'd been sent straight after victory was declared in Europe to Okinawa, as the Americans were still fighting the Japanese. The sisters spent many hours together in the first few weeks of being reunited. Grace thought as she saw them go off for a walk one Saturday mid-July, that they were strikingly beautiful in contrast. Lizzie was fair, with golden hints of red in her hair, amber eyes, tall and slender, although probably not that slim for much longer. She laughed to herself. She did look a lot like herself at that age and Victoria was so much like Alex.

She was tall and slender too, but had taken the darker looks of her father. Victoria had almost black hair and her eyes were a blue-green. Both women had their hair long and wore it like many young women curled up against the front and sides and fastened, so not to be in the way as they worked for practical reasons. It was a warm day and both were in summer dresses and no stockings. They'd linked arms and strolled of towards the park, chatting all the while. She hadn't given birth to these two wonderful girls but they looked so like her and Alex, it was unbelievable. She was so proud of all her family and loved them all dearly. Amelia would be home in the next few days. Paul had been home nearly a fortnight. She knew she wouldn't be seeing much of Amelia as the two young love birds would want as much time together as they could, but at least another one of her children would be home safe. But still there had been no word from Michael. She and Alex worried and she knew from telephone calls from Maggie that Mary was beside herself. Surely, he would be home soon.

Paul asked Grace and Alex if it would be acceptable if he alone went to meet Amelia from the station. Alex had said it would be fine, but Grace was a bit put out.

"They're all grown up now, Gracey. We have to let them have their own lives."

"I know, it's just that I haven't seen her in a long time. And in a short while, once Paul's met her, she'll be here probably longing to see us as much as we want to see her."

He cuddled his wife close to him and kissed the top of her head.

"I know I'm being silly, but I just want them all home."

"And they will be and in time to come, we'll be kept on our toes by all the grandchildren."

"I can't wait."

"Make sure you leave time for us, darling. With all the children ready to fly the coup, we can finally go travelling. I expect there will be a trip to the United States if Victoria marries Liam."

"Oh, I think she'll be dragging him up the aisle of St Mary's here in Bideford as soon as he steps back in England", Grace laughed.

"Poor lad, he won't know what's hit him," Alex laughed too. "I'm serious though, Grace. Once everyone is settled, you and I are going to enjoy ourselves. I think we deserve some peaceful times and some sightseeing."

"I've got to keep an eye on Mother, still."

"I know. Maybe she'll want to travel too. She's still quite sprightly and she's always ready to take on the next adventure."

Grace agreed. Her mother was now eighty-two. She knew Elizabeth still deeply missed her father and Helen's death had hit her too. Maureen and Iris had written many letters to Elizabeth, which had cheered her greatly. She missed having the girls around. Everyone being home would help lift Elizabeth's spirit too. Maybe she would want to travel too.

Paul waited patiently for the train, bringing Amelia back to him. Finally, he saw the steam engine coming around the corner into Bideford station. Once the train was stationary, Amelia opened the compartment door and stepped onto the platform and lifted her case down. As she looked up, there was Paul right in front of her. They didn't speak. She threw her arms around his neck and held him close. After a few minutes, they released their hold of each other, tears were rolling down Amelia's cheeks.

"Why all the tears?" he asked smiling at her. "Aren't you pleased to see me?"

"Oh Paul, of course I am. I'm so happy."

They kissed passionately, not caring who was around them. They were in their own world. "I love you, Amelia. I missed you so much. Your letters kept me going and then I was worried for you when you went to the military hospital. I didn't want you to see the horrors I've seen."

"It made me feel close to you, Paul. I needed to understand what you were going through."

"But now, I'm back and we are going to have a life together now, aren't we?"

"That's what I want, my love."

"So, Miss Whitfield," he got down on one knee, "will you do me the honour of becoming my wife?"

"Yes, Yes, Yes."

Paul rose and kissed Amelia firmly on the lips. The train had departed but the station master and a few passengers clapped and congratulated the couple.

"That's what we need to see," the station master said. "Happy smiling faces and people enjoying peace time."

The happy couple left the station, chatting about when they should marry and happy to be back together. Everyone was waiting at the house in the Strand to greet Amelia and Paul. Elizabeth, Grace and Lizzie had prepared a light lunch for everyone and Millie, Jane and Bryan had all arranged time away from the farm to come and welcome Amelia home. Victoria had come home from work early to welcome her twin home. She'd seen them both as they passed the cinema and ran to meet them. The sisters kissed then hugged.

"It's good to have you home, Amy."

"It's good to be back, Vicky." The girls laughed. Neither liked their names shortened by anyone, but occasionally did it between themselves out of affection.

"Come on now, everyone is waiting for you."

Inside, Grace and Alex were the first to welcome them. "It's lovely to have you home, darling. Alex kissed his daughter.

"It really is," echoed Grace.

Amelia embraced her parents and finally began to feel the tension of the last year starting to evaporate.

It had been hard at Haslar and many times, she'd felt like giving up, but Jessica had helped her get through it. After all the greetings, they sat and had tea and the lunch prepared. Grace watched her quiet twin.

She turned to Alex, "She's exhausted. She is going to need to rest. I hope she's not going to go straight back to work."

"She's been through a lot. I think being home, she'll soon perk up and she's got Paul, hasn't she?"

"Yes, they do look good together, don't they?"

Alex nodded in agreement. "Wedding Bells soon, I don't doubt."

"Oh, Alex aren't they too young?"

"No, not after what they've had to cope with. I think everyone should do what they want and be happy."

"You're a romantic, darling."

Lizzie told Amelia about her pregnancy and Amelia kissed her big sister. "That's great news. When is William going to be demobbed so that you can be together?"

"He should be finished by the beginning of August and I can't wait. What about Jessica? Is she leaving Gosport yet?"

"Yes, she's leaving at the end of the week. Patrick's been back to England. They had a few days together before he left for Canada and he asked her to marry him."

"Did she say yes?" Victoria asked.

"Yes, she did," replied Amelia, "and he promised to get back as soon as he could. He's written to Aunt Maggie and Uncle Arthur for permission."

"Well, we'd better make our announcement then," said Paul. He cleared his throat to make an impression of the announcement. "I asked Amelia today if she would be my wife and she agreed." He looked towards Alex, "If that's still alright with you, Mr Whitfield."

"Of course, it is dear boy," Alex shook hands with his son-in-law to be. "I'm delighted for you both."

He kissed his daughter and she hugged him.

"Thanks Papa," she said softly.

Grace kissed them both and asked, "When do you think you'd like to marry? Any thought yet?"

"I'd like Christmas," said Amelia. "Hopefully by then, Michael will be home," she looked at Victoria, "and so will Liam, and we can all be together."

"Christmas it is then." Grace looked over to Jane who was congratulating her son.

"Christmas is good for you Jane?"

"I believe it will be the best Christmas in a long while." Everyone was happy and enjoying being back together.

Amelia put her arm around her twin. "He'll be back soon, Victoria, don't you worry, and then you too can plan a wedding."

Victoria smiled. "Thanks sis, but we'll have to plan yours first, won't we? And Lizzie will want to help."

"I'm going to need all the help I can get; rationing hasn't stopped. I don't think I'll have the best wedding dress ever, but I'll be the happiest bride."

"I'm sure you will be," Victoria agreed.

William made it to Devon and to his new home the same week the Americans attacked the Japanese. The first B29 bomber dropped an atomic bomb on Hiroshima on 6th August and then another on 9th August on Nagasaki. In total, 105,000 people were killed, 97,000 were injured and another 343,000 died after from the effects of these new bombs. The events shocked the world and finally, on 14th August, Japan surrendered. Victoria cried with relief. Liam had written to her and she received it only a couple of days ago. He was fine when he wrote the note and she prayed that now the fighting had ended, he would be home soon. 15th August was celebrated as VJ Day; Victory in Japan day throughout Britain and the United States. The world was finally at peace.

On the morning of Saturday, 15th September, the household had breakfast together and then started busying themselves with the day ahead. It was a beautiful autumn morning; bright and sunny, with a slight chill in the air. Elizabeth said she was going to do some baking before she carried on with sewing for Amelia's wedding dress. Grace felt restless; perhaps, a walk alone would do her good.

She mentioned this to Alex and he asked, "You feeling all right darling?"

"Yes, Alex. I feel fine, good actually, I just feel like a bit of exercise on this fine day. Once I've helped Mother with the baking, I'll take myself off and enjoy the fresh air."

"Well, if you're sure, I'm going into the office for a couple of hours with William, then if you are still out, I'll come and find you. Where do you think you'll go?"

"Not sure, maybe up to the Fort."

"That's quite a walk."

"Yes, it is, but I'm raring to go. If the weather holds, let's go to Westward Ho! later."

"Sounds like a plan," he kissed his wife on the lips. "See you later my love," and then he left.

Once the baking was done, Grace freshened up and after saying goodbye to Elizabeth, she set off on her walk. She was wearing brown trousers and a cream blouse. She'd picked up a cardigan but at the moment, it was warm enough that she didn't need it, so she tied it around her waist. She had her hair in a bun earlier but just before she left, she let it down. She walked out of the Strand and made her way to the river. Along the way, she spoke to people she knew. Once over the bridge and past the station, she made her way up the hill to the remains of the old Civil War Fort. She was quite warm when she reached the summit and wished she'd brought some water to drink. Within a few minutes, she recovered from the climb, leaned on the wall of the fort and looked out over the town of Bideford, her home. She recalled that she hadn't been sure of the move from London many years before. She'd loved Devon for holidays, but to leave the city for good and live in the country full time was another matter, but she and Alex had discussed the pros and cons and they had been right to bring their family here.

Her father, Frederick, had embraced country life and had seen out his days here. Alex's mother was buried close to Frederick in the graveyard of St Mary's, the local church. She missed them terribly. Elizabeth was still fighting fit and taking on her next mission, to make Amelia's wedding the best possible. Amelia had rested and was back working at Bideford hospital, but it wouldn't be for much longer. The wedding was set for 22nd December and then she would be a farmer's wife. Her gentle, quiet Amelia had seen so much. Mother and daughter had spoken a lot about her nursing experiences at the Military Hospital. Grace had empathised with her daughter. They had both experienced caring for soldiers during a war. Amelia was a more confident young woman now and Grace was sure that her marriage to Paul would be a good one and they would be happy.

Jessica was going to be a bridesmaid at the wedding. She and Amelia had kept in touch ever since they'd left Haslar and became close friends. Jessica was going to Canada in the New Year to meet Patrick's family and then they would travel back together to marry in London.

Grace had also heard from John Gregson and his wife, Irene, just a few days ago. The couple had kept an eye on Amelia and Jessica during the time at the military hospital and as usual, were keeping up to date with all the news. They would try to make it to the wedding but as it was close to Christmas, it might be a little difficult.

John had finally retired and Irene was pleased to have him at home. They and their family had remained relatively unscathed through the war, although their son's home was completely demolished during a daylight raid. But they'd all survived and were getting on with life in peace time.

Ruth and Robert were in Devon at the moment. They had called to say they'd arrived and were happy to be at the farm again with Rachael, Edward and little Adam. Ruth had told Grace that she and Robert had been talking a lot and agreed that they wanted to move to Dawlish to be near their family. Grace told her she was pleased and hoped they would be able to get together soon. Rachael was pregnant again and was hoping for an easier time than before. Ruth was hoping to be there to ensure Rachael took it easy.

Grace thought of her dear brother, Michael. She had loved him so much and still felt his loss greatly. He would be proud of Rachael and his grandson and a new baby on the way. He would have liked to see Ruth happy. Ruth had lost Michael to the Great War and then her son, Matthew, in this war. She deserved some happiness and the move would be good for her. Grace thought of Ruth and Michael's wedding day and then of her own. She had been so happy and excited on that special day. She was marrying the most handsome man in the world and he had stolen her heart. Grace smiled. *Those eyes bewitched me from the start,* she thought. She recalled their wedding reception and their honeymoon in Torquay. They had hardly got out of bed, couldn't keep their hands off each other. She was lucky, she thought. It could have been so different. Alex might not have made it back from the Great War. What would she have done without him? Then she nearly died after giving birth to Michael and then Alex had been stabbed. They really had been through some hard times. She loved Alex so much, she didn't know where she finished and he began, they were truly one. *I'll make sure he knows just how I feel tonight,* she thought. *I'll show him how much I love him.* At fifty-four, Alex was still a strong, fit, good-looking man and when she thought about him caressing her, she would melt. *If Amelia and Paul are even half as happy as Alex and I, they'll have a good life.*

Then there was Lizzie. She had William back home for good and he hadn't wasted much time getting into the law practice with Alex. It was good for them both. William was young and bright, good for new young clients and Alex for the more mature already used to his advice. It would also give Alex more free time which she was looking forward to. Lizzie's pregnancy was going well, she looked a picture of health. Her hair shone brightly and her skin was rosy. She had started to get a little bump but not much. Grace knew this couple would do well too. They were a match in intelligence and shared common interests. She had once thought Lizzie would have gone to university and gone onto a career, but looking at her just this morning, Grace realised Lizzie had exactly what she wanted. *Just like me really, I'd wanted a career, to be a pioneer for women but then came Alex. Then allI wanted was to be a good wife and mother.*

Victoria, dear Victoria. Her once selfish and vain daughter had become her most home loving and cautious of all her children. The war had changed her so much. She'd had to share more, especially when Maureen and Iris had arrived. Once Michael and Lizzie had left home and become involved in the war, Victoria had started to feel vulnerable. She had always had a family around her that doted and cared for her. Slowly, everyone had gone. Grandma Helen dying had left Victoria more upset than anyone. She had clung to her and Alex, not wanting to go too far from home and then there was Liam. The dashing American had stolen her daughter's heart. He was fun, loving and had the same energy for life that Victoria had. They would be a good match. A letter had arrived yesterday to say that Liam was on his way back and he would be coming to England first. Victoria was so excited. Another wedding!

Her adopted children never ceased to amaze her; Grace reflected. No one ever spoke of their adoptions and she and Alex had never thought it necessary to tell them. Lizzie looked so much like her. Victoria was so like Alex and Amelia had a combination of Grace's colouring, like her eyes but the darker hair of Alex. No one would ever guess they weren't truly born of Alex and Grace. Then there was her son Michael, the only child she'd given birth to. He was now a grown man of twenty-seven years, married with two children. She still didn't know when he'd be home, but she was sure he would be. He had been a miniature Alex as a child and had also grown up to look like his father. He was six-feet tall and strong. He was a doctor, mostly influenced by Arthur and John Gregson. Michael's son, James, took after his father and grandfather in looks, but as yet neither, she nor Michael had seen little Helen Margaret. Lizzie said she was gorgeous and looked a lot like Mary. She really couldn't wait to see her grandchildren and her son. Suddenly, she sensed she wasn't alone. As she turned, Alex was by her side. He put his arm around her waist and stood next to her, holding her close and looking out over the town.

"It's beautiful up here. Do you remember when the children would play up here?" Alex said.

Grace had put her arm around him. "Yes, Victoria always wanted to be the princess."

"Amelia was her servant," Alex laughed

"I've been thinking of the past as I've stood here. Looking back at our lives and our children's lives and I think we've become quite a clan, haven't we?"

"Yes, The Whitfield Clan. We certainly have produced quite a brood and it's about to get bigger with Lizzie's baby on the way."

"Any regrets, Alex? "Grace turned to look straight at him.

"Some," he took her face in his hands. She looked a little hurt.

"Some, "she repeated.

"Yes, I regret I never took you to Paris before the war started. I regret that fate has made us see two world wars and I regret that I haven't been able to stop your worries and strains over the years. Apart from that, I have enjoyed and loved every minute of my life with you since that first dance in December 1912 and I wouldn't have lived my life without your love, Grace Whitfield."

She kissed him passionately. "I love you so much, Alex and I'm looking forward to many more years of peace and happiness well into our old age."

Alex kissed her again. She looked at this moment as young as she had that first Christmas. "Come on now, wife dear, it's time we walked home, you've been out a while."

"I know and I've enjoyed looking back and realising I'm a very lucky woman."

They chatted as they made their way back down the hill towards the station. Unknown to Grace, there had been a conspiracy at work.

Maggie had telephoned at the beginning of the week to say Michael was at home. He wanted to keep the surprise going as he and Mary and the children were coming to Devon and wanted their arrival to be a surprise for Grace. Maggie had been overjoyed to see her daughter's husband back. She was now going to have to prepare for the departure of her daughter Jessica to Canada in the New Year, but there was Amelia's wedding first and she, Arthur and Jessica were definitely not missing that. Alex had agreed a little reluctant to keep the secret, but Michael and Maggie convinced him. He used the excuse of going to the office with William as a ruse. They had worked for only two hours and then the two men had gone to the station to meet Michael and his family. Grace's impartial walk had made things a little easier with the subterfuge.

Alex had hugged his son. "Good to have you home, my boy."

"It's good to be back, Dad."

Alex had greeted and kissed Mary, tousled little James's hair. "You're growing up quickly, my little grandson." Then he looked at the bundle in Mary's arms. Just waking was little Helen.

"Say hello to your Grandpa Alex," said Mary, as she showed Helen to Alex. He took the four-month-old little girl in his arms. Lizzie was right, she did look a lot like Mary. He'd held Mary at that age too. So much time had gone by. He was now holding his granddaughter.

"She's beautiful, Mary. Michael, you must be so proud!"

"I am, Dad. I just wish I could have been around more since they were born."

"I know, son, but you've all the time in the world now. Enjoy them Michael, they soon grow up," they greeted William and then William set off with their luggage back to the house in the Strand. Alex explained that Grace had gone for a walk and hadn't returned yet.

"Why don't you get some refreshment in the hotel here at the station? Your mother has been up to the fort. I'll get her and meet you back here."

"Will do."

The plan had worked, thought Alex, as they reached the station. He had spotted Michael on the bridge. He was holding James up so he could look at the water.

As they crossed the road, Grace cried out, "It's Michael, Michael's on the bridge. Alex, it's our son." Without waiting for a response Grace started to run. "Michael, Michael!"

Michael turned with his son in his arms and saw his mother running towards him.

"Mum". He put James to the ground and took the few paces forward to meet Grace.

"Michael, it is you, Oh God, I can't believe it," they hugged. Tears flowed from Grace's eyes. She turned to Mary. "Hello, Mary, my dear daughter, you should have let me know you were coming."

"We had let Father know but we wanted to surprise you."

Alex had caught up with them and reached down to pick up James.

"Surprise me, that you have but you are all very naughty too for keeping it from me. You, especially, "she said to Alex.

"Hello, James"

"Hello, Grandma."

"You are very handsome and it's so good to see you."

Grace turned and looked at Helen. "And you are my granddaughter Helen."

Mary handed over the baby. Helen was wide awake now and looked straight at Grace.

"She's beautiful," her tears still flowed. She couldn't believe how happy she felt. How had they kept such a secret but she didn't care. She now knew why she'd felt the way she had this morning. She'd known somewhere deep inside that everything was all right. But this was better than all right. This was all her wishes coming at once. Her whole family was home; the Whitfield Clan together again, war-weary but full of hope.

Keeping hold of her granddaughter, she looked at both Michael and Mary and said, "You have made my day. Today is one of the best of my life. My son's home safe and well with his wife and two wonderful children and the man I've trusted for most of my life has kept a big secret from me. For how long?"

"A week, darling."

Grace hugged him. "Thank you, my love, this surprise was wonderful."

"Let's get home then, the rest of the family are waiting for Michael and Mary's arrival. I think it will be a bit of a party tonight."

"Good," said Michael. "We Whitfields have always thrown a good party as did the Richardsons and The Smiths," he said, kissing Mary's cheek.

"You're not wrong there," Alex boomed. "Without one of these parties, I'd never have met your mother."

Laughing and enjoying the moment, Grace and her family made their way back to the house. As they walked, Grace looked back to the fort where she had been reminiscing this afternoon and smiled. It had been a beautiful day. She'd been lost in her thoughts and memories and now in the present, her family were back together and complete. She prayed for those that had not been so lucky.

We've made it through, she thought. *The Whitfield Clan goes on.*

THE END

201